Grizzly Lies

Grizzly Lies

by

EILEEN
COUGHLAN

SUMACH
PRESS

Library and Archives Canada Cataloguing in Publication

Coughlan, Eileen Patricia, 1960-
Grizzly lies : a mystery novel / Eileen Coughlan
ISBN 1-894549-41-4

I. Title.
PS8555.082282G75 2005 C813'.6 C2005-902023-7

Edited by Catherine Marjoribanks
Cover photograph © Stephen J. Krasemann/DRK Photo
Design by Liz Martin

Sumach Press acknowledges the support of the Canada Council for the Arts and the Ontario Arts Council for our publishing program. We acknowledge the financial support of the Government of Canada through the Book Publishing Industry Development Program (BPIDP) for our publishing activities.

ONTARIO ARTS COUNCIL
CONSEIL DES ARTS DE L'ONTARIO

Printed and bound in Canada

Published by
SUMACH PRESS
1415 Bathurst Street #202
Toronto ON Canada M5R 3H8

sumachpress@on.aibn.com
www.sumachpresss.com

This book is for
Don
my whole world

It takes two to speak the truth —
one to speak, and the other to hear.

— HENRY DAVID THOREAU

ACKNOWLEDGEMENTS

My sincere thanks go to everyone at Sumach Press for believing in this book and for all you have put into it. Much gratitude also goes to Catherine Marjoribanks for being a wonderful editor. I am indebted to RCMP Staff Sergeant Joe MacDonald; RCMP Cpl. P.C.M. (Patrick) Webb; Banff Park Warden Doug Martin; toxicologist Peter Singer, PhD; hunting guide Rick Guinn; Paul Vargis; Mike and Diane McIvor for sharing their expertise. Many thanks to Lesley McNutt, the Banff seniors, Rick and Suzanne Lee for sharing their stories. Eric & Viva Balson I thank for their hospitality and for letting me glimpse their life in Africa. Eric, you are a true hero to the elephants of Tanzania. I am indebted to the Banff Centre Leighton Studios for providing a quiet, creative space. Thanks also to The Banff Book & Art Den. I thank Connie Varnhagen and John Ellard for their support. My appreciation goes to Mystery Writers Ink and The Crime Writers of Canada and especially Cheryl Freedman. Gracious thanks go to the late Catherine McKay. Cathy's spirit lives on in the work we do, through her husband Greg and everyone at Pages Books On Kensington. A special thank you to Gail Bowen for being a great mentor. Thank you to my writer friends: Carla Daum, Julia Vryheid, Catherine Gildiner, Nina and George Johnson. A special thanks to Katherin Edwards for her promotional help and friendship. Elizabeth J. Owens, Heather Bertram, Lisa and Robert Savin and the Johners I thank for their support. Margaret Gee I thank for her help with music and art. To my sister Catherine and brother Sean, much thanks for their continued support and generosity. To my sister Coleen I extend a very special thank you for her enthusiastic promotion and constant encouragement. Patti Hannigan I thank for her tireless promotion, trust and friendship. My deep appreciation goes to Michelle Leoppky for her cherished friendship, for reading everything I write, but mostly for being the original true heart. I am deeply grateful to Evelyn Carignan for her continued spiritual guidance. Tuff-Tuff I thank for always being my loyal writing companion. My mother Patricia I thank for her support and ace editing skills. I am also grateful to my mother and father for teaching me compassion and respect for animals, and for my mother's belief that no living creature ever belongs in a cage. To my husband Don, I am forever thankful for your love, wisdom, and patience. And for your strength to never, ever give up.

CHAPTER 1

IT WAS HARD FOR ME TO SAY WHO WAS MORE AGITATED, THE CAPTIVE or his tormentors. There were at least a dozen of them and only one of him. I held my breath as I watched a woman, dressed all in white, inch her way up from the back of the crowd until she was within spitting distance of the beautiful creature's black, wet nose. The elk's eyes remained alert, twitching, scanning. He stepped back from the woman, stole a glance over his massive right shoulder and searched for an escape. He found one. I exhaled.

But as the elk focused on his avenue of escape, the crowd took its cue and fanned out, creating a semi-circle. A man and a woman chatted to one another, seemingly oblivious to what could soon transpire; or perhaps they were bored, just killing time until things really got underway. One last person stepped into place and closed the circle, forming a human corral. The captive lifted his head.

Now he was trapped.

I was watching the scene play out from the kitchen window of the house I had been entrusted to sit. And this was the third time I'd watched the same scene in the past week. Last time, the people had taken their pictures and moved off without incident. The time before that, however, things had turned ugly and violent, ending with a tourist taken away, bruised and bloody, on a stretcher.

The woman in white took a step back. The captive scraped at the earth and kept a wary eye on her as she extracted a palm-sized video camera from her bag. She moved in for the shot. He looked straight into the lens and curled his upper lip into a sneer. It was a reflex, of course. But the crowd didn't seem to care. They loved this display of animal emotion and responded with hoots of laughter.

In a slow, bizarre kind of dance, the white-suited woman circled the elk, letting her camera take in every detail of the animal's majestic form. The bull elk responded by lowering his head and presenting his impressive rack of horns, as though striking the perfect pose.

I tapped on the window and waved to the tourists, motioning for them to leave. Some just waved back, and others turned their video cameras on me. There is a sign posted at the edge of the property warning people to leave the elks alone and of the inherent dangers if they don't. But the woman and her tourist friends had apparently ignored the sign and seemed to think the ungulate was just a big, impassive lawn ornament. It was as if they thought he should accept their attentions and intrusions as simply another part of his Parks Canada job. The bull lowered his head and munched casually on the grass, giving the woman one last chance to get the hell away from him.

When she didn't take it, the bull made a swift butting motion, stopping his horns within a breath of the camera lens. The woman let out a yelp and jumped back. The others shrieked.

I'd seen enough. I went to the phone and dialled the wardens' office. A female voice answered on the first ring. "Banff Park dispatch. Is this an emergency?"

"It will be," I said. "This is Hellie MacConnell. Can you ask Warden Bauer to get over to Doc Rivard's right away? Tourists are back at it with an elk."

"He's on his way," the operator said.

I threw on a fleece vest over my sweater, then slipped out the front door and made my way to the river path until I was behind the crowd of spectators. The woman with the video camera was inching closer still to the elk as he pawed at the fresh layer of snow, a sure sign he was ready to charge.

"Please," I said in a low voice. "Move back. He'll hurt you. You've got him cornered."

The bull lowered his head one final time, aimed the spear-sharp antlers and charged the woman with the camera. She tripped and fell. The others fled in all directions, running into and over the wire fence. The elk reared up on hind legs. Hooves hammered the ground next to the woman's head. He reared up again and again, dealing the camera a series of crushing blows.

No one moved, except one young guy who was filming the attack with his own video camera. "Get back," I hissed. At the same moment, a gunshot shattered the mountain air and echoed down the valley, obliterating my words.

The elk let out a wild cry that sounded like train wheels seizing up on a steel track. Out of the corner of my eyes, I spotted Des Bauer on the edge of the property aiming a banger pistol into the air. But the elk didn't retreat and continued his attack. The woman in white was still on the ground screaming, too frightened to move.

Des fired another shot. When the second blast failed to scare the elk off, Warden Des raced across the lawn. With a long pole and a yellow flag attached at its end, Des frantically waved at the elk. On hind legs, the angry ungulate pivoted away from the flag and dropped down on all fours. His hooves dug into the lawn, spraying great divots into the air as the terrified creature made a dash for the street.

Des crouched next to the terror-stricken woman. I was about to call an ambulance, but after Des had the woman on her feet again it was obvious the only thing that had experienced any real damage was her video camera.

My pulse roared in my ears as I stepped aside on the path to quell my thumping heart. The woman in the white suit was lucky. In fact, she had no idea just how lucky she was. With gulps of fresh air I breathed away the image of the other elk attack that had ended so badly.

I took in another deep appreciative breath. It was a beautiful autumn day. The air was crisp and fragile with ice crystals carried in on the breeze from the glaciers and snow-capped peaks that surround the town of Banff. During the night it had snowed, leaving everything covered in a diamond-studded, downy blanket sparkling under the morning sun.

I moved aside on the path while Des gave the tourists a good talking-to about leaving the wildlife alone, particularly during rutting season.

This was my second rutting season (as a visitor, I might add, rather than a participant), in the Rocky Mountains. It was the thirteenth of October, exactly one year to the day since I'd abandoned my groom at the altar, fled Toronto and shown up in Banff as a runaway bride, with a guilty conscience and all my worldly possessions stuffed into the trunk of my car. Twelve months later, my conscience was still no clearer. But aside from my weird encounters with uninvited visitors, I did like where I was living.

Des was herding the tourists off the property, each one of them tramping another bit of the fence on his and her way out. A few were reluctant to leave, though. The young guy who had filmed the elk attack earlier was busily tearing up and down the steps of the gazebo letting his camera take in every detail of the pretty white-columned, domed structure. In a single leap he cleared the rail, barely missing a wrought-iron garden chair, and landed with a thud in the rock garden, managing all the while to keep the film rolling.

"Okay," Des said to the young man. "Let's wrap it up."

The young guy held up an index finger to indicate he needed one more minute to finish his cinematic epic.

Des rolled his eyes as he came toward me on the path. He was carrying a bent aluminum fence stake. "Jeez," he said under his breath. "What's the matter with these people?"

"Blame it on Disney. They think the elk are all big Bambies."

"Yeah, well we'll be paintballing that big Bambi when we shoo him out of town. Hopefully, he'll stay put. But keep an eye out for him and let me know if you see a big elk with a red splotch on his flank."

"Sure will," I said.

"And thanks for calling this one in. Could have been real bad." Des crossed his arms over his chest and shook his head.

I shrugged and smiled. "At least no one was hurt."

His gaze narrowed. "This isn't like you, Hellie. You usually want to take after them with a hockey stick."

"I'm feeling uncharacteristically charitable today. The Doc's coming home tonight." Dr. Michael Rivard was my landlord, and my great-uncle. Our deal was that I would house-sit his lovely, historic home while he travelled. For the past year, he'd been in Tanzania, but he was on his way back for a visit.

"Is that a fact?" Des said with a bright smile. "Thought Doc wasn't going to be around for awhile yet." He pushed his round wire-rimmed glasses up the bridge of his nose and leaned against one of the poplar trees that lined the path.

Des and I met shortly after I'd moved into the house when, in a not-so-subtle attempt at matchmaking, Doc invited Des over for dinner under the pretense that I'd need the warden's help from time to time. As it turned out, I *had* needed Des's help. I'd called on the warden quite a few times to give me a hand with park animals and the tourists.

A stream of soft yellow sunlight filtered through the branches and set the red highlights of Des's thick, wavy hair alight. With his open, eager grin, boyish good looks and unbridled enthusiasm for everything he did, Des Bauer looked closer to nineteen than to the thirty-one-year-old man he actually was.

"He mention why the sudden trip home?" Des said.

"Nope. Just left a phone message the other day saying he was on his way back. I'm having a late dinner …" I paused wondering whether or not I should ask him to join us. We were friends, just friends. And for the moment, that's the way I wanted to keep things.

Des caught my hesitation and let his glance slide tactfully away from mine. Then I felt bad.

"You should come," I said quickly. "Pumpkin cheesecake for dessert." Now he hesitated. "Don't worry," I said. "I didn't make it." My inability to even nuke a hotdog without exploding it was legendary. "And I'm ordering — "

"Hey! There's something down here," a male voice called out.

The young guy with the video camera was kneeling beside the gazebo, his camera trained on the small lattice door that led under the building to a storage area. People were drawn to the gazebo. Doc had warned me to be on the lookout for drunken partiers who sometimes liked to crawl under there and sleep. Every so often I'd find the door open and evidence that someone had been sleeping amid the dilapidated gardening equipment and firewood. The lock had been broken so many times the Doc said he'd given up fixing it and just checked regularly to make sure no one froze to death under there in the winter.

"I'll remind him it's private property," Des said.

Before Warden Des was even off the path, the young guy opened the lattice door and stuck his head in. He brought it out just as quickly and began pointing and shouting. "There's … there's a dead body under here!"

I flashed Des a skeptical look before I raced across the lawn, losing my footing on the slippery snow-covered grass. I landed on my butt, scrambled to my feet and pushed past the gawking tourists. All the while, my mind was telling me that someone was probably just injured. The word *dead* had not registered.

Only when I was staring into the lifeless face of Doc Rivard did the word *dead* become devastatingly clear.

CHAPTER 2

His eyes were open, hands clenched at his chest. The silver shock of hair was brushed back off his forehead as if he'd just run a hand over it. The bright orange ski jacket covering his torso was almost an exact match to the orange tarp covering the woodpile.

I crouched closer to him in the gazebo's shallow crawlspace, and whispered his name. "Doc." It came out on a puff of steam that rose from my mouth and dissipated like a tiny spirit in front of my eyes.

Des crawled in behind me. "Jesus," he said.

We stayed there, not moving, barely breathing for what seemed like a very long time. Then Des's years of training kicked in.

"Come on, Hellie. Don't touch anything, and try to retrace your steps." He tugged my coat sleeve and we backed out together.

Voices floated in the autumn air. *Who is it? What happened? Who is it?* More tourists had congregated on the Doc's back lawn. I faced the crowd. I was calm. No hysterics. Not like in movies, where they scream and faint. The numbness had taken hold. People call it shock. It's not. It's a shot of something, a medicine that enables you to carry on in a detached, unfeeling way. It's the stuff that staves off the socially inappropriate hysterics, the low animal moans of anguish — it keeps them at bay and it gets you through it all.

One woman kept saying, "Is he dead? Is he dead?"

"Yes, damn it," Des snapped. "He is dead."

The woman began to cry and said she was going to her hotel. When I asked her where she was staying, she pointed up toward the street.

"The Wild Rose?" I said.

She sniffed and nodded then looked intent on heading that way. Des stopped her. "I'm sorry," he said ignoring her tears. "You'll have to wait until the police get here."

Now Friend Des was gone and replaced by Warden Des — a man who had assisted the police in many investigations. Through stories the Doc had told me, and what I'd seen myself, I'd come to learn that a

Banff Park warden was a combination of sheriff, cowboy, search and rescue expert, tourist guide and zookeeper. Des had done everything from wrestle a rifle from a poacher to bottle-feed a baby deer. And he'd seen his fair share of death: He'd told me about digging out avalanche victims, pulling drowned tourists from the Bow Falls and once finding the body of a young woman mauled by a cougar.

Yes, Des had been around tragedy. He knew the routine, the procedures. But I doubted he often stumbled upon the body of a very dear friend. Nevertheless, Des Bauer rose to the dreadful occasion.

"All of you will have to wait for the police," Des instructed the crowd. "And please stay on the path right where you are. Don't touch or disturb anything." He turned to me, "I'll call the police and get Nathan down here. You better check the cabin."

"Arthur! Oh God, you're right," I said. Arthur Elliott, another friend of the Doc's, lived in a log cabin on the property. "He was going to meet Doc in Calgary and drive back with him," I said, and then took off down the path at a gallop.

My mind was racing with fearful questions as I ran past the half-acre of treed property that separated the Doc's house from Arthur's cabin.

When I came around to the front of the squat log building, a breath caught at the back of my throat.

The door was ajar.

"Arthur?" I said in a raspy whisper. I cleared my throat and tried again. "Arthur?"

Nothing.

With the tips of my fingers, I pushed the door open a little farther and stood back.

"Arthur?"

The only response was the wind whooshing through pine trees and spruce bows. I took a tentative step forward and peered into the cave-dark room. "Arth — "

Something or someone moved in the far corner. My mind told me to run, but it was too late. A dark head lunged at me. A scream tore from my throat. I stumbled, fell back and landed with a thud, just as a great horned owl flew overhead, brushing its wing along the top of my short, spiky hair.

Once I'd collected my wits and brushed the dirt and pine needles off my — now stained — hiking pants, I felt foolish and nearly laughed. That is until I caught a terrible smell wafting from the cabin. I knew what it was: the acrid stench of rot and death.

For nearly a week, the cabin had been unoccupied. Autumn was Arthur's time to be away. No one ever seemed to know where he went, and those of us close to him knew not to ask. Two days earlier, I'd checked the door and found it locked. Arthur didn't like anyone going in his cabin when he wasn't there. I'd always respected his wish, but now I had to look. Had to know if Arthur was in there, dead or alive.

With the toe of my boot, I nudged the door open then braced myself against the doorframe. I flipped the wall switch. Dusty yellow light filled the cabin, and the putrid smell grew stronger. My pulse raced.

On the other side of the room against the wall, Arthur's cot was neatly made up with a Hudson's Bay blanket and a single pillow. Above the bed, paintings of mountain scenes and snapshots of Arthur's beloved grizzly bears hung on the wall.

Closer to the door was the kitchen, which consisted of a sink and a black pot-bellied stove that sat like a fat little monk in the centre of the room. All seemed well in the galley: no meat, fish or vegetable matter left out.

On my right was a shelf lined with books about various religions. Tacked to one corner, dozens of paper-chain moose trailed to the bottom shelf and dangled above rows of intricately carved wooden bears and miniature folk art weather vanes. Arthur made all these little masterpieces and sold them in town for fundraising. All were in perfect order. In fact, everything seemed to be in order.

Another step inside and I could just barely see to the far end of the cabin that lay in darkness. Tartan-patterned curtains were drawn over the two small windows, making the room cool and gloomy. The stench was nauseating. Yet, strangely, nothing seemed out of place. Arthur certainly wasn't there.

My eyes drifted under the rough pine table and settled on a half-eaten hare — no doubt the owl's lunch. In the dim light, I could see its head was gone and its stomach was slashed, exposing the dark guts.

Light poured in when I opened the curtains and revealed that the rabbit could not be the source of the smell. Its fresh crimson blood told me it had probably met its end within the last hour. But farther along the wall, tucked in the shadows under the desk, I noticed a dark shape. At first glance it looked like a pile of dirt about half a metre tall and equally as wide. As I knelt next to it, the smell grew stronger. I breathed through my mouth and tried to make sense of what I was seeing. It was definitely not dirt. A closer inspection revealed long curved claws and grizzled brown tufts of fur protruding from the rotting heap. I blinked and took a closer look. Then I knew what it was. I reared back and re-flexively shuffled away on my knees, but my gaze remained fixed on the yellow claws and black gore.

I was staring at bear paws.

Stacked like macabre pancakes, there were five, maybe six paws. Flies crawled between the black, fleshy cracks in the torn pads. Something white wiggled its way out and into the light. I forgot to breathe through my mouth and took in the awful smell. My eyes watered and the sour taste of bile rose to the back of my throat.

I ran from the cabin to the riverbank, threw myself down on a bench and breathed clean air. Dumbly, I stared at the water and let my eyes follow a stick as it floated by on the river's gentle current. I was trying to comprehend what had just happened, what I'd just seen. But nothing made sense. All I could do was concentrate on the obvious and tell my-self that this was bad. Very, very bad. The Doc was dead, I had no idea where Arthur was, and there were bear paws in his cabin.

Bear paws!

I knew that possessing bear paws at anytime was illegal. Being caught with them in a national park, I was sure, would mean jail time. For one idiotic second, I considered getting rid of those paws and covering for Arthur. I shook my head. I wasn't thinking clearly.

I had to call someone. The Society office in Calgary seemed like the most logical place to start. Doc Rivard was a founding member of the Save the Bow Valley Society, an organization with an office in the city that lobbied to halt development in and around the park. The Doc wasn't always popular with local business owners and ski hill operators, who found the Society's conservationist ideals were at odds with tour-ism and business dollars. Arthur worked with the Doc's group, but he had his own Save The Grizzlies Project, which mostly entailed working alone to thwart the annual grizzly hunt that took place outside the park boundaries. Both men had a lot of friends and enemies in Banff.

Leaves crunched behind me and made me look back at the cabin. I caught a flash of something orange and red, brilliant as a flame, moving through the trees.

"Hello," said a familiar voice.

It was as though thinking about Arthur had been enough to make him materialize out of the thin mountain air. His greeting, however, was not directed at me. He hadn't seen me yet. Arthur was talking to a Steller's jay perched in a spruce tree. He called another hello to the handsome black and indigo bird. The jay seemed to recognize the odd little man in the peculiar outfit and hopped down to a lower branch to squawk a greeting.

Arthur spotted me, gave a wave and hurried down to the riverbank. He sat next to me on the bench and said, "Hello, Hellie. I've just gotten in. Have you seen Michael?"

I was momentarily rendered speechless by what he'd just said and by what he was wearing. In public, Arthur usually wore regular Banff attire: flannel shirt, Gore-Tex jacket and cotton khakis. Today he was wearing his Arthur-at-home outfit, an African kikoi — a bright orange, yellow and red wrap tied around his waist then looped over his shoulder like a sari. He'd completed the ensemble with a grape-coloured parka. On his feet he wore rope sandals. The entire outfit begged for a staff and a flock of multi-coloured sheep. Occasionally Arthur could be spotted in town sporting this getup, which — along with his bald head and bushy calico beard, not to mention the silver rings in his ears — tended to garner long stares from tourists and locals alike. But for obvious reasons, he usually wore the outfit outside of his cabin only during the summer months.

"Someone stole my suitcase. I think," Arthur said by way of explanation.

"Ah. When?" I asked with trepidation, afraid his answer might have something to do with having been arrested.

"I'm not sure. It may not have been stolen at all. Simply misplaced. A friend loaned me this parka," he said and touched the collar. "Well, I am glad I've found you, Hellie. I stopped up at the house, but of course you weren't there." He smiled his shy smile. "Because you are here."

When I'd first moved into the Doc's house and met Arthur, I'd been misled by his simple, seemingly innocent Pooh-Bearish mannerisms. I'd soon learned that this man was anything but simple.

Like me, Arthur was a transplant to Banff. The story I'd heard was that Arthur had shown up six years earlier, not long after the Doc's wife passed away. He'd stood on the doorstep and announced that he'd come to save Banff National Park's grizzly bears. He'd spent the last thirty years, he'd said, saving the elephants of Tanzania. Now the grizzlies had him, and he wasn't about to stop at letter writing to protect them. Arthur was well known for sabotaging bear hunts and chaining himself to earthmovers. Saving the bears was a full-time job for Arthur. And since part of my rent-free house-sitting deal with the Doc was that I would keep an eye on Arthur, I had my hands full too.

As an ex-reporter for *The Toronto Star*, I'd spent enough time around the police to know that when they discover a dead body everyone, especially those closest to the deceased, is a suspect until foul play is ruled out. With Arthur's penchant for getting himself into trouble, and the severed bear paws in his cabin, I knew chances were pretty good that Arthur Elliott would be at the top of the cops' list.

"Didn't you see Des?" I asked. He shook his head. "The tourists down by the gazebo?"

"No. I went to the front door," Arthur said. "When you didn't answer I took the path through the woods." He ran a hand down his shaggy beard. "What is it, Hellie? Has something happened?"

"Oh, Arthur. Yes, something terrible has happened. It's the Doc — he's dead."

He closed his eyes as if to shield himself from my words. "Heavens. No," Arthur whispered. His eyes snapped open. "Who told you this?"

"No one. We ... Des and I ... tourists ... they found him ... under the gazebo."

Arthur shook his head. "It doesn't seem possible. I talked to Michael before he left Tanzania. His plane was to get into Calgary sometime after eleven last night. He told me he was going to rest at the Marriott then meet me this morning at the Society office. He planned to rent a car ... " Arthur hesitated. "Then we were going to drive home together this evening. But you know all this, of course. When Michael didn't show up at the office this morning, I contacted the hotel. They said he checked out last night, shortly after he checked in."

"Did he leave a message for you?" I asked.

"No." Then he added, "Michael can be forgetful. And he doesn't like hotels. I simply assumed he changed his mind and drove home. One of the Society staff gave me this coat and took me to the bus depot."

"Why didn't you call me from Calgary when the Doc didn't show up?"

Arthur's hands worked a corner of his kikoi into a tight orange and red knot, but his eyes were focused on the opposite shore of the river. I could see the devastation in his eyes, but I feared others would not see it and would not understand that from years of discipline and meditation, Arthur had learned and perfected the art of being still. They would interpret his calm demeanor as callous and uncaring, or worse, as guilt.

As if seeking help, Arthur looked up to the sky. I squeezed my friend's hand and said, "There's something else, Arthur. I found bear paws in your cabin." He nodded, and from where I was sitting he didn't seem too surprised. This worried me. "Do you have any idea where they may have come from?"

"I'd rather not speculate at the moment."

Not exactly a definitive no, which was what I was hoping to hear. In the distance a police siren wailed. "We better go," I said.

"Wait, Hellie. Did you see him yourself? You are sure?"

"Yes. I saw him. I'm sure." In an attempt to offer some comfort I added, "There wasn't any blood. I mean, I don't think he was hurt." An odd thing to say since the man was dead. "What I mean is perhaps it was his heart."

Arthur held my gaze. "Michael did not die of a heart attack. He was murdered."

"What! Why would you say a thing like that? Do you know something?"

"Yes. I know he was murdered."

I closed my eyes and heard myself sigh. That was about all I could expect for an answer. Over the past year, I'd become accustomed to and accepting of my neighbour's cryptic responses. "Come on then," I said. "Police will be here by now."

"You go along, Hellie. I need a moment alone."

Reluctantly, I left him and walked back to join Des.

***

Sergeant Nathan Delaware was hurrying down the path. His big weathered face was fixed and determined as he approached the gazebo. Des would already have told him what he was going to find under there: his buddy of thirty years. But Nathan had been with the Royal Canadian Mounted Police for nearly four decades. He was a good, experienced cop and he'd have to see it with his own eyes before he could believe.

With a grunt, the big man went down on his knees and stuck his head in the doorway under the gazebo. He kept it in there a whole lot longer than I would have expected. But I guessed Nathan was a cop first, and he was doing what he had to do.

The crowd murmured behind us. Finally, Nathan sat back on his haunches and stared down at his beefy, gloved hands. A hush fell over the crowd as the sergeant slipped a glove off and ran a bare hand down his face. He drew himself up and leaned against the gazebo rail. His mouth was turned down in a frown and the lines across his furrowed brow were so deep they looked like scars. Sixty-four years old, Nathan looked his age and then some.

The Doc had told me that Nathan had stayed with the police force longer than most officers just so he could get himself and his wife transferred back to Banff. After being posted in Banff during the seventies and then sent up north for the next twenty-odd years, Nathan's dream had been to return to Banff and retire in the mountains. Two years ago, he had finally got his wish and been made staff sergeant of the Banff detachment. Shortly before Doc left for Africa, Nathan had found a modest condo he felt he could afford. I remembered the day Nathan came by the Doc's with the good news. "Well, Rivard," he'd said with a broad smile. "We'll be drinking beer and playing cribbage on my new deck just as soon as you get back from Africa."

"Damn," Nathan said as he picked his way across the lawn to join us on the path, carefully watching that he didn't disturb any of the footprints in the snow.

Des placed a comforting hand on the older man's shoulder. "What do you think, Nathan?"

"I think my job stinks." He swiped a thick index finger across his eyes and turned his attention to me. "What the hell happened, Hellie?"

"I have no idea," I said. Then I added somewhat defensively, "I didn't even know he was home."

The few times I had met Nathan before the Doc left for Tanzania, I'd found him pleasant but a little gruff, and somewhat standoffish, especially when Arthur was around. When I asked the Doc about it, he just laughed and said Nathan was just a bit anti-social from all his years of being stationed up in remote northern posts. Nathan had a good reputation in town, but he was definitely old school, known for turning a blind eye to kids getting drunk on Banff Ave, yet not hesitating to haul the same kids in for smoking pot.

Arthur didn't smoke pot, but he had been in trouble with the law, and he was anything but old school. My guess was that Nathan's apparent shyness toward Arthur would be best described as wariness.

"Did you know Doc was coming back?" Nathan said to me. "My understanding was that he was extending his stay for at least another six months."

"Mine too. But then he called from Tanzania to say he was coming."

"When?"

I couldn't think. When had he called? "Few days ago," I finally said. "Uh, Tuesday maybe. Didn't say much, just that he was coming home for a week or two. He was going to meet Arthur in Calgary tonight and they were going to come back together."

"Where is Arthur now?"

"Here, at the river ... by his cabin." My breath was shallow and I couldn't stop my hands from shaking, so I slipped them into my vest pockets. "He, uh ... he needed a minute alone. He's been away for the past week and just got back." I took a deep breath.

"Where's he been?"

"Didn't say."

"Never does, does he?" Nathan said vaguely. His gaze swept over the property and came to rest on the gazebo. He blew out a long breath and readied himself for the unpleasant task that lay ahead.

"Okay, who discovered the body?" he said, flipping through his notebook to a clean page.

"That fellow there," I said pointing to the young guy with the video camera. Then my eyes drifted to the gazebo, and I caught sight of the Doc's gaping mouth. I looked away and tried to blink back the sting in my eyes. "What do you think happened, Nathan?" I said.

"Don't know. No blood. Nothing around his head. I'm thinking his heart. But it's too early to speculate."

"How long would you say he's been under there?" Des asked.

"Hours would be my guess. Not days, that's for sure. Special crimes unit is on its way from the city. We'll get more from them. In the meantime, I'll send in a couple of officers to do the interviews." He passed Des a roll of police tape. "Okay, cordon off the area, will ya, Des?"

One of the tourists tapped Nathan on the shoulder. "Excuse me," she said. "How much longer are we going to have to stay here? I'm getting cold."

Nathan was keeping his composure, but the pain in his eyes bespoke the emotions he was suppressing. Des saw it too and jumped in. "We'll all have to stay put a little while longer. You'll just have to hang on," Des said to the woman as he led her back to the others.

"Can we let them go in the house?" I asked Nathan.

He barked out "No," in his rough, gravelly voice. I blinked at his tone, and imagined that over the years Nathan Delaware must have scared many a youngster away from a life of crime just by having a talk with them.

"Sorry, Hellie," he muttered.

"It's okay," I said.

He ran a hand over his mouth. "Go see if Suzanna's home. Ask her if we can use her place to do the interviews."

I hesitated and stole a glance down the path. There was no sign of Arthur. If I was going to help him I knew what I had to do and fast.

"You going, Hellie?" Nathan said.

"Yes. But there's something else. I found ... " I was having trouble getting it out. "Bear paws. I found bear paws in Arthur's cabin."

The big cop was staring at me as if he'd never seen me before. And I suspect that's precisely what he was wishing.

He said, "Holy hell! What next?"

CHAPTER 3

I RAN UP THE PUBLIC ACCESS PATH AND ACROSS THE STREET TO The Wild Rose, Suzanna LaChaine's self-proclaimed "marvelously successful" bed and breakfast inn. Her Volvo wagon was parked on the street. I'd noticed it wasn't there when I went to bed the night before. Seeing it now, it struck me that this was the first time I'd ever been relieved to know that my neighbour was home.

With a deep breath, I pressed my back up against the building's smooth, cool river rock and tried to steel myself for what I was about to do. But the Doc's visage invaded my thoughts: the gaping mouth, the wide-open glassy eyes and the lifeless gray pallor. Dead. The word rolled over and over again in my mind. Dead. But how? His hands were clenched at his chest. His heart? Nathan could be right. There was no blood. That gave me some comfort.

But ... we were supposed to be having dinner tonight to celebrate the Doc's arrival and my new story assignment. My mind was in overdrive, spinning out unanswerable questions. How long had he been home? Why hadn't he told me he was back? What in the name of God was he doing under the gazebo? And why would Arthur say he was murdered?

Murdered!

Not in Banff. Murder was something that simply did not happen in this town. But there were those bear paws ... Waves of panic and grief surged up from my gut.

Come on, Hellie, you can do better than this, I told myself. I had to do better because I was going to need every bit of strength and fortitude I could muster when I faced Suzanna LaChaine and told her that the man I suspected she had always been in love with was dead.

I pressed the bronze doorbell and listened to the muted sounds of chiming bells announcing "the messenger" had arrived.

The door swung open and the elegant Suzanna with jet-black hair and cosmetically-enhanced ivory skin greeted me with her customary, "Yes, Hellie, what can I do for you?" The ubiquitous cell phone was clasped in her right hand.

"There's been an accident," I said. "Some of your guests are at my house and — " She cut me short with the raise of one quizzical eyebrow. "The Doc's house," I corrected myself.

The eyebrow went down, and her mouth tilted up in that self-satisfied, half smile I'd come to despise. "What happened? Is it that marauding elk again?" she said.

I shook my head.

"That fool woman in the white ski suit?"

"No, Suzanna," I said softly.

"Then who? What happened? Is someone hurt?"

"Yes," I whispered. "The Doc."

Her face was a perfect blank. "But he's not back yet. Is he? I wasn't called. I told you to call me just as soon as he arrived."

"I didn't know he was back."

"What are you talking about? He's all right, isn't he?"

"No. He's dead." It was an unfair way to tell her, but there was no alternative. It was unfair to us all.

Her disbelief was immediate and emphatic. "That's not possible. He's not coming in until tonight. Isn't that what you told me? I saw ... Who told you this?"

"No one. I ... we just found him. I'm sorry, Suzanna. I truly am. Nathan sent me over. Can you help with the tourists? Let them stay here for a little while?"

She narrowed her eyes at me, grabbed her coat and headed out the door. We met Nathan and the tourists on the street.

"What's this all about?" Suzanna demanded. "Hellie says Michael is hurt. That he's ... " Her words trailed off as she bit down on her lower lip.

"I'm sorry, Suzanna," Nathan said. He lowered his voice and stepped closer to her. "It's true. We just found him. Michael is dead."

Suzanna's face crumpled, and I half expected the layers of makeup to crack and fall away like a smashed theatre mask. She brushed past us and headed up the walk to Doc Rivard's house. Nathan stopped her.

"You can't go in there, Suzanna," he said gently.

"But I have to see him," she protested.

"You can't."

With fingers splayed and outstretched arms, she reached to Nathan. A look of helpless confusion distorted her face as she spoke. "What happened? Did someone hurt him?" Just as quickly, her eyes narrowed and her mouth pressed itself into a hard red line. "This has something to do with that overgrown hippie, doesn't it? It's him, isn't it? He's done this." She pointed at Arthur, who was coming up the wooded path with Des. "I knew it was only a matter of time before something was going to happen."

"Hello, Suzanna," Arthur said sadly.

She ignored him and kept her focus on Nathan. "He should never have been allowed to stay here. He used Michael. And now look what's happened. He's ... Michael's ... oh dear God." She turned on Arthur again, her voice raised to a near scream. "You've done this, haven't you?"

"Suzanna, please," Nathan said. "We don't know anything yet."

She inhaled deep, halting breaths. "You listen to me, Nathan Delaware. He knows. He knows." She hissed the words. "Michael was going to kick him out. That's why he was coming back. Because he knows what they — " She stopped herself when she caught the warning look in my eyes. "What he's been up to."

Arthur remained impassive, but the tourists seemed to shrink away from her. Even the usually unflappable Nathan was alarmed by Suzanna's venomous attack. Though he shouldn't have been. Suzanna had a history of becoming unhinged to the point of being violent. According to Des, Suzanna had once pelted her neighbour's house with dog feces when he refused to stop letting his dog poop on her front lawn. When the neighbour retaliated by leaving a bag of dog poop in Suzanna's mailbox, Suzanna went in to hysterics and flew at the man like a feral cat, leaving deep scratches down his face and neck.

"I want you to arrest Arthur Elliott," Suzanna said to Nathan.

"Pipe down. That's quite enough, now," Nathan said.

"All right. All right." Suzanna repeated the phrase as if she was trying to convince herself it was true. She spoke to the tourists and pointed to The Wild Rose. "You may all go to my inn. Wait for me on the front porch."

But the tourists appeared apprehensive and looked to Nathan, who gave them a nod. They murmured to each other and then started up the front walk to The Wild Rose.

Nathan turned back to Suzanna. "Did you speak to the Doc before he arrived home?"

I was standing next to her watching her expression. Her eyes flashed to me and then back to Nathan. "Yes. Of course I spoke to him. He … I … well, I always call him at the clinic in Tanzania. I keep him up-to-date on things."

I was having trouble holding myself back. "Up-to-date," in Suzanna-speak meant hunting the Doc down every other day to let him know what new infraction Arthur or I had committed against the property. Everything in Suzanna's eyes was Arthur's or my fault. When a piece of the rockery fell away from the garden, we were careless. When the tourists left garbage on the front steps, we were irresponsible. When wild animals wandered into the yard to munch the flowers and fruit, we were reckless for having invited them in.

Nathan said to Suzanna, "You can give all the details when one of my constables takes your statement." He turned away from her and pulled Arthur and Des aside to talk.

Suzanna remained beside me. She laid a hand on my wrist; her acrylic-tipped nails bit into my flesh. "Are you absolutely certain it is Michael?" she said.

I pulled my arm away and rubbed at the spot. "Yes. I am certain. And I'm so very sorry."

Her gray eyes bore through me and her chin quivered ever so slightly as she pushed a hand up through her dark, perfectly trimmed bangs and then let them feather back into line with her perfect Cleopatra-style hair cut. I was never sure how old Suzanna was, and I never asked. My best guess was that she was somewhere in her mid-fifties; however, with the aid of carefully applied makeup she could easily have passed for forty-five. But that day, Suzanna's Lancôme line was not holding up, and her skin tone was taking on an unnatural greenish tinge. I was watching her out of the corner of my eye, waiting for the next verbal attack. Predictably the wait was short.

"This is all just dreadful," she blurted. "This should not have happened, Hellie."

"No, it should not," I said.

"I can't believe you didn't know he was back. I mean, for God's sake, he was dead or dying back there and you ... I just don't understand."

I held my tongue. It didn't matter that she was blaming me. None of that mattered. He was dead. That mattered. I screwed up a little kindness. "This must be terribly hard for you, Suzanna. I know how much the Doc," I hesitated, "means to you." I couldn't bring myself to use the past tense. Not yet.

Her face went tight against my words as if I'd spit in her eye. "You don't know anything," she said. "You don't know anything at all."

As she spoke, Suzanna's countenance was as hard and defiant as I'd ever seen it, but I saw something else in the artfully made-up face that the expensive foundation, powders and creams could not hide, something unnerving I couldn't quite identify.

Another patrol car pulled up. Two officers jumped out and jogged over to Nathan. I wondered why they were running. It wasn't as though they could save anyone.

"Okay, we got a body under the gazebo," Nathan said to the officers. "Witnesses in the house across the street at The Wild Rose B&B. One of you get their statements. Suzanna, lead the way please."

Suzanna did as the sergeant instructed and took off at a charge, black dress billowing behind her as she led the constable up the steps to her home.

"Hellie, you're going to have to move out for a few days, so go with the constable here," Nathan said pointing to the other RCMP officer. "Give her your statement and pack some clothes." He turned to Arthur. "And I'll take your statement myself."

Normally the Sergeant would assign the task to one of his underlings. But this was a small town where murders were rare, and ... Nathan Delaware had a personal stake in this case.

"You must be freezing in that ... uh ... dress," Nathan said, looking Arthur up and down. "Okay, let's go in the house. Don't touch anything."

Trailing behind the police, I felt like an intruder in my own home. Arthur and Nathan set themselves up in the kitchen and I, with the constable in tow, went upstairs to pack up a few belongings.

When my suitcase was packed and I was through giving my statement, I followed the constable downstairs. She left me with Arthur, who was seated at the table staring out the kitchen window. The crime unit had arrived, and at least half a dozen police officers were combing the back grounds. Nathan was among them.

"How'd you make out?" I said to Arthur.

"I haven't said anything yet," he replied. "I think Sergeant Delaware is, as the saying goes, letting me sweat. I suspect he thinks I'm guilty of something, though of what he's not sure."

Outside, I caught sight of a black body bag being delivered up from under the gazebo. Two attendants placed it on a gurney before they trundled it down the river path. I leaned against the windowsill and considered how many times the Doc had strolled that path taking in Sulphur Mountain's Christmas-treed slopes and the crystalline waters of the Bow River. This was the last time he would make that trip, and it was devastating to watch. It was also utterly incomprehensible that the man who'd helped me so much and been a friend when I'd really needed one was gone.

"Are you all right, Hellie?" Arthur said.

I took a seat across the table from him. As if to mock this dark, sad day, the late morning sun was shining brilliantly, setting the beautiful breakfast nook in a bright, cheery glow.

"Are you going to tell Nathan what you told me?" I said.

"That Michael was murdered?"

"Yes."

"I don't know."

"If you know something, Arthur, you have to tell the police. Did the Doc … " I hesitated and tried to come up with the right words. "Is there something about the Doc you know that you should tell the police?"

Arthur set his quiet eyes on mine. I'd never seen eyes like Arthur Elliott's. They were the colour of maple syrup, with emerald flecks surrounding the irises, and they were always calm. They were eyes that belonged to a man who thought out every word carefully before he uttered it — a characteristic that often drove me to distraction because I grew up in the city where everyone possessed quick eyes and quicker tongues.

"No. There's nothing," Arthur said.

"Do you know why he was coming home?"

"Yes. Because he was concerned about me."

"Why? What's going on?"

"I don't know, Hellie. Which is why I've told you. Now you and I can look for the answer."

I rubbed a thumb and forefinger over my eyes. "If you think you know something, you have to tell the police."

He lowered his voice. "I will tell them I know Michael was murdered. But they won't listen to me, Hellie, because I can't tell them why I know. Those paws. They'll tell — "

Arthur's words were cut short when Nathan came in the back door. He'd been watching us the whole time from the backyard.

"Okay, Arthur. You can come with me to your cabin now," Nathan said. "What about you, Hellie, you ready?"

I nodded. Then turned my attention back to Arthur. "I'll wait for you out front. We can go into town and look into finding someplace to stay."

"Thank you, Hellie, but I have somewhere to stay," Arthur said. He wrote down a phone number on a piece of notepaper and handed it to me.

It was a Canmore number. Canmore is a town twenty minutes outside the park gates. This was unusual. Arthur rarely let people know where he was going. But then, this wasn't a usual day. Even so, as I folded the paper and slipped it into my pocket an uneasy feeling swept over me. With no other choice, I left the house and Arthur.

Outside I thought about asking Nathan if I could take my car, then I decided against it. A walk would help to clear my head. Besides, I rarely used my car anyway. Everyone in Banff walked.

I crossed the street and headed for town. As I passed The Wild Rose, icy fingers tingled up the back of my neck and sent a shiver along my scalp. Instinctively I looked back.

Suzanna LaChaine was standing in a window, watching.

Our eyes met. I turned away quickly and focused on a white Ford Taurus parked on the street. But all the way down the block, I felt her penetrating gaze follow me until I turned the corner and was out of her sight.

***

Along Banff Avenue, I passed shops and people, seeing neither store-fronts nor faces. Everything was out of focus, blurred. I even overshot my destination and had to double back to Church's Tea & Gifts.

I stood outside watching Bernie Church through the window. She was behind the counter talking to a customer, and I was trying to think how I was going to break the news that Doc Rivard was dead. Bernie was my closest friend in Banff, and she had helped make it possible for me to stay.

When I'd arrived in town the previous autumn, I hadn't intended to stay. In fact, I'd had no intentions at all, which I suppose made stay-ing inevitable. All I'd wanted was a little time to clear my head after my near-marriage debacle. So I checked into the posh Rim Rock Hotel where I ate well and floated around the hot springs pool across the street. I knew I had a distant relative who lived somewhere in or around Banff. I also knew his name was Michael Rivard, that he was from my mother's side of the family and that he was a doctor of some sort. I'd never met him, and coming from a family that lived by the maxim: *our relatives are wished upon us, thank God we can choose our friends*, I had no intention of contacting my great-uncle Michael. I opted instead to seek solace from strangers. So in the evenings, I wandered Banff Avenue and eventually met Bernie Church at her tea and gift shop.

Bernie and I didn't stay strangers for long, though. In fact, from the moment we met, she had treated me like an old friend. And according to her we were in fact old friends, just from another time. She never did specify when exactly that other time was and, quite frankly, I was afraid to ask. But it really didn't matter because Bernadette Church was one of those rare people you meet and trust immediately. She was a true heart, to use her own expression.

During one of my many visits, I told her how I'd done the "I do and dash" after catching my fiancé in a compromising embrace, and she was very sympathetic. I also mentioned I'd been a writer for *The Toronto Star*. Bernie seized the news and suggested I write for the town newspaper *The Peak*. After a week of eating and floating in the pool, boredom was set-ting in so I took her advice and whipped off a story about the Zen of rock climbing. The editor loved it and fed me more story ideas.

By the close of week two, I'd written four stories and was getting paid enough to keep me in beer money. But my tab at the Rim Rock was a whopping three grand. I hadn't been in touch with my parents, so there wasn't much chance they were going to top up my Toronto bank account, as they were once wont to do. This, I knew, was a ploy on my mother's part to smoke me out and drive me home. Poverty, in Helen MacConnell's mind, would bring me to my senses, back to Toronto, and back into the forgiving arms of Brock Hanlan, my ex-fiancé.

Helen's plan might have worked if Bernie and I hadn't consumed a great deal of blackcurrant liqueur one evening, and if I hadn't told her the truth about who I'd discovered my fiancé locking lips with just before the wedding. I'd also told her that I had nowhere to stay, and that I couldn't go home because to do so would only cause more pain for everyone involved. After Bernie and I wracked our brains and still couldn't come up with a solution to my problem, my thoughts turned to my great-uncle Michael. I wondered if Bernie had ever met him. But I hesitated to ask her when I remembered a family vacation. I was twelve years old at the time. We were visiting Banff, and we'd just arrived in town when my litter brother — who had recently completed a family tree for a Boy Scout project — said, "Hey, we have a great-uncle who lives here. We should try and find him." My mother's response was to cough into her hand and change the subject.

Maybe it was the liquor, or the thought of having to go home to Toronto, but whatever the reason, I did mention Michael Rivard's name to Bernie.

"Of course I know him," Bernie said. "Everyone in Banff knows the Doc. Do you?"

That's when I opened Pandora's box the rest of the way and admitted that he was my great-uncle. "But I've never met him," I added quickly.

Bernie clapped her hands. "You're related! This is perfect. Hellie, don't you see? Fate has brought you here. You leave it to me; I'll arrange for the two of you to meet over coffee. I just know he's the answer to your prayers."

Somehow I doubted Michael Rivard was going to come anywhere near to being the answer to my prayer. The last time I could remember my mother saying anything about my great-uncle Michael was when we'd returned home from our family Banff vacation and I'd pressed her about why she didn't want us to meet our great-uncle. My mother let out a long sigh and said, "Because Michael Rivard is a very odd man, who lives a very odd life in the mountains."

I came away with the image of my great-uncle Michael being some kind of weird mountain-man recluse. So the afternoon I showed up at Coyote's Café I was on the lookout for an old guy dressed in bearskins and a coonskin cap. Instead, I was greeted by a wiry seventy-one-year-old guy dressed in baggy jeans and a papaya-pink running jacket, whose height just matched my own five foot seven inches.

"Hellie!" he said pumping both of my hands in his. "You are the spitting image of your grandmother."

"Hi … uh, Uncle Michael," I said awkwardly.

"Call me Doc."

I wondered if I should call him "Uncle Doc." But he threw his arm around my shoulder and led me through the narrow restaurant to a table before I had the chance to ask. For the next twenty minutes he talked and I listened as he mapped out, on a serviette, our common lineage to my mother's mother — the Doc's sister — and then back about four generations to our ancestors who came from Scotland and Quebec.

"I'm ten years younger than your grandmother," Doc said as he pushed the serviette aside.

I just nodded. I'd met my grandmother only a handful of times before she died when I was ten. I wasn't sure what else to say. But I needn't have worried about filling airtime; Doc burned up the next half hour chatting, mostly about running.

"My quack doctor tells me running isn't good for my old knees," he said, punctuating his words with a dismissive snort. "Shot or two of cortisone fixes things up just fine. Got a bad ticker, too." He thumped a fist against his chest. "Same ass tells me running's great for the heart." Finally he got to the matter at hand. "So, Bernie tells me you need a place to stay."

Suddenly I felt ashamed. Like I was one of those long-lost relatives who slither out of woodwork when some relative she's never laid eyes on wins the lottery.

"I don't … I mean … I'm not here to ask you for anything," I stammered.

"No? Bernie said you need a place to live."

"I do. It's just that … " I trailed off.

"But she did tell you that I'm leaving for Africa in three weeks to volunteer at a clinic, and that I need a house-sitter?"

My heart quickened. I shook my head.

"Here's the situation, Hellie," the Doc said, stretching his leg and giving his knee a good rub. "I really need someone to look after my place. Bernie said you're good stuff, dependable, honest. And I see you're writing for *The Peak*. That's great. I talked to the editor — she vouches for you too. And, well, we are kin."

"But you don't know me."

"Sure I do. I met you when you were this big." He held his hands apart. "And I know your mom. Haven't seen her in about thirty years." He shrugged.

I blushed.

"But I have seen your dad."

"Really? When?"

"A few years back when he was here dealing with some folks who were trying to build a resort. I've had quite a few dealings with MacHan Travel." My father was in partnership with Brock Hanlan Sr., my ex-fiancé's father, hence the clever company name.

"So I'll tell you what, we'll try each other out. You can move in right away," the Doc was saying. "That'll give us a few weeks to get to know each other before I leave. If it works out, you stay. If not, I find someone else. And, of course, you'll have to meet Arthur and meet with his approval."

"Arthur?" My head was spinning.

Doc sighed. "Here's a little background. Art's my good friend. No. My best friend. Wait, that's not true either. Arthur's my other best friend. Barbara's my first."

"Barbara your wife? Sorry, my parents never said much."

He nodded, his expression solemn. "Barb passed away. Seven years now."

"I'm sorry."

"Thanks, we keep in touch."

I smiled. He didn't. I took a sip of my coffee and tried not to let my face show the alarm I was feeling. Okay, maybe Mom was right about Great-uncle Doc being odd. Really odd.

"Arthur lives in a cabin on my property," Doc continued. "You could say I take care of him. It's a little tough to explain. See, Art's the same age as me, seventy-one. And he's okay. Not sick or anything, just needs someone to keep an eye on him. Art gets himself in trouble. I need someone who can get him out of it."

"What kind of trouble?"

"Mostly gets arrested for civil disobedience. He doesn't like bear hunters much. I figure since you worked for a big newspaper in a big city — " he paused and smiled. "Bernie filled me in on your background. Anyway, I figured you'd know how to handle things if … well, if things do get out of hand. Just keep an eye on him, that's all. But for God's sake don't ever tell Art I asked you to."

"I won't," I said, and I meant it because at that point I had no intention of meeting Arthur or moving into Doctor Rivard's house. Next thing you know he'd have me changing the old guy's diapers and making dinners for his dead wife.

He had, however, piqued my curiosity about the situation. "Can I ask you a question?" I said.

"Sure."

"Unless this Arthur person is mentally unstable or something, why do you take care of a grown man?"

He stared down at his coffee cup; the silver hair on the crown of his head glistened in the light. Silence passed between us before he finally looked up and said, "Arthur is trying to do something good here. He tried to do good things in Africa, too, but that's another story. I'd like to think that by helping him, maybe I'm doing something good too."

The expression in my eyes must have told him I was wavering. The Doc pulled his trump card. "I know you're in a bit of tight spot, Hellie."

My back was up immediately.

"Don't worry," he added quickly. "Bernie didn't give details, and I didn't ask. And I really don't care to know." He leaned across the table and placed a hand over mine.

From any other stranger, relative or otherwise, the gesture would have made me flinch, at the very least. But with the Doc, only a fool would have interpreted the act as anything more than kindness. And at that point in my life, I was a little starved for kindness.

"Let me tell you something, Hellie, about the people who come to Banff. Most of us come with secrets, and this town's a good place to keep them."

***

With the Doc's words still echoing in my memory, I drew a deep breath and opened the door to Church's Tea & Gifts. The bell tinkled its welcome as I stepped over the threshold and into the cozy shop.

Bernie looked up from her customer and gave me a warm smile. "Oh, hello friend," she said.

Obviously, news of the Doc's death had not spread as far as Banff Avenue. It was about to.

"Be right with you," Bernie said. "Have a cup of tea. I just made some orange spice."

I thanked her and went to the tiny kitchen where I poured a cup. Moving into the sitting room, I settled into the worn leather couch — amid all the antique teddy bears, china and books — and let the gentle scents of sweet, musky incense, handmade herbal soaps and floral potpourri fill my senses. The sounds of running water and chirping birds played softly in the background completing the tranquil setting.

I sipped the tea and watched Bernie brush her fingers through her long, straight auburn hair while she patiently waited for her customer to make a decision over two types of tea.

Bernie and the woman standing in front of her were a study in contrasts. Bernie's customer was a petite woman with grey curly hair, dressed in a bright mauve and tangerine jogging suit — a member of the seniors' tour bus crowd Banff attracts in the pre-ski season. Bernie, on the other hand, was just over five feet six inches tall, with a slim build, and looked like a throwback to the heyday of Haight-Ashbury. At thirty-eight, Bernie was only seven years older than me, but the circa 1965 peasant blouse and Indian cotton skirt she was wearing were the genuine articles. Bernie never bought cheap knockoffs. She didn't have to, because Bernie Church was a master collector of all things old.

"That girl stockpiles everything from old cars to old people," Doc Rivard had once told me. "That's how she got me," he laughed. "I like to think of myself as Bernie's most treasured relic."

Tears prickled my eyes. Doc was right, Bernie loved him. And so did I. Maybe it was the thin line of familial blood that connected us, but something extraordinary happened when I moved into Doc's house. Almost immediately I felt at home. And then for three terrific weeks we were able to get to know each other. We took long walks along the river path, made dinners together, laughed a lot and talked about solving the world's problems. The only thing we didn't seem to talk about was family and that suited me just fine. For that time, I think we were all the family we needed, because my great-uncle treated me like a daughter. After he left for Africa I really missed him, but we kept up weekly correspondence with phone calls and emails and grew even closer. Now he was gone, and it felt like there were steel bands wrapped around my chest.

After her customer left, Bernie came and sat next to me on the couch. She cocked her head and studied me. "What is it, Hellie? Your energy seems all out of whack today."

"Where's Paul?" I said. Paul was Bernie's husband.

"Out of town on a buying trip." She eyed my suitcase and worry creased her forehead. "When does the Doc get in?"

"He's ... he's already back. Oh, Bernie. There's just no other way to say this. He's dead."

Her hand flew up to cover her mouth. "Dead! I don't believe it," she said. "How? When?"

"A tourist found him under the gazebo."

"The gazebo? What on earth was he doing under there? Hellie ... " Her face was filled with confusion and disbelief. "This just can't be," she whispered. "What happened?"

"No one knows much yet."

She let her head fall back against the couch and stared up at the ceiling as she tried to make sense of what I'd just told her.

I got up from the couch and went to the door and locked it. Then I flipped the sign over so the *Closed* side was facing the street. From the kitchen I fetched a bottle of cassis and poured us each a generous portion. We sipped the dark purple drink and let the liquor seep into our bloodstreams and the news sink in to our consciousness.

"I just don't believe it," Bernie said. "This has to be a mistake."

I could see she was in shock, and I wished with all my heart that I could tell her she was right. That this was a mistake. But it wasn't.

"Tell me everything you do know, Hellie."

"That is all I know, Bern. He came home, and we found him."

"And the police didn't tell you anything else?"

"We have to wait for the autopsy report."

"Does Nathan know?"

"He came right away."

"Well, what does he think?"

I shrugged. "He did mention something about the Doc's heart."

"Yes. I suppose ... But he was in great health before he left last fall." She glanced at my suitcase again.

"I have to be out of the house for a few days," I explained.

"Then you are going to stay with Paul and me, aren't you?" There was a note of something like desperation in her voice.

I squeezed her hand. "Of course. I'd be most grateful."

"Where's Arthur? He'll stay with us too, won't he?"

"Said he's staying with someone in Canmore." I sipped my drink and weighed what else I was going to tell her about Arthur.

"Hellie, what is it? You've got this weird look in your eyes."

"It's something Arthur said, and I don't know what to make of it."

She sat up straight. "What?"

"He said he believes the Doc was murdered."

"What? That's ... well, that's not possible. Is it?"

"I don't know, Bern. Doc didn't happen to say anything to you about why he was coming back so soon, did he?"

"No. Paul and I only heard he was coming home through you."

"Arthur just told me Doc was worried about him for some reason."

"Hmmm." Bernie tapped her chin with nervous fingers. "He didn't mention anything like that to me yesterday. I asked him why the Doc was coming home so soon, and all Arthur said was that he guessed he wanted to."

There was a knock at the door and a man was pressing his face against the glass. Bernie went to the door and pointed to the *Closed* sign. Then she opened the door a crack and said, "I'm sorry, the store's closed for the rest of the day."

While I watched the exchange, I was wondering if I'd heard her correctly, if she'd actually said she'd spoken to Arthur yesterday. Bernie closed the door and took up her place on the couch.

"When did you say you talked to Arthur, Bern?"

"Yesterday."

"Mind if I ask why he called?"

"He didn't call. He came by in the evening. Around eight. Just before I closed up and met you at our place."

"He wasn't home last night," I said. "He just got in this morning. That's what he told me."

"Well, he was here. Dropped off those." She pointed to a shelf lined with Arthur's signature folk art weathervanes made from recycled tin cans. Each one had a little man or woman that sawed a perpetual log when the wind caught and turned the whirligig. "I didn't think to mention it to you because I assumed he was home early and you knew. And you didn't see him when you got home from my place?"

I shook my head.

"Oh."

"Yes. Oh." I said and let the word and all its implications hang in the air between us.

CHAPTER 4

THE NEXT MORNING I WOKE WITH A START, EYES WIDE STARING UP AT Santa and his reindeer sailing across a blue-black, star-studded sky.

I had no idea where I was.

Propped on an elbow, I squinted across the room to the far wall where miniature Christmas villages were arranged on two bookshelves like little subdivisions. It all came back in one great wallop. Doc Rivard was dead. And I was at Bernie and Paul's house, staying in the Christmas room. Bernie's inventory had grown to the point where she'd had to create theme rooms to accommodate her collections. The four rooms upstairs were decorated according to the seasons, with each one done either in a Christmas, Easter, autumnal or summer motif. The downstairs den housed the time room, filled with antique clocks of every imaginable type and style. The kitchen was done in a country farm theme, and the living room amounted to a giant tea party with stuffed animals and dolls occupying every square inch of space.

I let my head fall back on the pillow and felt my stomach squeeze into a tight knot. Doc Rivard's house was being searched, and Arthur was supposed to be staying with friends. I'd called the Canmore number and left a message on someone's answering machine for Arthur to call me. So far, I hadn't heard from him. Neither had I heard from my younger brother Danny or my parents. Though I really wasn't expecting Mom or Dad to call, since Danny was the only member of my family still speaking to me after the wedding debacle. And coward that I was, I'd emailed Danny, instead of phoning the house, to tell them what had happened.

On the bedside table, a snowman clock indicated it was nearly nine. Sleep hadn't found me until the wee hours, and now I'd overslept. All night my mind kept seeing the Doc, and hearing Arthur's voice: *Michael did not die of a heart attack. He was murdered.* And today I was starting work on a new article — my first assignment for *McMillan*, Canada's premier newsmagazine. In two hours I was supposed to meet a Texan hunter named Ansel Rock. This guy had outbid all his super-rich friends and fellow hunters to win the exclusive right to hunt a bighorn sheep in Kananaskis Country's South Ghost Wilderness Area. The area had been closed to hunters for over twelve years in order to give the wildlife a chance to build their herds. But once every two years for the past half dozen, a Provincial auction had been held that gave hunters the chance to bid on one licence. Each time that lucky bidder had been Ansel Rock. Now it would be my job to find out exactly why Ansel Rock has spent a million dollars to kill one Alberta bighorn sheep. Then I'd have three days to write the story and get it in to my new editor at *McMillan*. And right now, I wasn't even sure I wanted to get out of bed.

Through the woodcut design in the window shutters, I could see star-shaped pieces of brilliant blue sky promising one of those unseasonably warm autumn days Alberta tends to get just before a huge storm blows in winter for the next six months. I closed my eyes against the light and the prospect of facing the day. All I wanted to do was pull the patchwork quilt over my head and go back to sleep.

There was a tap at the door. Bernie poked her head in. "You awake, Hellie?"

"Yes, but I'm not sure I'm that happy about it." She was carrying a tray with juice, coffee and muffins. "Bless you, Bernie," I said, reaching for the juice.

She sat down on the bed and placed the tray between us. She looked drained.

"Were you able to sleep?" I asked.

"Off and on. Paul called late."

"When does he get back?"

"Hopefully by tonight or tomorrow."

"Good."

Bernie smiled that dreamy smile she wore whenever anyone mentioned her husband's name. Then her mouth turned down in a frown. "But I have some bad news. Suzanna called a few minutes ago."

"That is bad. Was she just checking in to see that we're okay?" The sarcasm was thick in my voice.

Bernie rolled her eyes heavenward. "Oh yes, that, of course. And she's sending over a man named John Morrow to see you."

"Who?"

"She said he's a friend of your Texan hunter. Staying at The Wild Rose, and he's apparently got something for you.

"Maybe I should give him a call."

"I don't think you have time. Suzanna wouldn't give me a chance to come up and wake you, just said he was on his way over. If you don't want to talk to him when he gets here, I'll tell him you'll call him later. Maybe you could put off doing this article for at least a couple of days."

I swung my legs out of bed. "That's okay, I'll take care of it. Probably better to be doing something to fill the time anyway. And I need the money. Who knows how long I'm going to be able to stay in the house, or even if I'm going to be allowed back in there … "

"You can stay with us," she said.

"Thanks, Bern. Don't suppose Arthur called?"

She shook her head and her eyes were full of sorrow. "This doesn't seem real, Hellie. Paul and I have known the Doc forever. I don't believe Arthur, you know. No one would hurt the Doc. Sure there are people here who don't like what he and The Society stand for, but no one would hurt him over it."

I was digging in my suitcase for a pair of slacks and a sweater. My back was to Bernie. "I'm sure you're right," I said. But there was something in my own voice that wasn't ringing true. "We'll just have to wait until we hear back from Nathan and the medical examiner."

The sound of a cuckoo clock announcing the hour came from downstairs. I cocked an ear, unsure whether it was really one of Bernie's clocks or the sound-alike doorbell.

"Doorbell," Bernie said. "I'll get it. You get dressed."

I threw on a pair of black heavy cotton pants, a long-sleeved white T-shirt and a black wool sweater. A year ago, I'd dressed only in design er suits, tailored slacks and high-heeled shoes. My hair had been highlighted and styled in the latest, trendiest two-hundred-dollar do. Now my wardrobe consisted of functional, comfortable pants, lots of sweaters, hiking shoes and all-weather jackets. And my hair was just short. Styling it took all of two minutes — I'd just slap on a little gel, spike and go. When I was dressed I went to the bathroom, where I splashed water on my face, ran fingers through my dark hair and went downstairs.

At the front entrance, a tanned outdoorsy-looking man I guessed was in his early sixties was leaning casually against the wall. His lustrous head of platinum and gray hair reminded me of the Doc's.

"Morning. I'm John Morrow," he said extending his hand. "Ansel Rock's friend. I do apologize for bothering you, especially now. The hostess at The Wild Rose, Suzanna, told me what happened yesterday to your landlord. I'm very sorry."

"Thank you." I shook his hand. "He was my great-uncle." Somehow it was important to me that this stranger knew Doc was my relative.

"Oh. I see. Well, again, I'm very sorry for your loss."

I nodded and gave him a sad smile. "Would you like to come in?" I said.

"Won't just now," he said. "I'm on my way out of town. That's why I came by. Ansel hasn't checked in at the Springs Hotel yet, so I thought I'd better stop by and see if you're still doing the story. With all that's happened, I'm sure the magazine and Ansel will understand if you decide to opt out."

He spoke with an odd, barely detectable southern drawl, tinged with what I imagined were British boarding school undertones. Overall, John Morrow looked more like a pampered golf pro than my idea of a Texan.

"I appreciate your concern," I said. "But I intend to do it. Although I may need a couple of extra days. My editor said I was to meet Ansel at eleven o'clock today. Has he been held up?"

"No. He'll be here. Taking an early flight," John said. He shifted a manila envelope from one hand to the other. "Since you're going ahead as planned, I have a few articles about Ansel." His face was kind as he passed me the envelope. "Full of his hunting stats, awards, things like that. If you follow these and come up with something similar, you'll do just fine. But then you must be an awfully good writer as it is," he said.

"Oh, what makes you say that?"

"Ansel doesn't like to give interviews. He's no fan of the press. But he's making an exception with this article, so I sincerely hope you are long on questions and even longer on patience."

"Thanks for the tip."

"I'll give you another one. Ansel's a very private man."

"My editor mentioned that."

"Good. Because Ansel doesn't want any undue publicity about this trip. I'm sure you know there's a fair bit of controversy surrounding this hunt."

"Yes. I'm aware of that."

"Ansel wants this to be an uneventful, peaceful hunt."

Peaceful hunt. The oxymoron was not lost on me.

"Keep everything confidential. Hunting itineraries especially. I'm heading out on a painting trip for a day or two and may not be around when Ansel gets in from Houston. Listen Hellie, I've known Ansel a very long time, so if I can be of any help, don't be afraid to ask when I get back."

"Thanks. I'll keep that in mind. And thank you for dropping this by," I said holding up the envelope.

"You're most welcome. And again, I am awfully sorry about your uncle."

After he was gone, Bernie came up behind me. "Hmm. He's handsome."

"He is," I murmured. "Reminds me of the Doc."

Bernie forced a smile and said, "Yeah, me too." Her eyes glanced up to the collection of clocks that covered a good portion of the wall. Most of them indicated it was somewhere around nine thirty. She was fighting back tears. "We should be having breakfast with the Doc right now. When you told me he was coming back, I planned … " Tears choked her words.

"Aw Bern." I gave her a hug. "We'll get through this. Are you going into the shop?"

"For a little while," she said and went to the hall closet to get her coat.

I opened the front door for her. "I'll call you later," I said.

When she was gone, I ran upstairs to take a shower and get dressed again. Then I packed up the things I'd need for my first meeting with Ansel Rock and headed off to my office in the clouds.

***

The quiet mile-and-a-half walk along the Bow River's north shore was a nice respite that led me through a trail of pines, spruce and poplars. But the respite was over when I peered through the trees across the water to Doc Rivard's home. Yellow police tape encircled the property and flapped in the breeze. Uniformed men and women came and went across the lawn. A mere twenty-four hours had passed since I'd found my Doc dead. I didn't want to even think about what the next hours would bring.

I hurried on and walked up and over an escarpment that led down to the base of the Bow Falls, where the water splashed and churned over jagged rocks. A steep climb up a labyrinth of rail-tie steps finally took me to Banff's *castle*. A uniformed doorman held the heavy brass and bevelled glass door for me and I entered the grand lobby of the park's landmark hotel, The Banff Springs.

I made a quick stop at the Castle Pantry to grab a latte. Then it was off to the Riverview Room — a ballroom-sized, cathedral-ceilinged space complete with a "walk-in" fireplace and two grand pianos.

I sank into one of the antique chairs and, for inspiration and solace, gazed out the twelve-foot windows across the Bow Valley to the spectacular Fairholme Mountain Range. Cumulus clouds hovered over its peaks like great dollops of whipped cream. Just outside the window, one-hundred-foot spruce trees swayed in the valley breeze.

The soothing sounds of classical music played softly in the background. A fire crackled in the fireplace that was flanked by two bighorn sheep heads carved in stone. The whole floor seemed to be deserted. My only company was the stuffed deer and antelope heads mounted on the walls, that watched the comings and goings of guests and interlopers such as myself.

Directly above me was the head of a mule deer that looked as though it had just come crashing through the wall. The taxidermist had captured the quick look in the deer's eyes. Perhaps the creature had heard the crack of the rifle just before the bullet hit. I wondered what a man like Ansel Rock thought when he saw those eyes just before he pulled the trigger. I'd make a point of asking him.

It was ten thirty, and I had half an hour to review John Morrow's background articles. My plan was to take Mr. Rock for lunch, keep it casual as my editor had suggested, then set up a couple more formal interviews. If I could stay focused, by next week I'd have a well-written article about a man who spends more money trying to shoot one bighorn sheep than most people make in a lifetime.

So far, my knowledge of Ansel Rock was limited. From the brief research I'd managed to do over the net and what I'd just read, I knew he owned a very successful development company called Lone Star Developments that specialized in building mega-malls and vacation resorts. I also knew he'd proudly shot enough animals to rival Noah's collection. Though curiously, according to my research and my editor, the two previous times Ansel Rock had done this hunt he hadn't taken a thing home. He'd never even taken a shot.

I had to wonder whether Mr. Rock might be better off spending a few of those American dollars on some hunting lessons. But from all accounts the Texan was a great shot. It seems he'd been holding out for one particular ram.

This was the first time he'd be staying in Banff. During the other bighorn hunts he'd camped in K-Country. That puzzled me. Why was Ansel Rock staying in Banff and not in Kananaskis, where he'd be hunting? I jotted a note to myself and kept an eye out for a man I'd never seen. None of the articles contained a picture. But with a handle like Ansel Rock and a company named after Texas's state moniker and the state's favourite beer, I imagined he'd be the genuine article — a big guy, tall, brushcut, mid-to-late fifties. Slow talking, foot pawing and gosh-ma'aming me all over the place.

Half an hour later when I saw a lanky Stetson-wearing fellow making his way across the expansive room toward me, I wasn't disappointed. Ansel Rock was indeed a fine specimen of a Texan, well over six feet, with ostrich-skin cowboy boots adding another inch to his already skyward height. He wore a fawn sheepskin coat that hung to just below his butt, and the creamy soft wool curled around his thick, athletic neck. Age-wise, I'd been off by at least fifteen years. My Texan was thirty-nine, forty at most, very handsome in a cop kind of way with a good strong jaw, deep-set indigo eyes and a small scar over his right eyebrow.

"Mr. Rock?" I said, standing up.

"You must be Hellie MacConnell," he said with just a hint of a Texan accent, which did disappoint me. I was hoping for a drawl as thick as a good Longhorn steak.

I extended my hand. "Good to meet you."

"Let's hope so," he said and accepted my hand.

"Uh, have a seat," I said.

He took off his hat and sat down.

"I thought we'd just have lunch today if you're free," I said. "Then we can talk about your schedule and set up some interview times. Also, if you have any pictures you'd like the magazine to use I can pass them along. Of course, I'd like to take a few myself."

He leaned forward and rested his elbows on the table. "Look, let's get off on the right foot here. I'm not going to mince words. I don't want to get involved in any political stuff."

"The magazine told me."

"Good. So no pictures of me. Keep my hunting schedule to yourself. Don't introduce me to any weirdos. I make the rules, I set the agenda, and we get along just fine."

I stared at him with my mouth half open.

"Look, I have a friend who was hunting bears up north. They fire-bombed his truck."

"Oh my God! Was he hurt?"

"He wasn't in his vehicle, but his dog was."

"Someone blew up his dog?"

"Yes, they did."

"Why would they kill his dog?"

"He was a hunting dog. I guess they decided he was an accomplice."

"They? Animal rights activists?"

Anger ignited his eyes. "Animal rights terrorists," he corrected me. "But that's not what we're going to be talking about, is it?"

I made a quick mental note to avoid environmental discussions. "No, it's not," I said. "Unless you think it has some bearing on why you spend the money you do to take part in this hunt."

"It has none," he said through clenched teeth.

"Okay, then, if you have time, why don't we get started now?"

He put his hat on and rubbed the back of his neck. "I'm hotter than hell in this coat. Listen, don't worry about getting what you need for this story. We'll have plenty of time together. By the end of the week, you'll have more than enough to write about. I guarantee it." He tipped his hat.

The gesture eased my disappointment, but not my wariness. The accent was also taking on texture. "Thanks. But my editor did mention he'd like to see a draft of this article in about three days, so … "

Ansel stood and pushed his chair into the table. "So, we'll just have to tell your editor it'll be done when this hunt's done. Anyway, I'm starved, let's eat."

The guy was about as subtle as a bull and I had to wonder who was going to be writing this story because so far it certainly didn't look like it was going to be me. My sense was that Mr. Rock saw me as his typist.

I collected my belongings. "Okay, since you're all dressed up for winter, why don't we walk into town for lunch?"

"All right." It came out sounding like aw-rite.

"We're about a mile from the center of town, so it's your choice, Mr. Rock, we can — "

"Ansel will do," he said.

"Okay, Ansel, there are two ways into town: along Spray Avenue or the pathway that goes down past the Bow Falls."

"Falls sound good," he said. "That's one of my favorite walking spots. Other one's Tunnel Mountain."

I eyed his cowboy boots and wondered how well they'd double as hikers. I was about to ask him if he wanted to change into something with better grips, when footsteps clicking behind us on the Tyndall stone caught my attention. It was Ryan, a waiter I knew from the cocktail lounge.

"Hi, Hellie. There's a call for you in the lounge," Ryan said.

"Really?"

"Yeah, really," Ryan said with a smirk.

"Is it Bernie?"

"No. It's a man."

Ansel was watching the exchange with interest. "Do you work here?" he said.

"Yes. Sometimes. But I'm not an employee, if that's what you mean," I added with a shrug, trying to brush off my embarrassment. "Didn't think anyone knew I was here."

Ryan gave me the *yeah right* look and said, "Everyone knows you do your work here, Hellie. We all know. Security guys know. The cleaning guys too. And the general manager, he's on to you, but he says he's letting it go as long as you don't hire a secretary and put in your own phone line."

"Gee, I thought I just kind of blended in with the guests."

Ryan pulled another face. "You can take the call at the bar."

Ansel gave a low chuckle. "I'll meet you downstairs at the front doors," he said to me, then strolled toward the exit.

I followed Ryan to the bar in the Rundle Balcony Lounge and picked up the receiver.

"Hellie, Nathan here."

My heart pounded against my ribcage at the sound of his gruff voice. If the sergeant had taken the time to track me down here, I knew it was probably bad news.

"Glad I caught you," he said. "Bernie told me you might be there. Couple of things: First, we found the Doc's rental car parked down from the house. A white Ford Taurus."

"I passed that car on my way into town," I said. "Why would he park it away from the house?"

"That's what we'd like to know. Also, just got word from Des about one of those bear paws. It was a grizzly, and it's looking like it came from a park bear that was collared as part of a research project. Had a de-formed claw or something. Anyway, we'll know for sure when we get the DNA results back. And if it is that bear, according to the people heading up the project, it was alive and well three weeks ago. So whoever took it did so well out of season and most likely in the park. You know where I can reach Arthur?"

"In Canmore. I gave you the number."

"People there haven't been home the last few days and say they haven't seen him."

My heart sank. "Nathan, Arthur doesn't know where those paws came from." Out of the corner of my eye, I noticed Ryan was staying within earshot. I turned my back to him and lowered my voice. "This is ridiculous."

"Did he tell you that?"

"What?"

"That he doesn't know where the paws came from?"

"No. But — "

"Hellie, I'm not saying he killed those bears. I'm saying he might know who did. And if he does, he needs to be telling the wardens and me, instead of playing vigilante."

I knew he was referring to the incident last spring when Arthur had been arrested for harassing bear hunters outside the park. Arthur claimed the hunters were poachers. As it turned out, all the so-called poachers had legitimate permits.

"Are you thinking those paws are connected to the Doc's death?" I said.

"No, I'm not. Let me know if you hear from Arthur. Shouldn't have taken off without telling us. Oh, and the people he claimed he stayed with in Calgary the night the Doc came back, they said Arthur wasn't with them. Know who else he might have stayed with?"

"I ... ," I hesitated when I remembered what Bernie had said about seeing Arthur earlier that night in her shop. "I have no idea," I said. "But I'll check with some of the people from the Bow Valley Society in Calgary. I'm sure they'll — "

"Already did that," Nathan cut in. "Didn't stay with any of them."

"Well, then we'll just have to ask Arthur when he gets back."

"Sure will," he said and hung up.

"Damn," I said as I replaced the receiver. Arthur was getting himself in deeper, and I couldn't understand why he was doing it. He lied about when he'd come home. Not lied, exactly. He just hadn't bothered to tell me he was in Banff the same night the Doc came home and died. And now I hadn't bothered to tell Nathan. But at that moment I really didn't have time to think about it; I had to meet Ansel Rock.

I raced down the stairs to the front entrance. Ansel was seated in one of the oversized lobby chairs. "Sorry about that," I said.

He stood and gently slipped his hand under my elbow and led me out the revolving doors.

"I didn't realize you'd stayed here before," I said as we were coming around to the back of the hotel.

"Yup. First time I saw Banff, must be twenty years back. Can't beat the scenery."

"And the exchange rate," I quipped.

He smiled. "Yup. That too."

"Don't you usually stay in Kananaskis when you do this hunt, and camp out there?"

"Yes, ma'am. That's what I usually do. Camp out. And that's what we'll be doing this time too."

"What made you come to Banff now? Just a visit? Or is the camp cook better here at the Springs?"

His smile grew wider. "Yeah, and the spa. Almost as nice as a mountain stream."

"And a lot warmer," I added. "I'd hoped I might be able to show you around town, but since you're a regular you probably know more about this area than I do," I said.

"Probably not. Haven't been in Banff for, oh, about ten or so years. Things change," he said. We rounded the corner and he stopped abruptly. "Except that. That does not change."

We were above the golf course looking out over the Bow Valley to the Fairholme Mountain Range. "*Semper eadem*," I said.

"How's that?"

"Means 'always the same'. One of the original railway officials said it. His vision of Banff."

"I like that," Ansel said. "Must be why I keep coming back here. Can always count on those big ol' rocks bein' here. Never look quite real though, do they? My wife and little — "

He stopped himself and seemed surprised he'd almost slipped. So was I, because I knew Ansel Rock had no intention of discussing his personal life with me. So far, I hadn't found one word in any of the back articles to indicate if he was single, married, divorced or otherwise. But now I knew he was married and had at least one child. Things were moving along far better than I'd hoped. By lunchtime, I'd be listening to the guy relive his first love affair.

"And all that pretty white snow on 'em. Looks like someone got out there and painted us a spectacular backdrop," Ansel was saying. "Hollywood couldn't do any better." He pulled a disposable camera from his pocket and popped off a few shots. "Forgot my camera. I like showing off the pictures back home. Half the time they don't think they're real or accuse me of buying doctored-up postcards."

"Maybe you should just send postcards then, save yourself the trouble."

He laughed, and in spite of his earlier diatribe and the lecture on his rules and the code of conduct I was supposed to follow, I found myself liking Ansel Rock.

We ambled down the driveway that corkscrews past The Waldhaus

Restaurant and stopped to look over the railing to the spot on the golf course where, in only a few weeks, the landscape would be transformed into a winter paradise for skaters, cross-country skiers and tobogganers.

The weather was perfect, and the approaching winter seemed an impossible prospect. Thin wispy clouds streaked the otherwise flawless blue sky. This was summer's last hurrah. The early snow was going fast under the bright sun, and the little that was left was sticky and wet.

Ansel took off his coat and tucked it under his arm. "This really is something, isn't it?" he said and bent to collect a ball of snow in his gloved hand. "Now would you look at those." He pointed to a herd of elk grazing just below us on the fifteenth green. "Don't often get to shoot a few rounds with those fellows."

We continued down to the path past the Bow Falls. "Your timing is good," I told him. "Last couple of weeks have seen minus fifteen Celsius at night." The vision of Doc Rivard's lifeless face suddenly filled my mind. Did he freeze to death? Right under my window? I pushed back the thought and said, "But I heard on the radio this morning it's supposed to be staying around the plus five or ten Celsius mark with lots of sun."

"What's that translate to in English? Texan English," Ansel asked.

"I don't know. Maybe fifty degrees Fahrenheit."

He tossed his snowball against a tree, startling a chipmunk in the process. The frantic little creature made a dash for the next stand of pines and let fly a stream of staccato chatter and what I imagined was a string of chipmunk profanities.

"Heard you found a body in your backyard."

I stopped in my tracks. "That's right," I said slowly. "But it's not my backyard. I'm just the house-sitter. It belongs ... " I paused and swallowed. "It was my great-uncle who died. He owned the house."

"I'm sorry," Ansel said. "You all right? Sure you want to do this with me today?"

I cleared my throat. "Thank you, I'm fine. Did you read about it in the paper?"

"No, John Morrow told me. We talked yesterday. He's been — "

"Right, John. We met when he dropped off some articles."

Ansel nodded. "John and I have been passing each other in the sky these past few weeks."

"Is John a hunter too?" I asked as we started up the steep steps that parallel the falls.

"Yes ma'am. John Morrow is one of the finest hunters I have ever had the pleasure to know. He was a friend of my daddy's."

"Will he be hunting the bighorn with you?"

"No. Only one hunter gets to hunt in that area for the next three weeks. And that hunter is me. I outbid everyone for the tag."

"Yes, I realize that. But I thought he might be going along for the company."

"Yup. He'll come along. I usually only hunt with a guide and sometimes John. And now with a reporter."

"You mean me?" I said.

He looked down at me with an amused expression. "You haven't been at this too long, have you?" he said kindly.

I felt myself blush out of annoyance. "About a year. I used to write for *The Toronto Star*. Mostly lifestyles, human interest pieces." Now I was babbling, and bragging. I told myself to stop it.

"I know that. I've read some of your work."

"Really? Which articles?" Watch it, Hellie, my inner voice warned. Pride always cometh before a fall.

"The piece you did on the Canmore development. I liked how you handled it. Balanced. That's why I agreed to let you cover this story."

"Oh. My editor didn't tell me." We were on the path following the river into town.

"I liked your angle. That Canmore development was very controversial. You did a good job. I'm hoping you're going to take the same well-balanced approach on this one." His tone told me this was more than a wish; it was an order.

"Thank you," I said. "But you won't have to worry about this story being controversial. It's just a human interest piece."

"Oh yeah?" He picked up another glove full of snow. A breeze set the pines moaning around us. "What are your views on hunting, Hellie?"

I was completely unprepared for the question and suddenly felt off kilter. I was the one who was supposed to be asking the insightful, edgy questions.

"I ... um. I don't think that's at issue is it?" I said.

Ansel eyed me appraisingly. "Yup, sure is. So how are we going to deal with this, Hellie? Because if you're going to write this story, we'll need to know where you're coming from. And I'll make something clear right here and now: I have no intention of letting anyone make me out to be the bad guy. I'm a hunter, not a killer or murderer or whatever else those lunatic animal rights terrorists like to call us."

"Why don't we talk about this over lunch," I suggested.

"No thanks. I'd like to clear this up right now. Or else there is no point in having lunch or anything else." He threw another snowball into the river. "I told your people at the magazine that I won't be part of anyone's political agenda. I agreed to do this because I want people to know our side."

"Our?"

"Ethical hunters. We're sportsmen. We hunt by rules and we don't like anyone who breaks those rules. But never mind all that now." He jammed his fists into his jeans pockets. "We can cover that later. If there is a later," he added. "Right now I want to make sure we both know what we can expect from each other."

I was making my own snowballs, aiming them at a poplar and missing by at least three or four good feet. If he'd heard about the Doc and had taken the time to look into my work, then my guess was that he knew about Arthur. Which meant he knew I shared the same piece of land with Banff's most radical environmentalist. If that was the case, then I had to wonder why he'd agreed to let me write the article.

"Okay, I'm glad you brought this up," I said, and faced him. "Here's what you can count on from me. I'll write the truth. What I think really doesn't matter."

"Oh yes it does. What do you think?"

"I'm a journalist. I'll put what I think on the back burner."

"Really?"

"Yeah really. You're right, I don't like hunting, and I don't like someone coming from another country who pays buckets of money to hunt our animals in a protected area next to our national park. But that's not what this story is about. This story is about what makes a man spend all that money to come here and hunt an Alberta bighorn sheep. That's what I'd like to know because that's what I'm going to write about. I live in Doctor Michael Rivard's house. The late Michael Rivard." I lowered my voice. "And Arthur Elliott is my neighbour. I suspect you already know that."

"Yes ma'am, I do know that. And I know all about Arthur Elliott."

"Fine. Then I'll also assume you know that I'm not involved in Arthur's projects. So there is no conflict of interest, hidden agenda, or anything else. What Arthur thinks about this hunt is irrelevant. I have a story to write. So now if we can get going, that's exactly what I'll start working on."

"You done?"

"Yes."

He smiled down at me. It was the kind of smile a father gives his little girl when he thinks she's being clever. I made a mental note to stop my habit of liking people within the first five minutes of meeting them.

"Oh, and by the way. Personally, I didn't agree with the Canmore project," I said.

"Wouldn't have known that from reading your article."

"That's right, you would not."

"So where you taking me for lunch?" he asked.

"What do you feel like?"

"Some good ol' Alberta steak and eggs."

"Then we better go to Melissa's."

***

Melissa's was crowded as usual, but we managed to get a table. Ansel was pretty happy with the historic ambiance, but particularly so with his enormous lunch.

"You Canadians tend to be cheap with your servings," he pointed out. "But this is terrific. Look at all these hash browns, and I swear there must be half a dozen eggs in this omelet. Don't know how I've missed this place before," he said and wolfed down a forkful of blood-red beef.

When we were sipping coffee and going over Ansel's hunting itinerary for the next week, Larry Melwheeler spotted me and headed toward us. Which meant I was about to break one of the rules in Ansel's code of conduct for journalists. Larry Melwheeler was definitely a weirdo.

"Hey, hey, hey, Hellie," Larry said and turned a chair backwards against our table before straddling it — or in Larry's case mounting it. He thrust his hand out to Ansel. "Larry the Party Moose Melwheeler, pleased to make your acquaintance, Mystery Dude."

Ansel gave me an is-this-guy-for-real glance before he accepted the Party Moose's hand. "Howdy. I'm Ansel Rock."

I held my breath and waited for the next asinine thing to come out of Larry's mouth. Predictably, the wait was short.

"Say now, you're the dude who's come to take out a bighorn."

"That's right," Ansel said. "But if you don't mind I'd prefer to keep it quiet."

Larry made a zipping motion across his lips. "Your secret's safe with me, Mystery Dude," he said and tapped a finger against his forehead. "See you got yourself a nice Weatherby eyebrow."

Ansel stiffened and ran a finger over the scar.

Larry turned to me. "Know what a Weather — "

"I'll tell her," Ansel said. "Okay, Hellie, take notes. I use a 300 Weatherby rifle, which has a lot of kick. That means when you fire, the rifle butt can give a guy a good smack in the head. It happened once to me. Ages ago. I can handle a great deal more calibre than that."

"Hey, Dude, no shame in a Weatherby brow," Larry said.

I stole a glance at Ansel's taut face and steeled myself for his response, but Larry kept going before the big Texan had a chance to respond.

"Heard you're covering the story for some big Toronto magazine, Hellie. Nice score." He gave me a high-five. I returned his gesture with a half-hearted brush of my fingers. "You hear about Hellie finding our Doc Rivard dead?" Larry said to Ansel. "Overdose or something."

"Larry!" I snapped. "What are you talking about? The police suspect he died of a heart attack." No matter how many times I said it the words never rang true. Regardless, I was not going to let the Party Mouth spread vicious rumours.

"Yeah? Weird shit," Larry returned.

Larry and I shared a sad bit of history and mutual animosity that stemmed from an article I'd written about his now defunct dogsledding and backpacking business. For the piece, Larry had insisted that I "experience the story." Against my better judgment, I'd let him take me miles outside the park boundary to a remote trapper's cabin in Kananaskis Country, where I was supposed to experience the champagne tour. This apparently amounted to nibbling Camembert cheese, swilling champagne and commingling naked with Larry in a double sleeping bag. I drank the champagne, ate the cheese and wrapped myself *alone* in the sleeping bag. Larry slept on the other side of the room with only a space blanket for company. When I was safely back home, I wrote the story, just as it happened. Business dropped off. But Larry said he didn't care and that he held no grudge, since he was venturing into a new business opportunity. I always suspected he lied about the grudge, though.

Thankfully Ansel changed the subject. "Do you live in town, Larry?"

"Sure do, Mystery Dude. That's why I came over. I'm having a deep fall fling at my place tonight. Got the booze luge all set and ready to go in the backyard and the hot tub's heatin' up as we speak. So come by and bring your suit. Oh, and if you're in to it, Ansel Rock, we're doin' the wet-boxer shorts competition. Got a bunch of university kids in from Calgary for the weekend ... " He trailed off when he spied a group of very young women leaving the restaurant. "Gotta go. The ladies are getting away on the Moose." Larry popped a ball cap over his blond Rasta dreadlocks, tilted his head back and let loose with a reverberating noise that to Larry's walnut-sized brain sounded like a moose call. The Party Moose made a charge for the door.

Ansel was laughing and shaking his head. "What was that?"

"Our resident Valley boy. Or I should say man. I'm sure Larry's over forty now."

"I'm forty. He makes me feel old. What's he do when he's not chasing underage skirts?" Ansel lifted his cup to our waiter for a refill. At the same time he asked for the bill.

"Larry's in the guide business," I said. "He used to do dogsledding and backcountry ski tours, but his latest venture has something to do with guiding hunting trips. He also arranges skiing and hiking trips for college kids."

Ansel arched an eyebrow. "That guy's a hunting guide?"

"In training, or something. I heard he just hooked up with a guiding company. To be honest, I really don't keep tabs on Larry."

"Why does he do that howling thing?"

"I was afraid you'd ask. He says it's his moose-in-heat call and he does it whenever he sees young, pretty women. I've asked the wardens to tag him, so we women can identify him as a local pest. In fact, I've suggested to the Alberta government that instead of the bighorn hunt auction we should have a Party Moose hunt where all the women in town pay a hundred dollars to get a shot at paintballing Larry."

Ansel let loose a roar of laughter so loud people at other tables stopped eating and turned to stare. "This trip is shaping up to be a whole lot more interesting than I had anticipated."

I reached for the bill but Ansel placed his hand over mine. "I'll get that," he said.

His hand felt big and warm against my skin, and I noticed he wasn't wearing a wedding ring. "It's okay. Magazine's picking up the tab," I said.

Ansel kept his hand on mine and increased the pressure. "Which is why I'll be getting it."

I eased my hand back. I wasn't going to win, not this time.

***

Outside the sun was still shining brilliantly as we strolled down Lynx Street. I was beginning to relax with Ansel Rock, and I was looking forward to spending more time with him during the course of our interviews. I figured two, maybe three more hours would give me what I needed. Of course, I wasn't so naive as to assume it was going to be a breeze. Ansel was no talking machine, and I sensed that something besides privacy ran deep in the Texan. He struck me as a man quick to anger. It was the set of his jaw and the way he laughed; his face smiled but his eyes remained dark.

We turned onto Bear Street and stopped to look in the windows of the Canada House Art Gallery. "What's your pleasure, Hellie?" Ansel said squinting through the glass.

My eyes were on one item only: a one-hundred-and-seven-pound alabaster grizzly bear carved by artist David Riome. Over the past year, I'd stopped by to see that bear more times than I could count. We went in and I ran my hand down the slick, cool sculpture.

"Very nice," Ansel said. "Do a good job on this article and maybe I'll buy it for you."

"Thanks. That'll be the first five-thousand-dollar tip I've received."

He lifted his eyebrows suggestively as if to say, maybe it will.

"Are you trying to bribe me, Mr. Rock?"

"Might be. Now this is what I'd like to take home." He was looking at a Carl Rungius print of a bighorn sheep poised on a steep mountain cliff. "The original, though. This one's just a print."

"Of course, only the original will do," I said.

"I have a couple of his back home. One of a moose and another of an elk. I want a bighorn. You familiar with Rungius, Hellie?"

"Yes. He had a home here. He also painted a lot of his subjects when they were dead," I blurted.

Ansel eyed me. "Imagine they'd keep still a whole lot longer that way. Well, tomorrow, with some good planning and a lot of hiking, we just might get to see some of these fellows live on the hoof. It's quite a thing, Hellie. Ever been on a hunt before?"

"No."

"Didn't think so. This will be a new experience for you."

"Oh, I'm not going on the hunt. I thought we'd — "

"You're what?" His mouth twisted in disgust. "And just how were you plannin' on writing this article?" he said, his voice rising to an angry pitch.

Bingo on the temper, I thought. A clerk and a couple of customers were staring at us. "Why don't we go outside," I said.

He pushed through the door. I followed close behind. "Mind explaining how you figured you'd do this story without going on the trip?" he said when we were on the sidewalk.

"Interviews."

"Interviews! Oh, that's great." He sucked his teeth and jammed his fists into his jeans pockets. "What happened to being neutral and all that other crap? I thought we worked through this."

"We did. I don't see any need to go on this hunt with you. This isn't an article for *Hunter's World*. It's for a newsmagazine. It's a human interest piece. My editor didn't say anything about going on the hunt. That's not part of it."

"Aw shit. You don't get it, do you? I thought you were brighter than this. I assumed your editor got it too."

"I can write it — "

"You can write it my way or not at all. And my way is: You come on this hunt. You're supposed to be a journalist. And in my world journalists have to experience things to get it right. That's why some of the good ones get their heads blown off in wars. Because they're there. This isn't a story about me. It's a story about hunting. Get it?" His fingers tapped irritably against his thigh. "Here's the deal. My deal. You're up at five thirty tomorrow morning and I pick you up at six. Shit, you're not even packed, are you?"

I shook my head.

"Bring warm clothes. Personal stuff. Women's things."

"Women's things?"

He continued as if I hadn't spoken. "Mike Sands, he's my guide out of Canmore, he'll bring anything else you'll need. All our gear's being choppered in. We'll probably be gone five to seven days. I might have to be back earlier, though."

"I'm not going," I said flatly. "I have other work to do and other stories to write beside yours, Ansel. More importantly, my uncle died yesterday. I'll need to be here for the funeral."

Ansel's face softened. He took a deep breath, exhaled and said, "Look, I'm sorry about that. But can you tell me something? And I want you to be dead honest with me. Why did you agree to write this article when you can't stomach the idea of hunting?"

I swallowed. "It was an opportunity for me to get into a big magazine."

"Fine. Good answer. Now tell me this. And be straight, dead straight. Why won't you come on this hunt?"

I thought for a moment. There was only one answer. "I don't want to watch something die."

He nodded and ran a hand across his mouth. "Okay. Do you eat meat?"

He'd just seen me eat three slices of bacon. "Yes. I eat meat."

"Then you're a hypocrite and a coward."

"Maybe."

His right boot tapped out an impatient rhythm on the concrete sidewalk. "I'm willing to compromise, Hellie, because I want this story written."

"Why now, Ansel? Why not the other two years you've done this hunt?"

"Because I'm sick of hearing the bullshit. I want people to know that the money I bring to this country is put to good use."

"Which people? People like me, because I live next door to Arthur Elliott?"

His eyes blinked and a muscle twitched his jaw. "That's right. People like you. I want people like you to face up to your hypocritical thinking. So here's my deal." His tone was more befitting an ultimatum than a compromise. "The first couple of days are usually spent scouting and glassing — "

"What's glassing?"

"Using binoculars," he said impatiently. "Better read those stories John gave you."

"I did read them."

"As I was saying, we rarely get anything on the first day. Be a right miracle if we did. So you come, and at the end of the day if you can't take it we'll talk."

"No. The guide takes me out."

"I said we'd talk. I can't make you stay. And whatever happens, I'll make sure you're back for the funeral. So what do you say? We got a deal, Ms. MacConnell?"

I'd lose the story if I didn't go. I held up my index finger and said, "One day. See you at six."

CHAPTER 5

AT EXACTLY 6:25 A.M., ANSEL ROCK PULLED HIS RENTED DODGE Durango into Canmore's Apex Helicopter Tours parking lot. Ansel's guides were arranging to have all of our camping equipment and food supplies flown in to the campsite. For this I was most grateful, since it would save me the trouble of hauling in a hundred-pound pack full of Gore-Tex, grub and "women's things".

Ansel wanted to check in with the pilot to see that everything was in order before we started our long hike up to the camp. I was in the passenger seat trying to keep from nodding off as Ansel parked across from the chalet-style office building. When I spied a couple of fellows loading gear into a helicopter at the far end of the lot, a brilliant idea came to me.

"You know, Ansel," I said through a yawn. "We could save ourselves a lot more energy and time if we caught a ride up in that helicopter, along with all our stuff."

He turned off the ignition, tilted his head toward me and gave me a withering look. "Take another note, Hellie. By law, hunters are not allowed to ride in a helicopter for twenty-four hours before they hunt, because it might give the hunter an unfair advantage over the animals."

"Good law," I said trying to save face.

Ansel didn't bother to respond before he leapt out of the driver's side and jogged to the office. I couldn't help but smirk at the retreating figure all dressed up in full camouflage gear — the brave soldier on his way to do battle with a bunch of unarmed sheep.

When he'd picked me up at Bernie's half an hour earlier, it was all I could do to keep a straight face. And I was relieved that no one else was up at that ungodly hour to see me taking off with a guy who looked like Rambo. But there had been a big elk lying on the front grass, and I was certain the ungulate did a double take when Commander Rock came around to open my door.

Another car pulled into the spot next to me. It was John Morrow. I got out of the truck to stretch my legs.

"Good morning," he said getting out of his car. He was dressed in fawn-coloured Gore-Tex pants and jacket.

"Morning, John," I returned.

"Lovely day," he said gazing up at the clear sky. "Perhaps this trip will give you a bit of a rest from … well, from what you've been through."

"Hope you're right," I said. And I meant it. Underneath, I was sincerely hoping this trip would be no more eventful than a quiet hike in the mountains. I, of course, would be rooting for the sheep's team.

Ansel was jogging back across the parking lot. From the look on his face, I could tell he was none too happy.

He said, "We got a problem — "

"Houston?" I said with a smile

He didn't crack a grin. Then I saw "the problem" bouncing toward us on the balls of his feet, blond Rasta dreadlocks jumping in time with each jaunty step.

"Hey, Mystery Dude, forgot your hat," Larry The Party Moose Melwheeler said. He was sipping an extra large cappuccino and holding out a hunter's cap. Ansel took the hat, but his jaw was tight and his eyes stared hard at Larry. Larry didn't seem to notice and turned his limited attention to me. "Hey Hellie-girl. How's it hangin'?"

I was just about to ask Larry what he was doing here, when the sound of tires crunching gravel stopped me. A bearded man who looked as though he belonged to the mountains pulled his truck up beside us, rolled his window down and said, "Morning folks."

"Hey there, Mike," Larry said.

Mike Sands squinted his eyes at Larry as if he was inspecting him, then gave a slight nod before he looked to Ansel. "Sorry about the change of plans, Mr. Rock, but my kid's not feeling too good … " He trailed off at the sight of Ansel's taut expression. "Everything okay?"

"You sent the wrong guide," Ansel said. "I hunt with Becker Peterson."

"Well, I'm awfully sorry," Mike continued. "Becker is out with another camp. But Daniel's here. He went up with the chopper earlier to get set up. You'll meet him at camp. I would have called you, but my kid is real sick, and Larry was good enough to fill in."

Larry gave the thumbs-up sign, and I noticed his hand shook just enough to tell me that the Party Moose was either nursing a wild hang-over or he was still drunk. Either way, Larry Melwheeler was in for a very unfortunate day.

"That's just great," Ansel said and slammed his open palm on the truck's hood.

I jumped. Larry didn't — a bad sign. The liquor had anaesthetized him. Like Ansel he was dressed in camouflage gear. But with the dread-locks poking out from under his matching camouflage hat, Larry looked more like a Vietnam War vet than a hunting guide.

"Mr. Rock, I'm sorry," Mike said.

Ansel took a couple of deep breaths and gave Mike a quick, courteous nod. "I understand. And I am sorry about your child. But I would like another guide."

Larry, who was licking the milk foam off the top of his giant beverage, looked up with the expression of someone who'd just had ice dumped down his pants.

"It's your call," Mike said. "But I will tell you, Larry's been doing a fine job. And I know Becker would back me on that."

"Fucking eh, dude," Larry said.

Mike winced and shook his head at Larry, then turned his attention back to Ansel. "And Larry's had a good deal of backcountry and dogsledding experience. He's been on a lot of hunts with me. As for to-day, not much chance you'll be doing anything other than glassing, and Larry will only be taking you as far as the camp. Tomorrow, Daniel will be your guide and Larry will assist. But it's your decision, Mr. Rock. I'll be happy to find you another guide. It will delay things, though."

Ansel looked at his watch then back to Mike. "Do I have your guar-antee that Daniel Peterson will be guiding tomorrow?"

"Absolutely. And I understand you're flying in with us," Mike said to John Morrow.

"If I can," John replied politely. "Like to get a little painting in with the morning light."

"John's about the best wildlife painter you'll ever meet," Ansel an-nounced.

I wondered if the term wildlife was a misnomer, and if John, like Carl Rungius, actually painted wild dead life.

"If you're all set Mr. Rock," Mike said, "I'll let the pilot know. We'll chopper in the rest of the equipment and I'll meet you at camp some-time late this afternoon then I'll have to come back out."

Ansel gave Mike a nod and turned to me. "While we're getting ready out here, I want you to change into these hunting clothes," he said and handed me a duffle bag. Since he was already angry about Larry being our guide, I decided not to argue and scuttled off to the restrooms inside the office building, where I changed into the camouflage-patterned vest and pants.

An hour later, after we were bumped and jostled along a rough service line road that eventually turned into a dry creek bed, we entered a nar-row canyon at the mouth of three valleys in the Ghost River Wilderness Area. We left the vehicle and started hiking up a rutted dirt road toward the South Ghost region — a once popular area for hunters who would lie in wait for fat horned rams to step out of the park's safe zone and into the target zone. According to my research, this was precisely why the area had been closed to hunters: The pickin's were just too easy, and the bighorn sheep had been decimated through over-hunting.

Ansel was well ahead of us on the trail. Larry was in front of me, and I was bringing up the rear. I was Larry's doppelgänger all dressed up in my own camouflage outfit. I felt ridiculous, dressed up to look like the forest floor. But I did have to admit the matching down-filled vest was warm.

For the past half hour, I'd been watching Larry's shoulders heave and shiver spasmodically against the cold. "You should wear your vest, Larry," I said. "Blood's probably a little thin with all that alcohol still floating around your system."

"Very funny," he said back over his shoulder. "Lucky for me we were just about to fire up the luge, otherwise when Mike called me at about two a.m. I woulda been O.D.-ed."

The expression reminded me of something and sparked my anger. "By the way, Larry. Why did you say the Doc died of a drug overdose? What would possibly make you say that?"

Larry looked up the trail to where Ansel had disappeared over the crest. "I better get up there," he said. "Or it won't be the cold killin' me."

"Hold it a second. I hope you haven't said the same thing to anyone else. You'll start a really nasty rumour. It's ignorant. Why would you say something like that?"

"I don't know," he said, and hoofed it up the trail.

I kept pace and grabbed his arm to slow him. "Hold it, Larry. You have told other people, haven't you? What were you thinking?"

"I don't know," he said shaking loose from my grip. "Doc was always giving himself stuff. Shot of this, shot of that. Figured maybe he gave himself too much."

"He gave himself cortisone. I've never heard of anyone overdosing on cortisone, have you? Don't you think it'd be wiser to keep that type of speculation to yourself?"

"Yeah I guess. But it made sense. Paper said there was no sign that he, like, got killed or anything. You have to think about where I'm coming from, Hellie. I've had tons of kids take a little too much of this or that and then crash under my deck when it's been, like, twenty below. I always check under the deck before we close up for the night, or morning." He sniggered. Larry took great pride in his partying prowess.

Ansel reappeared like a warrior on the crest of the trail. "Lawrence!" His voice boomed and bounced off the mountain walls. "You with me?"

"Thanks, now I'm in trouble again. What is this, shit-on-the-Moose day?"

I jogged up the trail staying close to Larry.

"So now where, Lawrence?" Ansel said.

Larry brought himself up and in what I thought was a very professional voice said, "We're going to follow the trail there on your left." He indicated a narrow dirt trail that cut through the valley and eventually went straight up at a vertical angle, steep enough to break your heart.

"Very good, Lawrence," Ansel said, his voice thick with sarcasm.

I wondered if the Texan was going to ease up on Larry, or if this was the way the next few days of Larry's life were going to play out. I also wondered how long Larry would take it.

We continued on in silence, until we came upon a clearing with what looked like a small concrete building at its centre. I moved off the trail and leaned on the chain-link fence for a closer look. The building was actually more of an entranceway set into the hillside. Above the door and tacked along the fence were signs that read: "Keep Out. Danger." I assumed it was some kind of power station, or something to do with mining.

Larry joined me at the fence. "Know what it is?"

"Power station?"

"Nope. A Diefenbunker."

"A what?"

"Bunker. Bomb shelter. Government built a bunch of them across the country in the sixties in case we got nuked. Named them after Prime Minister — "

"Diefenbaker," I said.

"Right. One near Ottawa is like an underground city."

"Do they ever actually use them?"

Ansel leaned up against the fence. "Last time we were through here, my regular hunting guide, Becker Peterson, told us this one was privately owned."

"You thinking of buying it, Mr. Rock?" I asked.

"No thanks. I don't like being underground."

"Couldn't even if you wanted to," Larry said. "Government wants them all back now because a bike gang tried to buy one."

"That's comforting," I said.

We left the bunker and puffed our way up the trail until Ansel stopped to scan the area with his binoculars.

"Sheep usually come back near the meadows close to Stenton Lake," Larry said to Ansel's back. "If we're lucky, your big ram will still be hanging around."

"I'm not particularly interested in luck, Lawrence," Ansel said over his shoulder. "It's skill that will make or break this expedition."

I mentally rolled my eyes, but jotted the line down anyway in my notebook for the article. I glanced at my watch; it was just after one p.m. We had been hiking for nearly two hours, and so far I'd enjoyed every minute. As we climbed higher, new snow from the previous night clung to evergreen branches and dusted the rocky peaks, sculpting hard lines and deep contrasts in the rocks. There wasn't a breath of wind. There was silence, broken only by the sound of our boots treading on the snow-dusted trail, and the odd grey jay swooping past our heads giving a hoot and a whistle to remind us that we were still on this earth and not at the threshold of heaven.

I finally breathed. It was as though I'd been holding my breath since we'd found the Doc. Patience is not one of my strong points. I'd called Nathan again before going to bed the previous night. He had told me that they had nothing and we'd have to wait for the autopsy. And there was still no word from Arthur.

We hiked over a final crest and stopped before we made our descent into the South Ghost drainage area. Stretched before us was a mottled emerald-green, rust-red and golden-brown meadow that rolled to the base of a jagged rock face. It was so quiet. We all stood still and listened. Listened to the peace and quiet of the gentle mountain sounds: the wind breathing across the tips of evergreen trees, a bird's single sharp note piercing the day, a pika's high whistling response.

Then I heard a different sound: a clicking in the distance, and the echo. Like the click, click of castanets, tapping out slow irregular rhythms that bounced off the tons of rock surrounding us. It was coming from the range directly in front of us. But I couldn't see the source at first glance. Their forms blended too well with the limestone wall. Only when they began to move, to leap and dance, did my eyes catch sight of a dozen or more tawny spirits gliding up and down the craggy cliffs, each one bounding effortlessly and almost silently from steep ridge to steeper ridge, coming to land on all fours with the precision of an Olympian high jumper, making only the slightest click, click when its delicate hooves made contact with stone. Light hooves prancing on a tile roof: the ghosts of Saint Nick's reindeers. Curly horns like primitive headdresses protruded from their temples. They were the Rocky Mountain bighorn — Ansel's prey.

We moved closer; steam rose from their nostrils as they stared out across the meadow sensing our presence. All looked to be about the same size and age. I scanned the herd wondering which head it was Ansel was so intent on mounting on his rumpus room wall.

I looked to the Texan, who was scanning the herd with his binoculars, aiming the high-powered glasses to the rocky ridge above. He put his hand on my shoulder and placed the binoculars to my eyes. The ram's visage filled my sight. One onyx eye seemed to look straight into mine. I drew back, then looked again. Ansel's ram was massive compared to the other males. Its head was weighted with horns thick as tree stumps that curled back, then up and around, ending in ragged points parallel to his eyes. In that one luminous moment, I thought I understood why a person would spend a million dollars to have this animal. To possess it, yes. To kill it, never.

The ram's gaze swept out over the valley to where it seemed to catch and hold Ansel's. Both stood stock-still, locked in a stalemate. A chill went up my spine as I glimpsed the bond that existed between hunter and hunted.

"Let's see if we can get up higher. Maybe up to that ridge," Ansel said, pointing to a rocky spot above the ram. We ducked into the bush and followed a meandering creek before we came out and stopped less than a hundred feet from the herd. They all watched us; not one bolted. Our presence seemed only to arouse their curiosity. Ansel's ram came into view again and caught our scent on the breeze. He remained above the rest looking down on us like some kind of medieval king.

"I don't think we'll need to go to the ridge," Larry said in a whisper. "They're not skittish."

Ansel nodded. Without taking his eyes off the ram, he pulled his 300 Weatherby Magnum rifle from the side of his pack.

My eyes were wide with horror. *You can't, you can't! You said you wouldn't! Not today. We're just scouting. You said we were scouting!* Came my silent protest.

Ansel's hands were slow and steady as he pulled back the bolt then eased it forward, feeding the bullet into the chamber. I listened for the "ka-chick." None came. Ansel was a practiced, silent stalker. He slowly turned down the bolt then lifted the gun and fixed his sight on the unsuspecting creature.

Not while I'm here!!! The words screamed in my mind. I felt Larry's hand on my shoulder. *Say something, say something,* the voice in my head demanded. *Make a noise. Scare the damn thing.* But I couldn't. I was an observer. A writer. A writer who had been set up. I closed my eyes and waited for the air to be filled with the dreadful, deafening sound of gunfire.

It never came. Instead, the valley was filled with the sound of someone calling my name.

"Hellie!"

I turned in the direction the voice had come from, just in time to see something sail past Ansel. One of the mischievous grey jays swooping in to mooch a little lunch, I presumed. But when the object thwunked into the trunk of an old spruce, I saw that it was not a bird at all. It was an arrow.

We all froze: Larry with his hand on my shoulder, me half turned and Ansel with the rifle still to his face.

Larry was the first to speak. "Jesus Christ, someone's shooting at us." He pushed me down and my face hit the ground. Ansel was on his stomach in front of me. We all lifted our heads and stared in the direction the voice and the arrow had come from.

I think I spotted him first, but it was Ansel who spoke. "Look, there," he said pointing a finger at a hooded figure running up the trail and out of the valley. Ansel called out to our assailant to stop. When the man did not slow his pace, Ansel lifted the Weatherby and trained his sight on the retreating figure.

Larry and I screamed in unison: "Don't shoot! It's Arthur!"

CHAPTER 6

Cautiously, we lifted our heads and scanned the horizon for more flying arrows, though none were really expected. We had all witnessed our assailant disappear out of the valley.

"Nice work, Hellie," Ansel said. "You nearly got me killed."

I was still in shock and not really listening. The image of the retreating, hooded figure was still occupying my mind.

"What the fuck was he thinking?" Larry said looking back over his shoulder and around the valley. "He could have hit any one of us."

Ansel yanked the arrow out of the tree trunk. "He wasn't aiming at you. And he sure as hell wasn't aiming to hit his partner here. Was he, Hellie?" Ansel said, waving the razor-sharp arrowhead in my face.

"What are you talking about?"

"Game's done, Hellie. Your partner missed. And now you're in one deep bucket of shit."

"What the hell are you talking about? I didn't shoot at you. That guy did."

"That guy," Ansel scoffed. "What were you planning to do? Tell the police it was a hunting accident?"

"I don't — "

He turned his attention to Larry and cut me off. "And what's your part in this?"

"Me!"

Ansel lifted his rifle and held it lengthwise across his chest.

I swallowed.

"Yeah you," Ansel said. "Move over next to Hellie. And both of you dump out your packs."

"Hey, easy man. Listen — "

"Shut up and empty your pack."

I swallowed again, and tried to work up a little saliva in my dry mouth. "Ansel," I said trying to keep my voice even and steady, "what are you on about? Larry didn't know anything about this." I turned to

Larry. "Did you?"

"No way, man. I haven't talked to Arthur in, like, weeks."

"But you sure have, Hellie," Ansel said. "Now dump your pack."

I was about to protest, but with an angry six-foot-four Texan cradling a 300 Weatherby, I figured I'd best keep my mouth shut and do exactly what he ordered.

Larry and I went down on our knees and set about unloading our packs.

While we pulled trail mix, flashlights and various other weighty items from our packs, Ansel continued his diatribe. "Did you and Arthur really think I was stupid enough not to figure out this whole bullshit article idea was a set up? Come on, Hellie, tell me how Arthur didn't have anything to do with you getting this story."

I kept my head down and watched Ansel's hunting boots come in and out of my line of vision while he made agitated laps around us. My hands shook as I picked items out of the pack.

"You know all about me and Arthur, right, Hellie?"

I finally looked up at him. "You won't believe anything I have to say anyway, so why don't you stop asking me questions."

"You're right about that. I don't believe a thing you say."

I sat back on my haunches and waited until he went through each of the pockets in Larry's and my packs. He patted us both down, and when he was satisfied we didn't have any concealed weapons, Ansel told us to put everything back in our packs. Then he led us out of the valley.

Mike Sands was the first one to notice us coming across the meadow as Ansel marched Larry and I into camp like a couple of prisoners of war.

"Mike," Ansel hollered. "I want you to call the Apex office and get them to send a chopper back up here, stat! These two," he was referring to Larry and I, "had me ambushed."

Mike Sands was as flabbergasted as I was at the bizarre turn of events. He stood up from where he was unloading cooking gear from a pack. "They what?" he said.

A big man with a shaved head was setting up a tent behind Mike. He abandoned his task and came over to us. "Mr. Rock," he said. "I'm Daniel Peterson." He cut a glance to me and then to Larry. "Is there a problem?"

"Yeah, there sure as hell is," Ansel said. "Arthur Elliott was doing a little bow hunting, and I was his target."

"Larry, what's going on?" Mike Sands said.

Before Larry would answer, John Morrow came out through the bushes at the side of the camp. "Ansel, is everything all right?"

"No, it's sure not, John. But I really don't want to get into it right now. You can hear all about it when I tell the police."

John scratched his neck and looked worried. "Ansel, maybe we should go and have a talk. Let's all just take it easy."

"John's right," Mike said. "I'm sure there's some reasonable explanation. Maybe we could ... " Mike stopped. It was obvious to him and everyone else that the Texan wasn't about to listen to reason. "What do you want us to do, Mr. Rock?" he said instead.

"I told you. Call the Apex office and tell them to get a helicopter up here. And make sure the police are waiting when we get back down. I want Hellie to tell them exactly what she and Arthur have been up to."

***

Nathan was waiting for us in the Apex Helicopter Tours' office. Sergeant Delaware's calm, systematic way of dealing with the cranked-up Texan bespoke his years of service with the RCMP.

When Ansel was finally finished raving about how I was working with Arthur to sabotage this hunt, not to mention kill him, and how Arthur Elliott was a very dangerous person — as was I, because I was using this story as a front, Nathan thanked Ansel politely, then turned to me. "Well, Hellie, what do you have to say?"

Ansel piped in, "Whatever it is, I don't think you want to put too much of it in your back pocket."

Nathan put his hand up to quiet the younger man. "Let's hear what Hellie has to say. Hellie?"

"I didn't tell Arthur anything. I couldn't find him. And I didn't even know we were going on this so-called scouting trip," — I shot Ansel a dirty look — "until he told me yesterday." I flipped a thumb in Ansel's direction. "And for the record, Nathan, we only saw the back of the shooter's head, and the guy was wearing a hood. We didn't see the shooter's face. It may not have been Arthur."

Ansel snorted. And Larry, who had been uncharacteristically quiet, finally spoke. "Yeah, but Hellie, it did pretty much look like him. Even from behind. It was his coat. We both said his name."

I pressed my fingers to my eyes. "I just can't believe he'd do something like this."

Nathan, however, seemed to have no problem believing it. "Are you certain you didn't have any communication with Arthur about where you were headed today?" Nathan asked me in his brusque voice.

"Not a word."

"I wasn't aware Arthur was into archery," Nathan said. "Hellie, is he?"

"He learned it from the villagers in Tanzania. I've never seen him practising or anything," I added, as if that was going to undo the damage I'd just done.

Nathan nodded. "What about this article? That have anything to do with helping Arthur?"

"I queried the magazine with the idea a few months ago after I ... " Where had I heard about it? I was so rattled I couldn't think properly. The paper! Yes. "I read about it in *The Herald*," I said. "There was no set-up. I was assigned the story. Phone my editor at *McMillan*, he'll confirm everything." I wrote down my editor's name and the phone number and handed it to Nathan.

Out of the corner of my eye I could see Ansel was watching me, listening with interest. The sardonic expression was gone.

"My only motive for writing this story was to get an article in *McMillan*," I continued. "Nathan, you know I am not involved with Arthur or his projects in any way." I let my eyes drift over my shoulder again and rest on Ansel. "But you might want to ask Mr. Rock, here, why he chose me." Nathan's eyes shot to Ansel. "He hand-picked me," I said. "Might be nice to know why, since he knew I was Arthur's neighbour."

Ansel straightened up. "I picked Hellie for two reasons. And one of those reasons was precisely because she is Arthur's neighbour. I figured something was up when I heard her name and I wanted to find out what. I sure as hell didn't think it was to kill me, though."

I was crestfallen. I'd been hoping he'd say he picked me because of my writing.

"What is your connection to Arthur Elliott, Mr. Rock?" Nathan asked.

"I'm sure Hellie can tell you."

"Well, I'm sure I can do no such thing," I said. "I had no idea you two even knew each other."

"Right, Hellie. Fine, I'll play your game," Ansel said, and turned back to Nathan. "I ran up against Arthur in Tanzania when I was on an elephant safari. I figured I was running up against him again when I saw Hellie's name on the magazine's list of writers."

"How'd you know Hellie was Arthur Elliott's neighbour?" Nathan asked.

"Now isn't that an excellent question," I said.

"Simmer down, Hellie," Nathan said.

"Friend mentioned it to me," Ansel said.

Liar! I wanted to yell. I could see Nathan didn't buy it either but he let it slide for the moment.

Ansel sensed the cop's skepticism. "When you're in my position, Sergeant, you have to be careful. I make it my business to know who my adversaries are. I'm a hunter, and I don't like what Arthur Elliott stands for. And I'm damn tired of the garbage he and his lot spread about us decent hunters."

Nathan nodded thoughtfully. "Well, I'm awfully sorry about this, Mr. Rock. I'm a hunter myself, and I can understand your frustration. And the police certainly don't like it when our visitors are treated poorly."

"Oh, but it's okay for our visitors to threaten us locals with rifles," I said.

"I did not threaten you," Ansel said. "I never once pointed my weapon at you, and I never would unless you pulled one on me first."

"I think you're splitting hairs here, Ansel," I said.

"Hellie, please," Nathan said. He turned back to the Texan. "Were there any other incidents with Arthur the last couple of times you were in the area hunting, Mr Rock?"

Ansel shook his head. "Guess he was just biding his time."

Seemed to me it was Ansel who was biding his time.

"You should have told us, Mr. Rock, about your background with Arthur when you got here. The police could have helped."

"No way. No sir," Ansel said emphatically. "I wanted him caught red-handed this time. I want him doing the jail time he never did in Africa. Now I've got him."

"We'll take it from here," Nathan said. "One of my corporals and an officer out of Exshaw will come by your hotel to speak with you again. And they'll want to talk to you two," he pointed to Larry and me. "So make sure you guys stick around Banff the next couple of days."

We all left the office and picked up our belongings outside in the parking lot. Nathan brushed past me on his way to his patrol car and said, "I hope to God you're telling the truth about this, Hellie."

His words hit me like a slap, and I felt the powerlessness that comes with being accused of something you didn't do. The accusation alone has the strength to make you question your own innocence.

I followed Larry to his truck. As I was fastening my seat belt Ansel appeared at my window. I reluctantly rolled it down.

"I know Arthur Elliott had something to do with you being on this story," he said. The deafening whirl of a helicopter overhead drowned out most of what Ansel said next. "You ... give ... Fine ... "

The chopper came down and John Morrow hopped out, ducked under the blades and joined Ansel. The helicopter engine died, and quiet was restored.

"How's everyone?" John asked.

"I was just asking Hellie to admit that she and her friend Arthur were trying to kill me," Ansel said not taking his eyes off mine.

I rolled the window down lower and said very slowly, "I did not know a damn thing about all of this between you and Arthur. Let's go, Larry."

Ansel banged the hood of Larry's truck with his fist. "Damn, you're a laugh a minute, Hellie."

John put his hand on his friend's shoulder. "Come on Ansel, let's go."

Larry backed the truck out. Ansel shrugged John's hand off and kept in step with the moving vehicle. "I strongly suggest you come clean about this and tell the police the truth before you get yourself into more trouble," Ansel said through my open window.

"And I suggest you tell the police you set me up. You insisted I come on this hunt because you knew something was going to happen, and for some strange reason you wanted me there to witness it. But I'll tell you what I witnessed. From the looks of the way you were aiming your weapon at Arthur, or whoever was up on that mountain, I'd say it was you who was planning to do the killing today. Or maybe you just sent someone up there who was dressed up like Arthur so you could make your point to me." I pressed the button and the window buzzed up into place.

Ansel hauled open my door. Larry braked. I drew back reflexively and leaned into Larry. I don't know what I thought Ansel was going to do, but I caught a glimpse of his right hand balled into a fist.

"I was not plannin' on taking a shot at him." Ansel spat the words at me. "I was just getting a good look at him through the sight. Look, Hellie, I did not have to dress anyone up. I know Arthur set this article up, so you can cut the bullshit just about any time. And yeah, you're right, I did want you up there because I want the press to know there are consequences for backing the likes of Arthur Elliott." He tipped his hunting hat. "Now you have yourself a real nice day." He slammed the door.

Larry was staring at me wide-eyed.

"Let's go," I growled. He pulled the Land Rover out and we headed back to Banff on Highway One.

CHAPTER 7

NATHAN CAME BY BERNIE'S HOUSE THE NEXT DAY. IN HIS UNIFORM AND boots, the big cop looked superhuman amid the precious inventory in Bernie's petite world.

Nathan's eyes roamed the room seeking out a place to sit. Teddy bears dressed in kilts, sundresses and lederhosen, along with antique dolls in period costumes enjoying a cup of tea and a slice of lemon cake, occupied every available chair. Bernie relocated a couple of her "friends" to make room on the couch for the sergeant. Nathan took up the seat. Bernie and I remained standing, our shoulders touching for support.

"Nathan, I'm not ready for any more bad news," Bernie said between anxious sips of tea. "And for the record, I don't believe it was Arthur up there on that mountain shooting at Ansel Rock. Arthur chains himself to earth movers and makes noise, he doesn't shoot people."

I had been saying as much myself, but in truth I wasn't so sure. Whoever shot at us looked and sounded an awful lot like Arthur.

Nathan listened patiently. Then he said, "Arthur's not what I came to talk about. Autopsy report's back."

My fingernails bit into the flesh on my palms.

"Official cause of death is cardiac arrest. Doc died of natural causes," Nathan announced.

"Thank God," Bernie said. "I just couldn't stand the thought that someone may have hurt him."

I wasn't quite so relieved or enthusiastic. "But that report doesn't exactly give us any clues about why he was under the gazebo in the middle of the night with the door closed behind him, when he just happened to have a massive heart attack."

"No it doesn't," Nathan returned. "But that's all I've got to go on — natural causes."

"Arthur doesn't think it was natural causes," I said.

Nathan blew out an exasperated breath. "So he said. But unless he shows up real soon and tells me why he was shooting at Mr. Rock, and gives me something more than a knowing feeling about the Doc's demise, then my hands are tied. The examiner's office found nothing unusual except a few injection sites. Which, it turns out, aren't unusual since the Doc injected himself with cortisone."

"His knee," Bernie said.

"Yeah, his knee and his tennis elbow. Doc tended to be more careful with his patients than with himself," Nathan said. His voice was thick and rough with emotion.

"Isn't finding him under the gazebo unusual?" I insisted.

"Might have been looking for something."

"In the middle of the night? I didn't see a flashlight under there with him. Did you?"

"No."

"The door was closed behind him," I pressed.

"That's a fact." Nathan blew out another long breath. "It's all we've got. Doc died of a heart attack. His body wasn't moved after he died." Nathan leaned forward and let his hat dangle between his knees.

"So he just crawled under the gazebo and died?" I said, my voice a little too sharp. Bernie put a hand on my arm.

"Looks that way," Nathan said.

"Don't you think it's a bit weird he didn't bother to tell me he was on his way home? That he was home? And why would he park his rental car down the street like he didn't want me or anyone else to know he was there?"

"Would have been late. The report says the body wasn't there more than twelve hours. According to the hotel's front desk, Doc checked in a little before one a.m. Then checked out half an hour later. Which means he would have been back here somewhere between three and three thirty in the morning. Probably didn't want to disturb you."

"But he would have disturbed me if I'd heard him come in. He would have scared me to death if he'd come sneaking in at that hour."

"Doc wouldn't do that," Bernie said and sat next to Nathan.

"No he wouldn't," Nathan agreed. "I got a couple of theories. First one is he was probably heading down to Arthur's cabin. Doc knew he was supposed to meet Arthur in Calgary the next afternoon, so he knew Arthur's cabin was empty. Maybe after being away so long he just decided to drive home. I can see that. I hate hotels."

"Arthur says the Doc does … did too … " I said. "I guess that would explain the car being down the street."

"Right. He wouldn't park it in the garage or the driveway because he didn't want to wake you."

"Okay, I can buy that. But how do we explain the Doc's sudden urge to stretch out under the gazebo?"

"That's got me, too," Nathan said and scratched at his bristly brush cut. "Unless he saw something under there."

"Like an animal," Bernie offered.

Nathan shook his head. "Thought of that. But unless it was howling, you know, hurt or something, I can't see it. There was no evidence to suggest anything or anyone else was under there with him. And it still doesn't explain the door being shut behind him."

"Or on him," I said.

"Yeah, someone could have shut it after. But I doubt it. My guess is the wind shut it." He ran a hand down his face.

"I'm sorry, Nathan," I said softening my tone. "It just doesn't add up."

"Yeah, I know. It's hard for everyone. My other theory is that the Doc panicked."

"Over what?"

"His heart. See, I'm wondering if he was feeling sick. Maybe he was coming home because he knew he was in trouble. And that stubborn old goat would never admit to anyone he wasn't feeling well."

Bernie gave a mirthless laugh. "Isn't that the truth? It was all I could do to keep him in the hospital after his surgery. The way he told it, you would have thought he'd just had his tooth filled instead of having his chest cut open." She shook her head. "What a guy. I think you're on to something, Nathan. Doc knew the signs better than anyone. He probably did need help."

This one was making sense even to me. I took a seat on the corner of a chair.

Nathan nodded his agreement. "The old goat nearly died before he had that last bypass. And people do some mighty strange things when they panic. Kids hide under the beds in fires. People try to find the number eleven on their phone pads when they're dialing nine one one."

"If he was having a heart attack he could have been disoriented,"

Bernie added.

"That's what I'm thinking," Nathan said. "And he could have had that heart attack just as easily on the highway. Old bugger shouldn't have been driving."

"Does this mean the investigation is over?" Bernie asked.

"Officially, yes. Unless we get something else."

"Any news on those bear paws?" I said. "Where they might have come from?"

Nathan shook his head. "Might get something later today. You sure Arthur didn't say anything else to you about those paws, Hellie?"

"I wouldn't have just asked you if he had," I said testily.

"What in God's name did he think he was doing up on that mountain?" Nathan said.

"We don't — "

He cut me off. "I know, Hellie. You don't think it was him. But Ansel Rock sure does." He scratched his head again. "Let's not get into that right now. You can move back into the Doc's place." He looked past me, lost in his own thoughts. "I can't think of anyone who had any reason to hurt the Doc," he said quietly.

"Neither can I," Bernie said.

Nathan stood to leave. "I expect you've notified your family, Hellie."

"Yes."

He studied me a moment. "I don't remember the Doc ever mentioning your name or your family before you showed up."

"My family doesn't have many relatives and the ones we do have … well," I shrugged, "we aren't close to them."

"Is there anyone else on your side we should notify?" Nathan asked.

"Not that I can think of. I'm sure there are distant relatives, but really I don't know who they are."

Nathan nodded, and sucked at his teeth. "I know there isn't anyone left on Barb's side. So it looks like you and your folks are it as far as Doc's family goes."

Hearing that made the Doc's death seem all the more tragic somehow.

"And just one other thing," Nathan said. "Examiner's releasing the Doc's body. It'll be sent back here for the funeral. We'll need to arrange something.

"We'll look after it," Bernie and I said in unison.

"Thank you, girls," he said, making his way to the door. The sadness in the big man's voice hung in the air.

After he was gone, Bernie poured us both more tea. "Well, I guess that's it," she said. "We'll never know what really happened, or how Doc ended up under the gazebo."

"I want to know what happened, Bern. Doc died outside my bedroom window."

"But what can you do?"

"I don't know. But I do know Nathan doesn't believe any more than I do that Doc Rivard died of natural causes. But like he said, he can't do much unless he has more to go on."

"I can tell you're planning to try and find more for him. So how are you going to do that, Hellie?"

"Follow the crumbs."

"Pardon?"

"When I was working at *The Star* there was this one reporter who always dug up the best stories with the best sources. When I asked him how he did it, he said, 'I start with the guy everyone's mad at and see what crumbs of information he gives me. Then I follow the trail of crumbs until I find my next source. And I keep doing that until I score the big one.'"

"Okay, I like it," Bernie said. "So, we know who everyone's mad at ... "

"Arthur." I leaned against the fireplace and sipped my tea. "Bern, we've tried to come up with some explanation, some motive to explain Arthur's behavior. He and Ansel Rock share a past. That we now know."

"Would have been nice if Arthur'd shared that past with you," Bernie said.

"Or if the Texan had," I said. "He never mentioned a thing other than to admit that he knew who Arthur was. It's clear the crazy Texan has a pretty sharp axe to grind with Arthur, and with the press and now with me. He said something about making the press accountable, which explains why he's gone to all this trouble to let me start writing an article he knew I'd never finish."

"So he was expecting Arthur to do something," Bernie said.

"Absolutely. Now I'm afraid to think what he's going to say to my editor at *McMillan*, but it will be something along the lines of how I misled and used the magazine to further my own cause. Which is the absolute worst sin a writer can commit. And now Ansel will probably take the story to a competitor. Second worst sin: losing a story to the competition."

"Oh, Hellie, I hope you're wrong about that. I know you've been counting on this assignment."

"Yeah, well, not much I can do now. What makes me really mad is that I think the Texan was just delighted Arthur showed up on that mountain and took a shot at him. If, indeed, it was Arthur," I added.

"You still don't think it was him?"

"I wouldn't say that, exactly. But I do know we need to find out what happened in Africa."

"And doesn't it seem a little coincidental to you that the Doc just happened to be coming home from Africa at the same time Ansel Rock was coming to Banff to settle some old score with Arthur — "

"For something he claims Arthur did in Africa," I said finishing her thought.

"Didn't Ansel say it had something to do with Arthur getting in the way of his safari?" Bernie said.

"He did. And Nathan obviously believed him because he didn't press Ansel for more information. But why has Ansel shown up now, Bern? Arthur hasn't been in Africa for ... what, seven years?"

"About that."

"Arthur said the Doc was worried about him. My guess is that worry had something to do with Ansel Rock. Did the Doc or Arthur ever talk about Africa with you?"

She shook her head. "Not much. Everyone knew the Doc went there to the clinic and that he and Arthur met somewhere in Tanzania. But that's it. They never really told me a lot."

"Me neither," I said.

"But there is someone they've probably told a great deal to," Bernie said. I finished the last of my tea and set the cup and saucer on the table.

"I think I know who it is you've got in mind. Except she's already told Nathan and me that she doesn't know where Arthur is."

"True, but that was before he started shooting at people. Now she might be a little more motivated to point the way. Crumbs, Hellie. Think crumbs."

I gave her the thumbs-up sign, grabbed my coat from the closet and headed out the door.

***

"Fold in thirds. Header facing," Miriam Bauer said as she passed me a stack of flyers. The header was a picture of a dead grizzly bear splayed in the ditch alongside a dangerous stretch of the Trans-Canada Highway that runs between Banff and Lake Louise, noted for its high human and wildlife fatalities. Under the header the caption read: "Give Them Back THEIR Park."

I was in Miriam's cozy living room sitting on her well-worn couch folding flyers and listening to the dramatic, booming sounds of a classical music piece. A fire was burning in the river-rock fireplace, filling the room with warmth and the scent of woodsmoke. I'd been there about fifteen minutes, folding flyers and chatting mostly about the weather. I hadn't mentioned Arthur, and she obviously hadn't heard about his latest escapade.

"So," Miriam said in her slight German accent. "Enough about the climate. Des tells me they have completed the autopsy. They say our dear Michael has died of a heart attack." She looked me directly in the eye. "But I don't believe it. What do you believe, Hellie?"

I sat back. "I — "

"Wait, I'll turn Mr. Beethoven down so we can hear ourselves think," Miriam said. She moved across the room and turned down the old stereo.

The first time I met Miriam I knew she was Des's mom even before we were introduced. Like him, she had a head of thick, wavy hair that must have once been the same ginger colour as Des's. Now it was the colour of pewter spun through with silver highlights. She had bright eyes that matched her son's, and a generous spirit. Des and his mother were very close, something I envied him for.

Miriam was also Doc and Barbara Rivard's most trusted friend. And she was the first and most ambitious member of the Rivards' Save the Bow Valley Society project. More recently, she joined forces with Arthur as his dedicated assistant and co-conspirator on protest pageants and anti-bear-hunting excursions. She is also a storehouse of Banff history. If anyone knew where Arthur was, it would be Miriam.

"Well, what do you think?" Miriam said when she sat back down.

I hated the thought of being the bearer of more depressing news. She was taking the Doc's death hard. Now, I'd have to tell her that Arthur was in trouble, again. Big trouble. But while I considered the question, I reminded myself that Miriam Bauer was a tough sexagenarian, a sturdy, big-boned woman who chopped her own wood, walked five kilometres a day in summer and cross-country skied twelve in the winter. She only wore slacks; I'd never seen her wear a dress or skirt. Miriam Bauer was no little old lady. Being straight with her was my best bet.

"I'm sure you know what Arthur thinks," I said. "That he believes Doc was murdered."

She nodded.

"I really don't know what to think about that yet. But yesterday, Arthur took a shot at Ansel Rock with an arrow."

She sat back in her armchair and let the news sink in. "Are you sure it was Arthur?" she asked.

"I'm not certain, but it sure looked like him from behind. His coat. Green pullover with the hood pulled up."

"We don't do that sort of thing," she said, shaking her head slowly from side to side. "We've always believed in peaceful resistance."

"Miriam, I need your help. We need to find Arthur. And I need to know what his connection is to Ansel. Can you tell me what happened in Africa?"

"How much do you know already?"

"Not much. Come to think of it, whenever I did bring up Tanzania with either Arthur or Doc, we always seemed to end up talking about something else. Now with Ansel Rock here going on about how he wants Arthur to pay for what he did in Africa, I'm beginning to see why they avoided the topic. All I know is that Doc and Arthur met in Tanzania, and Arthur came here for some reason. Can you tell me anything else?"

"Yes. I can tell you the background, but I don't know how that will help."

"At this point I'll take what I can get."

"All right. Let me get us coffee and some pastry first," Miriam said. On her way to the kitchen she stopped at the fireplace where a couple of logs were smouldering on the grate and ready to capitulate. She threw on a fresh log. It ignited immediately and sent orange flames reaching up the chimney.

While I waited I looked around at the pine-panelled walls covered in family photos. I liked the Bauer home because it was nothing like my family home back in Toronto. Here the furniture was old, the hardwood floors were scuffed and the house was always comfortable and welcoming.

On the outside it was a modest, weathered wood structure with a screened-in porch and flower gardens bordering the property. It was one of the few remaining original houses on Spray Avenue — the busy road leading up to the Banff Springs Hotel — and a reminder of the way Banff once was.

Through Des, I'd learned his parents had bought the place back in the early sixties when they were first married. Des's father was a Canadian — the son of Austrian immigrants — who had grown up in the area. Miriam was born in Germany and immigrated to Canada when she was in her early twenties. Miriam had told me that at one time, she knew all the families who lived along the street. Now her neighbours were wealthy leaseholders, who paid in the millions for their sprawling homes, and whom she rarely saw.

"Here we go, Hellie," she said, appearing with two steaming cups of coffee and a plate of oatmeal cookies on a tray.

I stirred sugar into my coffee, munched a cookie and sat back to listen.

"Stop me if I'm telling you things you already know," Miriam said. I nodded.

"In the seventies," she began, "the Doc and Barbara, she was a nurse, were doing volunteer medical work in Tanzania in the villages around the Selous Game Reserve. Did he tell you that much?"

"Mentioned the reserve. Never gave any details," I said.

"It's a fabulous piece of geography. Full of rhinos, leopards, hippos, giraffes and elephants, of course. Fabulous." She shook her head in delight. "I went there once with Michael and Barbara." Miriam's mouth turned down in a frown and her forehead wrinkled. "And the diseases," she said. "Dreadful. Malaria, cholera. High infant death rate. Terrible poverty."

"Did they always go to the same place?" I asked. "The Doc and his wife?"

"Oh, yes. Went every year for over a decade. Then Barbara took sick. This last trip was Michael's first time back there in … let's see." She did the mental calculations. "Sixteen years. Anyway, back in about eighty-one, Barbara and the Doc ran into Arthur. Mind you, they had heard rumours about him long before they actually ever met."

"What kind of rumours?" I asked.

"Arthur was a well-known activist fighting to save the elephants in the reserve. He was essentially waging his own war on poaching and il-legal ivory sales."

"Wait a second, I didn't think it was illegal to sell ivory until the early 1990s."

"It has always been illegal to sell poached ivory in Africa. We're talking about black-market ivory. Terrible what was happening. Arthur said they started with about a hundred and ten thousand elephants. By 1981, half of them were gone. The ivory was smuggled out of Africa and sold to the rest of the world. People who bought it either didn't understand where it was coming from, or didn't care. Only when there was finally a complete ban on all ivory sales did the world start to get it. And by then it was almost too late for the African elephant. In the western world most of us didn't really know much about it … " She trailed off, lost in her own thoughts for the moment. "Michael and Barbara only came to understand about the plight of the elephants through meeting with Arthur … " She hesitated again, and cleared her throat.

"But they were there helping people. Can't do everything," I offered.

"No, we can't all be like Arthur. In Tanzania he was raising a great deal of money for his Selous Elephant Project, or SEP as it's known. And he never kept a cent of it for himself."

"You mean he didn't take a salary?"

"Not a cent. In Tanzania he didn't even have a home. He lived only where a friend or fellow activist provided a bed. Otherwise, he slept outdoors. Extraordinary, Hellie, it really was. Arthur divided up his time between two towns on the coast at either end of the reserve, the villages, and the reserve forests, where he literally fought the elephant poachers."

"How did he and the Doc cross paths?"

"Some of the village people Michael treated in a town called Mikindani told Arthur about the Canadian doctor and his wife at the clinic. Arthur often stayed with a friend in Mikindani."

A shadow passed over Miriam's eyes. It was gone in a flash and replaced with their usual brightness. "Anyway," she said picking up her story, "Art came for a visit one day and Michael told him they were from Banff. Well!" Miriam let out a howl of laughter. "That's when Art told them the story about his father, Cougar Joe. He has told you about Cougar Joe?"

"Doc told me Cougar Joe was Banff's original hunting guide — who brought in a lot of hunters to the area who took out a lot of game — and that he'd built Arthur's cabin back in the 1920s. They joked about Cougar Joe being Arthur's father."

"That's right. Arthur grew up in England with his mother. Apparently Bertha, that was Arthur's mother, met Joe Thompson when her parents brought her over to the colony for a summer holiday when she was just a girl of nineteen. The story goes that Joe took her out horseback riding, and they ended up at Cougar Joe's cabin. Well, one thing led to another," she said with raised eyebrows, "which eventually culminated in producing Arthur. Joe tried to do the right thing and went to England where he married Bertha. But Joe had the mountains in his blood and couldn't stay in the city. So, he returned to the Rockies. But Bertha was a city girl and she and Arthur stayed behind."

"Doc and Arthur didn't tell me that part," I said. "It's a good story. Should have it written up at the museum."

"I think it is," Miriam said. "Anyway, when Arthur visited the Doc at the clinic and heard he and Barbara were from Banff, Arthur claimed his dad was Cougar Joe Thompson. The Doc said to him, 'By God, Arthur, your father's cabin is on our property.'"

I could hear the Doc in her voice.

"Then offhandedly Michael said, as one does when one is on the other side of the world, 'If you ever find yourself in Canada, Arthur, please look us up and come stay in your father's cabin.' And by heavens, twenty years on, he did just that. Knocked on the Doc's front door and announced that he had come to save the grizzlies."

"Didn't the elephants need him anymore?" I said.

She hesitated when her attention was diverted by the sound of a tiny tinkling bell as a big orange tabby cat emerged from under the couch.

"Ah, you've come out to say hello to Hellie, have you, Mr. Ruffy?" Miriam said to the cat.

Mr. Ruffy sniffed the air and eyed me with mild interest. He jumped up on my lap, swished his fluffy tail in my face then manoeuvred himself around until we were face to whiskers.

"He wants you to scratch under his chin," Miriam said.

I brushed a couple of fingers along Mr. Ruffy's throat until he settled into my lap and pressed his paws into my thighs, sinking his claws into my soft tissue every now and again for laughs.

"You know Michael loved that story about Cougar Joe," Miriam said, smiling at the memory. "Arthur told him he'd always intended to come back to Canada and fulfill his obligation to save what he believed his father had begun to destroy with his hunting and guiding business. Now isn't that something?"

"It is. Quite a story," I said. "Did the Doc believe it?"

Miriam laughed. "I asked Michael the very same question. And he said, 'Doesn't matter whether I do or not. Makes a wonderful tale.'" Miriam's face darkened again and the smile was gone. She looked out her window to Spray Avenue. A tour bus roared past, belching out a cloud of black smoke on its way by. "Barbara died about a year before Arthur showed up," she said.

"Yes. I knew that."

"A lot of people thought Arthur's timing was pretty convenient. Michael told me he didn't care if Arthur's timing was by coincidence or design. Even if Arthur Elliott had bamboozled him, the Doc said he couldn't give two hoots. He was just happy to have someone to share a meal with every now and again. And Arthur has repaid his generosity by keeping up the grounds, along with helping to keep the Society going."

She sat forward in her chair and looked at me intently. "He's quite extraordinary, Hellie. He's not a madman, as some would have you believe. Arthur changes the way people look at things. And when someone has the power to do that, they scare other people. When the Doc and his wife returned home after meeting him, they were so motivated they started the Save the Bow Valley Society."

Something I remembered brought a smile to my face. "Doc once told me he believed Arthur could get money out of a nunnery."

Miriam laughed. "He was right." She paused. "Thank you, Hellie."

"For what?"

"Letting me talk about Michael. It helps."

"My pleasure. And I'd like to help more, but you need to tell me about Ansel Rock."

Her mouth was pinched to a straight line. "I'm afraid Arthur is the only one who can tell you what his relationship is with Mr. Rock. And why he was up on that mountain shooting at him ... if it was Arthur."

"Right, but since I don't know where he is ... "

She looked down at her hands and studied her short fingernails. "Will you tell the police?" she said.

"Not until I speak to him first."

Miriam's sad eyes looked deep into mine. "He's mourning Michael. We all are."

"Yes, we all are," I agreed.

She was watching the cat on my lap, but her calculating eyes told me she was weighing what she was willing to tell me. I waited.

Eventually she said, "My husband's uncle had an old trapper's cabin in Kananaskis."

"Is Arthur there?"

"I expect so," she said, and sketched a map on the back of one of the brochures. She handed the rough directions to me and stood. "Wait just a minute." She left the room and returned a moment later and passed me a key. "Just in case he's not there."

I pocketed the key, and I extracted myself from under Mr. Ruffy. "Thanks," I said. "I should probably go."

"You promise me you'll get his side of the story before you tell the police where he is?" she said.

"You have my word," I said. We walked out to the street. Another tour bus soared past, spewing out exhaust on its way up to the hotel.

"The cabin's pretty secluded," Miriam said waving away the smoke. "Not too many go up that way. And it's a good hike in. You'll never make it in before dark today, so you'll have to wait and go in the morning."

"Thanks, Miriam," I said.

"You're welcome. I just hope Arthur will thank me too." She turned to go back up the walk to her home, then stopped and turned back. "Oh, and Hellie, when you do go, watch out for the bears."

"Why, have there been sightings up that way?"

She let her gaze slide off my shoulder and up Rundle Mountain's massive plane of jutting limestone that towered behind me. "Possibly," she said vaguely.

CHAPTER 8

FROM MIRIAM'S, I HEADED INTO TOWN AND STOPPED ON THE BRIDGE to look at her rough map. It was a good hike in to the trapper's cabin, and I was going to need some things. Bernie and Paul had a lot of hiking gear, so I would borrow that and leave in the morning. The prospect of hiking up there alone was more than a little daunting. But I couldn't see not going and I didn't want to bring anyone with me.

On tiptoe I glanced over the river-rock railing and past the proud concrete native heads inlaid along the Bow River Bridge, to the flowing water below. The sun sparkled on the surface and turned the water from shades of aqua to a deep sapphire blue. For the past few days, my life had not been my own. It was as though I was being carried away like the water below me on a perpetual stream that was taking me farther away from what I knew and closer to something completely incomprehensible.

I moved off and continued into town. Once the funeral was over, I'd have to start looking for a new place to live, and I'd need more work. At the moment, I had a couple of travel pieces to do for a magazine out of Vancouver, which would pay about enough to cover one week's worth of groceries. All my hopes had been riding on the *McMillan* story. I'd had visions of being their western correspondent. Now I was back to where I'd started. "Damn," I muttered, as I stood on the corner waiting for a light on Banff Avenue. A man standing on my left was watching me out of the corner of his eye. I didn't care. "Damn," I said it again.

I still hadn't contacted my editor at *McMillan* to fess up to what happened. Though I suspected Ansel would have filled him in by now. And I was sure there would be messages waiting for me when I got back to the Doc's house. The light turned green and the man next to me made haste for the other side.

When I passed the Jump Start coffee shop, I took a right and heard someone call out: "Yoo hoo, Hellie."

I froze, and a sense of dread swept over me. I knew what I had done.

I'd been so lost in my thoughts I hadn't been paying attention to where I was going, and I'd made the wrong turn onto Lynx Street. But there was no escaping.

By the time Sandy Kole had me perched on one of her Apres Alpine Cafe lunch-counter stools, I was still searching for an excuse to leave.

"What'll it be, Hellie?" Sandy chirped from behind the counter. "Oh wait, never mind, we have something new. Just came out of the oven."

"Thanks. But I'm not really — "

She slipped out of sight through the swinging doors and into the kitchen. I looked around the cheerful, albeit empty, restaurant and couldn't help but admit that they'd done a nice job with the place. Everything from the booths to the floors was done in a golden lacquered pine, giving the joint a kind of mountain cabin/retro soda shop feel. They specialized in old-fashioned milkshakes, pies and trendier fare like wraps and special coffees. The atmosphere was cozy, and the inviting smells of vanilla beans and fresh-baked breads and cookies spiced the air. I suspected the only reason the restaurant wasn't popular had to do with Sandy and Doug's unwillingness to leave customers alone and their incessant blabbing about "relaxing because we're all in the mountains now," which tended to drive away repeat business.

"Okay, Hellie, this is our Cave and Basin muffin," Sandy said skipping back into the room with what looked like a miniature bundt cake sprinkled with sparkly blue candy chips. She set it in front of me. "What do you think? Doug doesn't think people will get it, but I do. See, it's a blueberry muffin with — "

"Blue candy to match the mineral pools." I picked up the pastry and examined it closer. "Yes, I see. Very clever, Sandy."

"Doug!" Sandy hollered so loudly, I nearly dropped my muffin.

Doug Kole appeared through the kitchen doors holding a long wooden trough. "Hello there, Hellie. What do you think of our new Cave muffins?"

"Cave and Basin, Doug," Sandy scolded. "People won't get it if you just call them Cave muffins." She looked at me and rolled her eyes.

"I'd prefer just Cave," Doug said. "What'd ya think of this?" He held the trough under my nose. The Koles's latest addition to their business was a fudge counter, where Doug and Sandy, but mostly their slave cook, made the stuff by the twenty-five-pound slab in twelve different flavours, then sold it to the tourists for about the same price as a gram of high-grade cocaine.

I breathed in the thick, sweet chocolate aroma. "Heavenly," I said. And it was, but I was so keyed up, I could barely stomach it. I looked down at the big muffin I hadn't touched. Doug and Sandy stood on the other side of the counter, expectant smiles pasted on their faces. I bit into the muffin. They smiled. I smiled.

Side by side Doug and Sandy looked like window mannequins from one of those leisure-wear stores geared to the fifty-plus crowd. That day the Koles were wearing matching white flannel shirts left open to expose cotton turtleneck shirts — Sandy's in mauve, Doug's in navy — tucked smartly into matching tan polyester trousers with permanent creases stiff enough to slice the fudge.

"Is it still a hot seller?" I asked, meaning the fudge.

"Oh my word," Sandy enthused. "We can't keep up with the demand."

"And did Sandy tell you we're shipping the darn stuff out now?" Doug shook his head in that disbelieving, self-congratulatory way of his.

"That's great. Where to?"

"Vancouver, if you can believe it."

I could not. Last time I was in Vancouver I remembered seeing an overabundance of overpriced fudge. "Oh, did this come about through some of your advertising connections, Doug?" I asked.

"Nope, just out of the blue. Fellow called up last week and said his daughter had been here skiing a month or so back and brought him back a few slices. And holy doodle didn't he get hooked. He's got gift shops in and around Vancouver and wants our fudge." Doug leaned over the counter, his forearm touching mine. "Now I'm working out the logistics of shipping it and keeping it fresh. Got a storage problem."

I nodded, feigning interest.

"Can you imagine, Hellie — our name's going to be all over the place."

"You'll be famous."

"And speaking of famous," Sandy said, her rabbity nose twitching. "Your name's been flying all over town since all that nasty business happened with the Doc."

My back went rigid.

"So what the dickens happened, Hellie?" Doug asked while he cut and stacked slabs of fudge. "Heard it had something to do with drugs."

"What? No. It was a heart attack."

"Really?" Sandy chimed in. "Larry told us the Doc shot himself up. In Winnipeg we knew a doctor who used to do that. Had to go into detox. But we never suspected the Doc."

"All hopped up on something, eh," Doug said and shook his head. "You just never know."

I kept my voice even. "Listen you guys, Nathan got the report back from the medical examiner's office. They did an autopsy. It was a heart attack. No sign of any drugs. Okay? The only medication the Doc took was cortisone. For his knee. That's it, no drugs."

My words were pointless. The rumour mill was already spinning out tales of the fantastic. By dinnertime, Doc Rivard would be a drug lord kingpin, who had been operating a multi-million dollar heroine operation out of his home and staged his own death.

Doug gave me a knowing smile. "They never tell you the whole truth. Don't forget Sandy and I grew up in the big city too, Hellie. Probably all hopped up on smack and hallucinated he was on the beaches of Hawaii."

Yeah, that's probably it. "Well, you two," I said, and reached for my bag. "I'd love to stay and chat, but I really have to get going. I'm trying to get the Doc's funeral organized."

A light went on for Doug and he sidled up to me. He was going to ask to cater the affair. I could feel it, and I readied myself. With that winning smile he'd cultivated from twenty-some years in the advertising business, Doug said, "Sure, Hellie, we know you're busy. Larry told us about the big magazine story you're doing. Who knows, maybe you could mention our little place, you know, local colour and all that."

The tension eased out of my shoulders. "Gee, you never know, Doug."

Sandy's eyes were bright with possibilities. "That fellow's from Houston, isn't he? Gosh, he paid an awful lot of money for a sheep, don't ya think?"

Doug rubbed the tips of his fingers across his upper lip. "A million dollars is what I heard," he said.

Sandy piped in. "Well, Hellie, you just make sure you tell that rich Texan to stop in at the Après Alpine Café." She placed a bill next to my half-eaten muffin. "I'm not charging you full price since we used you as a guinea pig."

"Great. Sure thing," I said, reaching for my wallet.

As I was inching my way to the door, Doug suddenly came up with another brilliant idea. "Say, Hellie, maybe you could help us out with something else."

Here it comes. The planets are aligned.

"Larry and Suzanna tell us there's a cold storage room in the Doc's basement," Doug said. "Might just be the perfect temperature for our fudge. It'd only be there until we ship this lot out. After that we'll have a new fridge. What do you say?"

Bless your hearts, Suzanna and Larry, is what I wanted to say. "Uh, yeah, okay. You can use the basement," is what I actually said. "But I don't know how long I'm going to be able to stay in the house. I'm going back tonight." I shrugged. "But I could be out anytime."

Doug flashed me his dazzling, triumphant smile. "We'll be in touch," he said.

I made my escape.

***

"I'll come in with you," Bernie said.

We were parked in front of the Doc's, sitting in her 1956 turquoise Chevy Bel Air, staring up at the imposing white and black-trimmed house that was cast in the evening's shadowy gloom. Even at night the Doc's place had always looked warm and inviting. Now the home was gone along with the Doc, leaving only the house.

"Thanks, it's late," I said. "And Paul should be home anytime, Bern. You should be with him."

"Are you really going up to Miriam's cabin tomorrow?" she said.

I nodded.

"I don't think you should go alone. I'll talk to Paul — "

"No, Bern. Let's keep this to ourselves, for now. I'll be fine. Where I'm going isn't all that far from where I was with Ansel."

"Oh, that certainly puts my mind at ease. You'll get shot at."

"No I won't." I hadn't actually thought of that. "Well, if it was Arthur doing the shooting, then I won't."

Bernie dug in the glove box and pulled out a black cord with a quartz crystal hanging from it. She handed it to me. "At least take this."

"What is it?"

"A necklace."

"I see that. But what's it for?"

"Protection. Wear it." She tied it around my neck and gave me a hug.

"I'm not going into battle, Bern. I'm just going for a hike."

"Yes. Alone."

After we said good night, I stood on the sidewalk and watched the Chevy's red tail lights until they disappeared around the corner at the end of the block. I turned away from the street and faced the house. My stomach and chest muscles tightened and I wished I hadn't been so quick to send Bernie away. I took a deep breath and walked up the steps.

When I stepped through the door, the scent of chemicals, paper and strangers punctuated the stale air. I closed the door behind me. Up and down the hall, muddy boot prints stamped the hardwood floors. Then I sensed something else. A chill slid over my skin, making the hair on my arms prickle with electricity.

I felt a presence.

I'd felt a ghostly presence in the Rivard household before — that wasn't new. But this was different. Someone was actually in the house.

I stayed where I was, close to the door, and listened. Something scraped against the roof. I started and took a step back. My hand wrapped around the doorknob. I turned it and opened the door a crack. I listened again and decided it must have been a branch. The furnace gave its usual perfunctory ping and sigh just before it kicked in and sent a gust of warm air up through the registers.

From the back of the house came a metallic clicking sound, like a door lock being engaged. Curiosity overrode good judgment and I bolted down the hall to the kitchen. I flipped on the lights.

No one was there.

And I don't suppose I really believed there would be. If I'd actually thought someone was in there, I would have gone out the front door faster than a spooked cat. I tried the back door. It was locked up tight. In the solarium, the sliding patio doors were in the same state.

My nerves were obviously frayed to the breaking point. I was worn out, and all I wanted to do was to go to bed.

Back in the kitchen, I poured a glass of milk and leaned against the sink to drink it. When I was done, I placed the empty glass in the sink and was about to run the tap when a creak on the hardwood floors from somewhere down the front hall brought me up short. A second creak followed. Then a third. This time I didn't rush to investigate. From where I was standing, between the counter and the stove, my only escape was over the counter and out the back door.

"Who's there?" I hissed.

Silence.

Another creak. I moved to the counter, hoisted myself up and kept my focus riveted on the hall entrance. My eyes grew wide with terror as fingers curled around the doorframe.

I wasn't about to stick around to see who those fingers belonged to, so I swung my legs up over the counter, dropped to the floor on the other side and lunged for the back door.

Behind me someone sucked in a breath and spat the words, "It's you!"

I spun around. "Suzanna!"

"Hellie!" Her hand was at her throat. "You scared me half to death."

"I scared you! What are you doing here?"

"The front door was open. I thought someone broke in."

"Oh." I breathed in and out. "I guess I must have left it open." My knees were weak and my pulse was pounding in my ears. "I thought I heard someone at the back door when I came in. Was that you, Suzanna?"

"No it was not. I thought you were supposed to be off hunting."

"Change of plans," I said.

"I need to get away, Hellie, so I'm leaving today for a retreat," she said. In Suzanna's world "retreat" usually meant some form of facial reconstruction or an anti-stress, anti-aging spa visit. "Have you heard anything more?" she said, her eyes surveying the room like a suspicious chaperone searching to see if anything was out of place, or if I was hiding someone.

"About the Doc?"

"Yes, about Michael. What else would I be talking about?"

"I have no idea," I said in a weary, hostile voice. At that moment, I was in no mood to be treated like the hired help.

"Well?" She crossed her arms. Her lips twitched, and she wisely softened her tone. "Did Nathan tell you anything yet?"

"Yes. The official word is that Doc Rivard died of natural causes." While I spoke I made moves toward the front door in the hope she would follow my lead. She did.

"Good. That's good news," Suzanna said. "Now, what about the funeral? I'll be away … "

"Bernie and I will take care of it. And Miriam, she's going to help too. It'll be in a couple of days."

"Fine. I'll make sure I'm back for it."

She opened the door, stepped outside then paused on the steps. "Have you heard from the lawyer's office?"

"No. Why? Should I be hearing from them?"

"Yes. They'll tell you when you have to be out of here."

I closed the door even though I really felt like slamming it.

***

Green iridescent numbers on my bedside clock flashed 2:03 a.m. I'd been waking on average every fifteen minutes to the sounds of the night. Above me in the attic, the hardwood floors creaked with each of Barbara Rivard's ghostly footfalls. When I'd first moved in I couldn't sleep because the noises in the attic kept me up. I told the Doc, and he assured me it was just his wife Barbara who had apparently been an insomniac and liked to read up in the attic.

The look on my face must have told the Doc I thought he was truly out of his mind. But he just laughed and gave me a good hearty pat on the back and said, "Get used to it, Hellie, we've got lots of ghosts in Banff. You're a Banffite now. Ghost stories and bear stories, that's what we're made of."

I smiled at the memory. Doc was right on both accounts. I'd discovered a number of Banff's ghosts. Melissa's restaurant has at least one. The Springs Hotel boasts three, and just about every other old building in town has one or two dearly departed souls still hanging about. Doc said he just had the one. Initially, I wrote it off as nonsense, but when furniture seemed to be rearranged and the phone would go missing, I started to believe. After awhile I learned to tune the noises out, and Barbara and I got on just fine. Now I imagined I heard a second set of footsteps and wondered if the Doc and his wife were up there pacing together.

Through the window I always left open a crack, I thought I heard gravel crunching on the river path below. Probably late-night partiers weaving their way home.

Or Arthur!

I eased out of bed, went to the window and tried to make out the cabin's silhouette. I could not. The sky was overcast, blotting out the moon and stars. It was a black night trying to snow. Single white flakes fluttered and danced in the breeze before they came to light on my window ledge.

A breeze blew in, bringing with it the scent of cigarette smoke. A twig snapped somewhere to the east of the property. I opened the window farther. The smell grew stronger. A chair leg scraped along the patio flagstone directly below me. I squinted against the darkness but could see nothing.

"Hello?" I called down.

No reply.

"Hello?" I said again.

The smoke grew faint. At the edge of the property, near the river path, a single point of red light floated in the blackness. It grew brighter for an instant before it dropped to the ground where it smouldered and fizzled out on the damp shale. Footsteps echoed in the darkness as they hurried down the path toward town.

I knew that whoever was out there couldn't have been Arthur. He didn't smoke. At least I didn't think he smoked; however, after his behavior with Ansel, I was beginning to wonder if I knew the man at all. And I wondered if the person smoking on the path had been watching me. Somehow I had the impression he or she was. I closed the window and drew the curtains.

Back in bed I tried to force myself to sleep. It was no use. Thoughts about Arthur intruded whenever I started to drift off. Thoughts that ran from worry to fury. Why hadn't he told me he knew Ansel Rock? What else hadn't he told me? I'd lost the story because of him. A story that ... my thought trailed off when a scrap of conversation I'd had with Arthur a few months earlier drifted up to the surface of my consciousness.

I sat up and flipped on the bedside light. It all came back in one sickening flash.

Arthur had been edging the flowerbeds and I'd been sitting on the front steps making a list of story ideas I could run past a few of the bigger magazines.

"How goes the search for your next Pulitzer-prize-winning article?" Arthur asked from where he was kneeling on the grass.

"Okay, I have a couple of ideas for one about the new golf course in Canmore. And there's this guy building a straw bale house. *Urban Living* might want it."

"Sounds like good reading," Arthur said. "Did you hear that the mountain bikers are organizing a rally to protest the closure of two more trails?"

I jotted bikes down on my list. "Got any more?"

"Oh, yes. No end of them."

"Then fire away," I said.

"How about what's happening to the elk and what the wardens' moving them out of town has meant to the Fairholme wolf pack. Oh, and the Louise Convention Centre project. Very controversial. They were even campaigning against it in the US. And the bighorn hunt. And the grain on the rail tracks, we've lost another bear because of it. And the grizzly project, of course ... "

I was writing madly while he rattled them off. Then Suzanna came into the yard to complain about some infraction Arthur had committed with the flowerbeds.

Weeks later, when I saw the notice in the paper that the bighorn auction was taking place, I clipped it out and made it my idea. I completely forgot that Arthur had been the one to put the bug in my ear.

My head fell back and hit the headboard with a bang. Arthur had intentionally set me up to do this story. And I owed Ansel Rock an apology.

CHAPTER 9

I WAS IN A FOUL MOOD WHEN I STEPPED OUT OF THE SHOWER THE NEXT morning. I'd had all of about two hours sleep, and I was dreading the embarrassing task ahead of me. Outside my bedroom window, two black crows sailed past like a nasty joke. I'd be eating plenty of that, and Ansel Rock was going to get a real kick out of watching me choke on the feathers.

But first, I'd face the inevitable and check my email. There were only two messages: one was from Gordon Moser my editor at *McMillan*, asking me to give him a call when I got back from the big hunting trip. Hmm. Ansel obviously still hadn't called him. He would, though. It was just a matter of when. Instead of hitting reply, I thought it would be more prudent to call and speak to him in person, later.

The second message was from my little brother, Danny, telling me he was sorry to hear about Doc Rivard and that he'd passed the news on to Mom and Dad. He also said there was something important he needed to talk to me about and would try to call me today. For the past year, we'd been keeping each other up-to-date on our lives. Now I wondered if something was wrong at home. I looked at the phone and considered calling. My stomach squeezed into the familiar knot. I couldn't do it. He might not answer.

Danny, even more than my ex-fiancé, Brock, was the reason I'd been living in exile, why for the past year I'd kept my mouth shut about the truth and had been playing out in my mind that day, my wedding day, scene by scene, like a series of snapshots.

It always started with the one of me in my wedding dress surrounded by champagne-sipping, white-gloved women in sea green and violet dresses bearing down on me with their cameras. I don't want to be there, in that room, in that monstrous Gothic church. I can feel the claustrophobia weighing on my chest and in my heart. So I make an excuse — tell the ladies I have to go to the bathroom. They all laugh and give each other knowing winks and smiles. I drag my dress and myself into the hall and, momentarily confused as I look for the ladies' room, I open the wrong door.

And there they are.

My husband-to-be in his lover's embrace, their lips latched as though giving each other one final bit of nourishment before my fiancé is to join me in holy matrimony.

They look at me. No one speaks. No one moves. Until I, apparition-like, glide silently back out of the room. I close the door, and feel my elbows slip into my mother and father's waiting hands. They usher me to the back of the church. The string quartet is playing Bach's sweet, gracious *Air on the G String*. It ends abruptly when the organist takes over and launches into the first jarring chords of "Here Comes the Bride."

We ascend the stairs to the nave. I hear my mother's voice. "Well, this is it. We've finally made it," she says and straightens my veil. My mother has been planning this day since she and Mary-Jane Hanlan dressed Brock and me in matching christening gowns, thirty long years ago.

"Ready, kiddo?" my father says. He doesn't wait for my answer. "Let's get this train rolling."

We pass into St. James Cathedral's magnificent chancel, and I walk up the aisle. Five bridesmaids, giant lavender petals sent in on an autumn gust, drift in behind us.

Brock has materialized at the front of the church. Danny is beside him. Brock is smiling his flawless smile, and it assures me that what I thought I just saw was nothing more than an illusion born of my panic and icy feet.

I am beside Brock. The priest murmurs something. Brock responds. Their voices are muffled and sound as though they are coming from behind a wall. I feel the groom nudge me. He says my name: "Hellie."

"What?"

"Say it. Say, I do."

I look up into his eyes. They are kind and reassuring. They tell me all is well.

So I say it. "I do."

Then my eyes drift to the right and meet my little brother's. He's not holding up nearly so well as my new husband. Brock is a practised liar. Danny isn't.

It's the pain in Danny's eyes that makes me turn on the balls of my satin shoes and face our guests. My mother is sitting in the first pew. She cocks her head. The familiar lines of annoyance crease her forehead. She mouths the words: "What's wrong?" They are the last words she will speak to me.

It is then that I flee back down the aisle like some kind of burning bride. I hurl myself through the cathedral's massive doors and stumble outside. With a piercing whistle, I hail the limo driver to take me home. Like a thief, I stuff clothes, laptop, shoes, anything I can get my hands on, into my suitcase and garbage bags, before I jump into our new VW Beetle — a gift from the groom's side — and speed out of Toronto. The pearl-encrusted, mile-long veil is left on the 400 somewhere around Barrie. Frothy layers of wedding-dress taffeta are shed in a Petro-Can restroom. And the bouquet? I'd launched it back over my head on my way out of the church.

For the next two days I drive west, stopping only to catch a few winks in a greasy motel before pressing on and arriving in my favourite childhood vacation spot — Banff in the Rocky Mountains. And that was it. After I'd run out of that church, my life had played out like a movie. Time stopped. Scene shift. I was in Banff living a new life. And my old life in Toronto was left suspended, as though the director had forgotten it, neglected to get back to it and finish the story.

I stared at the computer screen and let the well-worn feelings of blame work their way up from my stomach and settle in my chest. Through Danny I'd learned that my mother had cried for days after I took off from the church. She said that I'd humiliated her in front of all her friends and Dad's business associates. And that neither she nor Dad had any intention of speaking to me until I came back to Toronto and did the right thing. The right thing being: Finish the ceremony and become Mrs. Brock Hanlan.

And once again I told myself how I shouldn't have let things go so far. How I shouldn't have agreed to marry Brock in the first place. Because that's what it had amounted to, an agreement. An arrangement. Our fathers were already business partners in MacHan travel — this was just a different kind of merger: "Mac" marries "Han". Everyone said we were perfect together. And I believed them, even though I really didn't know Brock. But then neither did anyone else it seemed, except Danny.

I didn't blame Danny. And I didn't hate him for what he'd done. There's no percentage in hating a teenager. There is, however, a fair bit of mileage to be had in blaming and despising a thirty-one-year old, lying, cheating bastard, who seduced and nearly destroyed my little brother.

After I'd left Toronto, I phoned Danny from the Petro-Can station where I was shedding my dress and found him at a friend's house. I was terrified he might try to hurt himself, do the pill thing again. We talked long enough for me to convince him that he'd actually done me a favour. Which was, in part, true. I would have found out later anyway, I reasoned. Better to know now.

I looked at the phone again and decided that if it was an emergency Danny would have said so, or called by now. Maybe I was stalling, but I sent a note to Danny, in the hopes he might be online, saying I was at home. After I'd waited as long I possibly could, I gave up and reluctantly left the house.

***

Ansel Rock was waiting for me at the hotel in Mount Stephen Hall, wearing snug-fitting jeans and a pale blue checked flannel shirt. Sitting in one of the straight-backed oversized chairs, he seemed to suit the grand medieval room. Though Ansel, I was sure, would see the room as suiting him.

"I hope you've come to tell me where Arthur Elliott is," Ansel said. He stood and towered over me.

"Nope. That's not it."

"Then why'd you come?"

"To make a confession."

We remained standing as I told him about the conversation I remembered having with Arthur, how he had suggested the story. I felt sick at heart because I was being disloyal to a friend.

"And you just remembered this now?" Ansel said, skepticism curling his upper lip.

"Last night. I want to be honest with you, set the record straight and apologize. If it was Arthur up there on that mountain, then I'm sorry for that, too. Do you mind if we sit down?" He took up his seat and I sank into the chair next to his.

"And now I was hoping you'd be straight with me, Ansel. You and Arthur obviously share some history — "

"Yup. Sure do. I'm a hunter and he's a dangerous man. And unless they catch him right quick, my guess is that no one around here will be seeing Arthur Elliott for a good many years."

"Why would you say that?"

"That's how he operates." Ansel studied me for a long moment. "You really don't know him, do you?"

My pride wouldn't let me answer because I wasn't sure if he was right. "Doc Rivard thought a lot of him," I said.

"I'm sure he did."

I didn't like his tone. It put the Doc in the same unsavoury category he apparently reserved for Arthur.

"You've been duped, Hellie. Let me pass on something I've learned about men like Arthur Elliott and people like you. You go looking for a saint and you'll surely find one. But there are no saints, Hellie. There are only good salesmen." Ansel Rock sat back. His right eyebrow arched expectantly.

"Are you waiting for applause?"

He gave an exasperated grunt and pressed his hands into his pockets. "No. I'm waiting for you to wake up. And I'm warning you. If Arthur does contact you, you'd better call the police right quick. He's dangerous, Hellie. You saw yourself what he's capable of."

I couldn't dispute that I had seen someone who resembled Arthur, but in my heart I had to believe Ansel was wrong. I'd lived next door to Arthur for over a year. He was a good soul. Or was he? I pushed away my doubts.

"And about Michael Rivard's sudden passing — "

"What about it?" I snapped.

"I expect the police will see some connection to Arthur."

"Goodbye Ansel." I got up to leave.

He grabbed my arm. "Wait a second. Open your eyes, woman. He shot at us."

"Arthur did not do anything to the Doc. Arthur was his best friend."

"Best friends kill each other all the time."

"Perhaps they do where you come from. They don't in Banff."

He was still holding my arm. "I surely do not want to see you get hurt. I believe you've been set up. So please, just be careful."

"I don't have anything to be careful about. Doc Rivard died of ... " I hesitated. "A heart attack."

"Sure he did."

"I'm leaving now," I said.

"And I'm going for breakfast. You interested?"

"Are you inviting me to join you?"

"Yup. You interested in finishing this story?"

"Am I what?"

"This article. I'd like to see it finished."

"Then you better tell the magazine to get someone who can write it."

"You write. You write good."

"Well."

"Well what?"

"I write well. Never mind."

"Yes you do. And when I read your work, I was thinking that it was a shame you weren't on the level, because if I were going to let someone do this story it would be you. I meant what I said the other day."

He was standing again, looking down on me. A boardroom tactic, I guessed, that had no doubt served him well. Always loom over your opponents and bring 'em to their knees.

"I'm being honest here, Hellie. And I'm asking you to finish this story. So what do you say?"

"I'd say yes, but haven't you already told the magazine I was off the story?"

"Nope. You?"

I shook my head.

"Good," he said and offered me his hand. We shook on the deal, both of us fully aware we were using the other for our own motives and our own gain.

"All right then, you better have breakfast with me."

"Thanks," I said. "But I can't. Have to see someone. About the Doc's funeral," I added, but just a little too quickly.

He eyed me suspiciously and rubbed a hand over his stubbled chin. "Now you're pushing it. If you know where he is, Hellie, I suggest you tell the police."

"I'll keep your suggestion in mind," I said, and took off out of the hotel.

At home, I packed my backpack with clothes and the other things I'd borrowed from Bernie. Then I emailed the magazine to say we'd run into a problem on the hunting trip, but that I was still on track with the story. There was no word from Danny. So I sent him another message saying I'd be back the next day and to please call me. Then I set out to find Arthur.

CHAPTER 10

FROM MY ROCKY PERCH, I WATCHED A WHIFF OF SMOKE IN THE DISTANCE snaking its way up into the sky. With it came a great sense of relief; where there is smoke there is Arthur, I reasoned. Trees blocked any view of the cabin, but I had been following Miriam's map pretty closely and felt confident I was on the right track.

After I struggled back into my pack, I made my way down the trail that meandered into a valley and continued along a thickly wooded path that, according to Miriam's map, would take me to her cabin.

The sun was low, but still warm and the air was thick with the tang of pine sap running in the autumn heat. My shoulders were aching from the heavy pack and I would be grateful to be rid of it. With a last push as I put my head down and plodded up the path, Ansel's words invaded my thoughts. *He's dangerous, Hellie. You saw what he's capable of.*

"No, Ansel, you're wrong," I said aloud.

I rounded a bend in the trail, and a sense of pride swelled in my chest at having made it this far. To my right, amid the thick brush, I heard twigs snap and dead leaves crunch. Probably a deer, I guessed. But I started to get edgy as the noises grew louder. Whatever it was, it was coming my way, and it was beginning to take shape.

I squinted into the dark forest. At first I didn't understand what I was seeing. Up the trail there was a rustling in the woods. Now my mind was telling me exactly what was ahead. I couldn't breathe. Fear had sucked all the oxygen out of my lungs and turned my legs to concrete.

Branches swished as a massive grizzly bear and her cubs stepped out from the cover of woods and into the light.

My first reaction was to run. But a voice in my head said: *Don't run. Never run.* It was Des's voice. I ignored it, and was about to turn on my heels and go for it when his voice stopped me again. *You'll never outrun a grizzly, Hellie. Drop your eyes. Drop your pack. And take slow steps back.*

It took every bit of physical strength and psychological will to stand there and let my fingers fumble for the pack clips. The straps slipped off my shoulders and the pack hit the ground. The mother bear's head swayed from side to side as if she was telling me no.

I stole a glance at the cubs. Dear God, they were coming toward me. I lifted my right leg — it felt like a thick dead log — and I stepped back. At the same time the big sow took one step forward as if we were doing some kind of terrifying dance. The cubs were on the path heading for my pack. The sow reared up and let out a roar. I felt dizzy, and I thought I was going to faint.

The cubs scrambled back into the bush. The sow went down on all fours. She was galloping down the trail coming right for me. My body swivelled, reflex took over and I was about to start running for my life. My boot caught on a root, and I was going down. Just before I hit the ground I caught sight of something white flash above the bear's head.

On the ground, my body curled itself into a fetal position — head tucked into my knees, one hand wrapped around my neck. I felt something sharp digging into my chest. Bernie's crystal. My fingers curled around it. My heart was pounding so hard in my ears I was certain it was going to explode.

The ground shook next to my head. Grunting sounds grew closer until I felt her snout pressing against my cheek. I could feel her hot breath on my flesh and her musky animal scent assailed my senses.

My eyes were squeezed shut, but I could see her. See those giant paws and yellow claws as she paced around me. Her eyes watching me, waiting for one muscle twitch to tell her I was still alive and still a threat. Her nose was in my ear, snuffling. It was as loud as a train, and I thought I would cry out. I squeezed my eyes tighter and steeled myself ready to feel her teeth tear into my scalp. My whole body was one aching knot of fear. *Please God. Please God. Please …* I prayed.

Abruptly the snuffing and snorting stopped. Tree branches shook nearby. Leaves crunched, twigs snapped. The sounds grew fainter until there was nothing, except the sound of my own breath flowing wildly in and out of my lungs.

I didn't move. I could still see her waiting. A whimper escaped from the back of my throat. Then I felt the pressure on my shoulder, as her paw came down on my shoulder. Oh God no …

"Hellie."

My eyes snapped open. "Arthur!" It came out on a gush of exhaled air. "Arthur." I blinked not sure he was real. "Did you see them? There were bears. Did you see them?"

"Yes. I saw them," he said, helping me to my feet. "You're all right."

"I think so. Holy God ... " I blinked again and took a couple of deep breaths. My eyes searched the trees, up the trail then down behind us. "We should go. They might come back," I said and pulled his arm. "Come on. How close is the cabin?"

"Just up ahead," he said and picked up my pack.

"I thought I was going to die, Arthur. I really did," I said as we made our way up the trail. I kept stealing glances back over my shoulder.

"Why?" he said.

"Why?" I shot him an incredulous look. "Because I was between a mother grizzly and her cubs. That's why."

"She wouldn't have hurt you," he said.

"Hey, Arthur. I know you see them differently than the rest of us. And I like them too, from a distance. You didn't see her charge me. She was coming for me. You bet she was."

We entered a secluded clearing where a tiny log cabin was tucked amid evergreens with a patch of meadow doubling as its front lawn. Two chairs made from intricately woven willow branches sat near a river rock fire pit.

"Thank the Lord we're here," I said and threw myself down in one of the chairs. I was talking at lightning speed and couldn't seem to quiet myself. I ran a trembling hand over my forehead. "Whooee! I have never been that scared in my whole life," I said between deep breaths.

Arthur stood beside me listening patiently. He was wearing one of his colourful cloth wraps, and I felt I had just climbed The Mountain, slain the dragon on my way up, and met my Maker, or my Maker's garishly clad assistant, at any rate.

"Maybe she saw you," I said, "and that's why she took off."

My eyes darted around the clearing, imagining I saw something dark move in the brush. At the edge of the meadow, I spotted an old iron washbasin that looked like it was filled with apples. There were no apple trees on the property and as far as I knew, apple trees did not grow in the Rocky Mountains, except in Banff where residents planted them.

I got up to take a closer look. It was indeed filled with bruised apples, nuts and grain. My eyes swept the small property. "Do you keep horses here, Arthur?"

He shook his head and gave me a weak, guilty smile.

"Oh, then who ... " I suddenly remembered the flash of white I'd seen just before I hit the ground. "You're feeding them," I said. "Oh my God, that was Lulu! Of course ... Miriam warned me. She knows what you're doing."

I couldn't believe it had taken me that long to make the connection. The grizzly I'd just had a close encounter with was no stranger to Banff or to me. Everyone in town knew about the little grizzly who had beaten the odds.

Des had told me her story. Lulu's family had been attacked and killed by a large male bear when Lulu was only a year old. No one had held out much hope of the little cub surviving on her own through the winter, but the following spring she'd turned up on Banff Avenue, recognizable by the patch of white fur on her head. Lulu didn't much care for the busy street and took off out of town pretty quick. But she apparently held onto her hankering for fine hotels and would occasionally be spotted at the Post Hotel, stepping on the footpad to make the automatic doors open and close. The wardens moved her and did some aversion conditioning to convince her that it was a bad idea to get too close to humans. And it mostly worked.

Until one night, shortly after I moved in, Lulu and her cubs visited the Doc's property to make a midnight raid on his apple trees. From the kitchen window, I watched in awe as the cubs swung from the tree branches like little children and as Lulu stretched to her full seven-foot height, using her big paws and Brazil-nut-sized claws to pick the apples and shovel them into her mouth. I'd seen Arthur among the trees that night, too, standing perfectly still in the silvery light of the full moon. Later, I'd asked him what he was doing out there with the bears.

"I was talking to them," he replied.

Now, I asked him the same question: "What are you doing, Arthur?"

He gave me a half-hearted shrug and moved up the cabin steps. "Come inside Hellie. Please don't be angry. You've had a fright. I'll explain it all. Come," he beckoned. "We'll have tea." He jabbed a finger in the air. "The elixir of the mountains."

"I don't believe this," I said, and with that all my anger and energy dissolved. I was suddenly exhausted, and I followed him into the cabin.

Inside, the tiny home was far more rustic than Arthur's cabin in Banff. Miriam's relative had obviously opted for a hard, Spartan life. The single room contained a wood stove, rough pine bunk beds and a couple of pine chairs. Ghostly imprints lined the walls where traps had hung for decades.

"I got rid of them," Arthur said following my gaze to the wall. "Couldn't stand to look at them. This cabin has a dark history. I prefer to be outside. But for now, please, sit down."

While he fed the stove another piece of wood and prepared the tea, I took up a chair at the table and collected my thoughts. When the tea was done, Arthur poured me a cup and took up the opposite chair.

"All right, Hellie. Ask me what you wish," he said fingering one of the silver rings in his ear and running a hand down his calico beard.

I sipped my tea. It was jasmine, and it was wonderfully soothing. I took another couple of sips before I looked him straight in the eye and said, "Did you shoot at Ansel Rock?"

"Yes."

I think I was still hoping for a no. "That's great, Arthur. Did you set me up to do this story with Ansel?"

He looked genuinely bewildered. "No. I merely mentioned the auction, and you made the decision to pursue it. Which means you were meant to do it."

"Until this morning I would have argued that point with you. I was pretty sure I'd lost it."

"Ah, but you haven't. I didn't think you would."

"I can't imagine why. The man thought I was trying to get him killed."

"I know Ansel."

"Why didn't you tell me that?"

"I didn't think it was relevant to you writing the story."

"Shooting at him while I'm covering his story kind of makes it relevant, don't you think?"

"Yes. I suppose it does. I am sorry, Hellie."

"Are you really? Why did you lie about staying in Canmore?"

"Once again, I am sorry for that too. I had planned to go there, eventually. But I had to be certain those paws did not come from her," he said motioning toward the door. "And then there was the hunt with Ansel … well, I've been busy."

"Yes you have." I cut a glance to the door. "Are they here?"

"I think so." He stood and peeked out the window. "Yes, they're back. Why don't you come out and meet them properly."

"No thanks. I'll stay where I am. She wasn't too happy the last time we met."

Arthur laughed. "You must trust, Hellie. Somehow you've lost your ability to trust. Come outside. Even for a minute."

I shook my head. He smiled and went out. I stayed where I was, sipped my tea and looked around the bare room. The fire made it warm enough, but Arthur was right, there was something unsettling about the place.

When it appeared Arthur wasn't coming back inside, I acquiesced and went out onto the verandah where I stood close to the open door and watched the remarkable scene.

All three bears were near the feed bucket. The babies — this time I was able to get a better look at them — were about half their mother's size and just as plump. One was on its back, the male, bathing his tummy in the fading sun. The other was sprawled on her belly, head resting on a log.

The teddy bears' picnic.

Arthur was sitting cross-legged on a blanket, hands clasped and resting on his lap as if he were in prayer. I marveled at his agility and vitality. Sometimes it was easy to forget that Arthur was an elderly man. But at seventy-one he was probably more fragile than even he realized. And I was worried about him because things were getting complicated. I'd made a promise to the Doc that I'd take care of his friend; now I just had to figure out how I was going to do that.

At Arthur's side, his four-hundred-pound companion stirred and lifted her huge head to catch my scent on the breeze. The light patch on her crown glistened white as polar-bear fur in the dying afternoon light.

My throat closed just then, and I felt as if something heavy was sitting on my chest. Tears prickled my eyes. "This can't be real," I whispered. But it was.

"Come and sit with us," Arthur said, his eyes sparkling with mischief.

Lulu didn't seem to mind that I was around, and I guessed it was because I was with Arthur. With the cabin door left open behind me, I inched my way as far as the verandah steps. Arthur joined me and we watched Lulu and her cubs finish the last of their dessert apples. The air was laced with woodsmoke. I breathed it in and tried to relax.

Arthur sensed my unease. "Don't worry," he said. "She won't hurt you."

I cleared my throat and stared at the feed bucket. "Why are you doing this, Arthur?"

He shrugged. "Habit."

"Suzanna has always thought you were feeding them, you know."

"Yes, I do know," Arthur said. "The night you saw them in the apple tree, Suzanna saw them bounding across the front lawn," Arthur said. "She called Michael in Tanzania to squeal on me."

"Ah. But the Doc already knew, didn't he?"

"Yes."

"And Miriam?"

"She and Michael came once a number of years ago. But I'm the only one who comes here now," he said and went into the cabin. Thankfully, he was back in a moment carrying a bag with more apples. He went to the feed bucket and dumped them in. I watched him shield his eyes with his hand and look up to the sky. Lulu followed his lead and reared up on her hind legs — a giant Neanderthal towering above her friend, scanning the air trying to get a bead on a potential intruder.

I too shielded my eyes from the low sun and spotted a golden eagle circling high above us like a dark angel. I looked back down at Arthur and Lulu and suddenly put two and two together.

"You saved her, didn't you?" I said. "Des told me what happened to her mother."

Lulu dropped onto her front paws and stared at me as if she understood I was talking about her. Arthur laid a hand on her head and stroked between her ears.

"Yes. I think I did help her," he said and came back to sit with me on the steps. "She stumbled in one night. It was the year I arrived from

Africa. Miriam told me about the cabin and said I was welcome to it."

"This is where you spend your time, isn't it?"

"Most of it. I can operate better from here and keep my eyes on the poachers. That's how Lulu came to me. The wardens thought a male attacked Lulu's mother and her brother. But it wasn't a male grizzly that destroyed her. It was a human male."

"But Des said they found the mother all chewed up."

"They snared her, Hellie, poachers. The mother was caught in the trap and the babies were frantic. I couldn't get near her of course. You never want to approach them. Not here. Not in these mountains. We've taught them to fear us and to be aggressive. Lulu is the rare exception." He looked affectionately at the big bear.

"When I came upon Lulu's mother caught in the trap, I raced out and called the wardens. But by the time they got to her, Lulu's mother was dead, and yes, a male grizzly had come along and attacked her and dragged her off. Then he ate the little male cub. Lulu was nowhere to be found."

"Des didn't say anything about a snare."

"It was gone. The wardens didn't believe me. Those poachers must have come back. There was nothing left worth salvaging of the mother. So they took their snare."

"And the evidence."

"Yes, and the evidence. When little Lulu showed up all bruised and hungry, I had to help her. If I called the wardens they could have done only one of two things: put her in the zoo, or let nature take its course. She was too young to take care of herself. So I thought I'd help her first to get well, then let nature take care of her. I fed her and nursed her wounds. She bounced back very quickly. Nice and fat by the time she was ready to go to her den. I was so afraid she wouldn't make it." He clapped his hands. "She did make it. That little bear made it through the winter. That was six years ago. The next fall, she showed up again here. Bears have wonderful memories. Lulu is a miracle." He chuckled softly. "But of course, the Natives have always believed all bears were miracles."

"How so?"

"To them the bears died in the winter and rose back to life again in the spring. Bears are the symbol of resurrection. I think they're quite right. To survive in winter with no food or water for six months really is a miracle."

"And she's been showing up here ever since?"

"Yes. But when she came into town last year, that time you spotted her and the cubs in the backyard, I nearly died. I'd had to stay back in town a little longer because I had business to attend to."

"I remember," I said. "I know she came for the apples, but she also kept looking in the downstairs windows. I wonder if she was looking for you."

He put his hand to his chest. "Don't think I wasn't thinking the same."

"Maybe she wanted to show off her babies." I was joking.

Arthur was dead serious. "I think that was it. I thought I would lose her. It was terrible."

I told him what Nathan had said, about the paws in his cabin coming from a park bear.

Arthur nodded thoughtfully. "Perhaps now they will believe me when I tell them poachers are taking the bears."

For one terrible moment I wondered if Arthur planted those paws himself to make his point. I pushed the thought away. "Poachers?" I said.

"Yes. They take whatever they like. And there is no one out here to stop them."

"Except you."

"Yes. Except me. Oh, certainly the wardens do what they can ... but they can't be up here. They don't have the resources."

"Do you think poachers put those paws in your cabin?"

"I don't know, Hellie. I'm hoping I will find out soon."

The sun slipped away and dusk settled in over the mountains. Arthur finished the last of his tea and set the tin cup down beside him. "Now you know my guilty secret. I was trying to help her," he said.

I nodded and chose my words. "And that's why I came here. Because I was hoping I could help you. Will you come back with me?"

"I can't. Not yet."

"You're in a lot of trouble. They'll come for you. Des must know about this place. He'll figure it out."

"I need a little more time. Can you give me that, Hellie? I think I've discovered something and I need to investigate."

"Does it relate to the Doc?"

"Possibly. When I'm certain, I'll come back."

"For the Doc's funeral?"

"No. I don't go to funerals; they make me sad."

"Me too," I said and wondered why I went to them.

"Are you going to tell me what happened in Tanzania between you and Ansel?"

"Yes, of course, but not until after I've had a chance to talk to Ansel. Don't worry. It will all be straightened out. You'll finish your award-winning article and everything will be fine."

I liked his enthusiasm, but I wasn't sharing it.

***

When it was dark, we went into the cabin where Arthur fixed us a dinner of boiled, spiced lentils and dried fruit. While he cooked, I eyed the bunk beds, then gazed around the room and did some mental measurements. I decided the entire cabin was just big enough for two people.

"You can have your pick of the beds, Hellie. I have extra blankets," Arthur said from the kitchen.

"Thanks. Uh, they don't sleep in here do they?"

Arthur looked up surprised. "The bears?"

"Yeah, the bears."

"No, of course not. They're wild animals, Hellie."

I'd just watched him scratch that huge bruin's head like she was a golden retriever, but I wasn't going to argue the point.

When the meal was ready we put our coats on, lit a fire in the pit and ate under the dazzling canopy of stars. The bears were still there. A few times they wandered around my chair, sniffing the air, just generally checking me out. I managed to remain still, but my heart had taken on a life of its own and was thumping so hard I was sure the bears could hear it. Eventually they'd wander off and I could breathe again.

Arthur lit a few lanterns that cast the scene in a silvery, milky glow. Every now and again, a six-inch claw or a black-button bear eye flashed in the dull light. It was a surreal evening, both wonderful and devastating. The wonder lay in being so close to creatures so grand; the devastation in knowing how terribly wrong it was.

Forty years, millions of dollars and countless hours had been spent changing people's perceptions and attitudes toward Banff wildlife. And it was being undone by a man working at odds with himself. Had Arthur lived in the park thirty years earlier, he would have stood alongside the wardens appealing to visitors to stop spoiling and ultimately killing the bears. To forsake their photo-taking, stay in their Winnebagos and stop stuffing the brazen roadside bears and wily coyotes with marshmallows and honey-smeared crackers. Now I saw Arthur was one of them, part of the sector that comes to Banff each year and ignores the signs warning them: "A Fed Bear is a Dead Bear."

"Has Ansel Rock convinced you I had a hand in Michael's death?" Arthur asked casually. He kept his eyes on Lulu who was tipping the washbasin up to her face like a giant cup.

"Alluded to it," I said. "But I know it's not true. The autopsy report came back. Heart failure."

"We both know that's not true, Hellie."

"No, we do not know that," I said sharply. "Frankly Arthur, I don't know anything anymore." I looked at the bears and back to him. "I'm … I'm sitting in the middle of the forest having supper with three grizzly bears. How could I possibly know anything anymore?"

"I told you," he said, impassive to my outburst. "Michael was murdered and I suspect it's connected to me."

"In what way?"

"I don't know yet. Perhaps after tomorrow I will."

"I hope you're not planning to shoot your arrows at anyone else, Arthur. I'm sure I don't need to tell you that Ansel and Nathan are really ticked. You can't do that. Ansel's not a poacher. He's a hunter. You can't shoot at people."

"I usually don't. But Ansel was a different matter. And I wasn't shooting at him."

I wondered about that. The arrow had come awful close to Ansel. "What happened between you two? It must have had something to do with Ansel hunting in Africa."

"Oh yes, it was very simple. I was trying to save the elephants and Ansel was trying to kill them."

"Just like he was trying to kill that bighorn sheep, which he had every right to do since he paid a great deal of money to do it." I put up my hand to stop him. "I know, you don't think it is his right. But answer me this: Were you trying to kill Ansel?"

He rocked back and forth and laughed. "Heavens no. I was trying to help him."

"Really, how's that?"

"By stopping him from destroying that beautiful animal and from further destroying himself."

There was no point pressing the matter. Arthur often spoke in riddles, and, given time, I usually solved them.

The bears finished the last of their meal. Lulu stretched out on her back, front paws reaching luxuriously up over her head, a huge teddy waiting for someone to curl up with her. Suddenly I had the overwhelming urge to flop down beside her and give her a big hug. The two little ones romped and tumbled over one another. I realized I wasn't afraid anymore — and that was dangerous.

Lulu grabbed the washbasin and held it above her snout searching for any last morsel. The tub was empty, licked clean. She threw it over her head barely missing her two babies with the projectile.

"I think she wants more," I said.

"She knows she can't. This is our last meal together."

"You're not going to feed her anymore?"

"It's time. We both know this isn't good. I've told her," he said quietly.

I looked at Lulu then back to Arthur. "Uh, Arthur, do you really think you can talk to them?"

He smiled. "Of course. Try it yourself. Say 'Hello, Lulu.'"

I felt foolish. "Hello, Lulu."

She looked up.

"Dogs recognize their names," I said dismissively.

"That's true," Arthur returned. "So I guess they're almost as smart as bears."

"Do you really believe they understand you?"

"Certainly. Why else would I waste my breath? Saint Francis spoke to the wolf. Those ancient villagers spent all their time and energy being afraid of the wolf. They tormented him. But Saint Francis showed them that all they needed to do was offer him kindness and ask him to leave them be. The wolf listened. And the Natives, they have always communicated with animals. Really, Hellie, I'm not the first one to try it."

"Do they, uh ... talk to you?"

"Everything speaks to us. We need only open our hearts to hear. 'Speak to the earth, and it shall teach thee.'"

"That's nice. I'll remember it."

"Old Testament. As I said, I'm not the first." He laughed.

At the sound of her friend's laughter, Lulu the bear looked up and into the eyes of the man who was at once her saviour and her destroyer.

CHAPTER 11

WHEN I WOKE UP AT THE CABIN THE NEXT MORNING, ARTHUR WAS nowhere to be seen, but that hardly surprised me. I gathered my things together and headed home. Des was waiting for me when I got there. Just as I'd predicted, he'd figured it out and he knew where I'd been.

"Started thinking about the cabin and called Mom. Was he there?" Des asked, spying the pack I had recently shed and left leaning against the fridge.

From the worried look on his face, I truly believed he was hoping I'd say no. But I had to say, "Yes." There was no point lying, though I'd considered it.

"Did he come back with you?"

I shook my head.

"Aw shoot," Des said.

"He'll be back. He said he would."

"When?"

"Didn't say, exactly," I said.

"Did Arthur admit to taking a shot at you guys?"

I gave a rueful nod and added, "Well, not exactly at us … "

"Aw Jeez. What was he thinking? We're gonna have to bring him in, Hellie. He's really gone over the top this time." Des folded his arms over his chest, then unfolded them and put his hands on his hips. "Damn," he said.

At that moment, I was feeling more sorry for Des than Arthur. "It's okay, Des," I said. "You have a job to do. Your mom knows that too. Everyone understands."

He gave me a sad smile and then reached out to give me an awkward hug, something Des Bauer had never done before. "You really shouldn't have gone up there alone," he said in my ear. When he drew back his cheeks were pink and I know mine were just as rosy. "I'll call you when I know anything," he said and hurried out the door.

After he left, I checked my messages and email. Danny still hadn't called. So I took the phone with me upstairs where I fell into bed and caught up on the sleep I'd lost during my anxious night with Arthur.

Later, I helped Bernie and Miriam with preparations for the gathering after the Doc's funeral, and then I met with Ansel Rock to get some background for my article. Ansel honked on about his hunting life. How he got interested in killing things by following in his father's footsteps who, according to Ansel, was a superb hunter of all things winged and four-legged. Then he listed his best trophies and described his most exciting hunts. Like the time they nearly froze to death hunting a moose in the Yukon. I was glad I'd tape-recorded the interview, because I sure wasn't being a stellar reporter; my mind was wandering. And for the rest of the day and that night, while I tried to work on the story, my thoughts were with Arthur and his bears, and my ears were perked, listening for the phone or any sign that Arthur had returned home. But by the time I went to bed, I still hadn't heard a thing.

***

Des was supposed to give the eulogy at the Doc's funeral, but he didn't show. Miriam gave it instead and did a lovely job. The little stone church was filled to capacity with mourners who'd come to say goodbye to the Doc. When the service was over we all made our way down to the river path in front of the Doc's house to spread his ashes along the riverbank, where the Doc loved to walk under the shadow of Rundle Mountain. It was about the only time anything had felt right and appropriate since his death.

People were invited back to the house afterwards, and now here they were, milling around, sipping wine and chatting in hushed tones. Some I knew, or at least had seen in town. Others I'd never laid eyes on. The day was one befitting a funeral though — overcast and gray, spreading a dreary light that settled in like dust over the antiques and African artifacts in the lovely rooms of Doc Rivard's home.

I scanned the faces, wondering how many of these people had actually ever met the Doc, and how many had come simply to glimpse the inside of his house. In the solarium, two fellows in dark suits, standing among all the locals dressed in khakis and Gore-Tex, stuck out like a couple of city slickers at a barn dance. I thought I recognized one from a real estate office in town. He'd been scrutinizing the place as if he were conducting a professional appraisal. I wanted to tell him that the house was not for sale. Which was absurd because just as soon as the lawyers figured out who was entitled to what, the house would most likely be put on the block and sold to the highest bidder. And I would be without a residence once again. I told myself to stop being so selfish, but I couldn't help it. I loved the house and felt very protective of it. The Doc's voice filled my thoughts: *Treat this joint like it's your own, Hellie. I mean it. You belong here. I have absolute faith that you will look after it and Arthur.*

I squeezed past a dozen or so people and went to a side window to see if by some small miracle Arthur had made it back to his cabin. He had not. The curtains were drawn, the windows dark.

"Hellie."

I turned around. It was Des holding out a glass of red wine to me.

"Des, I've been so worried."

"Sorry I didn't call you earlier." He handed me the wine and gave me another brief hug.

I wasn't used to seeing Warden Des in anything but his Parks Canada uniform. Now he was dressed in a pair of taupe cords and a dark, checked flannel shirt. He looked very handsome and, for some reason, a little older.

"Sorry I missed the funeral," he said. "Got swamped after I came back from the cabin last night. A call came in about an injured bear. Couple said they saw it limping across the highway with something hanging from its hide. Probably got into fishing or climbing gear and got itself tangled."

Lulu immediately sprang to mind. "What kind of bear?"

"Black. Still can't find it."

"Oh, that's too bad. And Arthur?"

Des shook his head. "Must have taken off pretty quick. Left stuff out. Bears got into it."

"Really?"

"Yeah. I found apple cores and paw prints all around the cabin. And up on the deck. You're lucky you didn't run into 'em when you were up there."

"That's for sure," I said. I could feel my face heating up. I changed the subject. "Your mom did a great job at the funeral."

"I heard, and I'm sure sorry I had to miss it."

"Doc would understand," I said.

"Yeah, thanks. You look nice, Hellie."

"You too," I said.

"What you're wearing looks really good," Des said.

"Uh, thanks. It doesn't feel that good," I said on a nervous laugh. "Not used to dressing like this anymore." From my uptown-Toronto wardrobe, I'd resurrected a black, ankle-length wool crepe skirt, along with a white microfiber blouse and a pair of patent leather pumps. I'd even bought a pair of black pantyhose that were currently cutting me in half at the waist and amputating my toes.

With a shy smile Des said, "As the saying goes, 'It's better to look good than feel good.' And you look terrific. I ... " he trailed off. "Well, I should go and see how Mom's doing."

I didn't argue with him. I just smiled and turned my red face back to the window. I squinted through the trees toward Arthur's deserted home. My heart sank in the knowledge that Ansel Rock's prediction was coming true: Arthur Elliott had disappeared, again. Ansel had also been annoyingly sure that Arthur had something to do with Doc Rivard's death. Would he turn out to be right about that too? I scoffed at the notion. I would not to let Ansel Rock's wild accusations get the better of me.

My gaze drifted to the gazebo where I spied Larry Melwheeler straddling the railing and smoking a joint. I knew it was a joint by the way he held the thin cigarette between his thumb and index finger, and by the way he sucked at its end as if he were trying to extract poison from a snakebite. I was about to open the door and go have a word with him when he seemed to look past me and over my head. In the same instant the Party Moose, with a magician's sleight of hand, palmed the joint, slipped his legs over the rail and disappeared.

A hand came down on my shoulder and a gruff male voice behind me said, "How you holding up, Hellie?"

I knew it was Nathan Delaware even before I turned around. Though I hardly would have recognized him from across the room. Like Des, he was out of uniform, wearing a navy blue suit and tie. And like a lot of big men, Nathan did not look comfortable in a suit. The shoulders pulled, and the tie looked disproportionately small around his thick neck and hung too high on his chest.

"How are you holding up?" I said.

"It's tough." He placed his wine glass on the nearby bookshelf and picked up an antique African throwing spear that was leaning against the shelf. He ran an index finger along the edge of the flat leaf-shaped blade.

"Careful, that's sharp," I said.

The finger stopped and his eyebrows went up when he realized I was right.

"Doc told me a Zulu hunter could slice right through to a beast's heart with one of these." Nathan said. "Can you imagine tearing after a lion with only a spear?"

"No, I can't," I said, a little testy. My feeling was that the sergeant had something else on his mind besides African spears, and I was getting impatient for him to get on with it.

"Anyway," he said replacing the spear next to the bookshelf. "You've done a good job. Gave Doc a real nice send-off."

"Bernie and Miriam did almost everything."

"Well, pass along my thanks to them too. Those were nice flowers from your family."

My parents had sent a massive, no doubt hugely expensive, floral arrangement to the church. Once again, I felt ashamed that I was the only relative at my great-uncle's funeral. "Yes, the flowers were nice," I said in a clipped tone. "And it would have been even nicer if my parents had bothered to come."

"Well at least you were there," Nathan said. His eyes swept over the room as if he was searching for something or someone. "Any word yet from our friend?"

Finally. "No."

"Too bad. I was hoping he'd come back on his own. Take responsibility for what he's done. And listen, I heard from Des what you've been up to. Sure hope you're not going to pull any more stunts like this last one, Hellie. If you have even a hunch where he is now ... "

"I don't. He said he'd come back, and I believe him."

Nathan drank up the last of his wine and studied the empty glass. In his big hand, it looked as if he'd borrowed it from one of Bernie's dollhouses. "Say, I've been meaning to ask you something," he said as though the thought had just occurred to him. "Did Arthur say he actually spoke to the Doc in Calgary? On the phone even?"

I bristled. "You already asked me that. And the answer is still the same. As far as I know, Arthur did not see or speak to the Doc."

"And you're certain of that?"

"Of course I'm not. I wasn't there. But that's what he told me. Why, Nathan?"

"It's odd, that's all."

"What's odd? Please don't toy with me. This day has been hard enough."

"That it has." He tapped the rim of the glass against his lower lip. "Did you tell me you called the Marriott the night the Doc got back?"

I took a deep breath and exhaled. "No, I did not tell you that."

"Well now, that is odd too. A call came in to the hotel's front desk about eight o'clock that night. That call was made from this phone," Nathan said, tipping his glass towards the phone on the sideboard. "No one on the desk remembers taking the call or a message from the caller. But my guess is the caller wanted to know when the Doc was checking in. You sure you didn't call up just to see ... ?" Nathan stopped when he caught the annoyance in my expression. "Guess not. Okay, well another call came in to the Doc's room about a half-hour after he checked in. That one was from a phone booth down the street from the hotel. The front door guy puts the Doc getting into his car about fifteen minutes after he got that call."

"Did you just learn all this now?" I asked.

"Yeah. The hotel's got a one-eight-hundred service that just came through with the records. You're sure you didn't call the hotel, Hellie?"

I felt off balance. Did I call? No. Of course I didn't. What was I doing that night? I'd been through this when I gave my statement. Why couldn't I remember?

"She couldn't have made that call," Bernie said joining us. I hadn't noticed she was within earshot. "Hellie didn't leave my house until the movie was over at eleven. I told you that, Nathan."

"That's right. I was at Bernie's," I said.

"Then I guess it must have been Doc's wife, Barb, checking up on him," Nathan said with a straight face that gave way to a hint of a smile.

"Guess so," I returned.

"I thought the investigation was over," Bernie said. Pink spots flamed at her throat.

Nathan placed his wine glass on the sideboard next to the phone. "It is, officially. Well, I gotta be going. Did a nice job, a real nice job girls. Thanks again. I'll be in touch." He strode away down the hall.

"I think Nathan is beginning to suspect Arthur may have killed the Doc," I said bluntly.

"How? By scaring him to death?" Bernie said. "And giving him a heart attack?"

"Like I said when he came by with the autopsy results, the Sergeant's not buying the heart attack story. And I'm sure he thinks I've got Arthur tucked away in the basement."

"Do you?" Bernie asked poker-faced.

"Wish I did. You?"

"Same," Bernie replied. She opened the patio doors for a man and woman who were leaving. "Thank you for coming," Bernie said and then slid the doors closed behind them. "Good. Now I wish the rest of them would leave," she said.

"Me too."

"So why is Nathan looking at Arthur? He and the Doc were best friends, for heaven's sake."

"It's the Texan. He's making Arthur out to be some kind of terrorist and I'm worried Nathan is starting to buy it."

She lowered her voice. "Dare I ask how the story's coming?"

"Not great. With everything that's been going on it's hard to concentrate. I met with him yesterday and spent a cozy two hours listening to how his daddy bought him his first real gun when he was just out of diapers. And how he and his daddy used to hunt together, and boy, oh boy just being outside and experiencing the joy of killing things and all that other bullshit was the greatest thing to ever happen to him. God, Bern, he was so smug about Arthur disappearing. He's so right about everything. Can't wait 'till this story's over and he's back in Texas where he belongs."

Bernie was smiling kindly. "And he hasn't told you anything else about his connection to Arthur?"

"We agreed to stick to the story and avoid Arthur. Or I should say, he gets to say anything he likes, and I don't get to ask any questions. He's a strange guy. One minute I swear he hates me, and next he's all concerned about my safety. But the real annoying thing is that I know and he knows that Arthur is the only reason he's letting me do the story."

"Because he thinks you'll lead him to Arthur?"

"I can't think of any other reason."

"And why are you still doing the story, Hellie?"

"So I can make a living and keep a close eye on Ansel Rock and find out what he's doing in Banff ... and make sure I get to Arthur before he does, or at least at the same time."

"You think the only thing that's brought him here is Arthur?"

"I think that's the main reason. And Arthur knew it. Now he's disappeared just like Ansel said he would."

Bernie's eyes were wide. "You don't think Ansel — "

"I don't know what Ansel Rock is capable of. I do know that he's got some hate on for Arthur."

"But Arthur's the one who shot at Ansel."

"Technically not at him. Aw, Bern. He promised he'd come back and straighten — "

My thought was cut short when one of the fellows in his Sunday-go-to-meeting suit joined us. "Hi there, I'm Ralph Owen," he said. At the same time, he deftly slipped a business card into my hand. "And you're Hellie MacConnell," he said, pumping my hand with the card mashed between our palms.

Ralph Owen was a middle-aged real estate agent with a pleasant face and a slightly forced smile.

"Hear you're covering a story about Ansel Rock. Next time you see him, would you mind giving him one of my cards?" Another card went into my hand. Ralph moved a little closer and spoke out of the side of his mouth. "Has Mr. Rock been looking at anything?"

"Uh, bighorn sheep."

"I mean land or anything?"

"Nope. Just sheep."

"Don't be too sure. About ten years back he was here trying to get a five-star resort going, and what a place that would have been. Should've seen the plans."

"Where was he going to build it?" Paul asked as he joined us. He handed Bernie a glass of wine. And I watched with a pang of loneliness as Bernie gave him a peck on the cheek, and he slipped a protective arm around her shoulder. It made me wonder how I'd managed to blow it so badly when I was picking out a husband.

"Road to Cave and Basin," I heard Ralph say.

"I remember that project," Paul said. "But I don't remember hearing Ansel Rock's name associated with it."

"All done under one of his company names." Ralph scratched at his graying temple. "Can't think what it was though."

"Lone Star?" I suggested.

"Umm, no. It'll come to me. Should know. Worked hard enough on that deal. Woulda been huge … " Ralph suddenly looked downtrodden. "Then it all slipped down the toilet."

"Did the government stop it?" I asked.

"Yeah, in the end. But it was all undermined first by local pressure. Just bad timing." Ralph took a sip of his wine as the conversation died. "Anyhoo, maybe don't mention the resort deal to Mr. Rock, just casually slip him my card," he said. "Got a sure thing in Canmore." He raised his eyebrows as if he were imparting insider information. "Well, gotta go. Sorry about Doctor Rivard." He waved a hand and left.

When he was out of earshot Bernie said, "This is interesting."

"Very," I agreed. "What else do you remember about that project, Paul?"

"Only vague details," Paul said leaning an elbow against the glass doors. "Except I do know ten years ago was when the Doc's Bow Valley Society was really coming down hard on big developments in the park."

"Which means the Doc would have been involved in stopping the project," I said.

"He would have been at the head of it," Paul corrected me. "But I don't know the details."

"Think we better consult an expert," I said.

Bernie jabbed a thumb over her shoulder. "Try the living room."

***

I found Miriam sitting alone on an ottoman holding a mug of coffee and staring at the fireplace. I put my hand on her sweatered shoulder. She started at my touch, and stood. She held her mug at a precarious angle letting coffee drip onto her dark brown slacks. I righted the cup for her.

"Oh," she said staring at the cup in her hand. Her quick eyes focused on mine. "Has Arthur come home?"

"'Fraid not," I said and dabbed at the spilled coffee on her pant leg with a cocktail napkin. "Bernie and Paul are out back. Why don't you join us?"

"Don't fuss over me, Hellie," she scolded. "Or I'm liable to shed another tear and there have been more than enough of those today."

"We need your help," I said.

"Well, in that case lead the way."

Miriam screwed up her soft, lined face in thought as she listened to Bernie and I repeat what Ralph Owen said. "Sure I remember it," she said. "We put the kibosh on that monster project. It was a great victory for us. But there was no mention of Mr. Rock. And if I remember correctly, and I usually do, it was a company that started with a 'Z.' Zen something. Like Arthur's Zen."

"Zentex," Paul said.

"Righto. Zentex. Out of Vancouver."

"Not Texas?" I put in

"Let me see what I can find," Miriam said. She passed me her coffee cup and opened the front door.

"You don't have to go now," I said.

"Oh, yes I do. I feel something nasty coming in on the wind." She grabbed her coat from a chair and put it on in a hurry. When I held the door for her, I caught sight of what the wind was bringing — Suzanna LaChaine was sailing up the back lawn heading right for us.

I let out a resigned sigh that sounded more like a moan and said, "Maybe I'll join you."

"You wish," Miriam said over her shoulder on her way down the stairs. "I work alone."

Suzanna came through the door as if blown in by the force of her own storm.

Bernie and I said hello and scuttled out of her way.

"I was tied up at the inn with … " she paused, " … with a guest and couldn't get here any sooner," she said.

I wondered why she'd lied since it was obvious the reason she was late was because she'd gone home to change out of the midnight-blue dress she had been wearing at the funeral and into a new, equally elegant, black dress and matching jacket. On her head she wore a black scarf and dark sunglasses covered her eyes, giving her the Jackie Onassis look. I couldn't imagine why she had changed, but I did think she was wasting her time in Banff and that her exquisite fashion sense would be appreciated so much more in Toronto's trendy Yorkville.

"Who are all these people?" Suzanna demanded peering over my head and down the hall.

Bernie answered. "They're tourists, Suzanna. Hellie's charging ten bucks a head. Twenty if they want a picture."

Suzanna's mouth opened itself into a wide circle. "Bernie," I warned. "She's not being serious," I said to Suzanna.

A black-gloved hand moved the sunglasses down the bridge of her nose and Suzanna peered daggers at Bernie.

"Can I get you something to drink, Suzanna?" I said quickly. "Wine, coffee?"

She turned her gaze on me still peering over the rims of her glasses. Without a word, she moved off down the hall then stopped when she seemed to remember something.

"Here it comes," Bernie said under her breath.

"When can we expect you will be moving out, Hellie?" She undid the knot in her black scarf and let it slip off her head and into her hand.

A two-word expletive was on the tip of my tongue. I swallowed it back and stepped outside. Taking in deep, calming breaths of the cool autumn air it suddenly became very clear to me that Suzanna intended to be the highest bidder on the Rivard house.

I stared up at Sulphur Mountain across the valley, and let my eyes follow the white gondolas, mere specks floating their way up to the observatory. I thought how nice it would be to be up there instead of where I was. Should have stayed with Arthur and the bears. The thought saddened me because for some reason none of what I'd seen up at Miriam's cabin seemed real any longer.

I was about to go back in the house when, out of the corner of my eye, I thought I saw something moving through the trees. Probably just an elk. It seemed unlikely that Arthur was going to turn up that easily, but it was worth checking. So I made my way to the path that led down to Arthur's cabin, fully expecting to see a red-spotted elk. Instead I found myself tracking Ansel Rock, who was moving silently through the woods with the sure-footedness of a seasoned hunter. Though now, in his black trousers and black leather jacket he looked more like a successful developer than a hunter.

I kept my distance, making certain he wouldn't see me. When he went around to the front of the cabin, I crept up to the rear and waited. At my feet, stacked neatly along the back of the tiny log structure, were boxes filled with old magazines, tin cans and scrap wood Arthur used to create his folk-art weather vanes, candleholders and suncatchers.

A few more moments passed and I was beginning to wonder if Ansel had gotten into the cabin somehow. As far as I knew, there were only two keys: Arthur's and the Doc's. The Doc had given me his before he left. Something occurred to me, just then. If Nathan's theory was right and the Doc was on his way to the cabin the night he died, then he must have thought Arthur was there. Otherwise, how would he get in? Nathan obviously assumed the Doc had a key to the cabin, or he hadn't thought about it. So was Arthur there? He'd been in Bernie and Paul's store earlier. Had he stayed? Or had Arthur seen the Doc in Calgary and given him his key? But if that were the case, then why had he lied to me about seeing the Doc? The cabin door had been open when I found the bear paws. Someone had opened that door and left those paws. So the question was, who opened the cabin door?

I listened again for Ansel. The only sounds I heard were chickadees chirping in nearby trees and the wind swishing through evergreen branches overhead. Keeping close to the cabin, I snuck around to the front where I found no sign of Ansel. The door was locked tight. I raced back to the other side and was greeted by the sight of Ansel's backside sauntering up the path. He must have passed right behind me as I stood hiding like a lunatic. I stamped the ground and kicked a piece of moss on my way up the path after him.

"Looking for something, Mr. Rock?" I said catching up.

He stopped and whirled around so fast I started, lost my footing, stumbled and nearly fell into him. He grabbed my arms to steady me.

"You can't imagine how badly I wanted to scare the pants off you," he said. "But since it's your uncle's funeral today, I didn't have the heart."

"You're a bigger man than I thought," I said and tried to ease out of his firm grip.

He held on and looked into my eyes. "Lucky you were able to make it back in time from your hiking trip. Surprised you didn't mention it when you were interviewing me yesterday."

Nathan must have told him. "What I do on my own time is my business."

"You're going to get yourself hurt, Ms. MacConnell." He eased his grip and his expression softened. "So how you doin' anyway? It's never easy burying a friend."

Our eyes met and I felt an unexpected rush of pleasure. "I'm fine. Thank you," I said with caution and then added, "But I understand the Doc was also a friend of yours, Ansel. Well, not a friend exactly, more of a business associate."

He gave me a wry smile. "That's right. See you've been doing your homework. I came by to pay my respects."

"Reception is in the big house."

"I needed a walk."

"Down to Arthur's cabin?" I was so close to him I could smell his clean scent, soap and shaving cream. I shook free of his grasp and took a step back. The cold and my nerves sent spasms up my spine that shook my shoulders.

"You better go back in the house. You're shaking like a leaf in a dust storm," he said.

"What are you doing here, Ansel?"

"I told you. Came to pay my respects and see you."

"See me? About what?"

"Nothing. See if you were okay ... the story."

He was blushing. I wasn't taken in. "What are you doing in Banff?"

"You're gonna catch pneumonia," he said, and started to take off his coat.

I put up a hand to stop him. "Thanks, keep your coat. I'm fine." He came around behind me and placed it over my shoulders anyway. Warmth seeped into my skin immediately, and I took in his subtle scents trapped within the leather.

"Are you going to answer my question?" I said.

"I came here to hunt."

"Not in Banff you didn't."

"That's a fact." He crossed his arms over his broad chest, squared his legs and planted each foot in a solid stance. "Okay. Here it is. When the editor at *McMillan* mentioned your name, I knew who you were. I knew a gal named Hellie MacConnell was living in Doctor Michael Rivard's home. I also knew that you were working with Arthur Elliott."

"You got the first part right. How did you know who I was?"

"I've been keeping tabs on Arthur Elliott for half a dozen long years. Picked up your name along the way. Never saw you, or your picture, though. But when this article came up, I thought to myself, okay, this is it. I told my shrink ... "

Shrink? Hmm. This man was just full of surprises. Ansel Rock was the last person I would have expected to be interested in therapy. I actually admired him for telling me, and on a fleeting thought considered going myself and taking along my family.

" ... that I was off to Banff to get me some of this closure she keeps telling me I need so badly," Ansel was saying. "When your name came up, I figured Arthur was goading me. Getting you to write some character-bashing story about me and hunting. And I knew it was God's way of saying it was time."

"God's way? Time for what?" I asked.

"Time to face my enemy and maybe get some justice."

"Justice for what? What did Arthur do? Blow your chance at shooting an elephant?"

Ansel turned his handsome face up to the sky like a man searching for the Almighty to give him strength. Pain tightened the lines around his eyes and screwed his mouth into a scowl. Hands clenched at his sides. Chest heaved with each breath.

"What did he do to me?" His words came out on a thick rasp.

"Yes, Ansel, what did Arthur ever do to you?"

"He killed my wife and baby girl. That's what Arthur Elliott did to me."

CHAPTER 12

His words hit me with the weight and shock of a sucker punch.

"And now the sonofabitch is trying to kill me." Ansel took a step toward me. I stumbled back. Our eyes locked and Ansel looked at me in dismay. "I'm not the one you need to be afraid of, Hellie. Arthur Elliott is. He's the enemy."

Speechless, I stared at him. He brushed past me and slipped his coat off my shoulders. I found my voice. "Ansel wait," I called after him. He kept walking as if he hadn't heard. I didn't want to let him go. Let what he'd said go. But it was pretty obvious Ansel Rock was in no mood to stick around and chat.

Voices drifted from my left. Through a gap in the bush that separated the Doc's property from Arthur's cabin, I could see the gazebo. Larry was back sitting on the gazebo railing dangling his feet off the side. Behind him stood Suzanna, her mouth wagging in time with the finger she was shaking at the back of Larry's head. I couldn't make out what she was saying. But I did think it was rather tasteless, particularly on this day, that they were so casually hanging around the spot where the Doc's body had been discovered.

A big man with a jowly face, wearing jeans and a red and black checked lumberjack shirt, heaved himself up the steps and joined the unlikely couple on the gazebo. It was Daniel Peterson, Ansel's hunting guide.

Suzanna sat down on a bench, and Daniel sat beside her. I wondered what he was doing there and if he'd ever met the Doc. I didn't hang around to find out. Instead, I seized the opportunity and took off up the path to the street. I needed to talk to someone who could shed some light on what Ansel had just said.

John Morrow opened The Wild Rose's front door. "Hello, Hellie. I'm sorry, but Suzanna isn't in," he said.

"I know. She's across the street. It's you I've come to see. Can we talk a moment?"

"That depends what it is you want to talk about," he said. "But I suspect it's Ansel, so I'm afraid the answer is no. I'm sure you can understand." He gave me the PR smile and stretched an arm across the threshold. "All interview questions should be directed to him."

I wondered what happened to all the if I can be of any help stuff he'd ladled out the first time we met.

"Ansel just told me Arthur killed his wife and child," I said without preamble. John Morrow's ingenuous smile slipped down into a frown. "Now Arthur's disappeared, as I'm sure you've heard, and I'm kind of wondering if your friend had something to do with that."

"Don't be foolish," John snapped. "Your friend is surely in hiding after firing an arrow at Ansel."

"How can you be so sure?" The wind picked up and sent a cold blast through my thin blouse. I wrapped my arms around myself. "When the police hear this bit of news, I'm sure they'll find it intriguing."

A flicker of doubt flashed in John Morrow's eyes. "Where is Ansel now?" he asked.

I shrugged.

John looked over my head and up to Tunnel Mountain.

I followed his gaze and remembered Ansel mentioning it was one of his favourite walks. Tunnel Mountain, by Rocky Mountain standards, is little more than a geological molehill. But it's deceiving, and even though it's a relatively easy climb along switchbacks to reach the summit, the sharp cliffs off the back side are spectacular and dangerous.

"You think he's gone up there?" I said.

John nodded. "Likes to watch the sun set."

"Well, he's got all of about fifteen minutes. Can be a pretty treacherous walk at night. Hope he makes it back down before dark."

"He will," John said. "You'd better come in."

I ducked under his arm, headed into Suzanna's white leather-upholstered sitting room and took a seat across from the fireplace. A fire was burning so perfectly on the grate I took a closer look to see if Suzanna had converted the fireplace to gas. I marveled at my neighbour's ability to keep her house looking like a show suite. I'd been allowed into the place only once before and had wondered then if her guests were actually permitted to use the elegant toilets Suzanna had had flown in from Italy.

John offered me a drink. I thanked him but declined, lest I might have to use the facilities. He went to the sideboard and poured himself two fingers of bourbon from a crystal decanter then took up the chair across from me.

"Frankly, I'm shocked Ansel told you about his personal life," John said.

"Me too."

"He never talks about it. Never. Not even to me."

"Is it true?"

John swirled the amber liquid over the ice cubes in his glass and thought for a moment. "Is it true that Arthur Elliott killed Marianna and my ... " he paused and pressed a thumb and forefinger to the bridge of his nose. "My dear little godchild?"

"I'm sorry," I said. "I didn't realize ... "

"I'm sure you already know they were shot in Tanzania."

"No, I didn't know that."

"Well, they were. The police believed it was poachers. And Marianna and Nici were just innocent victims caught in the crossfire."

"That's dreadful. I am very sorry. But how does Arthur factor in?"

"This isn't for me to discuss. It's Ansel's business. But I'm sure you've pieced some things together from what Arthur has told you."

"Whether you and Ansel choose to believe me or not is beside the point. But the truth is before I met Ansel, Arthur never mentioned his name to me. He did, however, admit to shooting toward Ansel, but told me he wasn't trying to hurt him. Said he was trying to help him." John gave me a skeptical look. "I know," I added quickly. "That kind of help we can all do without. He also said he believes Doc Rivard was murdered. And I'm beginning to wonder if he's right. Maybe Ansel knows something. He did say — "

John got to his feet. I'd gone too far. "Ansel does not know anything about Michael Rivard's death. And any words, spoken or written, from you implying that will earn you and your magazine a big fat lawsuit. So if I were you, I'd watch what I say."

"I intend to. But can you tell me this? If the Tanzanian police say it was poachers, why does Ansel, and presumably you, think it was Arthur who killed his wife and child?"

"All I'm prepared to tell you is that what happened in Tanzania has been eating away at Ansel like a cancer for six years."

"Six years? It was six years ago that Arthur came to live in Banff."

"That's right," John said. "He had to leave Africa. Surely this isn't news."

"Is to me. My understanding is that Arthur was saving the elephants. That he was a hero of sorts."

John shot me a dismissive glare.

"Was Arthur ever charged with anything?"

"No. Nothing could be proven," he said.

"Maybe because he didn't have anything to do with it. But for some reason Ansel is certain Arthur's guilty, and he obviously came here to even the score. Eye for an eye and all that stuff you Texans are so fond of."

"He wants retribution. He wants to see Arthur Elliott pay the ultimate price for his crimes. Something you Canadians are not particularly fond of."

"Darn right, if we are talking about capital punishment. And what, Ansel is going to play judge, jury and executioner?"

"Once again, watch your words, Hellie. Ansel merely wants justice."

"Why now, John? Why not six years ago?"

"I can't talk about this anymore. He's my friend. I've already said more than I care to."

I sat back and let myself sink into the soft leather. The fire dared to crackle and sent a tiny spark into the air. John finished his drink and poured himself another. He offered me one again. This time I accepted. At least he wasn't showing me to the door. I had time. But I was also pretty certain I wasn't going to get any further with him unless I pushed. Just how far I could go was the question.

"You're a good friend of Ansel's, John."

He passed me my drink, took up his seat across the room and watched me impassively.

"A very good friend," I continued. "And it's my guess that's precisely why you're here." He blinked slowly. I felt sweat collecting under my arms. "Because you're not sure what Ansel's capable of, and you're hoping to save him from himself."

John put his drink down carefully on the green glass coffee table and moved to the fireplace where he picked up a poker. He squatted and stirred the ashes.

"I just learned about the development deal Doc Rivard messed up for Ansel," I said. The poker went still. "Now with the Doc suddenly dying ... It is kind of curious, don't you — ?"

John Morrow spun around and stood to face me. He held the hot poker tightly in his right hand like a jousting foil. "Now, you get this straight," he said between clenched teeth. "Ansel Rock is a good, decent man. And it would take one hell of a lot more than a quashed business deal to drive him to any kind of violence."

"How about losing his family? That be enough?"

John's face was red with fury. "I think you better show yourself out."

***

I walked back and stood on the steps of the Doc's house trying to collect my thoughts. To the west, Cascade Mountain was enveloped in a layer of graphite-gray clouds flying at half-mast as if in honour of the Doc. The door opened behind me. Bernie poked her head out.

"You okay, Hellie?"

"Not sure, Bern."

"Where you been?"

"Across the street."

"Oh. I just took a call from the Doc's lawyer. She's driving in tonight and said she was going to drop by here to see you."

"Did she say anything else?"

Bernie shook her head. "If it's about the house, Hellie, you know you can always stay with us."

"Hellie!" Came the shrill voice from somewhere down the hall.

"Cruella lives," Bernie said under her breath.

"I heard that, Bernie," Suzanna said and leaned past the younger woman. "Hellie, I've been looking for you. What are you doing outside?"

"Pretending to be a Swede."

"A what?"

"Nothing. What's wrong, Suzanna?"

"What isn't? This reception is a disgrace. The kitchen is a mess, there are no more clean glasses, and you're letting strangers ... " She stepped outside. "You're letting strangers roam all over the house." She spoke in low tones and said the word "strangers" as if she were uttering a dirty word.

Bernie was hovering behind Suzanna miming that she was strangling the older woman. The buzz in my head from what Ansel and John Morrow had just told me was now turning into a dull, thudding headache.

"Bernie, I know what you're doing," Suzanna said.

"I'll be in the kitchen," Bernie said and made a hasty retreat.

I stepped inside. Suzanna was blocking my way. "I just heard what Arthur has been up to these past few days," she said, "and I really think — "

"Suzanna, I'd love to stay and chat, but I've really got a lot to do right now." I pushed past her and went up to my bedroom and threw myself on the bed. I looked around the room taking everything in: the heavy oak dresser, the rocking chair, the wing chairs. In the closet, my sweaters were stacked neatly along the top shelf. I'd have to pack them. The lawyer was on her way, and I'd have to leave this beautiful house because it was no longer my responsibility. With that thought came a sudden clarity.

I propped myself up on one elbow. None of this was my responsibility. Not the house, not Arthur, not how or why the Doc died. The sounds of closing doors, shoes on hardwood floors and glasses tinkling on trays echoed up from downstairs. Outside car engines turned over and vehicles drove away.

The idea was taking hold and settling in. It was new and brought with it possibilities, a solution and a way out.

What was keeping me in Banff? Bernie, sure. But we'd stay in touch, visit. Banff was just one of any number of lovely places I could live. Now the idea was really picking up steam. I had to move out anyway, so why not move a little farther to a new town or city. Start over ... in my own place. Arthur was a grown man. I'd done my best. I'd tried to help him. But if he didn't want my help there was nothing I could do. And the *McMillan* story? I could scrape something together. I already had two hours of interview tape, and I'd experienced the "joy and thrill" of hunting first-hand. I also had all those back articles. Surely I could lift something from them.

Tension eased out of my body, and the headache was almost gone, replaced with that sense of peace and wellbeing that comes with making a decision. I'd start packing tonight.

***

With this new resolve, I went back downstairs. The last few mourners had gone and the house was suddenly cast in an unsettling silence. Bernie and Paul were just leaving. She gave me a hug and told me to call or drop by their place later.

Suzanna was still in the kitchen cleaning up and she didn't appear to be in any hurry to leave. "Thanks," I said. "I can finish up the rest."

She carefully folded and put the dishtowel away. "There's a load in the dishwasher," she said, "but otherwise it's looking pretty good."

I nodded and at the same time got the vague impression she was waiting for something. Then it stuck me that she probably didn't want to be alone. Aside from the Doc, Suzanna had few friends in Banff.

"It was a nice funeral," I said for lack of having anything more inspiring to say.

"Yes," she said. "It was nice. I was pleased."

I fought the urge to roll my eyes, and wondered why some people are so adept at turning what should be simple gratitude into authoritative approval? Didn't matter. I could be magnanimous. I was leaving and at peace with myself. I could afford to extend a little kindness. "Would you like something, Suzanna? Glass of wine, cup of tea?"

She treated me to a gracious smile. "That would be nice. Just a small glass of — "

A soft tapping came from the solarium. We both listened to the sound of the patio door slide open. I couldn't help wonder what new hell this intruder would bring to the day.

On cue, Larry the Party Moose stepped into the kitchen with eyes the same colour as his new cherry-red Land Rover and smelling like he'd just come from a Woodstock revival concert. I was about to tell him "the party" was over and that no, I didn't want to smoke cannabis with him, but he stopped me when he reached down the front of his coat and pulled something out that made me go soft in the head and emit a long, "Ooooh."

"He's for you, Hellie," Larry said placing an adorable black and tan puppy in my arms. "Thought maybe you could use a roommate."

"For me? Oh gosh, that's very kind. But I don't think so," I said, running a hand down the dog's silky little head.

"He's a beagle. I named him Tiger." Larry announced. "A friend of mine just had puppies."

Suzanna and I exchanged a smirk.

"Very funny," Larry shot back. "My friend's dog had puppies. And this little guy really needs a home. Otherwise, it's going to be … " He made a slicing motion across his throat. "He's two months old, but he's almost housebroken. So he's only a little bad."

"Which is a lot like being only a little pregnant," I said.

"Don't you want him, Hellie?" Larry said. He looked hurt.

"Sure. Of course. It's just that … " I stole a glance at Suzanna and was immediately cross with myself. This isn't your house. Not yet. I held the little creature up in front of me. His forehead scrunched into a worried look and his doleful eyes met mine.

"He's awful cute, but I'm sorry, Larry, I don't even know where I'm going to be living. I can't have a dog. It's really nice of you, though."

Suzanna, who had been unusually quiet throughout this exchange, descended on me, scooped the dog out of my hands and then really shocked me. I was expecting her to give Larry hell and tell him to get this furry chronic-carpet-soiler out of her house. Instead she said, "My God, he's just scrumptious. Never mind, Hellie, Larry's right. While you're still here, you need company and he'll be a good watchdog. These beagles bark at anything."

"Then you should take him," I said.

"No. Larry gave him to you. But I'll help you out with him. Michael's death has been hard on everyone. Maybe this little guy is just what we all need to take our minds off it. It might be nice … "

The woman before me was not the same woman I'd known for the past year. Or perhaps I'd misjudged Suzanna. She'd been in love with the Doc. That must have been rough when he obviously didn't return her feelings. Maybe I hadn't given her a chance.

"Thanks," I said. "But the lawyer's coming tonight … I have to move." I considered telling her I was about to start packing tonight. Then reconsidered in case she'd suspect I was planning to steal something.

She placed her free hand on her hip. "Really? Michael's lawyer is coming here? Tonight?"

"Yes," I said and waited for the old Suzanna to attack me for not telling her. But she was full of surprises that day.

"Never mind, they're not going kick you out tonight. In fact, they may even want you to stay for a while." She handed the hound to me. "And I think little Tiger is going to take good care of you."

Larry was moving toward the solarium. "I gotta go, you guys," he said and was out the door before I could give him back his dog.

I eyed Suzanna closely. "Why do I get the impression the two of you set this whole thing up?"

Her eyes were wide. "Larry and I?" she said incredulous. "Since when would I collaborate on anything with that vulgarian?"

"Since you started talking me into keeping this little guy," I said as Tiger nuzzled his wet nose under my chin.

CHAPTER 13

WITH A BUSINESSLIKE FLOURISH, KATHLEEN BENNER POPPED OPEN her briefcase and withdrew a file. The wistful sounds of Miles Davis's trumpet played softly in the background — one of the Doc's favourites. Earlier, while I was packing, I'd put the CD on in honour of the Doc and as a final farewell.

Doc Rivard's lawyer looked up from her file and gave me a quick, polite smile. "Just be a minute," she said. We were in the living room where a warm fire crackled in the fireplace. Tiger was curled up on a carpet taking in the heat. A scene right out of *Better Homes and Gardens*.

Ms. Benner glanced at the dog. "He's cute. Did you just get him?"

"He's not mine. Just spending the night."

She nodded and went back to her papers.

"Can I get you something to drink?" I offered.

"No, thank you," she said pleasantly. "This won't take long, and I'd like to get back to the city tonight." She straightened a sheaf of papers and steadied her professional gaze on me. "I was very sorry to hear about Doctor Rivard," she said, her eyes taking in the elegant, comfortable room. "He was a lovely man. And this is a lovely house. You're lucky. Right in the middle of Banff ... "

"Yes, I have been lucky," I said and waited for her to kick me out.

On the mantel was a photo I'd taken of the Doc and Arthur. Kathleen Benner was staring at it. "Is that Arthur Elliott?" she said. "The one shaking something at the camera?"

The image and the memory brought a smile to my face. Kathleen was watching me with an expectant look. "Yes. That's Arthur," I said. "I took that picture when we were having an indoor picnic. That's what the Doc called it when we'd roast hot dogs in the fireplace. Just before I snapped the photo, Arthur was trying to entice the Doc — who, I'm sure you know, was a diehard carnivore — to eat a tofu wiener."

Kathleen gave me a polite smile and waited the appropriate five seconds before she got down to business and said, "Yes. Well. I don't suppose you've heard from Mr. Elliott? The police informed me he's missing."

"No, I haven't heard from him."

"That's all right, I can go over the will with you." In layperson's terms, Kathleen Benner explained that Doctor Michael Rivard had left the house and its contents to Arthur Elliott.

Hurrah! Suzanna will not get the house! I thought merrily. Hurrah! Hurrah! I really couldn't see how this was any of my business, but this lawyer obviously thought it was. I'd let her finish and then tell her I was leaving Banff.

"If, however, Arthur Elliott dies, or is unwilling to accept the house and the estate, monies which equal approximately seven hundred thousand dollars and everything else will ... "

I was half-listening absorbed in my own petty thoughts. Suzanna can't buy the house. Suzanna can't buy the house. I let the singsong tune play over in my mind. I realized Kathleen Benner had stopped talking. She was staring at me, aware I was not listening.

"Sorry," I said.

She continued, "If Arthur Elliott dies or is unwilling to accept the terms of the will, the house and its contents and all monies associated with the estate will go to you, Hellie MacConnell."

Miles Davis played on in the background filling the room where all the air seemed to have been sucked out. I stared at the Doc's lawyer as my body rocked slightly from side to side.

"Impossible," I said. "A mistake. Surely."

Kathleen Benner assured me that all was in order. She had dealt personally with Doctor Rivard on the matter. The briefcase snapped shut and her final words were, "Until such time as Arthur is located you are, of course, free to live in the house."

Doc Rivard's lawyer left with the same crisp, efficient air as she'd arrived with. And I was left to deal with this new information and its implications.

Nathan's behavior at the funeral suddenly made sense. He must have known about the will. The lawyer had said it was the police who had told her about Arthur's disappearance.

Now I was a suspect.

Nathan didn't believe for a minute that the Doc's death was anything close to natural. He probably thought I'd done away with Arthur, just like I'd done away with the Doc. I'd been the last one to see Arthur. I'd claimed to have been home sleeping when the Doc crawled under the gazebo and died. A terrifying sensation overcame me. I felt as if I were looking down a steep, sharp drop.

In the kitchen I found a half-full bottle of wine and poured myself a big glass. Back in the living room, I drank my wine and paced up and down in front of the fireplace. If I left Banff now, I'd look even guiltier. The only option I had was to find Arthur. I was right back to where I'd started: I didn't have a clue where to begin searching. Something soft brushed against my leg. I looked down. Tiger was doing the beagle-with-a-full-bladder rumba at my feet.

"Great, you're a big help. Tomorrow it's back to Larry's for you, my little friend," I said.

Since I didn't have the proper accoutrements, a Velcro watchband and a piece of cord served as makeshift collar and leash. Tiger took to the lead without hesitation or complaint as we hurried down to the river. On the shore, he watered every tree and scrub he could find. When he was done he whined until I picked him up.

"This is not going to work," I told him and kissed his smooth head. "You're not staying."

But I was. I looked up the sweep of lawn to the house. The porch and second floor balcony lights were on and cast the home in a cool white light. The New England structure sat well in its mountain surroundings. The fact that this million-dollar-plus property had been willed to me, even indirectly, was sitting less well. It had to be a mistake. Had to. There was no reason Doc Rivard would include me in his will. Arthur, yes. That made perfect sense. But me? Sure we'd grown close over the past year, but ... I wondered if this was some kind of joke or, more likely, a very stupid mistake on someone's part.

Farther down the shore, the sound of footsteps on river rock echoed in the night air. I squinted and tried to see if someone was there. It was too dark and the brush too thick to make out anything farther away than a few feet. Yet I sensed a presence. A fellow dog walker, I presumed.

River water gurgled its way by and lapped at the shore. Then I caught something on the breeze: the scent of cigarette smoke. This time it smelled mustier, like a cigar or those French cigarettes Brock had smoked occasionally.

The footsteps grew closer. I'm not a skittish person, but my senses were telling me to get going. Banff may not be the murder capital of Canada, but it was surely in the running for drunken assaults.

Arthur's cabin was closer than the house, and I wanted to stop in and have a poke around anyway. As I fished keys out of my pocket, I looked back and listened. There was no one that I could see on the path or on the shore. The cigarette smoke was gone. I exhaled a breath I didn't know I'd been holding. I was beginning to wonder if my nerves were so shot I was imagining sounds and smells.

Inside, I flipped a wall switch and let my eyes adjust to the dull light until everything came into focus. I hadn't been in the cabin since the police had searched it. It was a little messy, but nothing seemed too out of place. With the door closed, I let Tiger off his leash. He ran around the cabin like a windup toy, investigating and sniffing everything. I sat down on the cot feeling like a trespasser and wondered if the cabin came with the deal. I hoped not. I didn't want it. I didn't want any of it. All I wanted was to find Arthur and get my life back. Or at least what it had been before the Doc died.

In the kitchen, the few dishes Arthur owned were stacked neatly on the shelf above the sink. Cups dangled on hooks under stacked plates. I'd always felt relaxed and comfortable in this cabin when I visited my neighbour. Now I just felt confused.

On the wall, above the table, was a rough sketch of a grizzly bear cub. I'd never really paid much attention to it before. Now I saw it was Lulu. My thoughts drifted to my meeting with her in the woods and to the man who talked to her. Never had I met someone so married to his convictions. Arthur lived and breathed for his bears.

"These bears, Hellie," he would say in a low, emotionally-charged voice, "these bears represent the power and the spirit of the forest and mountains. We must stop the dreadful machine that is destroying them. Do you know that spraying moths in one part of the country can affect the weight of a grizzly bear hundreds of miles away? Or that introducing a fish that doesn't belong in a water source can wipe out a significant part of a bear's food supply? It's so simple to stop. We need only be mindful. Remember, it takes only one minuscule part of a machine to cause it to malfunction and the whole thing stops."

I let my eyes trace Lulu's image in the painting. Where are you, Arthur?

I moved around the cabin searching. Searching for anything that might tell me where Arthur could have gone. My suspicion was that he was still hiding in the woods. But where? And how long could he manage out there? And when he couldn't manage any longer, where would he go?

I had to ask myself, was that the only thing I was looking for? No. I was also looking for something that might tell me the truth. Too many things were adding up against him. No one knew where Arthur was the night the Doc died. Nathan's theory that the Doc had been heading down to Arthur's cabin was probably right. Why would he do that if Arthur wasn't supposed to be there? And now the house, the money. Arthur had nearly hit Ansel with that arrow. Was he capable of killing his best friend for the money he needed to further his cause? I had to know.

The desk was a likely place to start, though I suspected there wouldn't be much in it. The police would have taken anything that might be seen as evidence anyway. A quick search of the drawers confirmed this. The kitchen cupboards and the cedar chest turned up zip as well. From there it was on to the recycling bins. I dragged each one inside and plowed through the piles of magazines, tin cans, newspapers and bottles.

An hour later, I had nothing to show for my efforts except filthy, newsprint-stained hands. I washed my hands and started to pick up after myself.

Medicine bottles in various sizes and shapes were strewn around the floor. I picked up one vial that looked like a squat little milk bottle with a rubber stopper at the top where the needle goes in to extract the medicine. There were half a dozen other vials of the same shape. Four were labelled *cortisone*. The others had lost their labels, or never had any.

Next to my foot was a plastic tube of some sort. A closer inspection revealed it was an EpiPen with the words: *Sterile Epinephrine Injection U.S.P.* printed along the tube. I knew epinephrine was adrenaline. I also knew that it was used to counter allergic reactions to things like bee stings. I held the EpiPen up to the light and idly wondered if Arthur or the Doc ever said anything about having allergies. I'd ask Bernie or Miriam. I turned the pen over in my hand; it felt light and was obviously empty.

Tiger whined behind me. I tossed the pen back in the bin with the rest of the bottles and turned to pick him up. I couldn't find him. Then scratching noises alerted me to a bulge of little dog trapped beneath the threadbare Turkish rug. I knew what he was trying to get at. He was directly above a trapdoor that led down to a root cellar. Beagles must have extremely sharp noses, because Arthur kept everything tightly sealed in jars, and the only item of interest to Tiger would have been a bit of salmon jerky Arthur continually tried to foist on the Doc. *Your heart will not thank you, Michael, when it has to deal with all that fatty red meat you insist on gorging yourself on.*

You were probably right, Arthur, I thought sadly as I flipped the carpet back to expose Tiger and the trapdoor he was so intent on scratching through. The brass hinge ring winked under the lamplight.

I was in a cabin alone at night. Did I really want to open that door? No. And yes … maybe yes. My heart sped up and drummed in my ears. I told myself I was being ridiculous. What did I expect to find? A dead body? After having found the Doc under the gazebo, that was precisely what I expected. But again, that was ridiculous. Nathan and his officers had already been down there. Nathan had said as much.

I knelt and lifted the door a few inches. No smell. Good sign. I pulled it all the way back. Tiger jumped up and down like a miniature wild pony, then stuck his head down into the hole, his tail wagging madly.

"See, I told you. There's nothing down there except food and stuff," I said. A narrow set of stairs, a ladder really, led down into the dank hole. On either side, the walls were lined with equally narrow shelves that held jam, flour, coffee, sugar and the like. A quart sealer was filled with strips of the salmon jerky. I reached down for the jar, unscrewed the lid and promptly fumbled it. The lid bounced down the steep stairs and disappeared under the bottom shelf on the right. And there it would have to stay. I broke off a piece of jerky and gave Tiger his treat. He devoured the fish and was begging for more.

There was a thud at the back of the cabin. I started and stared in the direction the noise had come from. In the split second my eyes were off Tiger, he was gone, tumbling down the steep steps. I dropped the jar this time and slipped down the steps right behind him.

"Please don't be hurt. Please little dog, don't be hurt," I said as he landed on his back. He gave a high-pitched yelp, jumped up and scooted off under the bottom shelf.

There was just enough room for me to squeeze my rear end up against one wall and stretch a hand out under the shelf on the other side to get at him. I looked up at the trapdoor, pulse roaring in my ears. I fully expected the door to slam shut. Just like they always do in horror movies.

Tiger had run under the right-hand shelf. It was dark and cramped but I could just reach him. I had my hand on his haunches and was pulling him toward me, and nearly had him, when he decided to turn this into a game and slipped his sleek little self out of my grasp. There was only so much room for him to hide in. I knelt down further and ran my hand along the base of the cool concrete wall.

No dog. He was gone.

Under the other shelf, same thing, no dog. I called his name. Nothing.

He had disappeared.

Now, feeling completely creeped out, I called him again. No response. No dog. What was this, the missing sock in the dryer thing? No, it was the missing dog in the scary cellar thing. Then I heard him whimper, but it was muffled, as if he was in a container or something. I got down on my knees and felt along under the shelf again. He simply wasn't there. He whimpered again. I bent lower, craning my neck until my head was resting on the bottom step. My hand traced the wall under the shelf until it slipped into an opening. I pulled back. An animal's den? Mercifully we don't have rats in Alberta. But we do have skunks and weasels, and beavers with huge yellow teeth. Somehow I didn't think a beaver would be living under Arthur's cabin. Weasels? Maybe.

Gingerly I put my hand back just inside the hole and tapped the floor. I called the dog's name. He responded to the tapping and poked his head out the opening and into my hand. I grabbed his watchstrap collar and gently pulled him toward me. While I was doing so my hand scraped against something else that was in that opening. The something felt like plastic.

I held Tiger in one hand and tugged at a piece of the plastic with the other. It came forward, but it was heavy. A couple more good tugs and the whole thing came out. It was an object about the size and weight of a rolling pin, wrapped in heavy, very dusty plastic. There was another noise up in the cabin. I looked back up the steps. My chest went tight and I had an urgent need to get the hell out of that pit. With Tiger under one arm and the rolling pin thing under the other, I went bum first back up the steps. News headlines ran through my mind: "House-Sitter Finds Human Bones Under Neighbour's Cabin." "More Grisly Discoveries At Doctor's Home."

Safely back up in the cabin, I listened again for the noise. None came. Might have been the wind or a tree branch, I reasoned, and I began to unwrap the package. The plastic came away in layers, each one prompting a deeper sense of dread and the mounting expectation that I would find a human femur. What I actually unveiled was almost as shocking.

CHAPTER 14

BEHIND ME, TIGER GAVE A LOW RUMBLING GROWL THAT, FOR A LITTLE hound, was surprisingly menacing. I spun around. A gasp caught in my throat at the sight of a man's face pressed up against the window.

In one sweeping motion, I flipped the plastic over the object and tucked it under the carpet. A pointless act. The peeper had seen everything. I was on the floor, my eyes riveted on the door handle. I hadn't locked the door. It clicked and turned. The door swung open.

"Evening, Hellie," my intruder said. He tipped his cowboy hat and ducked under the doorway.

"Shit."

"Yes, ma'am, once again you are gettin' yourself deep into that, all right," he said. "Mind if I take a look?" Ansel Rock knelt beside me.

Tiger was jumping around the big Texan's legs vying for his attention. Ansel reached down and gave the dog's head a scratch. "Looks like you got yourself a bird hound."

"He's not mine. He belongs to your hunting guide: Larry the Party Moose."

Ansel shot me a mordant look.

I moved aside as he pulled the carpet back and unwrapped the polished piece of ivory. He was about to pick it up. I stopped him. "Don't, Ansel. Police will want prints."

His hand hovered above the tusk as he turned his distrustful eyes on me and said, "Good thinking."

"Do you have a cell phone?" I asked.

"I do. And who would you be plannin' on phoning, Hellie?"

"Nathan. I think he's going to be very interested to see this. And to see you."

"That right? Where do you think this piece of ivory came from?"

"Probably the same place as those bear paws came from."

"Then I guess that would be Michael Rivard."

My head snapped to the right. "Nice try, Ansel. Now you're being ridiculous."

"No, Hellie. You're the one who's being ridiculous. It's time you faced the truth about Arthur Elliott and Michael Rivard. They are hypocrites, and they have been lying to you." He lowered his voice. "I do not want to see you get hurt."

"Well, here's a news flash, Ansel: I don't believe you. You could have planted this ivory, just like you, or someone you know, could have planted those bear paws. You've been hanging around this cabin, and you have access to this type of thing. Let's not forget, you're the big game hunter."

"Yeah, well so was your Doc Rivard."

I let out a bark of laugher. "Okay, now I really see how desperate you are. Look, are you going to give me your cell phone, or do I have to go up to the house to call the police?"

He handed over the phone.

While we waited for the police, Ansel wandered around the cabin taking in every detail of his enemy's home. In the kitchen he studied each cup, then the plates. He ran a finger over the cast iron frying pans that hung on the wall on horseshoe nails, then he moved to the book-case, squatted and read the titles aloud. "The Old Testament. Buddha's Book of Meditations. The Dalai Lama On Peace. Oh, here we go. Zen In Daily Life. Ah, and of course, the Holy Bible."

I played with Tiger and pretended to not be listening.

"Quite a collection, wouldn't you say, Hellie?"

I didn't respond.

"This here's a perfect example of what he's all about."

I couldn't hold my tongue any longer. "Yes it is. Arthur studies religion."

"No he doesn't, he uses religion to get what he wants. He's a charlatan, a chameleon. Changes his skin to suit the day. What's he stand for? I'll tell you. Nothing. He stands for nothing but his own gain. He's got you brainwashed. Know what I'd like to do with you?"

"I can't possibly imagine," I said.

"I'd like to pack you up and take you home with me and get your brain cleaned out."

"Kind of like a mental enema, huh, Ansel?"

"You are so … " He stopped in front my chair and loomed over me.

I continued to focus on the dog.

"For the past five years, I've had a private investigator working for me in Tanzania," Ansel said. "And here's what he's found out so far. Listen to me, Hellie. You can make jokes and pretend you're not hearing me, but I know you're too smart to ignore the truth. And the truth is, your Doc Rivard liked to collect ivory and he, just like me, was a big game hunter."

I looked up at him. "I have lived in that house for a year, and I can assure you there is not even a hint that Doc Rivard was a hunter, unless he was hunting with antique spears and shields," I said sarcastically. "And I haven't seen a scrap of ivory. Until now. Until you showed up."

"I'm sure you're right," Ansel said. "I'm sure there isn't so much as a trace of your Doc's former life. Because he gave that up after Arthur Elliott showed him the error of his ways. Then he started helping Arthur in his causes."

I ran my hand over Tiger's head and played with his silky ears.

Ansel bent and put his face close to mine. "About the time my wife and I were in Tanzania there were rumours that someone was smuggling illegal arms in through medical clinics. And guess what? One of those clinics was where your Doc Rivard worked. Everyone thought those weapons were going to the poachers. They weren't. Arthur was bringing them in for his lunatic fringe group who were intending to use their new high-powered weapons to fight their good fight against poachers and against us legitimate hunters. Because of that, my wife and little girl ended up dead."

I stared up into Ansel Rock's face and I knew he was the lunatic. "Stop," I said. "Listen to yourself. You're not even making sense now."

"No, it's you — "

Thankfully, the sound of approaching voices cut him off. There was a knock, the door opened and Nathan stepped into the cabin.

"Now what the hell is going on, Hellie?" the big cop said.

"I found that," I said pointing to the piece of ivory.

Nathan stared at it for a moment. And maybe it was because all his years of experience had taught him to hide his emotions, but to my mind, he didn't even look mildly surprised.

I pointed to the root cellar's trap door. "I found an opening under the right-hand shelf," I said.

"And I expect you're going to find a whole lot more down there once you start lookin', Sergeant," Ansel said from the doorway.

Nathan turned slowly and stared through the Texan. "Wait outside, please," was all Sergeant Delaware said.

***

For the next hour, I walked along the riverbank with Tiger and watched anxiously as more constables came and went from the cabin. Ansel was nowhere in sight, but I knew he couldn't be far. I just prayed that he was wrong and the police wouldn't find anything else. But then ... maybe Ansel was so sure they would find more simply because he'd planted something else down there. Or was Ansel telling the truth?

When I saw Nathan and the two constables going up the lawn toward the house, I couldn't stand it any longer and went to Arthur's cabin. The lights were on, but the door was closed and there were no voices coming from inside. I opened the door and peeked into the room. My mouth hung open in shock.

Arthur's home had been turned into a taxidermist's shop filled not only with more ivory pieces and figurines but with a dozen or more exotic skins and horns of African species, mostly endangered.

I went in and sat down heavily on one of the pine chairs and stared at the deplorable items strewn around Arthur's home.

Ansel was telling the truth. It just wasn't feasible that he could have planted all this in Arthur's cabin. It had been there too long; the dust on the plastic was proof of that. Arthur or the Doc must have put it all down there themselves. It wasn't the thought of the Doc being a hunter or even collecting ivory that was so devastating, it was that they had lied to me. And now I had to wonder if there was any truth to what Ansel said about the Doc and Arthur smuggling weapons. The implications of that were unforgivable.

Someone came in, and without looking up I knew it was Ansel. He knelt in front of me and, in his awkward way, tried to be consoling. He took my hands in his. "I can see you didn't know anything about this," he said. "And I am sorry you've been taken in so badly."

I felt like some force had picked me up and was spinning me out of control. I closed my eyes and took in a deep breath. The world stilled, and when I opened my eyes I was staring past Ansel at a zebra skin spread out over Arthur's bed. Next to it, kudu horns spiralled up the wall like curly sabers. The whole place looked like some kind of lifeless exotic zoo.

"I'm sorry too," I said, in a voice that didn't seem to belong to me. "Sorry I ever came here. Sorry I met you. And them."

At my feet was a leopard skin stretched out on the floor for its eternal nap. Glassy, accusing eyes stared up at me. I freed my hand from Ansel's and ran a finger up the beautiful creature's head to its nose.

"Fine specimen," Ansel said.

I was reminded of a conversation I'd had with Arthur. It was one of the few times he spoke about Africa, and what he'd told me was utterly dreadful.

"The leopards. Dear heavens," Arthur said. "The poachers used to kill them in a most disgraceful, painful manner." His eyes were moist as he spoke. "They used hot spikes … "

I made myself stop thinking about it and shook away the memory and the image. But my eyes were still focused on the dead creature at my feet. "I bet you'd be proud to have this specimen in your living room, eh Ansel?" I said it without a hint of sarcasm. "Tell me something, if you can. What makes someone want to hunt something like this? Why aren't you satisfied with a look, a picture? Why the need … " I looked into his eyes. "Is it need? Or is it just the desire to kill?" I asked in earnest.

He studied my face searching for judgment. He found none and rubbed a hand across to his chin. "Well, 'bout the best way I can put it is the way John Morrow once did. I think he hit it right because he's such a great wildlife artist. One time John and I were out duck hunting and I took down a lovely greenhead. When the dog brought it back and laid it at our feet, we both just stood there staring at it. At the beauty of it. It was autumn, and the sun was lightin' up and settin' everything on fire. The gold, red and yellow leaves were the likes of which I had never seen. We were knee-deep in colour. And the mallard's head was a gemstone sparkling in the middle of it. Not even the most brilliant emerald could compare. Not even the ones I bought my wife at the price of a house." He gave a low chuckle. "It was the most beautiful thing I had ever seen. John was having the same reaction, and when he bent down and picked up that duck he said, 'It's like owning a little piece of God.' I surely agreed. And that's the best I can do for an answer. It's like touching and possessing a piece of God."

"Or perhaps it's more like playing God for a moment, Ansel. That moment just before you pull the trigger."

Ansel set his deep Texas blue-sky eyes on mine. "And that's exactly why God gave us guns."

With a profound sense of despair, I wondered if he was right.

"Hellie. If anyone's been playing God, it's Arthur Elliott. Listen, Nathan and his boys will be coming back soon to take care of all this. Why don't you let me take you up to the house?"

"Thanks," I said. "But I'd rather be alone."

CHAPTER 15

THE START BELL KEPT RINGING AND RINGING IN MY EAR. I WAS ALREADY running as fast as I could, and I couldn't understand why it wouldn't let up. It rang louder, insistently. I looked down at my legs spinning like a cartoon character's. I was a human band saw burrowing a hole in the ground beneath me, a hole that would swallow me up and send me down through the centre of the earth and deliver me to China.

I came to in a foggy, sweaty haze and began to comprehend that the start bell was, in fact, the phone. Tiger jumped up from where he was sleeping at my feet and started howling. I hushed him. My heart hammered in my chest as I grabbed for the phone.

"Hellie. Its Miriam."

I exhaled. Heart rate slowed.

"I just spoke to Nathan. I need to see you."

"And I need to see you," I said.

"I guess you would," she said sheepishly.

"I'll be there as soon as I can," I said, then hung up and dragged myself out of bed. After I took Tiger out for his morning constitutional, I took myself to the shower and let the hot water wash over me until I felt almost alive.

There was another call. This one from Ansel, who was just checking to see if I was okay. Followed by one from Des who was also just checking because he'd heard from his mother what was going on.

After Des and I rang off, I checked the time. It was just after eight and I thought I'd better give Bernie a call. When she answered, I filled her in on what had happened the previous night. I did, however, leave out the part about Ansel accusing the Doc of smuggling weapons. I wanted to hear what Miriam had to say about that first.

"Doc? A big game hunter? I don't believe it," Bernie said. "Paul and I have known him for fifteen years. That's absurd. Someone put those things in Arthur's cabin."

"I don't think so, Bern. Nathan told me they probably were the Doc's."

"Nathan said that?"

"He's known the Doc for over thirty years. Said the Doc hunted back in the seventies. Anyway, I'll be able to tell you more once I've talked to Miriam. At least I hope I will."

"Does Nathan think all that ivory and those trophies have anything to do with the Doc's death?"

"I asked him the same question; he said he wouldn't speculate. Anyway, I've got to get over to *The Peak*. I want to head Zenna off before she talks to the Texan. And I'm sure the police will be back here again. Right now, I'd rather not be around when they show up."

"They won't search the house, will they?" she said. "What if they find something else?" There was panic in her voice.

"Bernie, do you know something about those skins and all that ivory?" She didn't answer. "Bernie?"

"No. No. I don't know anything. I'm just worried."

"Worried that they'll find out Arthur's a killer?" There was a moment of silence down the line. "It's okay," I finally said. "I've been thinking it too. It does look bad."

"That's right, Hellie. It looks bad. My grandmother always said appearances are fickle. Arthur would not hurt the Doc. And don't let anyone make you believe otherwise."

"Thanks, Bern." Something occurred to me. "Say, speaking of your grandmother, she had a heart condition didn't she?"

"Same as the Doc, only Nana had a quad bypass."

"Was there anything you weren't supposed to give her?"

"Eggs."

"Take a long time to kill someone feeding them eggs."

"It would."

"Anything else you weren't supposed to give her or do?"

"I don't know. I tried not to scare her or get her too excited. Sometimes she'd have chest pains if she got too excited and she'd have to use her nitro spray. Why, Hellie? What's on your mind?"

"Probably nothing. What about cortisone?"

"Her doctor never mentioned anything about it."

"She ever use adrenaline or something called epinephrine for her heart?"

"Not that I know of. Why?"

"What about allergies? Did the Doc or Arthur have allergies?"

"Couldn't say about Arthur. And I don't think the Doc did. If he did, I can't remember him ever mentioning anything. What's up, Hellie?"

"Last night I found a used adrenaline pen in Arthur's cabin along with used vials of cortisone."

"What kind of pen?"

"It's a syringe-like thing. People carry them to counter allergic reactions, bee stings, things like that."

"Oh sure, I know what you're talking about. Doc probably kept it around for emergencies, and somehow it ended up in the recycling."

"I'm sure you're right," I said.

Before we rang off, I promised to keep her posted. As I replaced the receiver, the nagging feeling that she knew more than she was saying refused to go away.

On my way out, I stopped in the den to check my email. There was one message from Danny that said: "Missed you again. Don't call. Still need to talk."

I looked at the phone lying on the desk. "Talk? About what?" I said through clenched teeth.

I hit reply, and wrote: "Hi Danny. If it's important, work something out so I can phone you at a friend's. Then email me with a number and the day and time I can reach you." I hit *send* and felt a little better.

While I was online I did a quick search for information on cortisone and adrenaline. First I read about all the nasty things cortisone does to one's body, but found little mention of it relating to the heart. Adrenaline, however, made for far more interesting reading. I found one site that said:

> Adrenaline: A hormone secreted by the adrenal glands that stimulates the sympathetic nervous system; also called epinephrine. Helps to prepare the organism for an emergency or a stressful situation.

I wondered if a person could use up too much of the stuff and if it was possible to get recharged. After the week I'd had, I figured I was due for a booster. I continued to read:

> Adrenaline causes the blood vessels to constrict in the stomach and intestines and causes the heart to beat faster.

That made me sit up. Could it make a heart beat too fast? I imagined it was possible, but the police had been through those bins, and in the autopsy nothing was found in the Doc's system. I was wasting my time. And no one would be stupid enough to leave the evidence in the recycle bin. I put my computer to sleep, leashed Tiger and we headed over to *The Peak's* office.

***

Zenna Duff, the managing editor, was behind her desk talking on the phone. She waved me in and motioned for me to take a seat. Zenna, like me, was a fairly recent journalism graduate. Unlike me, though, Zenna had followed the straight path out of high school and into university. She was at least four years my junior and she was a great editor who inspired her writers and knew a good story when she saw it. If she'd talked to the Texan or heard about the Doc's will and the animal skins we found in Arthur's cabin, she'd already be on it, and I wanted the details to come from me.

"Right, right," she said into the receiver. "Ah, sure, I'll think on it." Her Newfoundland accent was just detectable in the rolling "err" she pronounced in "sure." The half-dozen silver bracelets she wore on both arms tinkled when she put the phone down.

"Hellie, good to see you. Hey, cute pooch." She reached across and gave Tiger a pat on the head.

This time I didn't bother to say he wasn't mine.

"Gosh it's sure sad, this business with the Doc and all. Can't stop thinking about it. I'm glad you stopped in. Don't rush yourself with the Arts Centre piece. We can run it anytime," she said.

I said, "Thanks." I was supposed to be working on a feature about the history of the Banff Centre for the Arts, a piece I hadn't even begun to think about, let alone write.

"So. How are you doin'? Didn't get much of a chance to talk to you at the funeral. Was a nice one though."

She hadn't heard yet. If she had, Zenna would have been asking questions, not making small talk.

"I'm hanging in," I said. Then I got right to it and told her about the previous night. She listened and made some notes. When I was done, she put her pen down and steepled her fingers under her chin. Her face was grave.

"This is quite a story, Hellie. I can't believe Doc Rivard was doing the likes of that. I mean, what with Arthur running around annoying hunters, and Doc Rivard backing him up and saving the valley. Well, I'll tell ya, it's disappointing, and it's news. He deceived the whole community. And everybody loved and respected the Doc."

"Exactly. Everyone thought the world of the Doc, and I don't want anything to ruin that. Which is why I'm about to ask you a huge favour."

"I've got to run it, Hellie."

"I know that. But can you do it without quoting Ansel Rock?"

She gave me a dubious look.

"Just for now. Run the bare bones. Talk to Nathan, only."

"And not Ansel Rock?"

"Believe me, he's not your best source. And if you do happen to talk to him, I expect he'll make some outlandish comments."

Zenna's eyebrows shot up. "But are they true?"

"I don't know yet. I'm on my way over to Miriam's. Anything I hear, I pass on to you first thing. In the meantime, call Nathan, quote him."

She tapped her pen against the desk, her silver bracelets tinkling in time. "All right. Leave it with me. You've got twenty-four hours."

I went to the door. "Thanks, Zenna. I owe you."

She said, "You bet you do."

***

"You should have called me last night," Miriam said.

"I was too tired and too depressed."

"Yes, of course you would be. Ah, I see you have a new friend. Where'd you get him? Or is he a she?"

"Him. His name's Tiger. Larry gave him to me."

"Really?" Miriam's eyebrows shot up.

"Yup. Don't ask, long story. But the short of it is, little Tiger is going back to Larry."

"Oh, I see," she said, leaning down to give the dog a pat. "You're very cute." She straightened up. "Well, come in. Sit down." She ushered us into her living room where I took a seat on her couch.

"It's so maddening," Miriam said.

An interesting response, I thought. "Maddening? How so?"

She perched on the corner of an armchair. "Once everyone hears the police found ivory and African trophies in Arthur's basement, they will think Michael and Arthur have deceived them."

"Well, haven't they?"

"No. Michael Rivard and Arthur Elliott are the most ethical men I've ever known."

"Then why wasn't the Doc upfront about being a hunter and collecting ivory?"

"I don't know. It was a long time ago. Perhaps he thought it would just muddy the waters. And … well, he would have been embarrassed. The ivory he and Barb collected could well have been poached ivory. And most likely it was." Her eyes went to the ceiling then back down to me. "I thought he'd got rid of all that," she said.

"So you've seen it?" I said.

"Back in the seventies Barbara and the Doc kept Michael's trophies and Barbara's ivory upstairs in the house, some in the attic, some in the guest rooms. Not many Banffites would have seen it. Doc and Barb were private people. I saw it, though, and I didn't like it."

"Nathan would have seen it too."

"Oh, yes. Nathan coveted them. He's always been a hunter. But he was also a good enough friend not to mention Michael's hunting days once he changed his course. Michael and Barbara were not bad people, Hellie."

"I didn't say they were."

"And you have to remember we're talking about thirty years ago. Back then things were different. They were in Tanzania helping people. And they were doing a mighty fine job of it. We didn't think about the environment and animals the way we do today. Michael and Barb didn't understand the gravity of the elephant's plight and the ivory poaching situation until they met Arthur."

"Which is when they came back and started saving the Bow Valley," I said.

"Right. All the African skins and ivory disappeared. I never asked what happened to them. Now I guess we know."

"I guess so," I said.

Miriam was trying to coax Tiger onto her lap. Tiger, however, was far more interested in Mr. Ruffy, who was lounging on his pillow along the window ledge looking completely underwhelmed by the little dog's presence.

I picked up the dog and put him in Miriam's lap. "I still don't understand why the Doc wasn't honest about it," I said. "If he had been, he could have helped further his own Society's goals and Arthur's anti-hunting projects. Admitting that he was once a big game hunter, but quit because of what he saw going on in Africa with the elephants and other species, would have sent a powerful message."

Miriam shrugged. "Michael made a mistake."

"I wonder about that," I said watching her stroke the dog's floppy ears. "The Doc was a smart man," I said. "Is it possible he hid his past for some other reason? Perhaps he made other mistakes in Africa he didn't want to come out."

Her hand stilled on the dog's ear. "What are you getting at, Hellie?"

"Ansel Rock claims Doc was smuggling illegal arms into Tanzania for Arthur's group, through the medical clinic."

"Hogwash!" She put the dog down.

"Is it? After what I saw last night, I'm ready to start believing Ansel. Because the police think I'm involved in the Doc's death and now Arthur's disappearance. Nathan keeps saying the investigation is officially closed. Which is crap. I know he's always believed the Doc was murdered, just like Arthur said. And I'm convinced he's right. I was planning to leave. But since I'm a pretty likely suspect, I can't."

"This is tough, I know, and I am sorry."

"I need more than your sympathy, Miriam. I need your help. We have to find Arthur."

Her eyes flashed and revealed the mental calculations of someone who wanted to tell the truth, but couldn't. I couldn't wait. "If you know where he is ... "

"I'm telling you the truth when I say I don't know." She sank back in her chair.

For the first time since I'd met her, Miriam Bauer did not look like the tough, spry, sixty-four-year-old I knew her to be. The woman across from me that day looked tired and worn. The skin on her face hung limp, pale as paper.

"Do you know why the Doc was coming home?" I asked. She shook her head. "Come on. You must know. You've got to help me."

"I don't know anything."

"Did the Doc's visit have anything to do with what we found yesterday?"

"No. Absolutely not. Oh hell's bells," she said, her German accent becoming more pronounced. "I don't know. They stopped telling me anything."

"The Doc and Arthur?" She gave a nod. "When? Why?"

"Few months ago. Don't know what I did."

"Maybe nothing," I said.

"Maybe nothing," she repeated sadly. "They used to tell me everything. Everything." Her eyes brightened at a distant memory. "When Art chained himself to that bulldozer in Canmore last year — do you remember?"

"Yes."

"I knew beforehand!" she said with guilty pleasure. "But don't ever let on to Des, he'd kill me if he knew half the things I've done."

"I won't tell him," I said.

Her bright mischievous eyes dulled again as she focused on some spot on the fireplace. "Then they cut me out. Just like that. But I knew they were up to something. I knew. I talked to Michael in Tanzania, asked him why the sudden trip. 'Just a visit,' he said." She sniffed. "Hogwash."

"Was it because Ansel was here?"

"I assume so. But they certainly didn't tell me."

"So you knew about Ansel's wife and little girl."

She nodded.

"Why didn't you tell me?"

"Sorry about that. It's all gotten so damned complicated. When we heard Ansel was coming, we didn't think there was any need to panic. Ansel Rock hunted outside the park in the same area on two previous occasions and never once set foot in Banff, or near Arthur."

"Oh. But since he was coming, and since I was doing the article, you guys figured it wouldn't hurt to have someone you know sticking close to him."

"That's what we thought," she said sheepishly.

"A lot of secrets and lies seem to be surfacing around here, Miriam. Any more I should know about?"

"How about some tea?" She was up and out of the room before I could press her for an answer.

While she was gone, I picked up a flyer from the pile on the table. The heading on this one was in bold black print that read: "STOP THE SLAUGHTER." Under that was a dark picture, obviously taken at night with a flash, of two men in the back of a pickup truck with a dead grizzly. Under it another caption read: "The Poachers Are Winning. Help Us Save Our Bears."

A few minutes later, Miriam placed a tray with bagels and cream cheese and tea things on the coffee table.

"We're losing them, Hellie," she said when she saw me reading the flyer. "The wardens are doing their best. But they don't have the time or money to patrol the backcountry anymore."

I put the flyer back. "Do you know anything about those paws I found in Arthur's cabin?" I asked.

"I do not. Other than I'm certain it was some kind of message. A warning perhaps. But I can't prove it. Come on, Hellie, have a bagel."

I accepted the offer since I hadn't eaten a thing all morning. "Doc left the house and his estate to me," I said, and spread cheese on the warm bagel before I bit into it.

"Only with Arthur's say-so, or when he dies. But let's not consider that possibility."

"Did Nathan tell you about the will?"

"No, Michael did."

I put the bagel down. "Really. When was that?"

"You have to understand that of course he wanted to leave the house to Arthur. That was a given. But we also knew that Arthur would give it away, and he wouldn't have a place to live. It was a terrible dilemma. Then you showed up: Michael's niece. It was the answer to everything. Has the lawyer told you all the details?"

"I'm not sure."

"The money's in trust, of course," she continued. "And there's a proviso in the will that states that as long as you are in possession of the house and estate, you will provide for Arthur. In other words, you'll make sure he has a decent place to live."

"Isn't this all just great! I'm feeling pretty used here, Miriam." I took a long drink of my tea and considered asking her to spike it with something very strong.

"Yes. I can see how you would. But it is a lovely house."

"That's hardly the point. When did the Doc and you decide all this?"

"Just before he left for Tanzania."

"Sounds like he thought he might not be coming back."

"Not necessarily. We're not young, Hellie. That's why I didn't want Michael to leave the house to me. At our age, dying is always a concern," she said matter-of-factly. "And Tanzania can be dangerous, especially where Michael was, around the game reserve. There's a lot of violence."

"Apparently. Ansel claims Arthur killed his wife and child the last time they were all there. And that their deaths have something to do with Doc bringing in illegal weapons. Know anything about that, Miriam?"

"I know Arthur's version," she said, turning up the cuffs of her heavy wool sweater.

"Which strays from Ansel's."

"Considerably. Do you feel like a walk, Hellie? I need to get out of this house and pick up my mail."

"Hoping Arthur might have dropped you a line?" I said.

She gave me mischievous smile. "One never knows ... "

***

I took my bagel for the road, and Miriam, Tiger and I set out along Spray Avenue. As we were nearing the bridge, Miriam pointed down Cave and Basin Road. "Where those condos are and the land beyond them is the site of Ansel's failed mega resort. I looked into it after we spoke yesterday. The project belonged to Ansel and his friend, John Morrow."

"That a fact?"

"I did a little more digging," Miriam continued, as we crossed the bridge into town. "John Morrow, like Ansel, specializes in developing high-end resorts."

"John didn't mention that yesterday when I spoke to him. Mind you, no one seems to be telling me anything."

"I am sorry, Hellie. You're caught in the middle. Not a nice place to be. But I simply couldn't afford to divulge too much."

"Well you better start divulging now," I said. "My nerves are rubbed raw. And I need to find Arthur before Ansel Rock finds him, and before the Texan convinces the press Doc Rivard was smuggling weapons into Tanzania."

Miriam gave me a motherly pat on the back. "I'll help you, Hellie. We'll get through this. Come on," she said with a wink. "As Doug and Sandy would say: 'Relax, you're in the mountains now.'"

I gave her a mock death stare. We were passing The Banff Book & Art Den, and it would have been a perfect day to relax. People milled around the bookstore sipping cappuccinos and nibbling candy from Welch's Chocolate Shop. The weather had cleared and the sun was bright with only a scattering of cloud puffs suspended in the autumn sky.

We undid our coats and headed to the post office. I wasn't planning to go in because I wasn't in the mood to field questions. Everyone who lives in Banff meets at the post office. During the summer months, locals scurry down the back alleys and spend as little time as possible on Banff Avenue, where throngs of tourists crowd the famous street. But after the Labour Day weekend, Banffites reclaim the town and emerge from the alleys and make the trip to the post office along the main streets. Unfortunately, at that moment Suzanna was one such local making her way down the street toward us.

"Want to duck into a store?" Miriam suggested.

"Hellie! I've been trying to get hold of you," Suzanna called from half a block away.

"Too late," I said. "She's upon us."

"What's going on at Michael's?" Suzanna demanded. "This has something to do with Arthur, doesn't it? Did he shoot at someone again?"

"I don't know what you're talking about," I said.

"The police. There are police cars and people poking around the backyard."

I was right, they had come back. "I guess they're still investigating," I said. I couldn't bring myself to tell her what I'd found the previous night.

"You should be there keeping an eye on them. Make sure they don't take anything."

"They're police officers, Suzanna. I think we're safe."

She scooped Tiger up into her arms and fingered his makeshift collar. "You can't wear this. I'm taking you right now to buy you a proper collar and a proper leash," she said nuzzling the dog's head. "Really, Hellie. String!"

I was too exhausted to fight with her, and regardless of whom he was going to end up with, Tiger did need some new gear. "Ok, drop him off at the Doc's when you're done," I said.

"What if you aren't home?" Suzanna responded. "What if the police are still roaming around?"

"Then keep him at your place until I do get home."

"I'm going out in an hour. Do you have an extra key?"

I did, but I was loath to give it to her.

"For heaven's sake, Hellie, I'll give it back."

I handed her the spare key I kept in my wallet. It disappeared into her purse, and she rushed off down the street with the little beagle in tow. As I watched them go, I felt my first pang of separation anxiety.

Miriam was watching too. I realized that Suzanna hadn't even bothered to acknowledge the older woman's presence.

"Make sure you get your key back," Miriam said as we walked on past the shops.

"Don't worry, I will."

"When it comes to Suzanna, I always worry," Miriam said.

"Yeah well, forget her for now," I said. "Let's concentrate on you helping me."

"All right. How can I help?"

"By telling me what happened in Tanzania between Arthur and Ansel, and then giving me some idea of where I can start looking for Arthur."

Miriam was silent for a moment as we waited for a break in the traffic and then crossed Banff Avenue. "All right," she began when we were on the other side passing the Hudson's Bay store. "Arthur never talked about it. It was Michael who told me." As she spoke, I could almost hear the Doc's voice. "Terrible things were going on in Tanzania. The poaching was rampant and government agents and game wardens didn't have adequate vehicles and equipment to combat it. They still don't. And the methods some of those poachers were using to kill the animals — terrible! They would drive in their vehicles through the herds, shooting and wounding anything in their paths. They wounded the elephants and took their tusks and left them to die horrible, painful deaths.

"Arthur told me some of that."

"Fine. Then you know what he and his group were fighting against. Actually it would be more accurate to say Arthur worked in the name of the group. He started the project."

"Selous Elephant Project."

"Right, SEP. He raised funds for the group. But Arthur tended to work alone or sometimes with undercover agents hired by the Tanzanian government. My goodness they were brave, Hellie. During Arthur's time in the game reserve, there were very sophisticated poaching rings and some high-ranking officials were implicated. That's how the poachers were getting the trophies and skins out of the country with such ease. They had government backing.

"The poaching in Africa was nothing short of guerilla warfare," Miriam continued. "And it wasn't the village people. Both Arthur and Michael said the villagers were some of the finest people they'd ever known. No, it was the organized poachers, the higher-ups, the ones with the automatic weapons. Arthur used to go into the remote regions of the reserve and pretend to be a buyer. It was terribly risky."

"How did Arthur and Ansel's wife meet? Or did they?" I was considering the possibility that Ansel was insane.

"In '95, Ansel came to the reserve to hunt elephants."

"I didn't know you could still do that."

"Oh yes. It's still possible today. But it's very hard and tremendously expensive to get a permit to go on safari."

"Not a problem for our rich Texan, though."

"No. Money was not Ansel's problem. His wife was."

"Ah, marital discord."

"Exactly. And the discord was being fuelled by her conservation efforts."

"Well now, isn't this interesting," I said. We'd reached the post office and I kept walking.

"I'll just be a jiffy," Miriam said as she climbed the stairs.

I went across the street to the park. At the riverbank, I stared at the water and let my eyes follow a pintail duck riding along the water's surface. Banff somehow looked different to me just then. Maybe it was my nerves. Whatever the reason, it was as if every element was magnified, the colours intensified. The mountain ranges looked even more magnificent, and so still. The clean, clear sky and swan-feather clouds were vivid images mirrored in the transparent water. The air was so fresh and filled with the sharp scents of fall forests.

Miriam joined me. "Arthur send anything?" I asked hopefully. She shook her head. "See anyone?"

"Bert Mooney, he just heard what's been going on at Doc's house. So we'll avoid downtown and stick to Bow Avenue," she said. "Now where was I?"

"You were telling me about Ansel's wife, the conservationist."

"Righto. Arthur's group got wind that Ansel, the elephant hunter, was staying at a resort in a town called Mikindani."

"That's where the Doc's clinic is," I said as we strolled down the river path.

"Right. Well, some SEP members staged a protest outside the hotel. Arthur happened to be involved in it, although he wasn't particularly concerned about the hunters. It was the poachers he was after. Anyway, Ansel was furious about the protesters. Marianna, on the other hand, was delighted, and later, when she learned of a conservation meeting taking place in town, she managed to talk Ansel into attending."

"Wow, Marianna Rock must have had some hold on her husband to get him to a meeting with the same people who'd been protesting against him."

"He didn't know it was the same group until he got there," Miriam said. "When Ansel met Arthur, he made the connection and left."

I snorted. "Well, the irony's a little thick there, isn't it? Him going to a conservation meeting in the first place, since he was in town to whack a pachyderm."

"Not really. A lot of big game hunters and safari companies support conservation efforts. In fact, they're the original conservationists. Many of us are on the same side. Killing things, however, is where we part company."

"So what happened after the big meeting?"

"Marianna Rock became SEP's newest member and most ardent anti-hunting advocate."

"Uh-oh. I would have liked to see Ansel's reaction to that one."

"I doubt that."

"But anti-hunting wasn't what the group was about, was it?" I said.

"The group was divided. Most didn't like the idea of hunting, but their main focus was poaching. There were a few, though, who were very vocal and actively protested hunting of any kind. Arthur wasn't one of them."

"But Marianna was?" I said.

Miriam nodded. "After the meeting, Marianna stormed back to their hotel and delivered an ultimatum to her husband. Either he called off his hunting trips or she was taking their little girl and leaving."

"I can't see Ansel Rock backing down."

"You're right. He went on his trip and she went straight to Arthur."

"For what?"

"A place to live."

"Holy cow. She was serious about the cause."

"Very. The rest of the story is vague," Miriam said. "According to the police in Tanzania, and members of Arthur's group, an agent Arthur had been working with was trying to get hold of him to deliver a message. They presumed the agent was on his way to the house where Arthur, Marianna and Nici Rock — "

"Ansel's little girl."

"Yes, their little girl. The three of them were staying with Arthur's friend. On that same day, Ansel Rock claims Marianna and Nici were on their way to his safari camp."

"Why?"

"No one knows. She never made it. The poachers ambushed her before she got to the airport. They found the jeep and then they found Marianna and her daughter a few days later in the reserve forest. Dead."

"My God, they killed an innocent woman and child."

"Yes," Miriam said quietly. "And the agent. The agent's family had been receiving death threats, so they left the country. That's why the authorities assumed the agent was on his way to meet Arthur. Another agent verified this. Said the poachers must have followed the agent, seen him go to the house, then waited for Marianna to leave, thinking the agent had left the message with her, although that was very unlikely. Marianna probably didn't know anything."

"But I wonder why she was going to Ansel's camp."

Miriam shrugged.

I tried to put myself in Marianna Rock's place and came up with two possible theories. I put them to Miriam. "Marianna missed her husband and wanted to make up. Or, she was going out there to try and get him to stop the hunt."

"I pick number two," Miriam said.

"That'd be my guess too," I said. "Except Ansel seemed pretty convinced she died because of the illegal weapons being brought in through the Doc's clinic."

"Well, he's wrong."

"What a sad story." I was beginning to feel a little differently about Ansel Rock. He'd been through hell and he was still living it. "So why did Arthur have to leave Tanzania?" I asked.

"Because Ansel Rock made sure he had to. Ansel went on a campaign to prove that Arthur had used Marianna, put her in jeopardy and sent her out to meet with the agent."

"But that's not what the police thought?"

"At first they didn't take Ansel seriously. Then he went to Arthur's group and convinced them that Arthur was directly responsible for his wife and child's death. It wasn't a difficult task. Some of the SEP leaders were on the anti-hunting side of things anyway, and they were only too happy to get rid of Arthur. Also, Arthur was in favor of selling stockpiled ivory in countries that had a healthy elephant population. Arthur, as you well know, cannot abide waste. The group was dead set against it. So, politically, the timing was perfect. And ... weapons were discovered concealed within medical supplies at Michael's clinic."

"So it's true."

"Yes, it is true weapons were found there, but they were not going to Arthur or to his group. They were going to the poachers."

"Says who?"

"Michael and Arthur."

"Ansel's had a private investigator working on this since his wife and child were killed," I said.

"I'm not surprised."

"He believes those weapons were going to SEP, and he thinks Arthur killed the Doc."

"Hogwash. The man is consumed with grief. He needs an outlet. He wants some one else to pay for his loss."

We took a seat on a bench along the riverbank and gazed up at Mount Norquay. Fluffy white cloud strings were suspended midway down the slope like giant feather boas slung low on the nape of the mountain.

"If you're right, then we simply have to find Arthur before Ansel does," I said.

"Yes we do. And I have an idea where you might start looking."

"Thought you might," I said. When she finished telling me her idea, I said I had one more question for her. "Why did you wait so long to tell me all this?"

"Because Michael made me promise that I would never breathe a word of that story to anyone. Now I've broken the promise. In this business of saving the environment, Hellie, I've learned to keep my mouth closed." She thrust a forefinger into the air. "Those who speak least are heard most."

"Arthur. He's gotten to you."

She smiled. "I certainly hope so."

CHAPTER 16

At eight forty-five that evening, I entered the lobby of the infamous Baltimore Hotel — a three-storey establishment in Calgary's industrial southeast end, offering competitive room rates on a weekly, daily and hourly basis.

Against the far wall, a rock beat pounded behind black vinyl doors. To my right was a front desk of sorts, where a wasted fellow — I guessed he weighed no more than my one-hundred-and-eighteen pounds — was watching a hockey game on a tiny portable TV and shovelling fried noodles into his mouth. The mix of smoke, grease and old booze hung in the air thick as sauna steam.

The desk clerk wore a name tag that said: "Chad." Chad was affable when I showed him a picture of the Doc and Arthur and asked if he recognized the bald man with the beard.

Chad squinted at the picture and pointed an unusually long, yellow pinky fingernail at Arthur's visage. "Yeah. I seen him." He tapped the weird pinky nail against his lips. "Maybe ... uh, let's see. Maybe last week some time."

My heart leapt. "Do you know what he was doing here?"

Chad cocked an eyebrow that asked the question: *You kiddin' me?* He said, "Picked up one of the girls. Little Ruby."

"Who?"

"Ruby Mist. Works the lot. Only reason I think I remember him is 'cause your friend was dressed up like a psychedelic monk and opened the door for Ruby." He gave a mirthless laugh. "Not too many doin' that around here. I keep an eye on the girls," he explained. "See who they're gettin' in with, case the john gets mean and the girl don't come back."

Arthur a john? Picking up prostitutes? I was staring at the man behind the counter, but not seeing him. My mind was on what Miriam had told me. "Arthur's been going to the Baltimore once or twice a week at night for the past two months," she had said. "He usually borrowed my truck on Tuesdays and Thursdays, between nine and eleven.

He never told me why or what he was doing. And," she gave me a sad smile, "I knew better than to ask."

Well. If this was the reason he was frequenting the place, Miriam and I were better off not knowing.

"Ask Ruby," Chad said. "Wears a white coat, big boots and has green, or maybe it's blue now ... yeah, blue hair with blonde streaks."

"Oh. Um ... okay. Is she here?"

He checked his watch. "Left maybe twenty minutes ago. Should be back anytime now. Wait a bit. Or check the bar. She could've slipped in without me noticing. And if she is in there, tell her to get out. She's underage."

"Right. Okay." My feet remained planted.

"Say, uh ... you mind?" He pointed his fork at the greasy mess on his plate.

"Sure. Thanks. I'll get out of your way."

"Bar's through the double black doors," he said around a mouthful of noodles.

I opened one of the black doors a crack and poked my head into a hazy, smoke-filled room. Giant speakers pounded out Bob Seger's "Hollywood Nights." On a makeshift stage a young woman, with a bored countenance, was swinging her head from side to side in time to the beat and sliding her back up and down a pole. Her legs were splayed, and a naked breast was cupped in each hand as if she were offering them up to her equally bored audience of predominantly leather-clad, scruffy-headed men. Only five or six other women were in the crowd; none fit Ruby Mist's description.

Gingerly I closed the door and slipped back out to the parking lot. Three women, girls really, were huddled together sharing a joint near a pod of shiny Harley-Davidson motorbikes. On the other side of the lot, a fourth girl stood alone puffing a cigarette. I approached her and said I was looking for Ruby Mist.

"You her mother?"

I was completely taken aback. Then I did the math. If Ruby was fourteen or fifteen, it was certainly possible.

"No. I'm not her mother. I'm looking for someone ... a friend. He's — "

"Ain't your friend if he's hanging with Ruby," she said with a smirk.

"Oh, he's not … " Her bored, distracted expression stopped me.

"Ruby should be back pretty quick. And don't bother talking to those other bitches," she said, jabbing her cigarette in the direction of the threesome across the lot. "They'll beat the shit out of you if they think you're crowdin' their turf. Like they own the place or something."

I assured her I was doing nothing of the sort and made a hasty retreat back to my car, giving the three girls and the Harleys a very wide berth.

Safely ensconced in my car, I turned over the ignition and got the heat blowing. Across the lot, light from a bare bulb above the bar door bounced off the Harleys' chrome tanks and shot silver rays into the night sky.

Over the next half-hour, I kept a keen eye out for any sign of Arthur and the blue-haired Ms. Mist. A few cars pulled in and out of the lot. Eventually, all four young women were gone.

A car, badly in need of a muffler job, caught and held my attention when it roared up to the hotel entrance and came to a rubber-screeching halt. The car's front passenger door swung open and a pair of long white boots, just like the ones Julia Roberts wore in *Pretty Woman*, hit the pavement. Twig-thin thighs were exposed above the tops of the boots. What looked like half an elastic band was doubling as a skirt. The other half served as the top, stretched tightly over the woman's tiny chest. For warmth, a white rabbit-fur coat, that apparently didn't have any buttons, flapped open to expose her bare belly. Light from the street lamp illuminated the washed-out blue hair. When Ruby Mist turned her heavily made-up face in my direction, I saw that this "pretty woman" was all of about fourteen years old.

My heart hurt. It ached for this child, for the woman in the bar offering her breasts. And it hardened toward the man in the car in front of me.

The driver's side door suddenly swung open. Ruby Mist stole a nervous glance over her shoulder and made a dash for the hotel's front entrance. A pudgy figure in tight jeans hauled himself out of the car and took off after the little girl in the big boots. He grabbed her roughly by the arm. They exchanged angry words, and she tried to struggle free.

I scanned the lot for help. It was deserted. I had to do something but, save for smashing the guy's head in with my tire jack, I knew I'd be no match for him. So I flipped on the VW's brights, catching Ruby and her assailant in a blinding spotlight. I rummaged in the glove box for a ballpoint pen. The Beetle's horn had been damaged shortly after I left Toronto, when, in a fit of hormonal road rage, I'd hit the steering wheel so hard the air bag inflated, and the horn wouldn't turn off until I let some kid at a gas station tear the entire thing apart with a Phillips screwdriver. In order to honk the horn, I now had to poke a pen in the gaping hole that was left in my steering column. I did just that and the Beetle's horn sounded off like a semi-trailer's.

The man started. His eyes zeroed in on my car. He was still holding Ruby's arm, but now his attention was directed at me. I couldn't hear the words he was screaming, but I didn't have to be a professional lip reader to get the message. I scooted over to the passenger's side, rolled down the window and stuck my head out. "Can't get it to turn off," I yelled and threw my hands up in frustration. "Can't get the lights off either."

Chad, the desk clerk, poked his head out the front door. At the same time a couple of burly fellows — no doubt coming to see if some moron was messing with their bikes — stepped out the bar doors. Ruby called to them. The guy released her, took off back to his Camaro and roared out of the lot. One of the burly fellows stayed with Ruby while the other came toward my annoyingly loud, bright car. Miraculously, the lights turned themselves off and the horn went silent.

I stepped out of the car. "Thanks," I said. "Got it under control."

He turned back to Ruby, who was rubbing her arm and talking to the other guy. They said a few words to her then headed back inside, but not before one of them turned and gave me a thumbs-up sign, which gave me a sliver of hope for humanity.

Ruby caught the gesture. When the men were gone she tottered over, leaned in my window and pressed her tiny chest against the frame. The sight of that underdeveloped cleavage almost made me weep. Around her neck she wore a silver chain. Whatever was attached to it was tucked away under the tube top. I wondered if it was a Saint Christopher medal. Though garlic would probably have been a more effective amulet in her business. From the neck up, Ruby was covered with a thick layer of foundation that appeared to have been applied with a pallet knife in a vain attempt to hide her adolescent acne. The smell of cosmetics wafted in through the open window.

"Who the fuck are you?"

The harshness of her voice and words literally pushed me back in my seat. "I'm a … a … "

"Volunteer?" she said. "Where's the hot chocolate and the van? Lose your funding?"

"No. I'm not a volunteer. I'm a writer. I'm looking for someone. Thought you might be able to help me. Are you Ruby Mist?"

"Maybe. You a cop?"

"No."

"Social worker?"

"I told you. I'm a writer."

"Chad tell you to talk to me?"

"He said you might — "

"Chad's a dick."

"Can't be all bad, says he keeps an eye on you guys."

She screwed up her nose. "Are you, like, for real? Chad gets well paid for the dickless job he does. Keeps his nose filled helping us out."

Ah, ha! A coke freak. The weird pinky nail. I am sharp.

"He did a great job tonight. Only stuck his head out 'cause you blasted your horn. I'll tell him he owes you."

"No. That's fine," I said. "I was glad to help. That guy looked like he was going to hurt you."

"Duh. Yeah. He was plannin' on doin' some major damage." She spoke with the bravado of one who had handled many a similar situation. "Wanted half his fucking money back. Guy's got a broken pecker and it's my fault." She fished in her little white purse and pulled out a package of cigarettes. "So you gonna tell me who you're looking for?" She lit her cigarette, threw her head back dramatically and exhaled a cloud of blue smoke. Then threw her empty cigarette package on the ground.

Two cars pulled in a few spots down from us. Ruby kept a close eye on them as she puffed on her smoke. Two young guys got out of the first car and headed across the parking lot. Ruby stepped out of the shadows and into action.

"Hi guys. Want some company?"

"Hey Ruby, isn't it past your bedtime?" one of the fellows called over his shoulder.

She gave him an impish look. "Don't worry, boys, I just had a nap." Both guys laughed, and Ruby turned back to me. "They're dicks too." She stamped her feet against the cold.

"You want to get in? Warm up maybe?" I said.

Another flip of the hair and Ruby wobbled her way on those precariously high heels to the other side of the car. She slipped her minuscule self into the passenger seat, and I showed her the picture.

She flashed a smile of tiny Chiclet teeth. "Oh yeah, I seen him," she said stabbing a blue-lacquered fingernail at Arthur's face. The dread she caught in my expression egged her on and sent her into a fit of witchy laughter.

I looked out the window and told myself to be still. "What's so funny?" I said trying to sound casual.

"Noth ... Nothing," she snorted with laughter.

Her cheap perfume filled the car like a sweet gas. I had a deep desire to hit her. "Come on Ruby. This is important. So you've seen him, okay. Did he come here?"

She howled with laughter again. It was a forced, cruel laugh. "Oh, he *came* here a few times." She watched me, waiting to see if I got the double entendre. I pretended I didn't and kept my countenance in check. She stopped laughing, but her eyes remained amused and calculating. "He your dad or something?" she said, obviously enjoying inflicting pain on someone else for a change.

"No." I turned away. I couldn't look at her. "He's   "

"Christ! Not your husband?" she cackled.

"He's a friend." Friend. The word turned over in my mind. Was Arthur Elliott my friend? I could hear Ansel. *Go looking for a saint and you'll surely find one. There are no saints, only good salesmen.*

Ruby tossed her half-finished cigarette out the window. "Got a smoke?" she asked.

"No, but we could get some. And maybe something to eat?"

"No thanks, gotta work," she said. "And I want to hang out for a bit. See if Dan the Meat Man shows. He's not a dick, just comes to do his own business and sometimes gives me smokes or brings me a burger. He doesn't do us girls. What time is it?"

I looked at my watch. "Ten fifteen."

"He's late. But if Dan shows, your dad will probably show too. So you might want to hang."

"Who's Dan?"

"The Meat Man Dan. Do you know the Meat Man Dan. The Meat Man Dan." She sang the words to the tune of the "Muffin Man" song, and stared out over the dash tapping her feet. "And heeere he comes," she said.

A light-coloured pickup turned slowly into the lot and parked in the shadows. A big man jumped out of the cab and went around to the back where he hopped up onto the truck bed.

"What's he doing?" I asked.

"Unlocking his freezer."

He jumped off the truck bed and ran to the bar's side entrance.

"Watch for your dad. Last time he was here he went to talk to the Meat Man, but when Dan saw him he fucked off outta here. So your dad, he, like, had nothing else to do 'cause Dan drove away, so ... " she paused for effect. "So ... he drove me!"

I kept my eyes on Dan's truck.

"Home!"

I continued to stare straight ahead.

"Really, he just drove me home," she said petulantly. "Okay?"

I breathed a silent sigh of relief. "Okay."

"Paid me for my time. Two hundred bucks to drive me to my place."

I wished Ansel had been here. Hah! One for the Banff All Saints, and zip for the Texas Demons!

"So what's going on? What's in the freezer?" I asked.

"Meat. I told you he's the Meat Man." She studied me for a moment. "You don't get it do you?" I shrugged. "He sells meat?" She huffed in exasperation. "Duh! That's what we call the johns too, Meat Men. So it's funny."

"Oh, okay, I get it. Ha ha. So what kind of meat is he selling?"

"Animal meat," she said slowly. The sarcasm in her little-girl voice did not slip past me. Neither did the fact that she was flying high on something. I watched her out of the corner of my eye as she swayed from side to side, keeping time to her private tune.

"What kind of animal meat?"

"Are you, like, retarded or something? Illegal meat. Moose, deer, shit like that."

"Oh, poached meat." I did feel like an idiot. Arthur! Of course. That's why he's been coming here. By God, I congratulated myself. I am swift. I'm a natural investigative reporter.

"Dan gave me this." Ruby pulled at the silver chain around her neck. A long claw dangled at the end. "It's a grizzly bear claw," she announced. "Here, feel it." I rubbed my fingers down its four-inch length. "Debbie, this Native chick who sometimes works down here, said her grandfather has a whole necklace made out of these that's, like, two-hundred years old or something. Supposed to show strength. Like you're a really good hunter. And the bear's strength or spirit or some fucking thing stays with the person who wears it. I use it as my secret weapon. Scratched a guy's eye out with it once. Well, nearly out."

"It's certainly unique," I said. And at the same time hoped with all my heart that the bear's spirit would, indeed, stick around and protect this child.

"Does Dan sell bear meat?" I asked.

She shrugged and pointed to the bar door. Dan slipped back out and trotted across the lot. I still couldn't get a glimpse of his face. He was wearing a ball cap with the rim pulled down low. There was no sign of anyone else in the parking lot and no one followed him out of the bar. Dan was sitting on the side of the truck bed, his head bent to the task of sorting the freezer's contents. I told Ruby I was going to talk to him.

She grabbed my arm. "Wait, here comes customer number one. Hey, I think it's your dad."

Out my side window I saw a man's dark silhouette emerge from between two parked cars. He was wearing a hooded pullover and a dark field coat that looked just like Arthur's. He also was wearing dark trousers, not one of his colourful kikois. He continued toward the truck, his back to us. There was something odd about his gait, though. It was his arms. He seemed to be walking with outstretched arms, like a sleepwalker.

The man must have said something because Dan suddenly looked up, then stood and lifted a hand in greeting at the approaching figure. Dan's face glowed under the street lamp, and for a second I thought there was something vaguely familiar about him. Before I could get a better look, Dan's hands flew to his face as if shielding himself from a blow.

Ruby gasped. My eyes cut to her. Her blue-shadowed and mascaraed eyes were wide with fright. "Holy fuck, he's got a gun or something," she said.

I turned back and watched the scene play out through the windshield like a slow-motion drive-in movie. Dan The Meat Man slumped forward and clutched his chest. Then his arms flew back and he fell off the side of the truck.

Ruby pulled at my arm. Her childish voice hissed in my ear, "Get down! Jesus. Get down!"

We were face to face, our foreheads nearly touching. Ruby's eyes were closed and she was drawing deep, halting breaths. With each breath she exhaled came the powerful smell of booze and cigarettes.

Tires squealed and light poured in though the windshield. Ruby's breathing became more laboured. "You okay?" I whispered.

"Shut up," she snapped, and dug her fingers into my shoulder. "Don't fuckin' move."

Outside there was silence. I wondered if Dan The Meat Man was dead or dying. "We need to call an ambulance," I whispered.

A car door slammed in the distance. Footsteps echoed across the pavement. People yelled.

Ruby lifted her eyes over my shoulder to the driver's side window. "Shit!" she said, and was out of the car and tearing across the parking lot before I could sit up.

My door opened behind me. I looked over my shoulder expecting to see Arthur. But the man leaning over me was not Arthur.

"Ansel! What are you doing here?"

"Keeping an eye on you." He held out his hand. I accepted it and he helped me out of the car. "You all right?" he said.

Sirens cut the night air, and the parking lot was ablaze with pulsating lights, police cruisers and people running into and out of the hotel.

"I'm okay," I said. "But I don't think that guy is." I motioned across the lot. "Is he dead?"

"I don't know." He slipped his hand under my elbow. "Let's find out."

My mouth was dry as toast and my legs belonged to Gumby as we walked together across the parking lot to where the paramedics were already working on Dan. They'd cut away his shirt. I suppressed a gasp at the sight of the arrow sticking from his chest like a meat thermometer, dark blood pooling at the shaft.

His head lolled to one side. The emergency vehicles' red lights pulsed perversely in the night air, staining crimson the bloodless face of Daniel Peterson, Ansel Rock's hunting guide.

CHAPTER 17

I SWUNG MY CAR INTO THE DOC'S DRIVEWAY. ANSEL ROCK SWUNG HIS truck in right behind me. Nathan Delaware was waiting for us in his cruiser. I opened the electric garage and put the Beetle in for the night. It had been a little balky on the drive home, and I figured it could use a night indoors. Inside the house, I offered Ansel and Nathan coffee. Both declined.

"I'm losing enough sleep as it is," Nathan said. His voice was hoarse and even more grave than usual. "I'd like to get home. So let's make this quick, Hellie, and you tell me how you knew Arthur was going to show at the Baltimore tonight."

"I didn't know," I said. "Someone told me it might be a possibility." Impatience and fatigue in the sergeant's eyes told me I'd be wise to do better than that and fast. I weighed my options. I had two: rat on Miriam or shut up and take the consequences. No contest. "Sorry, Nathan. I'm not going to betray a confidence."

He tapped his pencil against his note pad, no doubt weighing his options.

"Come on, Hellie," Ansel said. "Don't you think you're in enough trouble already?" He was leaning against the doorframe in the kitchen.

"Oh, are you still here?" I said. "Didn't I mention I wasn't speaking to you?" On my way home, the shock had subsided and anger had taken over. Ansel had been following me and I didn't like it. Had he been the one hanging around the backyard? I didn't think he smoked cigarettes. But how would I know?

"You're getting yourself in deeper," Ansel warned.

"Thank you, Mr. Rock. Did you join the police force while I was away?"

Nathan cut in. "Okay. Enough. I spoke to Miriam," he said sharply. "She told me Arthur has been going to the Baltimore for the past month. I'm assuming she told you the same thing."

"I can't reveal my sources. But the real question remains ... " I spun on my heels and faced Ansel. "How did Mr. Rock know where I was going tonight? And isn't it interesting that Daniel Peterson happens to be Ansel's hunting guide?"

Nathan directed his attention to Ansel and waited for him to respond.

Ansel, unmoved, said, "I followed you."

"Isn't there some kind of anti-stalking law, Nathan?" I said.

"Why were you following Hellie, Mr. Rock?"

Ansel's face was impassive. "I was worried about her."

"Bullshit," I said. "You thought I'd lead you to Arthur so you could mete out whatever cowboy vigilante justice you think he's got coming."

"The only one I see engaging in vigilante behavior is your friend, Arthur Elliott. And, yes, I did think you might be meeting with him. And ... I was worried. I told you he's dangerous."

Nathan's head was bouncing back and forth between us like a Wimbledon spectator.

"Oh, and for the record, Nathan," I said, "I did not see the shooter's face."

"Did you, Mr. Rock?" Nathan asked.

Ansel grudgingly conceded he had not. "But the clothes and height were a match."

Nathan turned to me. "Hellie?"

It was my turn to grudgingly concede. "Yeah, looked like his coat." I tried to recover my advantage. "Kind of strange though, eh Ansel? Your hunting guide being a poacher and all?"

"Yes, it is strange and very disturbing. It's usually his brother Becker who guides — "

"Cousin," I said.

"What?"

"Larry said they're cousins." Both men stared at me as if I'd just told a senseless joke. Fatigue suddenly washed over me. "Can I go to bed now?"

"In a minute," Nathan said. "Hellie, after tonight I don't want you to go anywhere or do anything that's connected to Arthur unless you check with me first. That clear?" I nodded. "Mr. Rock is right. That was a very dangerous situation you got yourself into tonight. If that was Arthur, and it's sounding pretty likely it was — "

Something came back to me. "Arthur said his clothes were stolen," I cut in. "When he came back from Calgary, he was wearing his kikoi."

"Was wondering about that," Nathan said. "Cold day for a skirt."

"He was probably lying. Said his clothes were stolen so he'd have an alibi later," Ansel blabbed on.

I turned to Nathan and changed the subject. "What'd you hear about Daniel Peterson? Is he going to live?"

"Too early to tell. We'll know more in the morning. If he makes it through the night, that is," the sergeant added. "If he does, he'll ID the shooter and we can put this to bed."

I told him about Ruby Mist's bear claw. "And I'm wondering if Daniel had something to do with those bear paws in Arthur's cabin."

"Yup. I'm wondering that too," Nathan said.

I didn't like his tone. "Come on," I said. "Bears are Arthur's whole life."

"Yeah, and preaching lies is his life too," Ansel added. "And he'll do just about anything to convince everyone he's right and we hunters are wrong. My guess is that someone, i.e. Daniel, was supposed to drop those paws off in Arthur's cabin, so Arthur could take them to the wardens and the press and convince everyone how his phantom poachers are killing all the bears. At the same time he strengthens his case against bear hunters, since there aren't many bears left now. I'll bet Arthur paid Daniel well for those paws. But something went wrong. The timing got screwed up."

I ignored him. Nathan didn't.

"Not a bad theory," the big cop said. "It's looking like Arthur was meeting Daniel on a regular basis."

I piped up. "Or how about this theory: Arthur was meeting with Daniel to try and get him to stop poaching."

Nathan directed his attention to me. "Mr. Rock claims he has proof that Arthur was up to some pretty shady stuff in Africa."

"Did he also tell you that he believes the Doc was involved in that same shady stuff?" I said.

"He did." Nathan turned and squared off with Ansel. "Which, by the way, Mr. Rock, I find hard to believe. And I'll need some very solid evidence before I pursue that theory."

Oh, but you obviously have no trouble pursuing the theory that Arthur could be in cahoots with a poacher, I thought bitterly, but I said, "Ruby claims the last time Arthur tried to get near him, Daniel took off."

"Maybe their deal went bad, and Daniel knew Arthur had it in for him," Ansel said.

I let my mind play out what I'd seen. Daniel lifted his hand in greeting. Even though I couldn't see his face clearly, I could understand his body language. He wasn't afraid of the person coming toward him. He saw the bow, then he got scared. Not the other way around. Daniel knew his assailant. I had my doubts that Arthur was the assassin. Otherwise, according to Ruby Mist's version of things, Daniel would not have been interested in hanging around to chat with him. But at that moment, I was too tired to argue the point any further. I'd wait, see what else turned up.

"Unless there's something else you need Nathan," I said, "I'm going to bed."

"Just one more thing. Bernie staying here with you?" Nathan asked.

"No."

"Anyone else?"

"No," I said again. "Why do you ask?"

"What time did you head out of town tonight?"

"Around eight."

"Hmm." He scratched absentmindedly at the grey stubble on his chin. "No one else staying with you in the house?"

"If you're referring to Arthur, the answer is still no. Neither he nor anyone else is staying here. Why?" My nerves were frayed and I was about to unravel.

"Drove by about ten," Nathan said. "Rang the bell. No answer. Then I noticed a light on in the attic. Could've sworn I saw a shadow move across the window. Someone was up there."

Suzanna was my immediate thought. But I'd retrieved my key before I left for Calgary. She had summoned me over to pick up Tiger and to choose between two really ugly fake diamond-studded collars and leashes for him. When she left me for a moment to get a bag, I noticed my key hanging on her key rack, so I pocketed it. When she returned, she was so busy telling me how to walk Tiger properly I forgot to tell her I'd taken back the key. My mind raced trying to think up some logical explanation. Bernie didn't have a key. I had the Doc's keys. That left Arthur. As far as I knew, he was the only other person with a key. Unless Suzanna had made a duplicate.

Ansel stood watching, waiting, I was sure, for me to break down and confess that yes, I was hiding Arthur in the attic and that I couldn't take it any longer.

"Must be the ghost of Mrs. Doc," I said trying to sound casual.

"Barbara liked company. She would have answered the door," Nathan returned with a tired grin. "Mind if I take a look around before we leave?"

I said I'd be eternally grateful if he would. I went to the living room where I took a seat on the couch. Ansel stayed in the kitchen, which bugged me though I wasn't sure why. Did I want him to follow me?

Nathan returned a few minutes later.

"All clear?" I asked. As I did, I thought about Tiger and had to admit I kind of wished the little guy was with me. I'd dropped him off at Bernie's before I left for the city; now it was too late to pick him up. As it was, I doubted I would get much sleep.

"Seems to be. It's odd, though," Nathan said. "I rang the bell a few times. No one answered. When I went back to the car, the light was off in the attic. Thought it was you, trying to avoid me. But it couldn't have been you."

"No. It could not have been me."

With that comforting thought, I said good night to Sergeant Delaware and Ansel Rock, and I went upstairs to bed.

CHAPTER 18

I SAT BOLT UPRIGHT, MY BACK RIGID AGAINST THE HEADBOARD, listening. The room was in complete darkness. I'd slept fitfully, waking to the sounds of the house — the pings of the furnace, the drip, drip, drip from the bathroom faucet, a creak above me on the hardwood floors — listening, waiting for whomever Nathan had seen in the attic to return.

Now I thought I heard voices drifting up from downstairs. I leaned forward, my eyes blinking rapidly, as if that would help me hear better. The clock on the bedside table said it was 6:01 a.m. I relaxed, a bit. At least it was morning, though still dark. Somehow whoever was downstairs was far less menacing than someone who comes in the night. Night is the time to be afraid. Not six in the morning.

The voices grew louder. A woman's voice. A man's voice. They were coming up the basement stairs. I was no longer afraid. I was terrified and reached for the phone. Damn. Battery was dead. The voices grew louder still. They weren't whispering, which meant they had to think the house was empty. Just as suddenly, the voices grew faint. A door slammed.

I waited a few seconds. When they didn't come back, I crept down the stairs to the main floor trying to decide my best course of action: Find the phone? Or get the hell out? They were out there, so I decided to find the phone and call the police. Finding the other cordless phone was no easy task in the darkened house. Doc Rivard owned three phones: a wall phone in the hall and two cordless ones I was certain Mrs. Doc hid on me for fun. I'd have to go to the hall.

Light from the street lamps filtered in through the stained glass window above the door and cast the hall in a frail rainbow light. I made it to the phone and picked up the receiver. At the same moment, the front door flew open. I let out a shriek.

Sandy Kole let one out right along with me. Doug barreled in behind her. We all stared in disbelief at one another until our brains quelled our flight-or-fight response.

"Hellie!" Sandy's hand was on her chest. "You scared the life out of me."

"Gee, you scared me too, Sandy. How did you get in here?"

Doug manoeuvred a wooden trough filled with his over-priced fudge past his wife. "Hi ho, Hellie. Sorry we barged in on you. Didn't think you were around. Just going to slip this down to the cold — "

"How did you get in here?" I demanded.

Doug's eyes blinked indignantly. "Suzanna let us in."

I stormed past them and marched barefooted and pajamaed across the street to The Wild Rose, where I pounded my fists on the door. No one answered. I pounded again. Suzanna peeked out the side window. Our eyes met; both of us angry as yellow jacket wasps.

"What is it, for heaven's sake? I was in the bathroom," Suzanna said scrutinizing her door for damage.

"How did you get into my house?"

Her eyes bore through me. It was the word *my* that got her. I did it on purpose. I wondered if she'd heard about the will. If she hadn't she was about to.

"I used your key," she said coolly. "What's the big deal? I didn't think you made it home last night."

"What would make you think that?" I knew the answer. I knew she'd been watching the house and every move I made, every minute of the day and night.

"Lights weren't on when I went to bed. Have you forgotten you gave me — "

"I took it back."

She cut a glance to the spot where the key had hung beside the door-jamb.

"You made a copy, didn't you?" I said.

"I did no such thing."

"Then how did you let Doug and Sandy in? I'm telling the police, Suzanna."

"Go right ahead. I didn't copy your key."

"Then where did you get it?" I said, jumping from one foot to the other. My bare feet were freezing on the frost-covered step, and there wasn't much chance Suzanna was going invite me in to warm up.

"Michael gave me a key long before you showed up."

"Really? Then why would you ask for my spare if you already had your own key?"

"I … er … I misplaced the one Michael gave me, and I just found it."

"That's a lie," I said. "Doc would have told me if he'd given you one."

"Told you! Don't be absurd. He left explicit instructions with me to keep an eye on you and the house. Do you really think he'd entrust his home to you? He didn't even know you."

"You have no idea just how wrong you are, Suzanna. Doc Rivard willed the house to Arthur and me."

Her lips twitched spasmodically.

"Were you in the attic last night?"

"No."

"You're lying. Give me that key."

She crossed her arms over her chest.

"Fine, I'm calling the police."

She let out a shrill, hysterical laugh. "I don't think they'll be too interested. They think you murdered Michael. And so do I." She stepped out the door. I took a step back and promptly fell down the three concrete steps. I landed hard and skinned my arm. Suzanna turned away and went back into her house. "Get off my property," she said and slammed the door.

Doug and Sandy were hurrying to their vehicle when I came roaring back across the street. Doug gunned the engine and took off.

I banged around the kitchen in a rage trying to find a nonexistent stash of coffee beans. When I was close to tears I finally found a package of year-old coffee I'd swiped off a housekeeping cart at the Rim Rock Hotel. I didn't care if it was petrified, I held it up like a trophy. While I waited for the water to drip through my Jurassic coffee, I fumed and speculated about how many times Suzanna had been in the house without my knowledge. How long had she been in possession of that key? Had she just copied mine? Or had the Doc really given her one? No. He would have told me.

So, if Suzanna was roaming around the house when I wasn't home, the question was why. Was she merely checking up on me, or was she was looking for something? Perhaps Suzanna already knew what was in Arthur's root cellar and she was looking for more of the same. But why?

Armed with a cup of coffee, I headed upstairs to the attic. The skinny, half-sized door creaked open when I gave it a light touch. Through the small window on the other side of the room, a streetlight cast a single square of white light on the floor. The light switch was behind the door, or so I thought. This was a room I had been in only twice. Once when the Doc gave me the grand tour and once during my first solo night in the house when I was certain someone, a non-ghostly someone, was up there pacing the attic floor. I called Des because I was too embarrassed to call the police. We investigated the attic together. No one was there, of course. Or no one we could see, at any rate. Now I wondered if those sounds had been Suzanna. But was it possible for her to sneak in and out without me noticing? Yes, it was. This is a big house and the stairs to the attic are on the second floor, on the opposite side from my bedroom. She could have slipped in when I was asleep. And the night I'd called Des over, if Suzanna had been in the house, she could have easily gone out the back door when I was waiting for Des in the front.

I found the light switch and was startled to see a person standing on the other side of the room — a headless person! It was one of Mrs. Doc's old dress forms. Now I could tell Nathan I'd just cleared up the mystery of his nocturnal sighting. I could not, however, explain the light being turned on and off.

Near the dress form was an old desk pushed up against the wall. I opened a couple of drawers, each stuffed with old files and papers. I closed them and spied two worn leather suitcases stacked in the corner. Both were empty. Various spots along the walls were patched with swipes of plaster — the only remaining signs of the animal heads that had once hung there. There were no closets. In fact, there really didn't seem to be much of anything in that room.

I sat on one of the suitcases and considered the possibility that Arthur was letting himself in the house when I wasn't around. But why? Did I believe he was capable of murder? No. I did not. Yet, Arthur didn't have an alibi. No one knew where he was the night the Doc died. Now, after what had happened to Daniel Peterson, I was sure Nathan was even more suspicious of Arthur and me, and I wondered if he suspected Arthur and I killed the Doc. We certainly had motive — the house, the money. Arthur and I both made good suspects. Now with Arthur gone, I made a prime suspect.

I considered my options. If I told Nathan about the key and he confronted Suzanna, she'd simply say the Doc gave her one and twist things so that I'd look all the more guilty. All I could prove was that she'd opened the door for Sandy and Doug. They were the trespassers, not Suzanna.

And there was another twist. If Suzanna had a key, that meant she'd had access to the house the night the Doc died, and access to the phone. Nathan had said that someone made a call from this house to the Doc's hotel the night he died. That someone was either Suzanna or Arthur. My money was on Suzanna; now I needed to find out if I was right.

The attic's low ceiling suddenly pressed in on me. I hurried out and down the stairs to the kitchen. I called Bernie and asked her to come over with Tiger. When she arrived, I told her about my encounter with Suzanna and about the key.

"I knew it! That witch is not to be trusted," Bernie said. "She's been after the Doc for years. She's always wanted to be Mrs. Doc Rivard. Boy did she make a play for the Doc right after Barb died."

"I guessed that," I said. "She must have been furious when Arthur moved in instead of her."

"Got that right. She thought she was being real cagey when she'd point out things Arthur had done wrong, or when she'd tell the Doc how he had to careful not let himself be taken advantage of by hangers-on."

"Not mentioning any names, of course," I said with a smile.

"Of course. Like the Doc couldn't see through her. But he was always kind to her."

We were in the front room by the fireplace, sipping coffee and nibbling the fresh pastries Bernie, bless her, had picked up on her way over. Tiger was curled up at his place in front of the fire.

"She wants this house," Bernie said. "And I'm so glad she's not going to get it. Does she know it's been left to you?"

"Does now," I said and popped the last bite of a blueberry Danish into my mouth. At the same moment, a feeling of utter fatigue swept over me.

"What's wrong, friend?" Bernie said, watching me.

"Aw, Bern, I can't take much more of this. I've got four articles I'm supposed to be writing, and I haven't typed a word. The police consider me a suspect. And now either my psycho neighbour or my missing neighbour is prowling around the place when I'm not here, and maybe even when I am here."

"That's really creepy. Are you going to tell Nathan?"

"Not yet."

"Are you sure that's wise?" Bernie said.

"I don't really have anything to tell him. I don't have proof that she was in here."

Bernie nodded thoughtfully. I sat back and stared at the fire and said, "I've been thinking about something, Bern. When you just said you wonder how much Suzanna wants this house — "

Bernie sat up, ears perked. "Yes."

"Something's been nagging at me. The night the Doc died, I got home from your place at about eleven thirty. Suzanna's car wasn't there. Nor was it there an hour later when I went to bed. Reason I know is because I heard some people out front and looked out the window. There were no cars on the street."

"So?"

"So, the next morning when I ran over there after we found the Doc, her car was back. She had to have come back in the dark. But Suzanna won't drive at night. She told me that herself."

"Maybe she didn't leave Banff. Visiting a friend? Or she got back in the morning just before you ran over there."

"Maybe. I know it's a long shot, but later that morning when I went to get her I noticed something."

"What?"

"Her reaction. I thought she was in shock."

"I'm sure she was."

"Of course. But there was something else. I saw it in her eyes again this morning. It was fear."

Bernie offered me the box of pastries. "What do you think she's afraid of?"

I accepted a croissant. "I don't know. And I'm probably reading too much into this," I said smearing marmalade on the bun. "The woman just threw me down her stairs. I want to believe she's guilty of something."

"Me too," Bernie said.

"Well, maybe she didn't really throw me down the stairs. I kind of slipped."

Bernie nodded. "So the point is, much as we'd like to, can we actually believe she's capable of murder?"

"Like I said, it's a long shot."

"Besides, how could she have got the body, the Doc's body" — Bernie lowered her voice — "under the gazebo?"

"True. And Nathan did say he died under there. It's not likely the two of them crawled under there together and then he just happened to die."

Bernie was up pacing the floor. Tiger trotted behind her. "Are you going to tell Nathan about this? About the key?" she said.

"Not yet. If I start in on Suzanna, he might think I'm trying to take the heat off myself. All she did was let Sandy and Doug in the house. As far as I know, Suzanna didn't even step over the threshold. Looks like a neighbourly gesture. And she'll just say the Doc gave her that key. What's Nathan going to do? Arrest her for doing me a favour?"

Bernie stopped pacing. Tiger followed suit. "But she was in here sneaking around last night."

"We don't know that. It's suspicious, yes." I had an idea. "Do you have a picture of Suzanna?" I asked.

"I hardly," Bernie said. "But I can get you one." She went to the hall and returned with the phone book, open to a page with an advertisement for The Wild Rose B&B. Next to it was a photo of Suzanna LaChaine.

"Perfect. Aren't you clever," I said. "Now let's see if we can put Suzanna anywhere near the Doc's hotel."

"Does this mean you're going to Calgary?"

"Probably, but I need to make a couple of calls first, and then I'll need your help and Paul's. See, I'm not really supposed to leave Banff, and I'm definitely not supposed to leave if leaving has anything to do with finding Arthur."

Bernie looked at me suspiciously. "What happened, Hellie?"

"Long story. I'll tell you after I make my calls." I was on my way down the hall when the phone rang. It was Ansel.

"Morning," he said. "Just checking in to see how you're doing."

"I'm fine, thanks."

"Good. That's very good," he said.

A pregnant pause ensued. While I was waiting for Ansel to tell me why he really called, I noticed a couple of faxes had come in. One was junk and the other was from my editor at *McMillan* looking for a draft.

"I'm planning another hunting trip," Ansel finally said. "Like to head out tomorrow. So if you're — "

"Setting another trap, Mr. Rock?"

"No," he said. "I paid a lot of money to be here and I'm hoping to get some value for my dollars."

"Hmm. If Arthur shows up, as I'm sure you're hoping he will, that'll certainly get you some value."

An exasperated sigh came down the line. "Anyway, if you're interested in coming along — "

"Oh, I'm interested."

"Good. Because I'm interested too. Keep an eye on you this way."

"That's right," I returned. "When do we leave?"

"Tomorrow, early. I'm meeting with Larry tonight."

"You're using Larry? Not the Petersons?" I was being cruel.

"I had no idea what they were up to, Hellie. And for your information, it doesn't look like Becker was involved in that meat selling business with his cousin Daniel."

"Nathan tell you that?"

"No. John spoke to Becker this morning at the hospital. He's pretty angry about his cousin's stupidity."

"How is Daniel?"

"Looks like he's going to make it. That's all I know."

"So why aren't you using Becker?"

"He's running another camp right now. Anyway, I'm meeting with Larry this evening. Thought you and I could have dinner first."

I smiled in spite of myself. Then told myself to knock it off. This man was not to be trusted or smiled upon. "Sorry, I'm pretty tied up for the rest of the day and early evening."

"Tied up with anything I should know about?"

"No. And Ansel, quit following me."

"You could have got yourself hurt last night."

I scoffed. "I think I'm in more danger right here in my own neigh-bourhood," I said brushing gentle fingers along my scraped arm. "And I'm pretty sure my well-being is not the reason you're following me, Ansel."

"You might be surprised."

"I'm sure I would be."

He said he'd call me later with more details. We rang off, then I dialled the Marriott hotel in Calgary. The hotel operator told me that the clerk and doorman who'd been on duty the night I specified would be in later to work the evening shift.

There was one more person I was interested in talking to. A second call to Peterson's Outfitters in Exshaw got me through to Mrs. Becker Peterson, who said Becker would be delighted to be interviewed for a hunting story, since he's always up for that kind of free advertising. Mrs. Peterson then gave me explicit directions to Becker's camp and even ex-plained that Becker was at the hospital in Calgary visiting a sick relative, but would be back at his camp that afternoon.

I joined Bernie and Tiger in the kitchen and filled Bernie in on Daniel Peterson and what had happened the night before at the Baltimore Hotel."

"And now you're going to Becker Peterson's hunting camp?"

"Uh, yeah. I was hoping you and Paul could cover for me if Nathan starts looking for me."

Bernie groaned. "I really don't want you to go. But since I know you will, I'll tell Paul what's going on. And don't even think about arguing with me because I'm coming with you."

CHAPTER 19

DISTANT GUNFIRE SLICED THE WARM AUTUMN AIR. BERNIE, TIGER AND I froze on the trail, and listened.

"Must be getting close," Bernie said, her eyes scanning the valley.

We were hiking through the Burnt Timber Creek region — a wilderness and hunting area that borders Banff National Park. Next to us on the narrow path was a boulder, and on it Bernie was spreading the hunter's map we'd picked up on our way out of town.

"We're about half a mile from Becker's camp," Bernie said. "And we're standing in wildlife management unit number four one four."

"Which means?"

"Which means you can hunt black bears and grizzlies here in the Spring."

"Really? How do you know that?"

"Says so at the bottom."

"Ah." I leaned in for a closer look at the map. "Miriam's cabin is a few miles due east," I said. "Wonder how often Becker runs into Arthur up here?"

"You mean how often does Arthur run into Becker," Bernie corrected me. "I'm sure he picked Miriam's cabin specifically for it's great location, location, location."

"Have you been there, Bern? To the cabin?"

"Once. Doc took me up," Bernie said busying herself with Tiger's leash.

"So, uh … see anything unusual?"

Bernie kept her focus on the dog. "Like what?"

"Unusual wildlife?"

She bit her lip, and telltale splotches blossomed at the base of her throat.

"Thanks for not telling me," I said.

"I couldn't. I promised," she said defensively.

"No, Bern, I mean it. Thank you. You're a good friend. I know I can trust you with anything."

Her face softened to a humble smile. She folded the map and leaned against the rock. Tiger whined at her feet and she scooped him up into her arms. "It was the most incredible thing I'd ever seen," she said. "Paul was there too. We asked Arthur to stop feeding Lulu. I think he wanted to. But she kept coming back, and then she had the cubs and started bringing them to him too."

"He told me he's not going to feed them anymore," I said.

"Good. I hope he means it." Bernie looked up to the sky to where huge gray-fringed clouds collided and drifted apart. "God's bumper cars," she said absently. "Looks like rain."

"Bern, I think Daniel Peterson is poaching bears. Or he's connected to someone who is," I blurted. "And I'm betting Arthur knew it."

"What makes you say that?"

"A couple of things. Ruby Mist, the little girl I met at the Baltimore?"

"With the boots," Bernie said.

"Yes. Along with the boots, she was wearing a grizzly claw she claims Daniel gave her. I'll bet she showed Arthur that claw when they met. And when I saw Arthur at Miriam's cabin he said, 'They're taking the bears.'"

"They?" Bernie said.

"He wouldn't say anything else. But Ruby told me the last time Arthur was at the Baltimore, Daniel took off when he saw him. That would have been just before the Doc showed up dead."

"And bear paws showed up in Arthur's cabin."

"Exactly."

"You're thinking it's the Petersons?"

"Finger's pointing that way for me. Arthur obviously knew Daniel was selling poached meat. So he was probably thinking that even if Daniel wasn't poaching bears himself, he might know who was."

"One crook leads to another," Bernie said.

"Right."

"And if he thought Daniel was poaching bears that would explain why Arthur shot him."

"I'm still not convinced it was Arthur who shot him. Ruby said she's seen Arthur more than once around the hotel. If Arthur was the shooter, why would he have waited so long?"

Bernie shrugged. "But he did admit to shooting at Ansel."

"True. But you know what else is strange? Until the funeral, I don't remember ever seeing the Petersons around the house, or anywhere else for that matter. They showed up when Ansel Rock showed up."

"Hmm, that is interesting," Bernie said as she put the dog down. She dug a Tupperware container from her pack, filled it with water from a bottle and placed it on the ground for Tiger, who happily lapped it up.

"So, uh … exactly what are you going to say to Becker Peterson once we get there?" Bernie asked as she put the map back in her pack.

"I'm going to tell him what I told his wife, that I'm a writer doing research for a hunting article."

"Clever."

"Not really, since it's pretty close to the truth. And while I'm at it, I'll ask him if he's seen Arthur and tell him that I don't think Arthur shot his cousin."

"That ought to loosen him up. Especially if Daniel's spreading that it was Arthur."

"I'll say that finding Arthur will help his cousin."

"How so?"

"Arthur might lead us to the real shooter."

Bernie gave me a dubious look.

"Okay, then I'll just have to think of something else. Or perhaps you will, Bern."

"Yeah, or perhaps we'll get our heads shot off."

"Let's think positively, Bern."

She moaned, and I collected Tiger's water bowl before we set off down the trail.

Within the half-hour we entered a clearing and stopped in our tracks to gaze at the scene that lay before us. Tiger stretched his neck out as far as it would go while keeping his paws planted firmly. His hypersensitive nose twitched in the wind, picking up the scent of death.

About a hundred yards from Tiger's nose was a little village made up of about half a dozen army tents. Five or six men, all dressed up in full camouflage gear, stood around a fire sipping coffee from tin cups. Laundry flapped on lines in the breeze. Hunting bows were set against picnic tables, and white-tailed deer carcasses hung stiff from tree limbs.

Clouds parted overhead. The sun slipped out and cast golden streaks through the pine bows that glistened on the dead animals' cedar-toned flanks. The men were all staring at us. One lifted a hand and gave a friendly wave.

"We're okay," Bernie said. "Looks like they're allies."

We entered the camp. I made the necessary introductions and said we were looking for Becker Peterson. One of the fellows pointed behind him to a treed path and said, "Last I saw, he was down at the creek."

Another man offered us a cup of coffee. Bernie and I accepted a cup and, after a sip or two of the fine dark brew, agreed it rivalled anything Starbucks had to offer. We soon learned that it was indeed Starbucks coffee that one of the hunters, a lawyer from California, had helicoptered in the day before, along with a pizza and a case of Scotch.

We took our coffee and followed the lawyer down the path through thick brush until we popped out on the shore of a rushing creek. A burly guy, with a massive head and a grim countenance, was wading toward us through thigh-deep water, hands stretched above his head brandishing a heavy rifle. His determined, almost threatening expression was intensified by the black greasepaint smeared under his eyes and over his cheeks.

"That's Becker," the lawyer said.

"Thanks," we said, and he left us to watch the big man make his way through the water.

"Here comes Marty," Bernie said under her breath.

"Who's Marty?" I whispered.

"Martin Sheen, *Apocalypse Now*. Went into the jungle in Nam. Set up a freaky camp then went berserk."

"Thanks, Bern."

Becker spied us. "Help you?" he said, dragging his camouflaged bulk out of the water.

"I'm Hellie MacConnell and this is Bernie Church."

He nodded at Bernie. "Think I've seen you around Banff. What the hell is that?" He was referring to Tiger.

"A beagle," Bernie said.

"Yeah, I see that. What's he doing in my camp? Are you lost or something?"

Mrs. Peterson apparently hadn't told her husband about our nice conversation.

"Hellie's a writer for *McMillan* magazine and I'm her research assistant," Bernie announced.

"I already told the press I don't want to talk to anyone about that idiot cousin — "

"Hellie's covering a big hunting story," Bernie said. "The bighorn auction."

Way to go, Bern.

He turned his hard gaze on me. "Wait a second. Well shoot me with a ball of my own shit! You're that reporter woman Ansel Rock took down the mountain after that little freak friend of yours tried to kill him. What the hell are you doin' here?"

I put my hand up, palm facing Becker. "It was all just an unfortunate misunderstanding. Mr. Rock and I have straightened the whole thing out."

He crossed his arms over his big chest. "Is that so?" His tone told me he wasn't buying a word of it. "You still haven't said why you're here." His fingers drummed impatiently against his forearm.

"I was hoping I could ask you a few questions about hunting. Depending how it goes, I may quote you in the story. And ... " I thought I'd better be straight. "I was at the Baltimore last night."

He hesitated, and in that split second something passed over Becker Peterson's face. Shock? Worry? Maybe. I couldn't tell.

"Yeah? So you saw your friend try to murder my cousin." He shivered against the cold that must have been seeping into his bones from his soaked pants.

"I did see someone shoot your cousin, but I don't think it was Arthur."

He leaned against a tree and said, "Come on, lady. It was him. Why'd you come here?"

"I told you, I'm doing research. And I'm hoping you might help me. I need to find Arthur Elliott."

"Oh, yeah? Well I don't need to find him. He's cost my company Ansel Rock."

This was interesting. Ansel said the only reason he wasn't using Becker was because Becker was busy, not because he'd fired him. "I think you've got that wrong," I said. "Your cousin Daniel is the one most likely responsible for costing you Ansel."

Becker narrowed his gaze at me. "Well if Arthur Elliot hadda kept his nose out of other people's business ... " He bit off the words. "Look, that little freak has cost me plenty."

"I'm just wondering if you've seen him lately." I motioned with my arms. "Out here, anywhere."

He pushed off from the tree and took a step toward me. "Now why in hell would I want to help you?"

"Hellie could get Ansel Rock back for you," Bernie blurted. "She's still covering the story. In fact, they've become very close." I stepped on her foot. She didn't flinch. "You help us, Hellie helps you." Bernie crossed her arms and tugged her foot out from under mine.

Becker clicked his tongue and eyed us both. "That right?" he said to me. "You can square things with Ansel?"

I swallowed and tried to get some saliva going in my mouth. "I'll do what I can." My neck suddenly felt very hot. "How's Daniel?"

"Not too good. The arrow sliced through his chest and stuck in his lung."

I winced. "Was he able to tell you anything about what happened?"

Becker avoided my gaze and stared out to the water.

"Did he say it was Arthur?"

He looked back at me. "You have any idea how much damage one of those things can do to a person?"

"After seeing those dead deer you've got hanging back there, yeah, I think I might. And I'm truly sorry about your cousin," I added.

Becker hesitated again and sucked at his teeth. "Know what your Arthur did last spring?"

He's avoiding the question, I thought. Bernie gave me a sideways glance. She'd caught it too.

"Had a good group I was takin' up to hunt black bear around Rocky Mountain House, and that little fool and his idiot friend are jumpin' out of shrubs asking to get themselves killed."

I assumed the friend he was referring to was Miriam.

"And then there was the bait — "

"Steaks are on, Becker," a female voice said. Behind us a woman had appeared on the path. She had jet-black hair piled loosely on her head, olive skin and high cheekbones. Except for the hunting attire, she could have passed for a fashion model.

"Good," Becker said. "I'm starved."

She gave Bernie and me a shy smile, and said, "Hi, I'm Julie Sands."

"Hi Julie," Bernie and I said.

"Any relation to Mike Sands? The guide?" I said.

"I'm his wife, and — "

"They're reporters," Becker said.

Bernie turned back to Becker. "What's this about bait?"

Becker shivered against the cold. "When we were hunting black bear," he said. "Arthur and his friend would collect all the bear bait. Then they'd get real cute and replace it with fucking flowers."

"I'm not sure I get it," Bernie said. "You put out traps?"

"No," Becker snapped. "We — "

Julie turned to him and said in a soft, shy voice, "You should get out of those wet pants, Becker."

"Only if you help me, darlin'," he said through another involuntary shiver. He hooked a finger into a side pocket of Julie's hunting pants.

With narrowed eyes and fists clenched at her sides, Julie slowly turned away from him. Becker's hand dropped lazily from her hip, but his leering gaze remained fixed on her backside, and a satisfied smirk spread across his face as if he were actually waiting for her to comply.

It appeared that Julie worked for Becker, and I wondered why if this was the kind of crap she had to put up with. He finally took his eyes off her and started up the path back to camp, undoing his shirt as he went.

Julie rolled her eyes at me in an attempt to hide her embarrassment and brush it off. But her jaw was as tight as her fists as she spoke. "When people hunt bears," she explained, "they set bait out. Meat and stuff to lure the bear to it."

"And then you shoot it?" I said.

"No. We take a fucking picture and send it to National Geographic," Becker bellowed over his shoulder.

"That sounds fair." I couldn't help myself.

Becker charged back down the path toward me like an angry bull. "Look, if you're one of them goddamn enviro — "

Julie's eyes shot from Becker to me and back again. "It's ... it's okay, Becker," she said. "Everyone has an opinion."

"Not in my camp they don't." Becker spat the words. He took another couple of steps and closed the distance between us. My nose was within an inch of his soggy chest and a five-inch grizzly bear claw suspended from a heavy silver chain. I backed off slowly like a smart cat retreating from a fight she knows she'll never win.

"Julie, show these girls out," Becker said.

"I was going to give them something to eat," Juile said. "They've hiked in quite a ways." Her voice was timid, as if she was asking permission rather than making the statement.

Becker didn't answer. He started back up the path.

"That's okay, Julie," I said. "No need to feed us. But would you mind answering a few questions? Then we'll be on our way."

"Sure," is what she said, but her nervous fingers worrying her wedding ring suggested she was thinking otherwise.

Becker was halfway up the trail. I called after him. "Becker," I said. "You didn't answer my question. Did Daniel say it was Arthur Elliott who shot him last night?"

He stopped, but didn't turn around. "Course. Who else would he say it was?" Now he turned. "And as far as that moron cousin of mine goes, I didn't know nothin' about the shit he's been selling. I don't even know where he got it. I run a tight camp. Ansel knows that. So you remind him for me."

"Will do," I said. This time I didn't feel my neck or cheeks heat up. Lying was coming easier.

When Becker was gone, I turned to Julie. "I'm wondering if you've seen Arthur or if you've heard anything about him lately from," I shrugged, "maybe some other hunters?"

She shook her head. "Sorry."

It was clear Julie didn't have anything to tell us about Arthur, or perhaps she didn't want to tell us anything. I wrote down my phone number and handed it to her.

"If you do see or hear anything about him, could you call me?"

Again, she said, "Sure." But I had the impression the piece of paper was headed for the firepit.

"Well, thanks," I said.

"Yeah, thanks, Julie," Bernie said, and we left.

"Well, that was pretty much a bust," Bernie said. "And we still have to get to Calgary and back to Banff before Nathan knows you're gone."

We were just outside the camp. Tiger was watering a tree and I was looking back idly calculating how long it was going to take to get to the Marriott Hotel, when I saw a silver-haired man come out of one of the tents.

"I wouldn't say our visit here was a complete bust, Bern. That's John Morrow."

CHAPTER 20

IT WAS NEARLY NINE O'CLOCK WHEN WE MADE IT BACK HOME. BERNIE and I had grabbed a quick bite in the city. Then we dropped by the Marriott with the picture of Suzanna to show the desk clerk and the doorman who'd been on duty the night the Doc had been there. The doorman's response held the most promise. He was sure he remembered seeing a woman who fit Suzanna's description, wearing all black, enter the hotel around one a.m. "Even had a black scarf tied over her head," he said. "Looked just like Jackie O."

Now I was pretty certain it was Suzanna who had made the call to the Marriott from the Doc's phone because I was almost positive the mystery woman in black was her. The problem was I wasn't sure what to do with the information. During the drive home Bernie voted to tell Nathan straight away. I had something else in mind, but that would have to wait.

"I'll take Tiger out back for a quick squirt before he goes to bed," Bernie said. While she was putting on his leash, I checked my answering machine. There was one message. I pressed the button:

"Hi, Hellie. It's me, Danny. Uh, I … um, I'll try you again. Don't call me."

My heart skipped a beat. Something was wrong. "Damn," I said.

The phone rang.

"Danny?" I said when I picked it up.

"Hellie! Moose here."

It was hard to hear him over the loud music and the people shouting and singing in the background.

"What do you want Larry?"

"Plan to sleep in tomorrow. No trip. Me and the Rock are partying instead," he giggled. "And since I know you won't have a date or anything tonight, come by my joint. Bring booze," he laughed and hung up.

I blew out an exasperated breath. The day seemed to be stretching into an eternity.

I dialled the Springs hotel and asked for Ansel's room. I intended to find out what Larry was talking about and get the word on whether or not we were going hunting. I also intended to find out what John Morrow was doing at Becker Peterson's camp. Becker's camp wasn't that big. I suspected the only way we'd managed to avoid each other was because John had made sure we did.

The operator came on the line. "I'm sorry, Mr. Rock is not in his room. Would you like to leave a message?"

"Uh, no, thanks. I'll try later."

Bernie came back in with Tiger, who looked about ready to pass out from his long day. I tucked him into his bed by the fireplace.

"Ansel's not in his room," I said to Bernie. "So I guess I better go over to Larry's and see what's going on. I can't imagine the big Texan's partying with Larry, but … " I threw up my hands. "Anything seems possible today."

"I'll come with you," she said and looked back at Tiger who was sleeping soundly. "So, uh, are we going to return him to Larry?"

"Not right now," I said. "There's a party going on over there. He'd get trampled."

"Yeah. You're probably right. You can do it later," she said, not bothering to suppress her knowing smile.

***

Pearl Jam's molar-rattling beat pounded the night air as Bernie and I sidestepped young bodies strewn along the steps of Larry's palatial party palace. We entered the cavernous living room and squeezed our way into the thick of the party. Fresh-faced college kids in various states of dress and undress lined the open teak staircase — a randy choir belting out bawdy tunes between swigs of beer and tokes of pot. Young tanned women, some sporting only the briefest bikinis, sat beside other equally tanned young men in, God help us all, tiny thong bathing suits. Others were clad in warmer après-hiking, climbing and biking wear — wind pants, tights and snowflake-patterned sweaters.

In the middle of five thousand square feet of open, rustic but elegant space a winding staircase ascended to Larry's infamous Love Loft. Notwithstanding the innumerable salacious invitations Larry had extended me, I prided myself on never having seen The Loft where, according to legend, the Party Moose treated his female guests to hot tub soaks, hot oil massages and sexual gymnastics.

Larry was apparently in the midst of renovations. A sign that read: "Out of Bounds/Construction Zone," was tacked to a permanent gate at the top of the stairs. The gate was always locked, or so I was told. And anyone caught beyond it without invitation risked immediate expulsion from the Moose's crib.

Bernie and I stood on the bottom step and watched a man climb over the low gate, then pick his way down each riser, past girls and boys young enough to be his grandchildren. When he reached us on the landing I said, "You must be a very special friend of Larry's, Mr. Morrow."

"Oh. Hello, Hellie," he said with a smile. "Why's that?" He had to practically yell to be heard over the music.

I leaned close to him and said, "Not too many make it up to Larry's loft, and those who do are always female."

John chuckled. The music stopped and he could speak at a normal level. "I was having a look at his renovations. This is quite a house."

"Thinking of buying in Banff, again?"

His smile remained cordial, though he didn't respond to my comment, and turned his attention to Bernie. I made the introductions and they exchanged a handshake.

"Looks like we're on the same travel schedule today, John," I said evenly.

"It does," he returned. "Becker mentioned you were at his camp. We must have just missed each other."

"Not quite. What were you doing out there?" I asked bluntly.

"Meeting with Becker. I was trying to get some information."

"About Arthur or me? Or both of us?"

"No." His brow furrowed. "Haven't you heard?"

"What?"

We were interrupted when a very young, very drunk woman approached us. "Hi, I'm Tony," she said. "Want a hit?" Tony was wearing a teddy bear patterned sweater and size two black tights. She blew out a plume of smoke and waved a joint in my face.

When I shook my head, she offered it to John Morrow.

He smiled pleasantly and said, "I don't think so, but thanks."

"Aw you guys are no fun," Tony said, and then staggered away.

"Heard what?" I said to John.

John's face darkened. "About Ansel's bighorn."

"What about it?"

"It was taken. Hikers found the carcass. The head was missing. But we know it's the ram. Looks like poachers. Just heard myself this afternoon. So I went out to Becker's to ask him some questions. Police and wardens did the same."

"Becker must not have been too happy to see you," I said.

"I told him we weren't blaming him. I don't think Becker was involved in what Daniel's been up to. But Ansel can't afford to be associated with ... "

"Potential poachers." I finished his sentence. "Do you know when the ram was killed?"

John shrugged. "Within the past twenty-four hours."

"Then it couldn't have been Daniel," I said.

"No, it could not."

The music started up again. John slipped his hand under my elbow and we went to a quieter spot near the front door. Bernie had moved off to the kitchen.

"That's too bad," I said. "I mean, about the sheep. Is Ansel still going out tomorrow?"

John looked at me as if I was daft. "Hellie, this has been a terrible blow for him. He's taking this very hard."

"I'm sure he is, but I'm equally sure there are lots more big rams out there."

"You don't understand the situation. And at the moment, I think it's best if you leave Ansel alone."

"Is he here?"

I heard my name being called above the din of the music. Bernie was by the fireplace, which separated the kitchen from the rest of the main floor, waving me over.

"Please, Hellie. He's not doing well."

"I'll try not to upset him," I said and joined Bernie in the kitchen.

"Larry's outside," Bernie said.

We followed a drunken conga line of girls dancing their way out the back patio doors. In the yard, another swell of human life spilled off the deck and into the hot tub, where their wet heads glistened under patio lanterns.

Next to me a gas heater hissed above my head. The warmth from the bodies, coupled with the heaters, made Larry's backyard an unseasonably humid atrium.

A voice belonging to The Party Moose himself called out: "It's luge time!" A snow mogul was piled high to meet the top of a six-foot ladder, where Larry stood poised with a bottle of Blue Curacao in one hand and a bottle of vodka in the other. I'd heard rumors Larry trucked in snow from a Canmore arena, but I'd had no idea why. Now I did.

"Booze luge!" Larry screamed. He poured a stream of the clear liquor down a foil trough fashioned like a thin slide that ran down the length of the snow pile. "Glacier shooter!" Larry yelled and let a stream of the Curacao chase the vodka. Light from the heaters reflected off the foil and the sapphire liquid to create the image of a glacier-fed stream trickling down the mountain slope to where it landed with a splash into the gaping mouth of Ansel Rock, who was down on his knees, head tilted back under the base of the booze luge.

"Way to go, Mystery Dude!" another male spectator screamed. Others joined in and chanted, "Go, go, go, Mystery Dude!"

The scene was embarrassingly reminiscent of a frat house movie I'd had to live through while on an equally embarrassing date.

"Mystery Dude takes all!" Larry screamed. "He takes all! Okay ladies, give the man his prize."

Ansel Rock spread his arms and accepted victory kisses from two very young women. I felt a pang of something in my chest.

Bernie's gaze cut from Ansel to me then back to Ansel. "Uh, maybe we should go, Hellie. I think we're a little too sober for this crowd."

"I think you're right," I said not taking my eyes off Ansel. I didn't know him well. I did, however, think I knew enough to know this was completely out of character. Ansel Rock was not a partier. He was a straight shooter, long on pride and even longer on doing the right thing.

"Hey, hey. I am a man blessed tonight." Larry was off his perch and bearing down on us. "Hellie and Bernie, together at last with the Party Moose." He threw a heavy arm across my shoulders and hauled me toward the lawn. An unlit cigarette hung from his damp lips. "You're next, Hellcat. It's the booze luge for you. An experience not to be missed."

Out of the corner of my eye I could see Ansel was still accepting his congratulatory smooches. I didn't think he'd seen me yet, and I didn't want him to. I unwound myself from Larry and pulled him by the front of his shirt to a quieter corner of the deck.

"Hey, hey, Hellie, babe. What's this? Are you still trying to get me alone?" He leaned in close, breathing the sweet acrid smell of booze in my face. I placed my hand on his chest to stop him from making contact.

"Larry, don't call me babe. I'm not one of your sixteen-year-old dates of the weekend."

"Hey, don't worry, Hel. You still look good."

"Larry ... you are ... " I blew out a long breath. "Never mind." I lowered my voice. "Are we still going tomorrow?"

Larry giggled. "There's been a change of plans. Major Dad's not going anywhere except the hot tub."

"Are you sure, Larry?"

"I'm sure. Look at the guy. He's consumed at least a twenty-six. No one defeats the booze luge. Not even the Texan. Farthest he'll be draggin' his sorry ass tomorrow morning will be the Springs' spa. Drowning his sorrows, our Mr. Rock is. Because Mary stole his little lamb, baa, baa, baa." Larry giggled.

I glanced over at the booze luge. Ansel was on his feet now, his arms draped over the shoulders of the two girls whose combined ages would not equal his own.

"I don't think that's all that's wrong, Larry," I said in Ansel's defense, surprising myself in process. "He's got a lot on his mind."

Larry backed off and tried to focus on me. "You're pretty impressed with the ol' General aren't you, Hellie? Got a little crush on him?"

I felt my cheeks flare. "Give it a rest, Larry." My voice cracked and I cleared my throat. Bernie was trying, but not particularly hard, to suppress a grin. "I just want to know if there's any chance we'll be going tomorrow."

"Ask him," Larry said, jabbing a thumb in Ansel's direction. The Texan was now leaning against the deck railing, his back to us, with his two young friends tucked one under each arm like toys he'd won at a fair. "Hmm, looks like you got competition, Hellie," Larry said with a snort. "Young competition." He giggled and staggered off to the hot tub, where he threw himself, clothes, cigarette and all, headfirst into the steaming water.

As Bernie and I came up behind Ansel, we could just hear one of the young women flanking him saying, "My dad's a hunter too."

I took a silent step closer to eavesdrop.

"Yeah right," the other girl said. "If you count shooting magpies in your backyard."

"He hunts other stuff too," she countered.

"That a fact? Like what? He a big game hunner?" Ansel slurred.

"I guess. He shoots ducks. And I hate it when he brings them home."

"Why?" Ansel said with that kind of exaggerated astonishment only a drunk can muster.

"Because it's, like, yuck. I'm a vegan. And it's soooo gross. I refuse to park my car in the garage when he's got them hanging all over the place. I feed ducks at the park. They're, like, pets."

"Well don't worry, darlin' I won't be shootin' your little duckies. Not on this trip."

I considered dragging him back to his hotel before he embarrassed himself any further. But I wasn't fast enough. And as it turned out, I was glad.

"Want to know the biggest animal I ever took down?" Ansel said. He didn't wait for the girls' response. "Elephant. A goddamned one hundred and twenty-five pounder. That's tusk weight, each tusk. One hundred and twenty-five pounds each!"

"Oh my God," the one on the right shrieked. The other one put her hand to her mouth and gasped.

Through his drunken fog, Ansel interpreted the girls' reactions as awe. The great white hunter plowed on. "It's a once-in-a-lifetime experience."

Both girls leapt away from under Ansel's arms and stood before him, their eyes narrowing and their lip-glossed mouths pursing into tight little buds of indignation. "I think that's, like, really ... really bad," the first one said. The other followed suit. "Yeah. Like, you're not human to me. They should charge you. Or send you to jail or something. And I suppose you get your kicks from clubbing baby seals to death too!"

Their words were finally penetrating Ansel's booze-soaked brain. "Hey, come on. It was a long time ago," Ansel protested. "I don't do it now. I just thought you'd ... Hey," He lurched and tried to catch one of the girls by the arm. "Come on. Don't go. I give money. I'm a fucking hero. I save the goddamn things. Ever heard of Sal ... Selous Elephant Project, I'm a big 'tributor to Sal ... ous," he slurred. "In Tanzania. Know where Tanzania is?" His new friends weren't listening; they were already half way to the other side of yard.

Ansel fell back against the deck railing, his chin dropped to his chest. A rotund husky dog lumbered up beside him and slipped its puffy head under the hand of the dejected drunk man.

Bernie and I stepped away from the railing and looked at each other thoughtfully. Without a word we headed back into the house and found John Morrow on the front steps smoking a big, rich-smelling cigar.

"How's he doing?" John asked.

"Not great," I said. "You should take him home. But before you do, can you tell me why Ansel is giving money to Arthur's elephant fund in Tanzania?"

John looked startled, and Bernie too seemed surprised at my bluntness.

"That just doesn't make sense, John," I continued. "And I'm tired of the secrets. The agenda. I'd like some answers. So start by telling me why he gives money to SEP."

John dropped his cigar and ground it out with the heel of his shoe. He said, "Same reason he never shoots anything when he comes here each year."

"And I don't suppose you're going to tell me why that is," I said, and bent to retrieve John Morrow's litter. I handed it to him.

He studied the ruined cigar butt in his hand. Then he lifted his eyes and set them on me. "No I'm not, and you might want to consider leaving things alone that don't concern you. Leave Ansel alone, Hellie," John said before he strolled down the sidewalk and around to the back of the house to find his friend.

CHAPTER 21

LARRY WON. THE BOOZE LUGE DEFEATED THE TEXAN. IT WAS AFTER NINE the next morning, and I still hadn't heard a word from Ansel. Clearly, the trip was off.

I was packing up a few things to take into "the office" at the Springs. My editor from *McMillan* had just called — not faxed or emailed — to say he was now very anxious to see a draft of the article. His tone led me to believe that very anxious meant if I didn't have something to him within the next forty-eight hours, my career with *McMillan* magazine was going to be extremely short-lived.

As it was, I was thankful to the booze luge. Now I had the day to myself, and my plan was to go to my office at the Springs hotel and scratch out a draft of the Ansel Rock story.

But writing for the day wasn't my only plan. I had another one, and I was about to put it in motion. Based on our visit to the Marriott, I was convinced Suzanna had either seen the Doc or tried to see him the night he died. If I was right, Nathan would certainly want to know. If I was wrong and told Nathan my suspicions, I'd come off looking like an idiot, or a conniving murderer trying to deflect attention from my own guilty self.

I doubted Suzanna was capable of murder, but I wasn't so sure she was above prowling around the house when I was out. The locksmith was scheduled to come out later in the day to change the locks. In the meantime, I'd take the opportunity to at least rule Suzanna out as my prowler, or catch her in the act.

I dialled her number and watched her house from the front windows. Her car was parked in the drive, but the machine picked up. Out for her morning walk and Tai Chi in the park, no doubt. The tone sounded for me to leave a message.

"Suzanna, it's Hellie. I'm calling to say ... " I had to make this sound sincere. "I'm ... well, sorry about yesterday. Bad day. Nathan said someone was in the house, so I'm having the locks changed later. I'm just kind of on edge lately. Anyway, there's something else I need to talk to you about. It's important. I have to go out now, and I'll be back around two this afternoon. Could you come over about two thirty, say? Please come. It's very important."

Before I left the house, I wiped down the outside and inside handles on the front door, unraveled two pieces of dental floss and taped the first one over the lock and doorjamb on the inside. I repeated the procedure at the back door after I let myself out and locked the deadbolt. Only this time I taped the dental floss on the outside of the door at its base between the door and frame. This was a trick I'd learned from Danny, who used to set the same trap to catch my mother snooping in his room when he was at school. I was giggling at the absurdity of what I was doing. Tiger joined in and gave a few yips and piddled in his excitement.

We took off down the river path to Bernie's store. She wasn't in, but Paul said he was happy to doggy-sit Tiger. At the Springs, I wrote for four hours and managed to produce a run-of-the-mill article about the joys of hunting, getting back to nature and various other sundry bits of bullshit I'd plagiarized from a stack of generic hunting articles and the ones John Morrow had given me. Four hours and a thousand words later, I was still pondering the question: What possessed Ansel Rock to pay a million dollars and not shoot anything? It just didn't make sense. The day I was with him, he'd sure looked like he was going to shoot that ram. The only thing I knew for certain was that I didn't understand Ansel Rock. I looked up to the ceiling and wondered which room he was in and how he was feeling and … if he was alone. That thought annoyed me. Who cared? Not me. Ansel Rock was a stubborn, vengeful man.

I checked my watch. It was half past one. Time to go home. I strolled down the Spanish Walk and stopped to look down at Mount Stephen Hall, at the chairs where I'd sat with Ansel. His drunken words at Larry's party came to mind. *I'm a big contributor to the Selous Elephant Fund.* Arthur's group in Tanzania. Why would Ansel be supporting Arthur's group? The answer came in a flash: to make certain SEP supported Ansel's version of events and not Arthur's. He bought their support to drive Arthur out of Tanzania. Was that enough for Arthur to want to see Ansel dead? Was that the real reason Arthur took a shot at us? Daniel Peterson's assailant had looked an awful lot like Arthur. Was the Doc caught up in the plan? Or had the Doc turned on Arthur? Arthur had been the last person to talk to the Doc. But he was the first one to say that Doc had been murdered.

Neither the police nor I had found evidence to suggest that Doc had died of anything other than a heart attack … except the EpiPen. My mind kept going back to it. I needed to put it to rest. On impulse, I found a phone, dialled the operator and got the medical examiner's number in Edmonton. They had done the Doc's autopsy in Calgary, so I thought I'd better phone somewhere else, lest I make someone in the Calgary office suspicious when I start asking questions about a recent case.

The receptionist answered. "Medical examiner's office, can I help you?"

"Good afternoon," I said. "I'm a reporter doing research for an article I'm writing. And I was wondering if I could speak to someone who could give me information about how you go about determining if someone was murdered or died of natural causes."

I was glad I was calling from a pay phone so my own number didn't show up. I felt like a nut. But the receptionist didn't skip a beat and, after she'd apparently explained what I was after, put me through to a toxicologist named Dr. Blake.

"Blake here," he said when he came on the line. "What type of article is this for?"

"It's a piece on crime investigation. I was hoping you could answer a few questions for me."

"Which publication?"

"Uh … well, I'm a freelance journalist so I haven't actually submitted the story. I'm just gathering research at the moment."

"Okay, so what's your question?" he said.

"Actually, it's a scenario. A hypothetical case."

"All right, give me the details."

"A body's found."

"Male or female?"

"Male, and it looks like he died of a heart attack, but it's suspicious. The police found his body outside in an odd location."

"Was the victim taking any medication?" Dr. Blake asked

"Cortisone."

"That won't kill anyone," he said. "Well not right away, at any rate.

Does damage the body, but over the long term."

"That's what I thought," I said. "The only other thing found near the body was a used adrenaline pen."

"Okay, that's interesting. Adrenaline affects the heart."

"Yes, but what if the autopsy reports nothing in the victim's system?" I said.

"That would make sense. Adrenaline has a very short half-life."

"A what?"

"Half-life. It means it doesn't stay in the system long. So if adrenaline was injected into the victim's system before he died, an initial autopsy wouldn't find it. We'd have to know to look for it. See, adrenaline or epinephrine is naturally present in the system, so it's not easy to do an analysis. And if we are looking for it, it's a time-consuming process. It could take three months to get the results back."

"But could you kill someone with adrenaline?"

"Sure, if you inject enough of it, and particularly if the person has a weak heart to begin with."

My own heart sped up. My instincts were correct. I knew I was on to something.

"You've been a great help, Dr. Blake," I said. "Thanks a lot."

"Anytime, and good luck with your article."

I hung up and called the RCMP station. Nathan was on the other line but I left him a message. "Please ask him to meet Hellie MacConnell at Doc Rivard's house as soon as possible."

When I arrived back home I was so keyed up I nearly forgot to check my trap. The tape and dental floss on the back door were undisturbed. I let myself in and went straight to the front door. The floss was still in place there too. I was a little disappointed. But I was more concerned with getting hold of Nathan and telling him what the toxicologist had said.

I now had three other pieces of information I needed to pass on to Nathan. The first was my certainty that Suzanna had been at the Marriott the night the Doc died. The second was my absolute belief that Doc Rivard had been murdered. And the third was that I had found a possible murder weapon.

The only question remaining was, who did it? Suzanna? Arthur? Someone else? Suzanna wanted the house and the Doc. Which meant she'd have nothing to gain by killing him. And I just didn't believe she was smart enough to pull off a clever murder. Was Arthur? Probably. Or someone I hadn't thought of. But who? Who had the most to gain from the Doc's death? Arthur.

It always came back to Arthur.

The phone rang. I grabbed it on the second ring.

"Hi Hellie."

"Danny!"

"How you doing?"

"Okay. What about you? What's up?" I moved into the solarium and leaned against the patio door. "How's Mom and Dad?"

"Okay. The same. You know."

"Yeah, I know."

"That's what I'm calling about. Hellie, I've been thinking about things. And … I'm … I'm going to tell them."

"No! Absolutely not! Not yet." The vision of my little brother the night he'd tried to kill himself, ashen faced and staggering around a friend's living room filled my mind. He told me what he'd taken and how many, but not why. He was sixteen.

"You're still starting at McGill in January, right?" I said.

"Yeah."

"Okay, good. You'll be on your own. Tell them then if you want to. We can both tell them. But not now. Not while you're living there."

"We?" Danny said. "How can we tell them, when Mom and Dad won't even talk to you? I hate it, Hellie. I hate that you can't even call here." He dropped his voice to a whisper. "And I hate what they say about you."

I swallowed. "It's okay." And it really was okay, because whatever they said about me was nothing close to what they'd have to say about him. Our father, Mac MacConnell, was the original homophobe. All gays were "freaks of nature," according to Mac, who had an endless repertoire of "faggot jokes." And my ex-fiancé's father, Big Brock Hanlan, had even more.

I too was whispering. "Now is not a good time to tell them. Please, Danny. Listen to me."

There was a pause. Dead air hung between us. I took a breath. "Please," I said.

"Yeah. Okay," he said. "If you don't want me to, I won't. I gotta go. I miss you."

"Me too," was all I could manage before I hung up. The tears strangled my throat.

I opened the patio door. The mournful sound of a train whistle echoed in the distance. An elk bugled in response. Birds chirped happily in the trees. I leaned against the doorframe and kept my eyes focused on a nuthatch's zebra-striped head as it flitted and skittered down a tree trunk. I was so far away from Toronto and from Danny. The call had ended too abruptly. I wanted to call him back. But really, what else was there to say? I stayed there looking out to the mountains and thinking about Danny, until I heard a noise behind me.

My eyes glanced up. A woman's reflection stared back at me in the glass. I spun around.

"Suzanna!"

She moved past me, slid the patio door closed and locked it.

"What are you doing?" I said and reached for the lock.

"Don't," she snapped. Then she softened her tone. "I need to talk to you about something. It's private."

My heart was still pounding in my throat. I didn't unlock the door, but I stayed close to it.

She moved away from the door. With her arms crossed over her chest she leaned against the bookshelf making the appearance of being relaxed. The hard lines around her pursed mouth told me she was anything but. Her face was as pale as a geisha's.

"Tell me where it is," she said.

I suspected she was talking about the adrenaline vial. I drew a deep breath. My mind left like it was on speed going a million miles an hour as I tried to think what to say.

"Where's the damn will?" Suzanna demanded.

Will? "With the lawyer," I said.

"Liar. Tell me where it is, you little tramp. And move away from the door."

Dark circles of perspiration had formed on her royal blue blouse under her armpits. She licked her lips repeatedly.

I had to get out of there.

Just as my hand reached for the door, Suzanna screamed. "Get away from that door or I'll hurt you!"

My head snapped to the right. She was holding the African spear, looking like some kind of demented warrior. Her hand and arm were trembling so badly I was terrified she'd propel the spear at me accidentally.

I took cautious steps away from the door and into the centre of the room. "Okay, Suzanna, I'm moving. Now put that thing down."

"No. Not until you tell me exactly where the other will is. Or ... or I'll get you with this." She used both hands to grasp the wood shaft as she jabbed the spear at the air.

"You don't want to do that," I said as evenly as I could. "You know you don't. So put the damn thing down."

"No." She took a step closer.

I took one back.

"You're not going to ruin my life any more," she said in a high-pitched whine.

"Ruin your life? What are you talking about? I've never done a thing to you."

Her face flushed with rage. "Ha! That's a good one. You stole everything. I belong in this house. Not you. He should have left it to me. And I know you've done something with Michael's original will. You forged the one that lawyer has." She shook her head and the spear swung back and forth in time. I tried to swerve out of range.

"Don't move another step," she said.

"Suzanna, I don't know what you're talking about. There's only one will that I know of, and it's with the lawyers. Is that what you've been in here looking for?"

"Liar," she screeched. "You are a dirty liar. He left me this house. I ... I loved him." Her voice cracked and tears pooled in her eyes.

"I know you did. And he cared for you too. I'm sure he did."

"Yes, he did," she spat the words. "Until you came along."

"Me? What are you — "

"You moved in and stole him away."

"Stole him? Don't be so stupid, Suzanna."

"No. You're the stupid one. Don't lie. I saw the two of you. Walking together along the river. Laughing. I saw him touch you."

"He hugged me."

"You ruined everything." Tears were streaming down her face. She licked her lips.

"Did you kill him, Suzanna? Did you?" I took a step back in the direction of the kitchen archway.

She gave a mirthless laugh. "You must have been a pretty good little fuck. Good enough to get him you leave you my house."

"Don't be disgusting. He was my uncle for God's sake. And he didn't leave this house to me. He left it to Arthur." It came to me then: the crushing realization that if Suzanna had killed the Doc then she had probably killed Arthur too. "Oh, no," I moaned. "You didn't. You didn't … kill Arthur too?"

The spear vibrated in her hands and her eyes were wild and hysterical.

"Take it easy," I said. "We can talk. Why do you think there's another will?"

"Larry said there was another will and my name was mentioned in it. I think you slept with the Doc and you either got him to make a new will or you forged a new one. Larry dates a girl who works in the lawyer's office. She said something funny was going on."

"Larry's an idiot," I said. "So put the spear down and we'll discuss this rationally."

"I don't want to talk. I want that will and I want you out of my life you little whore." Her face was twisted with hate as she lunged at me.

Help me, God! I spun around intending to make a break for the kitchen. But I tripped over my own feet, lost my balance and went down hard. My face smashed against the hardwood floor, and something dug into my chest. I smelled dust and struggled to get back up on my feet. From somewhere to my left came a loud bang followed by a terrible sound of crashing glass. In my frantic mind I imagined Suzanna had fallen and smashed through the patio doors.

A scream pierced the air.

"Get her!" I heard a male voice yell.

I gasped for air and rolled over, clutching my chest. Ansel and John Morrow were wrestling with Suzanna. Ansel had his arm around Suzanna's waist and his hand on her wrist, holding her hand with the spear straight up in the air.

"Grab it, John!" Ansel said.

John reached up and took the weapon from Suzanna's hand. When he had it, Ansel swung Suzanna around and plunked her down on the wicker couch and said, "Now you sit right there." He turned to John. "Keep an eye on her. We'll call the police in a second."

"I wasn't going to stab her. I was just … scaring her," Suzanna said in a dazed voice.

Ansel crouched next to me and cradled me in his arms. I took long, halting breaths. "Are you okay?" he said.

I nodded. After a while my breathing calmed, and my heart slowed. When I placed my hand on my chest I felt the lucky crystal. Maybe there was something to it after all. I smiled. *Thank you, Bernie.*

"Are you hurt?" Ansel asked.

My eyes met his. He was staring down at me so intently and with such care and worry, I reached up and brushed fingers across his cheek. "I'm okay," I said in a shaky voice.

Then I glanced over at Suzanna. She was sitting motionless with her head bent and chin touching her chest like a doll whose neck had been broken. Tousled black hair covered her face. But I didn't need to see her eyes to know she was crying. "I … I'm … oh, Michael. I'm sorry," she sputtered through her tears. "I'm so sorry."

"Oh, God," I said. "She did do it. She killed the Doc," I said.

"Come on," Ansel said gently as he helped me to my feet. He pulled me close to his chest and whispered in my ear, "Thank God you're okay." Then he held me at arms length. "You are all right, aren't you?"

"Yeah. I'm fine. Thanks."

My foot hit something on the floor that tinkled. I looked down and saw a set of keys. A sickening realization came to me: Suzanna must have been in the house all morning, searching the place, and waiting …

***

Nathan showed up. He called in backup and they took Suzanna away. Ansel had called for the paramedics because I had a nasty bump on my head.

After a cute medic checked me out and said I'd live, I went back into the living room and listened to John explain to Nathan how he and Ansel happened to show up just at the right moment to save me from Suzanna. John and I were sipping brandy. Ansel was knocking back straight H_2O, no doubt trying to counter the ugly aftermath of the booze luge. John did all the talking. Ansel remained silent.

"I've been watching Suzanna for the past few days," John said. "Noticed she was receiving calls from the Petersons."

"How'd you happen to take notice of that?" Nathan asked.

"Call display. I've been checking for my own messages each day. Suzanna lets guests use her machine. I didn't think anything of the Petersons' calls because I assumed she set up trips for her clients through them. Then that business with Daniel happened, and the ram was poached."

We all looked to Ansel.

"I was sorry to hear about that, Mr. Rock," Nathan said in his gruff voice.

Ansel gave a polite nod and kept his eyes focused on the rim of his water glass.

"Is that why you went out to Becker's camp yesterday?" I asked John.

"Partly. But to be honest, I also noticed Suzanna was coming over here quite often, and there were those calls to her from the Petersons. I started wondering if maybe Arthur Elliott was here and she was meeting him. I saw her let herself in. That was about seven this morning."

"That's when I was in the shower," I said. I felt off kilter again at the thought. "She must have thought I was already gone, but then got caught short and had to hide somewhere." I snapped my fingers. "She was probably in the basement. The dog knew. He was hanging around the basement door all morning. But he didn't bark because he knows her."

"So what was she waiting for?" Nathan asked.

"For me to leave, so she could look around for another will she thinks exists. She would have heard me call you, Nathan. When she couldn't find this phantom will she waited for me to come home to tell her where it was. I looked back to John. "So why did you come over here?"

"Ansel came by — "

"And you told him Suzanna was probably over here feeding Arthur," I cut in.

John looked embarrassed. "Something like that. We peeked through the back patio doors and saw the struggle going on. Ansel threw a deck chair through the window."

"One of my guys will call in someone to fix it for you, Hellie," Nathan said.

"Thanks," I said. Then I told him what I'd been up to at the Marriott hotel. "I'm almost certain that the woman the doorman said he saw in the hotel the night the Doc died was Suzanna."

Nathan was taking notes. He looked up from his pad. "I thought I told you to let us handle this."

I shrugged. "You would have thought I was out of my mind if I'd come to you with this theory. I wanted to make sure I had something first."

He gave a grunt and said, "I'll get the Calgary police to check with the doorman."

"Do you think she killed Doctor Rivard?" John said.

"I'm certainly going to explore that possibility," Nathan said.

"I think Arthur's disappearance may have something to do with Suzanna too," I said, and felt my chest squeeze. "I think she might have killed him."

Ansel finally spoke up. "I doubt that. My theory is Suzanna has been working with Arthur."

"Oh, come on, Ansel," I snapped. "Suzanna has always hated Arthur. Believe me, he's the last person she'd be working with."

"Maybe that's what she wanted people to believe. Hear me out. You just told us she was looking for a will that leaves this house to her. So at some point she had reason to believe Doc Rivard was going to leave something to her. Why?"

"Because she was in love with him," I said. "But he didn't return her feelings. He was nice to her because he was a nice man."

"So she interprets his kindness as love," Ansel said. "Then she finds out the Doc left the house to Arthur and you, Hellie. And let's suppose it was Arthur who told her Doc left it to you."

"Why would he do that?" I said.

"So that she would get rid of the Doc for him in a fit of jealous rage."

"Why would Arthur want to get rid of his best friend?" I said.

"My guess is that Arthur has been up to his old tricks and he's been sending funds to his followers in Tanzania so they can keep bringing in illegal arms. I think Doc Rivard found out and was on his way back here to confront Arthur."

"Ansel," I said. "You told me before you believed the Doc was helping Arthur smuggle those weapons in. Now he's working against Arthur? Pick a team."

"Maybe the Doc never was involved in the weapons smuggling," Ansel countered. "Or perhaps it was like his hunting days, he had a change of heart. After my baby girl and my wife got killed he got a sudden case of guilt and he stopped. He was a doctor, after all."

Nathan rubbed a hand back and forth over the gray brush cut. He let out a long breath. "Mr. Rock, we're obviously going to have to have a very long talk so you can fill me in on this weapons smuggling business in Tanzania you're going on about. But not right now because I'm getting one banger of a headache listening to you two argue. And I'm frustrated as hell over this case. All I've got are theories, a suspect with motive and opportunity and a heart attack victim — not a murder victim. I've got no evidence, and no weapon." He rubbed his thumb and forefinger across his eyes.

I put my hand up.

"What is it, Hellie?"

"I think I've got your murder weapon."

CHAPTER 22

"Des, drink your coffee and knock it off," I said. He hadn't taken his eyes off me since he'd shown up at Bernie's teashop. We were sitting in comfortable armchairs arranged around a coffee table. I'd stayed at Bernie and Paul's the night before and come to the shop with them that afternoon. After my run-in with Suzanna, I hadn't been in the mood to spend the rest of the day, and certainly not the night, alone.

"What? What am I doing?" Des said.

"Staring at me. You're making me nervous."

"Sorry. I'm just kind of shook up. Suzanna could have killed you."

"But she didn't," I said.

"Close enough," he said, his eyes following Bernie, who was moving to the door.

She flipped the *Closed* sign over and turned the lock. "We need a little privacy around here," Bernie said, avoiding her husband's penetrating gaze. Paul liked to sell things a whole lot more than Bernie did.

As I watched her, my mind wandered back to the same thing that had been nagging me since my encounter with Suzanna. "What's wrong, Hellie?" Bernie asked.

"Oh. I was just thinking about Suzanna and how she acted yesterday. Unless it's just wishful thinking, I'm having a hard time believing she really would have killed me. Not intentionally, at any rate. She was a nervous wreck when she was handling that spear. She just didn't come off as a practiced killer. So if she did kill the Doc, I think she must have had help. There's a connection to the Petersons. John Morrow said she was receiving phone calls from them."

"And someone shot Daniel Peterson," Bernie said.

"Yes, but I'm quite certain it wasn't Suzanna. Did Nathan tell you anything more, Des?" I asked.

"Not much. We're hoping a couple more nights in jail might get Suzanna talking. She has admitted to going to the Marriott, though."

"I knew it," I said.

"Her line is she wanted to surprise the Doc. Apparently he was surprised but not pleasantly so."

"Told her to beat it, huh?" Bernie said.

Des gave a nod. "She claims that she and the Doc had a thing. But I don't believe her." He looked as if he was feeling badly about talking behind her back.

"I don't believe her either," I said. "Because he certainly didn't encourage her. Well, not that I ever saw."

"I sort of remember them spending time together shortly after Barb died," Des said. "Then it ended about — "

"About the time Arthur showed up?" I guessed.

"That'd be right." Des put his coffee cup down on the table next to two stuffed bears and a husky dog. "I kind of feel sorry for her."

Des was truly one of the good ones. Even after everything Suzanna had done, he still felt compassion for her.

"Well, it'll be a good long time before I ever feel sorry for her," Bernie said, as she placed Tiger in what looked like a rather permanent dog bed near the window.

Des watched the little dog spin around trying to catch his tail before settling down. "And the dog," Des said. "According to Larry, Suzanna put him up to giving you a dog."

"So she'd have an excuse for freer access to the house," I said. "She was probably planning to hang on to my key, just so it would look good in case I ever caught her. But she must have copied the Doc's key a long time ago."

Bernie looked up at me. "And I suppose this mystery will leaves everything to her."

"That's what she says," Des replied.

Bernie clucked her tongue against her cheek. "Dream on, sister. Suzanna LaChaine is the last person the Doc would've left his house to because he knew she'd kick Arthur out so fast his kikoi would spin. But I still can't believe she'd ... hurt the Doc."

"It's looking pretty suspicious. Things are stacking up against her, and she knows it." Des turned his attention back to me. "And your theory about the adrenaline is looking good, Hellie."

"I don't get that," Bernie piped in. "They did an autopsy. You still haven't explained that to us. But maybe you don't want to talk about all this yet," she added with a look of concern for me.

"No, no. I'm fine," I said. "It's good to talk about it. I was just kind of edgy before."

"Well I should think," Bernie said.

"You're right, though," I continued. "They did do an autopsy. So if she used adrenaline, it was a pretty ingenious way to get rid of someone." Bernie and Paul were staring at me. "I called the medical examiner's office yesterday," I said with a shrug. "Anyway, adrenaline's interesting. Speeds up the heart. In the Doc's case his heart was already in bad shape and it wouldn't have taken much to blow a gasket."

"But the autopsy didn't report finding anything," Bernie insisted.

"Exactly. Adrenaline only stays in the body about two to five minutes after it's injected. It does its job, then poof, gone. No trace of the murder weapon."

"I can't believe Suzanna's smart enough to think up something like that. But how will they ever know now that ... well, since the Doc's body is gone?" Bernie said.

"The medical examiner takes tissue samples during the initial autopsy," Des explained. "Nathan says they're sending those samples to the crime lab in Edmonton. Now that they know adrenaline is a possibility there's other things they can look for. But it'll take time. Three months maybe. Also, that EpiPen Hellie found may not have had enough adrenaline in it to kill someone. It might have, but we're thinking Suzanna had more. So Nathan and the crime guys are looking into that too."

The image of the Doc, dead under the gazebo, flashed in my mind. "One thing doesn't wash for me, Des. How would Suzanna get the Doc under the gazebo? The reports show he died under there."

"She could have had help," Paul said. He'd just returned from the back room.

"I guess. But if you're going to kill someone, why would you leave the body and the murder weapon so close to home?" I said.

"And why call the Doc's hotel room from the Doc's house?" Bernie added.

"To frame someone else," Des said.

"Ah. Like Hellie or Arthur, say," Bernie said.

"That's what it's looking like. Nathan and the crime guys swear that the adrenaline vial was not in those bins when they searched them.

Arthur's prints were on the vial." Des lowered his eyes.

The possible implications of what he'd just said was devastatingly clear. "Nathan thinks Suzanna killed Arthur," I said flatly.

"That's the theory," Des said softly. "Makes sense. I'm sorry, Hellie. You don't need to hear this. You've been through enough."

"I guessed anyway. That's why the vial showed up later. She couldn't plant it until she got his prints on it. And there's probably only one way she could have done that ... " I swallowed back the tears.

Bernie wasn't as successful. "What's the witch got to say about that?" she said, wiping at her eyes.

"Nothing," Des replied. "She denies doing anything other than seeing the Doc."

"What if she's telling the truth?" I said.

"We don't think she is."

The phone rang and Paul went to the back to get it. I got the impression he was grateful for the interruption. His eyes were moist as he left the room. A moment later he returned with the phone, his palm over the receiver.

"It's Ansel Rock," Paul said to me.

I took the phone. "Hi, Ansel. Where are you?"

"In my room at the Springs. Can I see you?"

"I'll walk up there," I said.

"Are you sure? I can come and get you."

"No thanks. I can use the walk," I said and rang off.

And just then I really did need the walk, the air and the time to digest the fact that Arthur was probably dead.

***

The door was open, and I didn't bother to knock before I stepped into the two-storey, condo-sized room, furnished with handsome, heavy dark furniture and multiple fireplaces. The wraparound windows and spectacular 360-degree panoramic view of the Bow Valley was enough to take my breath away. In the background, the twangy, woeful sounds of cowboy music played softly.

There was no sign of Ansel. I called out a hello.

He appeared in the doorway from another part of the suite and crossed the expansive room. On his way, he stopped to pick up a stack of papers off the grand piano.

"What happened, Ansel, couldn't get yourself upgraded?" I said deadpan.

"Oh. This is the Presidential Suite. It's the best — " he stopped himself when he caught my grin and returned the smile.

But the smile was different and didn't seem to belong to the same hotheaded Texan I'd met days earlier. The usual hardness around his jaw was gone. His eyes were tired.

"Thanks for coming, Hellie. How you doin'?" He tucked the papers under his arm, put his fingers to my chin and eased my face to the right. "Head looks not too bad."

"I'll live."

He gave me a wistful look. "That's good. Very good." We shared an awkward pause. "I'm leaving," he said.

"Leaving? As in going home?"

"Yeah. It's time. Tomorrow, I'll be outta here."

I felt a stab of sadness and, yes, regret. The music wasn't helping — a crooning cowboy singing his goodbyes to another cheatin' lover.

"Not going to finish the hunt?"

"Your friend finished it for me."

Blood rushed to my face. "He's dead," I blurted. "Suzanna killed him. Just like the Doc." My throat tightened around the words.

Ansel placed his hands on my shoulders. "I'm sorry for you. I know what it's like to lose someone you care about. Believe me I know. But he's ... " Ansel had the grace not to finish his thought.

The feeling of utter exhaustion finally swept over me, and when Ansel pulled me close, I didn't resist. I breathed in his clean scent. It felt so good to be close to someone. Which is exactly why I pulled away and let Ansel's hands fall from my shoulders. He kept his eyes on mine.

"So what did you want to see me about?" I said, and glanced down at my shoes.

"A couple of things. First to see how you're doin'. Called your place and then figured you'd be at your friend's. And second, to apologize."

"For what?"

"I feel like a damned fool for the way I acted at Larry's. Understand you were there."

"Forget it. We all go a little crazy now and then."

"I usually make a point not to," he said in a dry tone. "And I wanted to give you these." He handed me the papers he'd picked up off the piano. "Some things I've written over the years about hunting. Why I do it. Why I spend so much goddamn money to do it. Should do the trick for you. Lots of personal shit. Your editor will eat it up."

"Thanks, Ansel." Then I couldn't help myself and added, "Do you happen to mention anything about why you never shoot anything after you do spend all that goddamned money?"

"Just unlucky I guess."

"I don't think so. But it's your business," I said, flipping through the pages. "Well, thanks, again. I really mean it. Thanks for yesterday. You saved me. I'll do my best on the story."

"I know you will." He held out his hand and we exchanged a firm shake. Our eyes met. "Wish we'd met at a better time," he said, still holding my hand.

"Me too."

"Woulda liked to take you out for a nice supper."

"Yes. That would have been nice."

"So what about now?"

"Aw, I don't think — "

"We'll stay here. Room's big enough. I'll order something up. What do you say?"

"I say I should probably get going."

"Come on, you gotta eat."

When he flashed me a crooked, charming smile, I gave in. "Okay. What the heck. Probably be the only chance I'll ever get to eat a meal in a room like this."

"Great." Ansel picked up the phone in one hand and lit a match to the paper and kindling set on the fireplace grate with the other. I watched the tiny flames catch and spread. Then I went to the window and looked out at little Tunnel Mountain's beehive profile in the fading light.

Ansel finished his call and joined me at the window. He was holding a bottle of champagne in one hand and two flutes in the other. He held up the bottle. "Came with the room. I took the liberty of ordering for you. Hope that's okay."

"Just fine," I said. Dusk was rolling in and Tunnel Mountain was cast in a soft sienna light.

"Used to take Marianna up there to watch the sun set," he said quietly.

"I'd guessed as much."

"She loved it here."

"Is that why you were going to build that resort?"

"That was one reason."

"I'm sorry about what happened to you, Ansel. To your family. I can't even imagine what that would have been like for you."

He kept his gaze on Tunnel Mountain and said, "Thanks."

We moved to the couch in the living area. With the fire burning softly, lights dim and Ansel pouring the champagne it was the perfect setting, had we been on our honeymoon. I took up a seat on the floor next to the fireplace and leaned my head back against the sofa's exceptionally puffy cushion. Ansel was on the couch. I held my glass up over my head in a toast to him. "To better things to come."

Our glasses clinked and Ansel slid off the couch and took up the place next to me on the floor. The irony of us both sitting on the floor in this fifteen-hundred-dollar-a-night room did not escape me. I drank up and enjoyed the moment.

"So why are you leaving now?" I asked.

"Ram's gone."

"And there's only one?" That's when I got it. I understood exactly why Ansel had been so broken up when he'd learned it had been poached. "It was for her, wasn't it? For Marianna. You buy the tag so no one else can hunt that ram. You save it for her."

He lifted his glass to me. "Congratulations, Hellie. You found me out."

I touched his glass with mine but I forgot to drink. I was too busy thinking up questions. "But why all the pretense, Ansel? You made me believe you were going to shoot that animal. Why not just tell the truth?"

"Because a lot of other decent hunters who would give their eye teeth to hunt that ram would find what I do pretty damned annoying. And it would undermine what we stand for."

"Fine. I don't want to get into an argument about the politics of hunting," I said.

"And I don't want this to show up in your story. That clear?"

"Yeah. Whatever. For what it's worth, though, I think it's a lovely tribute to your wife's memory. I know she was involved in conservation efforts."

Ansel gave a disgusted snort. "Yeah, she sure was. And Arthur Elliott knew all about that, and he knew what I was doing here, and that's why he took out that ram. He's been trying to destroy me for years. And now," Ansel put his hands up in surrender. "He's won. That ram was a gift for her. And that sonofabitch knew it."

"You're right, he did know." I could hear Arthur's words as clearly as if he were standing next to me: *I was trying to stop him from destroying that beautiful animal and from further destroying himself.*

"Arthur shot at you because he did know. And he thought you were going to shoot the ram that day. He wasn't trying to kill you. And ... " I took breath. "And the police think Arthur's dead. So he couldn't have killed that ram."

"You still don't get it, do you? You've got to listen to me, Hellie. You are wrong about Arthur Elliott. Dead wrong. And you nearly got yourself killed because of it."

"What happened with Suzanna had nothing to do with Arthur. Other than that she probably killed him, too."

Ansel was shaking his head. "Arthur Elliott is not dead. He's too cagey to get himself dead." He looked at the empty glass in his hand, his face working itself into a fierce scowl. "I'm worried sick for you," he said. "I like you, Hellie. I might even ... Aw shit. What the hell am I saying?"

"I better go." I got up and moved across the room to get my coat.

"You runnin' again, Hellie?"

I stopped and turned slowly back to face him. "What did you say?"

"I know what happened in Toronto."

"What do you know?"

He got up, came around to the other side of the couch and leaned against it. "I know that you ran out on your wedding."

"How the hell do you know that?"

"I told you. Had you checked out when I heard your name. Wasn't hard. I knew your name. John does business with your daddy's company.

Everyone who owns resorts does business with MacHan Travel."

"John knows my father?"

"They met once when — "

"When you and John were trying to get that resort going."

"That's right. But John didn't talk to your daddy about you. He doesn't know him well. Neither did my investigator. Just picked up gossip here and there."

I was incredulous. I felt violated, and I was speechless. He was talking about my life as though it was public property.

"I'll tell you something, though," Ansel went on. "I think you made the right decision. Just left it a little long is all. That Brock fellow you were gonna marry, he'd have been all wrong for you." My face told him he'd better take a breath. "Right, well, I guess you kinda knew that and that's why you took off, huh?"

"You really did your homework, didn't you?" I spat the words at him. "You think you know an awful lot about me. Well I happen to know a lot about you too. I know that you have been lying ever since we met. I know you gave money to Arthur's group in Africa so they'd back you and blame Arthur for murders he didn't commit. You still give money to his group. Why, Ansel? Insurance? Make sure they'll always agree with you? You bought their votes. You framed Arthur. He was doing something he believed in. Something good. What were you doing in Africa?"

He kept his hard eyes on me as his long slender fingers wiped at his mouth. "I was hunting an elephant." He breathed in a harsh breath. "Hellie, don't run away on me. Stay and listen. Because I've got something you need to hear."

CHAPTER 23

I REMAINED STANDING, HOLDING MY COAT CLOSE TO MY CHEST.

Ansel sat on the couch and stared into the fire, letting his mind take him back to the darkest moment of his life. "My daughter ... my baby girl," he began. "She was five years old. Five." He took a deep breath and seemed to be struggling for words. It was pretty clear that talking about this — about anything personal — was not in Ansel's makeup.

"Her mother wanted to see Africa," Ansel said in a hypnotic monotone voice. "So I planned tours for her and Nici to go on while I was hunting. See, Marianna wasn't always against me. She came from a long line of sport hunters. My daddy and her daddy had been hunting buddies for years. She was never interested in it, but it was such a big part of her family I don't suppose she ever gave it much thought." He hesitated. "But then, I guess I was the one who never gave it any thought.

"She got into studying history," Ansel went on. "Especially slavery, and the town we stayed in, Mikindani, has historic slave markets. Said she wanted Nici to understand what terrible things went on in the world. I thought Nici was too young for it." He shrugged. "But what did I know? I was just the animal-killing male in the family. As soon as we checked in to our room, Arthur ... " He paused, the lines around his mouth constricting at the sound of his enemy's name. He cleared his throat and brought himself up. "Then Arthur's lunatic friends started holding demonstrations outside our hotel."

I slid onto the couch next to him. "But surely, Ansel, you would have been expecting some attention from environmentalists," I said gently.

"Oh yeah. No surprise there. In fact there wasn't much overt action, not against us hunters. What surprised me was how covert he was. I had to leave for a few days and go to Dar es Salaam on business. It's a bigger centre. Anyway, while I'm gone, I arranged for Marianna and Nici to go on a very nice, very expensive boat trip. When I get back, I find out she's been hanging out with Arthur Elliott instead. What's worse, she announces I can't go on my hunting safari."

Outside, a train snaked its way through the valley whistling its lonely call in the distance. Ansel stopped to listen. "When I hear that, I think of Marianna," he said, sorrow resonating in his voice. "She used to say it was the sound of Banff."

"She was right," I said softly.

Ansel cleared his throat again and took up the story. "So Marianna tells me I can't go on safari and — "

"It was a very hot issue, Ansel," I interrupted. "Your wife sounds like a passionate person."

"Oh I know how hot it was, and your friend Arthur was fuelling the flames of my wife's so-called passion. And don't sit there with that sanctimonious look. I wasn't a poacher, Hellie. I was a legitimate hunter who had paid a great many legitimate American dollars for the privilege of hunting an African elephant. Do you know how much money it costs to shoot one elephant?"

I shook my head.

"About fifty grand. Half that money goes to the game reserves. I shoot one elephant; my money saves a hundred. Hunting in Africa translates into millions of conservation dollars. The issue was, and continues to be, with poaching, not hunting. But Arthur and his people couldn't quite see the difference. And he worked on Marianna long enough until she couldn't see the difference either."

I had to say something. "Wait a minute. My understanding is that Arthur spent his time and energy on poachers. Isn't it possible your wife had her own agenda?"

"She never had that agenda before she met Arthur Elliott."

"I take it you didn't give up the elephant hunt."

His eyes narrowed and a look of deep suffering and regret crossed his face. "No. I did not give it up."

"And she never forgave you for it."

"Are all you women the same, Hellie? Do you all hang on to one thing and let it fester until it destroys everything else that's good? Do you all have to remake a man to fit your newest cause?" He wasn't looking for an answer. "Well let me give you one good bit of advice. Let it go. And let a man be a man."

"And being a man means killing something every other weekend?"

"You sound like my wife."

"Congratulations. You proved your theory. We are all alike."

We were silent for a moment, neither one willing to give in. Finally I said, "Ansel, I know this must be hard. I'd like to hear the rest if you want to tell me."

He shook his head and continued. "When I refused to give up the elephant safari she moved in with him. Hell, I was just as against poaching as she was. If only she'd been reasonable, compromised. I could have helped. Helped them put their time and money toward something more productive."

"And directed Marianna away from working on you?" I said, not unkindly.

"Damn right. And if you want to know the worst of it, Marianna was giving carloads of my money to Arthur. I barely saw her the whole three months we were there."

"Well, you were away hunting ... "

"Damn right I was."

I was beginning to get the picture. Ansel was away with the boys, doing boy things. Marianna was with her little girl doing little girl things. She was lonely and starved for adult company. Arthur was company, a friend. The question was, how long had they been friends? It struck me then that Marianna's desire to be in Mikindani may have had more to do with being close to Arthur than satisfying her hankering for local history. Marianna must have had contact with Arthur or his group before she and Ansel arrived in Tanzania. How else would Arthur's group have known that Marianna and her great white hunter husband were staying at that remote resort? Answer: Marianna told them. She chose Mikindani because Arthur was there and she was hoping to turn her husband around. She even went so far as to drag him to a meeting, a meeting he never would have agreed to. But Marianna Rock obviously had not known her husband very well. Turning Ansel Rock around on anything, I suspected, would be the impossible dream. I didn't bother to share my theory that his wife had set him up long before they left the States. I suspected that, underneath, Ansel Rock already knew.

" ... and it was my right," Ansel was saying.

"I'm sure it was very hard for both of you," I said.

"Hard? Oh yeah it was hard. It was particularly hard when I found out she was giving good ol' Arthur my money for the sole purpose of undermining and destroying something that had been a tradition in my family forever. I know you think I'm some kind of chauvinist. And maybe I am. But damn it, Hellie, I'm not a murderer. I hunt animals. It's your friend Arthur who is the murderer."

He got up and paced the room, then stopped in front of me. "Tell me something. If Arthur is alive, what do you think is going to happen? You think you'll find him, save him, and he'll come back and the two of you will live happily ever after in that big house? He killed my wife and my child, and he killed your Doctor Rivard. Get it? Why can't you accept that?"

"Ansel," I warned.

He put up his hand to stop me. "Just let me finish. After I found out how much money Marianna was giving that fool, I made her stop."

"You cut her off?"

"That's right."

"Because you thought once the money dried up, Arthur would send her packing."

He bit down hard on his lower lip.

"But he didn't do that, did he?" I said.

"Nope. Just had 'em killed."

"Ansel, I don't understand why you keep holding on to that. It's making you — "

"They found her in the jungle," he said cutting me off. "She was shot in the chest with an arrow. An arrow right through her heart." Tears pooled in his eyes. "Next to her was the agent Arthur supposedly worked with. He got one in the chest too. And little Nici, same thing, dead. Only with her, they shot her in the stomach, so it probably took a good goddamned many more hours to die, lying there next to her dead mother. I know that because when you wound an animal that way, it can take an awful long time for it to die. That's why you've got to track it and make sure you finish the job. And it can be a very long trail of blood."

I reached out to him and put my hand on his shoulder. "Oh, Ansel," I whispered. My heart broke for him. I moved closer and put my arms around his broad chest. Tears leaked from my eyes and spilled onto his shirt. He wrapped his arms around me and we held each other close. I felt him shudder against me and we stayed like that, just holding each other and crying for what seemed a long time.

Eventually, Ansel sat back, but he kept his hand on my leg and I put my hand over his. "I'm so sorry," I said. "I wish I had something more to offer you."

He gave me a sad smile and brushed fingers down my tear-streaked cheek. "There isn't anything else to give," he said.

"You're a strong man," I said. "I don't know how you've managed to live with that kind of pain."

"I really don't know how I did live through it without killing some-one. If John hadn't been there, I'm sure I would have."

"John Morrow was with you in Tanzania?"

"Sure, he's been my best friend through all this. He owns the safari company. John took your Doc Rivard on hunting safaris."

"Oh. That's how you knew … "

"That's right, John told me. And John is Nici's godfather. I think it nearly killed him, too. John's spent a lot of time in Tanzania. So did my father and Marianna's. John's known Marianna since she was a kid. He's a good man. Kept me sane. I wanted to kill Arthur, and I think I would have if John hadn't stopped me."

"But it was poachers who killed your family." I said it as gently as I could.

"No it wasn't. I'm convinced it was either Arthur himself or a mem-ber of his small anti-hunting group. Like I said, my investigator hasn't been able to find anything definite on Arthur. But I just know he was involved in that weapons smuggling operation. You want to know my theory?"

I didn't, but I didn't have the heart not to let him keep talking.

"Sure," I said.

"I think that agent who died alongside Marianna knew Arthur was smuggling in illegal weapons and, like other members of SEP, he didn't agree with it. My guess is he told Marianna and that's why she ended up dead."

"Ansel, that doesn't make sense. Why would the agent tell Marianna?"

"He was probably going to the house to confront Arthur, but Arthur wasn't there. So he told Marianna. Told her to tell the authorities. See, Marianna called John's safari company office in Dar es Salaam. Said she needed to get out to the safari camp to meet me."

"Maybe she just wanted to make up with you."

"No. I think she was afraid."

"Or maybe she was going to try and stop your hunt."

"No way. Marianna knew me too well."

I couldn't help but smile.

"She needed my help."

"If you're right, why wouldn't she have gone to the police?"

"She was scared. Marianna always came to me." He blinked back the tears. "Arthur knew she was coming to see me. And he got her. I didn't have to pay off Arthur's group — they were already against him."

"Some of them were."

"Yup. Well, it's no coincidence he turned up here in Banff. I still believe your Doc Rivard initially helped Arthur bring in those weapons. And later, when things got too hot for Arthur in Tanzania, your Doc offered Arthur a place to hide. Problem was, Doc didn't know how dangerous his friend really was, and he got himself killed for his trouble."

"The police think it was Suzanna who killed Doc."

"If it was her, she had help. And that help was Arthur Elliott. If she was going to kill the man who broke her heart she would have done it in the hotel room in a fit of rage, not planned an elaborate murder."

I'd been thinking along those same lines myself. My lines didn't include Arthur as an accomplice, though. "She really had nothing to gain from killing the Doc," I said.

"Not unless there was another will. Then maybe she'd get the house."

"Too obvious," I returned. "Suzanna wanted to be the next Mrs. Michael Rivard. Killing the Doc would definitely put her out of the running. Killing Arthur and me, now that has its advantages."

There was a knock at the door. Ansel got up to get it. On his way past he said, "In Arthur Elliott's case, getting rid of you, Hellie, has great advantages."

"How? That makes no sense at all. I've been trying to prove he's innocent."

"Yes. And he knows eventually you'll prove he's not."

Ansel returned shortly after, pushing a room service cart. He set an elegant table for two and opened a bottle of red wine. "What do you say we call a truce and avoid talking about everything we've just been fighting about," he said. "And allow ourselves to enjoy this meal together?"

"Okay. You've got a deal," I told him. Though underneath I knew it wasn't going to be quite that easy. My mind was spinning with unanswered questions. But I did want to give Ansel something. And the least I could do was offer him a pleasant dinner together.

So I focused my attention on Ansel as he poured the wine. With a grand gesture, he lifted the silver domes from our plates to reveal sumptuous offerings. "Who knows," he said, taking up his place across from me, "maybe we'll even become friends."

"Maybe." I lifted my glass in a toast to him.

The dinner was wonderful. I dined on sea scallops arranged in a tower atop a layer of wine-soaked cabbage, butternut squash and finished with a light golden truffle cream sauce. This was heaven. This was Banff — the side that only the very rich ever see. Ansel had wild game, venison done in a rich three-peppercorn sauce. I was tempted to ask if he was making a statement, but I kept my mouth shut and kept to the deal.

We chatted about music, books, his work, my work. After dinner, we rounded out the meal with a luscious crème brûlée, and somewhere along the way Ansel and I became friends.

Good friends.

So good, in fact, was our new friendship that Ansel asked me to stay the night.

"Nothing has to happen." He traced a finger over my ear and down my cheek. "Just stay."

The truth was, I had feelings for Ansel Rock. What exactly those feelings were born of was a matter for debate: Loneliness? Lust? Love? Desperation? Or perhaps fear. I hadn't been with a man in over a year. It was as if I'd put my emotions, just like the rest of my life, in limbo. And now I was too afraid to move out of that nowhere place.

"Don't think so much, Hellie," Ansel murmured as he put his lips to mine. Warmth, desire and longing coursed through my body at the touch of his skin. I wanted to draw him close and into me. I wanted to feel the heat and passion of our bodies together. I wanted to feel alive again.

It would have been so easy to stay. I was so tempted. Ansel was handsome, sexy, strong and available. He was also too wealthy, too arrogant and too unpredictable. And he scared me, because Ansel Rock was just the kind of man I'd been avoiding my whole life.

I went home alone.

CHAPTER 24

THE NEXT MORNING BERNIE CAME BY WITH TIGER. THE LITTLE DOG bounced up and down in the kitchen like a kangaroo until I picked him up and cuddled him in my arms. He licked my face until I was embarrassed by his affections.

"Thanks for looking after him again, Bern. Didn't get in until late."

Bernie leaned up against the counter and grinned. "Long meeting with Ansel Rock. Well, well. I trust it wasn't all business, then."

"We had dinner. That's it."

"It's a start."

"No it's not," I said. "He's had a private investigator check me out. He knows everything about me," I said, undoing Tiger's leash.

"So, hard part's over," she said with a wry smile.

"Oh, okay, Bern. I get you. So when the Texan and I decide to get married I won't have to tell him about my embarrassing past?"

"Exactly," she said.

The phone rang. "Just a sec," I said and headed for the hall.

I picked up the receiver and said, "Hello." There was no response, but the line was still open. "Hello?" I said again.

The line went dead. A shiver prickled my skin.

I replaced the receiver and noticed the answering machine light was blinking.

I hit the play button. The first message was from my editor saying the draft I'd sent was pretty good, but that they were hoping for more personal insights. He was looking forward to receiving the second draft. Then the machine beeped and a woman's voice came on: "This is a message for Hellie MacConnell. It's … um … Julie … Julie Sands. I need to talk to you. I'm going to be out so you can't get hold of me. I'll keep trying you."

The next message was also from Julie. "This is Julie calling again for Hellie. I'll try you later." The machine clicked off.

Bernie was filling the kettle when I came back. She looked up, her face expectant. "Mr. Rock?"

I shook my head. "There was no one on the line. But Julie Sands left a couple of messages."

"The woman from Becker's camp?"

"Yes."

"What'd she want?"

"Didn't say. She's going to call back." I took a seat at the kitchen table and rested my chin in my hands.

A knock at the back door announced Des's arrival. He looked anxious. "Hellie, I've been trying to get you since last night," he said and stepped inside. "I didn't leave a message because I wasn't anywhere you could reach me. Are you all right?"

"Yes. Fine. I was ... tied up. With writing."

Bernie glanced over at me. I felt like a coward. Why hadn't I told him the truth? Why didn't I just say I was with Ansel?

"Oh," Des said, and relief unfurrowed his brow.

Tiger was skipping around the warden's legs. Des scooped up the dog, and not a moment later, the back door creaked open and Ansel poked his head in.

"Hi," he said and joined us.

Bernie greeted him and filled the kettle with more water. Des gave the Texan a polite nod.

"You forgot these in my room last night," Ansel said and passed a stack of papers to me.

Bernie eyed Ansel then cut a glance to Des before she prudently busied herself with cleaning and filling dog dishes. Des's mouth turned down into a deep frown and he shot Ansel a death stare.

I shifted from one foot to the other. Des obviously had the wrong impression: He probably thought the big Texan had taken advantage of me. At that moment, I loved Des for his gallantry. But I'd have to straighten him out later.

"Can I get anyone some tea, coffee?" Bernie said.

Both men declined. "Got some bad news," Des said. "Daniel Peterson is dead."

There was a shocked silence. Then we all seemed to take a breath. Ansel spoke first. "Last I heard he was on the mend."

Des didn't look at the Texan. He kept his eyes on me and said,

"Someone got to him."

"What do you mean 'got to him'? Wasn't he under police guard?"

"He was," Des said. "But somehow someone slipped in during the night and slit his throat."

Dog dishes crashed to the floor. Shards of glass skittered over the tiles. "Oh my God," Bernie said with a gasp.

Ansel's response was predictable: "Arthur!"

Des finally acknowledged the Texan's presence. "Police don't know what to think. But they haven't ruled out that possibility. Hellie, did you get those locks changed yet?"

Ansel was on his feet. "I'll call a security company. You need a good system in this place."

"And," Des said in an uncharacteristically forceful voice, "I'll talk to Nathan about police protection."

"Hold it," I said. "What are you talking about, Des? Yesterday you and Nathan said Suzanna probably killed Arthur. Now he's going to come after me?"

"That's the thing, we just don't know. We — "

The phone rang. I went to the hall to get it. A female voice said, "Hello. Is this Hellie?"

"Who's calling please?" There was a pause. "Hello?" I said again. Traffic noise in the background filled the void.

"It's ... Julie," the voice finally said. "From the camp. Becker's camp."

"Hi, Julie. How are you?"

"Not so good. I need to see you."

"About?"

"Can't say on the phone. Can you meet me? Daniel Peterson was — "

"I just heard," I said. "You can come here if you like."

"No. I need you to meet me. I'll explain when you get here."

"Where's here?"

"Canmore. I'll give you the address."

Another person was just murdered. I wasn't going anywhere. "Sorry, Julie, I can't. You can meet me here, in Banff."

"Please. I have information about your friend."

My breath caught in my throat. "Arthur?" I said it quietly.

"Yes. Don't tell anyone or bring anyone with you to my house. It'll just be me, promise. Don't worry, you'll be okay. But if you bring anyone else I won't talk." She gave me the address and hung up.

I dialled the caller identification number. A mechanical voice said: "We're sorry, the number you are trying to reach is not available to your call return service." I replaced the receiver. She was either calling from a cell phone or pay phone. Or her number was unlisted.

Back in the kitchen, Bernie was alone. "Ansel left," she said. "He'll call you in a little while. And Des had to get back down to the station."

"Was he okay?" I asked.

"I don't think he likes Ansel."

"No kidding. I'll call him later."

"He's all right, Hellie. You didn't do anything wrong."

"I lied."

"Not really. Unless something more than dinner did happen last night," she said with a suggestive twinkle in her eyes.

I didn't want to lie to Bernie too. Something had happened between Ansel and I. Just what that something was, I still wasn't sure. But after I went home, I'd had a sleepless night thinking about how badly I'd wanted to stay and make love to him, and at the same time, how relieved I was that I hadn't.

Bernie was watching me. "Don't worry about Des," she said quickly. "He's a big boy. And right now with everything that's going on, he's a very busy boy. I can't believe someone killed Daniel Peterson. It's so … like a movie."

"I just hope it ends soon."

"Who called?" Bernie said.

"Julie Sands," I said, and got my coat.

"Where are you going?"

"Canmore." I wrote out Julie's address and handed it to her.

"You're not going alone. Call Nathan."

"I can't. She said she won't talk if anyone comes with me. I'll take your cell phone and call you when I get there. If I have even the slightest feeling something isn't right, I promise I'll hightail it."

"I don't like this," Bernie said. She went to her purse, dug out her cell phone and a small canister and handed them to me.

I read the label on the can. "This is bear spray," I said. "What do you want me to do with it, wear it around my neck with the crystal?"

"Very funny. It's for protection."

"I'm going to Canmore, Bern. Not Mount Assiniboine." I turned the can over in my hand. "Do you always carry this?"

"Ever since those cougars started hanging around."

"Bern, right now I think cougars are the least of our worries. It's the two-legged creatures we need to fear."

***

The Sands' house was a squat, white bungalow with a fresh coat of paint that glowed luminescent in the fall light. Notwithstanding the new paint, it had a deserted look, like a summer home shut up for the winter. Flowerbeds were dug up, the soil left barren save for two lonely cement dwarfs and a plastic squirrel. Shrubs flanking the front entrance were wrapped in burlap and looked like little beige sentries keeping vigil. Curtains were drawn, and all signs of children were conspicuously absent — no bikes or toys. The street was empty of vehicles. I wandered around back, where a petite gingerbread building that was either a play-house or a garden shed was locked up with a solid chain and padlock. I came back around to the front and rang the doorbell.

While I waited I looked closer at the house and guessed it was built sometime in the late fifties when Canmore was still a working-man's mining and rail town, and little more than a gas stop on the way into the park. Now the town was popular with city folks who bought up land at premium prices to build their fancy weekend chalets. The Sands' house, I guessed, would be worth at least twenty times its original value.

No one answered the door, and I was about to turn away when an odd sensation came over me that sent prickles up my spine and damp fingers curling around my neck.

Someone was watching me.

I cut a glance to my right. Behind a screen door, in the neighbour-ing house, an elderly woman wearing a faded floral dressing gown was beckoning to me. I looked over my left shoulder to see if it really was me she was after. No one else was around. I crossed the lawn to her house. She opened the door and looked past me as if she was searching for someone else.

"Hi, I'm — " before I could finish my sentence she grabbed my arm with a gnarled, claw-like hand and hauled me inside.

"Who are you?" she said, searching my face for any sign of a fib.

"Hellie ... uh, Hellie MacConnell. I'm looking for Julie Sands."

"You the reporter woman?"

"Yes."

"Let me see some ID" She tightened the falcon grip, her talon-nails bit into the flesh of my forearm. I pulled away and passed her my licence. She snatched it out of my hand, held it close to her face and made two or three comparisons against mine. The picture was about five years old. The old woman's eyes did a final check and match before she handed back my licence. "Your hair looks better short," she said. "Any chance someone followed you?"

I shrugged. "Don't think so."

She craned her neck to see out to the street. "Julie and her family took off. Said it'd be okay to tell you where she's gone, but you can't tell anyone else."

From deep within her dressing gown pocket, she produced an envelope, which to my trained eye looked to have been steamed open. I knew the signs — the wobbly edge where the steam curled the paper and the seal yellowed from new glue. Helen MacConnell, my mother, was a master letter steamer-opener.

Julie's neighbour handed me the letter. "Probably directions out there to the reservation."

Gee, I'll just bet you're right, is what I thought. I said, "Thank you." And made a move to the door.

"You're welcome. Julie's a nice girl and her hubby, Mike, he's a good fellow. I was the secretary down at the community centre for twenty years. Nice boy he was. Never used that foul language like the other boys. In fact, I remember ... "

I'd missed my chance, I should have bolted right after she handed me the envelope. Now I was trapped. Trapped by an old master well versed in the art of keeping unsuspecting souls verbally captive. She was part of that club of talkers who never take a breath between sentences and never, ever pause between topics. A skill so finally tuned it's like watching someone win a verbal giant slalom, effortlessly gliding from one topic to the next without the listener even being aware the subject has been changed.

" ... wouldn't say why all the secrecy, but I think it's old boyfriend troubles." She let out a nasty cackle. "That's what it's about these days. They stalk 'em. That's what he's been doing."

I took my hand from the door handle. "Who? Has someone been stalking Julie?"

Julie's neighbour gave me a sly, knowing smirk. "Been sittin' out there eyeing the place. Old flame, that's what I figure. Wouldn't look twice at him myself."

"Did Julie tell you who he is?"

The woman crossed her arms over her chest. "Didn't have to. Name's Peterson."

"How do you know?"

"Peterson Outfitters. Name was all over the truck. These fellows are so brazen today."

***

Forty minutes later, after travelling a road that was little more than tire ruts baked into clay, I went as far as I could, then parked in front of a line of boulders blocking the rest of the way. Signs nailed to trees warned trespassers that hunters were in the area. In the distance, intermittent gunshots punctuated the air in staccato blasts.

I called Bernie on her cell phone.

"Now you're going where?" Bernie said.

I relayed the directions to her. "I'll call you in an hour."

"You better. If I haven't heard from you in one hour," Bernie warned, "I'm calling the police and I'll come looking for you myself. Was that a gunshot? Am I hearing gunshots?"

"No, it's thunder. Gotta go." I slipped the phone back in my jacket pocket and made my way on foot up the road toward the sounds of guns and barking dogs.

Within the past hour, the sky had turned from a bright fall blue to steely gray. A crisp, westerly wind was coming in from the mountains bringing with it the assurance of an evening snowfall.

At a clearing, surrounded by brush and naked poplar trees, I spotted Julie, who stood out conspicuously in one-piece orange overalls. She held her rifle high and was taking aim at a mound of deadfall. A white and brown-spotted rabbit bounded from the underbrush. Julie squeezed off the shot and the rabbit flew into the air like a dropkicked stuffed toy.

It fell to the ground. Except for the scratching noises the animal's hind legs made as it kicked wildly at the dead leaves, it made no sound. Julie bent to the task of stilling the wounded animal with her bare hands. I turned away and tried to suppress the wave of nausea rolling in my stomach as I waited to hear the little animal's neck snap. When I didn't hear anything, I stole a peek to see if she was done. Julie got to her feet, holding the lifeless rabbit by its hind feet. She turned, and jumped when she saw me.

"Oh, Hellie. Hi. Didn't hear you. Thanks for coming. I guess you talked to Mrs. Leachman."

I nodded, trying not to stare at the limp creature suspended from her hand. My face, I was sure, was as white as the rabbit's belly. She flipped the rabbit up and cradled it in the crook of her arm.

"There's about a million of them out here," she said. "They eat every-thing. Want to give it a try?" Julie held her rifle out to me.

I shook my head vigorously.

"Started with hare myself. Didn't think I could do it either. They're pretty cute." She was speaking quickly.

"Yes, they are. And, no, I don't want to shoot one."

"Felt exactly the same way," she said. "But just before I turned twelve my dad took me out shooting. Got home that night, put my first dead bunny on the table, and told my mom I knew what I wanted for my birthday: a rifle." She giggled. It didn't suit her.

Julie ran a hand down the lifeless creature's flank. "Thought I got a good head shot on this one, but I missed. The thing is you don't want to get him any lower — there's really not much meat on these little guys, and you don't want to ruin any of it by hitting him in the back here."

"Not that the meat's all that important to you anyway, Julie," Mike Sands said coming up behind his wife. "How you doin', Hellie?" He lifted a hand holding a hunting bow. In the other he held a target.

"Just fine. Thanks," I said. Mike Sands, however, did not look fine. His mouth was set hard and dark circles ringed his tired eyes. This was not the same unflappable, fresh-faced outdoorsman I'd met in the Apex Helicopter's parking lot.

"Haven't see you since — "

"Our failed hunting trip."

Mike nodded. There was a lull in the conversation. Naturally I filled it with the wrong thing. "So you don't use the meat?" I said staring at the dead rabbit in Julie's arms.

Her eyes blinked. "I give it away. Friends like it. I just enjoy being outdoors."

Then why don't you go for a walk? I thought angrily, and yes, unfairly. "So what else have you been shooting lately and not eating?"

"Wait a second," Mike said taking a step toward me. Julie put a hand on his sleeve to stop him. "We didn't ask you to come out here so you could dump this attitude on us," he said.

"Why did you ask me?"

"Because Julie said you'd be a good person to tell our side of the story to, since you're a reporter. Maybe she was wrong."

"Mike," Julie warned. "Go see to the dogs and then get the kids."

The harrowing sound of howling, barking dogs was fading in the distance.

"I'm sorry, Mike," I said. "I shouldn't have said it like that. A lot has happened lately. I'm not thinking too sharp."

Mike's nostrils flared with each agitated breath. He spat on the ground then said, "Yeah. Ain't that the truth. Lots has happened." He took his ball cap off and stuffed it in his pocket. "And you don't want to know the half of it." He cut a warning glance to his wife.

"It's okay, Mike," Julie said. "Let me talk to Hellie. It'll help. I promise."

Mike tapped his foot a couple of times then reluctantly turned and walked away from us. Until then, I hadn't noticed what he was wearing. He had on a dark green pullover and a hunting vest. When he flipped the hood over his head, I knew then that I was staring at the man who had shot Daniel Peterson at the Baltimore Hotel. I wondered if he was the one who'd finished the job at the hospital, and if so, whether his wife knew what he'd done. Arthur said his coat and his clothes had been stolen in Calgary. Now I knew why and by whom. Arthur and Mike Sands were about the same height and weight. They both had beards and they both knew how to use a hunting bow.

"Sorry about that, Hellie," Julie said. "Why don't we go and sit somewhere and talk," she suggested. I let her lead me to a stand of pine and spruce trees where a wooden picnic table was tucked out of sight under the tree boughs. "You want a coffee or anything? I've got a thermos in my pack."

"No thanks," I said.

She was still holding the rabbit, stroking its head. "We used to keep some of these guys as pets," Julie said.

"So did we."

"When my dad took me out hunting, he was so proud of me. Maybe that's what hooked me," she said.

"Maybe."

"He was a great hunter, my dad. Real ethical." She lowered her voice to mimic her father's: "The kill isn't important, Julie. It's the hunt and being a good sportsman. Make sure it's a clean shot or don't shoot at all."

"So what happened, Julie?"

"You mean when did I stop being ethical?" A faraway look crept in and clouded her eyes. "My dad could skin a rabbit faster than any man I ever knew. He showed me how, and I think I'm just about as fast."

"Is it Becker? Are you afraid of him?"

"It's the knife and knowing your equipment ... " Tears filled her eyes until fat drops plopped from her high cheekbones and splattered on the rabbit's head. "I'm glad he's dead, my dad. I'd sure hate for him to see me in this mess."

"What mess, Julie?"

She sucked in a halting breath. "We had a really good life in Canmore. Bought years before the boom, when you could still get a place for less than the cost of a mansion. Now it's all gone down the toilet." She sucked in another breath. "I don't know what to do. Mike thinks we can just up and move and it'll be okay. But it won't."

"Why won't it, Julie?"

She thought for a moment before she began. "See, a few years back Mike wanted to go on his own. Been working for the Petersons for years. It was time. He's a good guide, Hellie."

"I'm sure he is," I said, and I meant it.

"But he wanted his own thing. So we borrowed the money against the house to get our own guide business going."

"I can guess what happened," I put in. "Becker didn't like the competition."

"That, and the fact that Mike wasn't under his thumb anymore. Mike and I knew too much. That was the real problem."

"Which is why you really wanted out. Because you and Mike knew they were poaching."

"Yeah. We knew," she said, and ran a finger down the bunny's head. I wished she'd put the thing down.

"It was mostly Daniel, at first. Becker would take a moose or two out of season and sell the trophy head. Daniel was into selling the meat."

"Was Mike poaching for them?"

Tears streamed down her face. "Becker worked against us from the beginning. Mike couldn't get any business. We were going to lose the house. So Becker bailed us out. The bastard. He had us from the start."

"Why didn't you go to the police?" I knew the answer. At least I thought I did.

"We were too scared."

"Julie, did Mike shoot Daniel?"

"No! Mike would never do that. Never. Mike told me Becker got someone who was just supposed to scare Daniel that night."

"Then why did that someone put an arrow in his chest?"

"Maybe the person panicked or ... " She looked me in the eye and kept her gaze a little too straight for just a little too long. I knew she was lying.

"Julie, I know. I was there that night."

She put a fist to her mouth. "Daniel moved. Mike panicked and missed."

"Why were they trying to scare Daniel?"

"Becker was taking park animals. Best trophy heads come from the park. Daniel's job was to get rid of the carcass. He wasn't supposed to be selling the damn meat. They were park animals, for God's sake. If Daniel got caught, the police and the wardens would be able to trace it back through DNA. Then they'd start asking Becker questions."

"Like where are the heads of these animals?"

"Right."

"You think Becker went to the hospital and killed his own cousin?"

Julie nodded and looked down to her lap and seemed surprised that she was still holding the rabbit. She put it on the ground next to her and wiped her hands on her pants.

"It's all getting too scary now, Hellie. Someone else is going to get hurt."

"Like you and Mike."

"And my kids." She'd said it so quietly I could barely hear her. As if even uttering the words was enough to cause it to happen.

She may have been right. If Becker was capable of strolling into the hospital and slitting his own cousin's throat, he probably wouldn't have too much trouble doing the same to Julie and her family.

"That's why I called you ... " she hesitated. "In case anything happens, someone needs to know. Mike's been doing favours for Becker for too damn long."

Her words triggered a thought: The scene at Becker's camp. What he'd said to her, how he'd acted toward her. "And what about you, Julie, what favours have you been doing for Becker?"

She looked away. "I cook for him and his clients."

"I saw the way he treated you."

"I'm not a ... a prostitute. Jesus I hate him. I'm just trying to raise my kids."

"I know that," I said.

She clasped her hands together as if in prayer. "Please don't tell anyone, Hellie. Mike doesn't know. Becker, he made me. My kids ... I'm just trying to protect my husband and my kids."

Becker Peterson was using and abusing both of these people and neither one knew the full extent. If they did, I was sure one of them would kill him.

Julie Sands' brow creased into a solid line across her forehead. She rocked back and forth. "I think they had something to do with your friend disappearing. And Doctor Rivard ... " She trailed off and stared into the distance. "He delivered my kids. God, I'm so sorry."

"What do you know about Doc Rivard, Julie? You've got to tell me what you know."

She looked around and stared at the dense brush at her side, as if she fully expected to find someone hiding there. She lowered her voice.

"Mike said — "

The sound of a truck rumbling in the distance cut her short. Fear shone in Julie's eyes. We both listened until we heard truck doors slam and children's laughter.

Julie sank back. Exhaustion was inscribed on her face. "It's Mike and the kids," she said with relief. "Becker said something to Mike about getting rid of that enviro nut," she spoke quickly.

"Arthur?" I asked.

"Yes," she said.

"Because he knew what they were doing?"

She nodded. "Becker sometimes snares bears and cats, trees the cats. He usually calls in a hunter from the States who flies in and ... " she trailed off again.

"And what? Shoots the poor creature while it's tied up?"

"Yeah, It's pretty disgusting, I know. But some people are lazy. A lot of those guys don't want to have to hike in anywhere. All they want is to get out of a vehicle, take their shot and take their trophy back home and brag about how they're such a great hunter."

"Why doesn't Becker just shoot it for them then?"

Julie shrugged. "Because the hunter wants to do it himself."

"My God, how long does it take the so-called hunter to get there?"

"Could be two, three days."

"Arthur knew," I said.

Julie nodded. "He stopped them a couple of times. Distracted the dogs, cut the snare."

"You think they killed him and the Doc? Why the Doc?"

"I don't know about Doctor Rivard. His name was never mentioned, only Arthur's. I just thought because he was a friend of Arthur's ... I don't know. Maybe it was just beer hall talk," Julie continued. "But it was the day before Arthur Elliott disappeared. I figured it out after you came to the camp." The children's voices grew louder. Julie talked faster. "That friend of Ansel Rock's — "

"John Morrow?"

"Yeah him. He was out at Becker's camp that same day you came."

"Yes, I saw him."

"I got a weird feeling," she said. "He and Becker were arguing."

"Becker wanted Ansel Rock's business back," I explained. "And the ram that Ansel bid on in the auction had just been poached."

"Yeah, I know. Maybe that was it."

"Did you hear anything they were saying?"

"No. But I could see into the tent and John was really giving it to Becker. Just thought I should mention it."

Two dark-haired children, a boy and girl about five and ten respectively, came running into the clearing.

"I have to go," Julie said and got to her feet. "Please don't say anything about me and ... Becker," his name caught in her throat.

She didn't have to ask. The pleading look in her eyes was sufficient to seal my lips forever. I would never mention a word about her and Becker Peterson. Although I wished I could. Guys like Becker get away with bullying because their victims are decent people who can't bear the prospect of public scrutiny.

"But Julie." I placed a hand on her shoulder. "I have to tell the police ... you have to tell the police about the other things. What Mike's done. You've got to protect yourself and your family from Becker."

She nodded and the flash of relief that comes from telling the truth was visible in her eyes. Julie's children ran up to me giggling and laughing with excitement. They held out their arms to show off their new prize puppies — beagle puppies.

Tiger's kin.

CHAPTER 25

AFTER I LEFT JULIE, I REPORTED IN TO BERNIE TO SAY I WAS ALIVE AND well and on my way home. I made a second call to Nathan. He wasn't in, and I really didn't think I could leave a message explaining everything Julie had said. I'd try him again as soon as I made it back to Banff.

When I rounded the corner to the Doc's house, my heart sank at the sight of Sandy and Doug's car parked in the drive.

"Hi ho, Hellie," Sandy said opening my car door for me. "Sorry we didn't call. Thought we'd take a chance. And looks like we lucked out." She laughed.

Bernie opened the front door and came out.

"Oh. Bernie, you're here," Sandy said.

Doug was pulling boxes of fudge from the trunk of their car. "Hidy ho, Hellie. Well, this is the last of it." He handed me a box and I led the way into the house. Bernie rolled her eyes as I passed her.

Inside, I excused myself and went upstairs to call Nathan. He still wasn't in, so I left a message for him to call me right away. Downstairs Doug and Sandy were in the kitchen stacking boxes on the counter. Bernie was just coming in with another load.

"Say, Hellie," Doug said. "We heard Suzanna is in the clink. Larry said she attacked you or something. Now what in the Dark Ages is that all about?"

"I think she lost her mind," I said in earnest.

"And that man in the hospital. We heard about that too. Our little mountain paradise is turning into a hotbed of crime," Sandy chirped. "And we thought we'd left all that behind in Winnipeg."

"Oh, I think you have. Banff doesn't see many murders."

Sandy let out a hoot. "Perhaps not by your Texan boyfriend's standards."

"He's not my boyfriend. He's — "

"Believe you me," she prattled on, "one murder is more than I wish to see. What with all their guns, I suppose murder in Houston is about as common as parking tickets."

"Not quite," I said patiently. But keep it up, Sandy, and it'll get that way around here real quick. "So how long before you ship this stuff out?" I asked as I picked up one of the boxes off the counter and followed Doug to the basement stairs.

"Truck will be here by seven tonight and it'll be out of your hair," Sandy said.

"For now," Doug corrected his wife. "But I thought the truck was coming for six. I've got it all mapped out for six."

"Larry changed it to seven," Sandy said. "The driver has a couple of stops to make to pick up ice cream or something."

"Ice cream!" Doug stopped on the stairs in front of me. "Frozen ice cream?"

"That's the only kind I know of. The frozen kind," Sandy said.

"Can't be frozen. This fudge cannot be frozen."

"Listen you guys," I said. "I really need to get some things done." I wanted to try Nathan again and fill Bernie in on what I'd learned from Julie.

Bernie came down the stairs behind us carrying two more boxes. "This is all there is from the car," she said.

When we had the last of the new boxes in place, Doug announced with great satisfaction, "Our man in Vancouver will have this on his shelves by tomorrow night. And by Tuesday, people all over BC will be hooked on our Too Goody-Goody Fudge."

"Do you like the name, Hellie?" Sandy asked.

"Sure."

"Clever, isn't it?"

"Sure it is. Well, your man certainly ordered a lot of it," I said. Half the cold storage room was now filled with boxes. "Okay you guys. If that's it, I wouldn't mind — "

"Say, Hellie and Bernie," Doug interrupted. "If you have a few more minutes, I sure could use a couple of extra hands rearranging and stacking these," he said hefting a box from one pile to another. "I want them organized by flavour."

I looked to Sandy.

"Sandy's got back problems." Sandy demonstrated the problem by pinching up her face and placing a hand on her lower back.

I grabbed an end, albeit grudgingly, and got down to it. Bernie did the same with Sandy who protested but managed to lift a corner of one box.

"So, uh, when is that new fridge of yours coming?" I asked after we'd rearranged about a dozen of the boxes.

"We're going to see what happens with this first order," Sandy said.

Translation: There will be no new fridge.

"I'd like the French vanilla to go over here," Doug said with authority to his wife and Bernie.

As they were placing the box on the floor Sandy let her end slip at the last moment and the box went down with a bang followed by a clinking noise.

"Now, what the Dickens was that?" Doug said.

"That sounded like glass, Dougy," Sandy said.

Doug tore open the carton. Inside the container, celo-wrapped fudge blocks were stacked in towers. Between the fudge buffers were three tall liquor bottles. We all stared in fascination. "Now, what the Sam Hill is this doing in with the French?"

"We have a vanilla nut and a French vanilla," Sandy explained helpfully.

Doug shot her a look to shut her up and pulled out a bottle of rye whiskey. He held it to my face. "Now, I don't know what the heck you're tying to pull here, Hellie. But if this is illegal, I'll tell you — "

"Me! What are you talking about? This is your property."

"Illegal!" Sandy said.

"What's going on, Doug?" I demanded.

Doug went pale and dropped the bottle back into the carton as if it were burning the tips of his fingers. "We don't know anything about this, Hellie. I swear. These boxes ... " he said, tearing open more cartons. "These boxes have been down here for a few days. Whoever put those bottles in with the French certainly did it without our knowledge."

"They sure did," Sandy chimed in. "We're not bootleggers." Her face was ashen, and her husband was wringing his hands.

Doug tore open another carton. "Well now, isn't this just a fine how-do-you-do," he said, holding up a block of chocolate fudge.

"Now what's wrong?" Sandy whined.

He unwrapped the cellophane. "Sandy and I always wrap these

individually. Someone put two portions together and rewrapped it." He separated the two blocks. Inside, each block had been scraped out and filled with what looked like a piece of dried leather.

Doug dropped it, and I could tell from the dumbfounded look on both Sandy and Doug's faces that neither had ever seen this before, and they didn't have a clue what it was. I thought I might have one, though.

"What in the name of the Holy Ghost is that?" Sandy said.

"Did you say Larry arranged the trucking?" I asked Doug.

"Yes!" he said, and snapped his fingers. "Ha! That's it, of course. It's Larry. He's just the type to be a bootlegger. Feeds all his degenerate friends stolen liquor."

I didn't bother to point out that the liquor was heading out of Banff. I was considering a few other things, though, as bits of information started to fit together to create an interesting pattern. The dog, for starters. Larry had obviously got Tiger from Mike Sands. Mike was working for the Petersons. Larry told Doug about the cold storage room. The truck. Larry arranged it for Doug. The Doc. It was Larry who said the Doc died of an overdose.

"Call Larry's dad, Hellie," Sandy said. "His father owns a trucking company. Larry got us a deal." She sank down on a stack of boxes.

I told them to stay put and not to touch anything until the police arrived. I ran upstairs with Bernie and went to the hall. As I dialled the RCMP station, I said to Bernie, "I'm going over to Larry's. Will you wait here for the police?"

"Of course," she said.

Nathan was in and came on the line. "Nathan, it's Hellie. I need you to send an officer over to the Doc's right away. Bernie will let them in."

"What's this about?" he asked calmly.

"I'll explain it all when you meet me at Larry Melwheeler's."

"I've got about a dozen drunk kids I'm dealing with right now. I'm a little pressed here."

"Trust me, Nathan. Please. I'll see you at Larry's."

***

The Moose's party palace was uncharacteristically quiet: no music, no dancing kids, no pulsating lights. Gatsby's house after the tragedy. The front door was ajar. I pushed it open and peeked in. Duffel bags and suitcases were piled at the foot of the stairs in the grand foyer. A door closed overhead on the second floor.

"Larry. You there?" I called out.

Silence. I knew someone was up there. I went up the stairs, jumped over the gate and entered Larry's lust loft. The entire upper floor was divided into two enormous rooms: a black granite and stainless steel bathroom, and one massive bedroom. In the center of the bedroom a king-sized waterbed was heaped with black satin sheets and a leopard print duvet. On the nightstands lava lamps burped up primary-coloured gel blobs in frosty glass tubes. Crystals and glass pyramids hung from the ceiling like stalactites.

A quick check of the bathroom revealed nothing. In the bedroom, an entire wall was dedicated to mirrored closet space; one of the panels was open. A tumble of clothes and sporting equipment spilled out onto the bedroom floor.

"Larry?"

"Hellie?" The voice came from somewhere inside the closet.

"Yeah, it's me." I opened the closet panel further. Pants and shirts were lined up neatly along the wall. But there was no Larry.

"Larry?" I moved the clothes aside.

"In here," came the muffled voice.

"Where?"

I heard a door open. Light poured out from the back of the closet through a door that was about three feet tall.

"Here."

I hesitated, debating whether I'd wait for Nathan before I started crawling into small spaces with Larry Melwheeler. I decided that if he tried anything, I'd tell him Nathan was downstairs. I crawled past the pile of laundry and sports equipment and stuck my head into a room that was about twelve feet by twelve. Floor to ceiling bookshelves covered one wall. The shelves were empty. A desk sat in one corner littered with magazines and books. Next to the shelves, dirty dishes were stacked on a small table. An armchair was pushed up against the far wall. Larry was sitting in it holding a brightly-coloured piece of cloth: Arthur's kikoi.

"Where did you get that?" I demanded

Larry's face was eggshell white. "He left it here."

A gasp caught in my throat. "Arthur's been here?" I scanned the room. "Living here?"

"Not by choice."

"You bastard. What have you done with him?"

"Nothing. I was supposed to kill him," Larry said matter-of-factly.

"You what? You ... you didn't?"

His head swayed from side to side. "Couldn't. Be like killing Gandhi or something. So I hid him up here."

"My God, Larry, what have you gotten yourself into?" My eyes took in the cramped space. "You built this room?"

"No. Guy who owned the house before was involved in some trust company fraud or something. Hid documents back here."

"Where's Arthur now?"

"I let him go. He probably went to find them." Larry twisted a dread-lock between his thumb and forefinger. "Shit, I gotta get out of here," he said and stood. "Thought you were them."

"Who?"

He pushed past me. "I gotta go. They're gonna kill me soon as they figure out Arthur's alive."

I followed him into the bedroom, where he madly pulled shirts, shorts and underwear from drawers, dropping it all at his feet.

"Hold it," I said. "Sit down. Nathan's on his way over here." He froze. "If you're scared, let the police help you."

Larry's eyes searched the room frantically trying to decide what to do next. "I can't find my fucking passport," he cried, and pulled at his frizzy locks.

"Sit. Larry. You're not going to get very far. And if you're afraid someone is going to hurt you, you're better off here." He leaned his back against the dresser. Beads of sweat glistened on his forehead. "Who's going to hurt you, Larry? Who wanted you to kill Arthur?" I knew the answer, but it was too painful to say.

He looked me in the eye. "Haven't you figured it out yet?"

"Ansel."

Larry watched me for a moment. "No."

"Then who?"

"John Morrow.

"Can't be."

"Sure can. He's a poacher, Hellie. A big-time poacher."

"Are you telling me John is working with Becker?"

"Becker works for John. We all work for John Morrow."

"But ... he saved my life, the day Suzanna came after me. Said he'd been watching her."

"He only saved you because Ansel Rock was there. John was watching Suzanna all right. And when he noticed she'd been in the house a little too long that day, he started to get worried. One other time she'd been in there at night, and he looked in the basement window and saw her snooping around, going in and out of the cold storage room. John figured she'd found something."

"Something like illegal animal parts and liquor bottles?"

"Yeah, that. And he was intending to let himself in and do something to stop her, but Ansel showed up. Saw John coming around the front of the house. John lied and told Ansel he was worried about you. They looked in the back window and saw Suzanna had a spear and that she was going after you."

"She could have killed me," I said. "All because you made her believe there was another will with her name mentioned in it. You made up all that stuff about knowing a secretary at the lawyer's office, didn't you?"

"Yeah," Larry said.

"Nathan thinks she killed the Doc. Did she?"

Larry shook his head. "Becker did. John made him."

The floor tilted beneath me. I dropped onto the bed. My hand went to my chest. I felt as though I'd been kicked. "Why?"

"John thought the Doc was on to him. See, they knew each other."

"I know. Ansel told me John took the Doc and his wife out on hunting safaris."

"Yeah, but I bet he didn't tell you that all the ivory, skins and trophies you found came from John."

"No, he didn't."

"That's because Ansel doesn't know that John has always cut a few corners for his clients. Everyone always goes home happy from John's safaris."

"I don't understand what you're talking about."

"Okay, we sometimes do the same thing here for clients. Let's say you come to shoot yourself a grizzly bear, and you don't get anything? Well, me and the Petersons might just find one for you to take home."

"So you go out and poach one and sell the bearskin to your client."

"Right," Larry said.

He looked only slightly guilty as he spoke and I wanted to slap him. But I gritted my teeth and let him keep talking.

"John has been doing that in Tanzania since the seventies."

"Did he do that for the Doc?"

"Maybe. But I know for sure he did get his wife, Barb, a bunch of ivory."

"But then they met Arthur," I said.

"Yeah, and Arthur knew they were ivory collectors and told them the ivory they were collecting was most likely coming from poachers."

"Did Arthur know it was coming from John Morrow?"

"No. The Doc never told Arthur where he was getting it. Doc went to John and told him he had to quit selling customers ivory. John played innocent and thanked the Doc for letting him know the situation, and said he'd make sure he followed everything by the book. They both agreed never to mention it."

"But John kept up his poaching business," I said.

"Sure did."

"And when the Doc went back to Tanzania this time, he found out," I said.

"John wasn't exactly sure what Doc Rivard knew, but he got scared when he heard he was coming home. Arthur was getting too close to the Petersons, and John was sure Arthur would make the connection back to him sooner or later with the Doc's help."

"Did Arthur tell you what the Doc said to him? Why he was coming home?" I said.

"Yeah, me and Arthur talked about all this. But the Doc just said he was worried because Arthur told him he suspected the Petersons were poaching bears."

"And when Doc heard that John Morrow was coming with Ansel," I said, "he must have been even more suspicious."

"That's what John figured. In the eighties, John brought in some illegal weapons through medical clinics."

My hand flew to my mouth. "Oh, my God. John is the one. He framed Arthur. Oh, dear God. Ansel has to know." I stared hard at the stupid, greedy man sitting at my feet.

"What?" Larry snapped. "Quit looking at me like that."

"How long has John been working with the Petersons?"

"I don't know. Ten, twelve years. But John's got stuff going all over the place. He's connected all over the world."

"What exactly is in that fudge?" I asked.

"Bear gallbladders. We pack it in chocolate because customs dogs can't smell it."

"You've really thought of everything," I said, my voice was full of disgust. "Ansel isn't involved with John in this, is he?"

"No. One time John and Ansel had plans to build a big resort here together, but that fell through because Doc Rivard had found out it was going to involve John Morrow."

It all came together for me. "So the Doc did all he could to stop it. Because he never really trusted John."

"That's what John thought, and it really pissed him off."

"So this is how you afford all this, huh?" I said spreading my arms. "This house, everything. Poaching animals for John Morrow."

"This isn't my house. It's John's."

"I see. You do his dirty work and you get to live here. Big deal, Larry. Look what you've done. You've destroyed people, animals, bears and now yourself. Did you put those bear paws in Arthur's cabin? So you could destroy him too?"

"Becker did. John told him to do it." Larry gnawed at his thumbnail. From my vantage point it looked like he was sucking his thumb.

"But John doesn't have a key for the cabin," I said.

Larry gave me a look. "Hellie, a ten-year-old could break into that cabin."

"Oh. I suppose you're right." I thought for a moment and let everything sink in. Choosing my words carefully I said, "So all this has been an elaborate plan. Even shooting Ansel's ram?"

"Yeah. John said he had to get rid of it — "

I cut him off. "Because he wanted Ansel to think it was Arthur who'd done it."

"Right. And John knew once the ram was gone, Ansel would leave town."

"Who killed the ram, Larry?"

He ignored my question, jumped up and started dumping more drawers. T-shirts and underwear cascaded to the floor. He was on his hands and knees digging through the pile like a madman.

"Damn. It's not here," Larry whined. "Shit." He slumped back against the dresser.

"It's okay, Larry. Calm down." I kept my voice steady. "Just talk to me." Underneath I was terrified. I had no idea what Larry Melwheeler was capable of. I kept listening for Nathan and wondered where the hell he was. "Tell me what happened with the Doc. You injected him with adrenaline, didn't you? Tell me the truth, it'll only help."

"You think?" Larry said and pulled his legs up to his chest, his knees knocking together in a nervous rhythm.

"I do. You've got nothing to lose."

"Yeah?" His face brightened pathetically. "And maybe if I tell you, you could, like, act as a witness or something?"

"Sure."

He rested his head against the dresser and seemed to relax a little. "I didn't kill Doc Rivard, Hellie. I waited outside the Marriott until he checked in. Then I called him."

"From the pay phone?"

"Yeah. I told him Arthur was real sick. That he had to come back right away. Said you'd been taking care of him, but that you were beat, needed to rest."

"That's how you got him to park his car down the block. He didn't want to disturb me."

Larry nodded.

"My God, how could you?"

"I didn't kill him."

"Well who the hell did, then?"

"Becker and Daniel."

"Oh, dear God," I whispered. "How could you? How could you, Larry?"

"Hellie, I didn't do it. They did. When the Doc got to Arthur's cabin, Daniel came running down the river path and told Doc someone was hurt. Then he led him back to the gazebo. Becker was under there, waiting. He made some moaning noises or something. You know, like he was hurt. Doc crawled under there to help him, and … " Larry paused and shrugged. "Then Becker injected him with the allergy stuff."

My eyes closed against Larry's words. "That is positively monstrous," I said on a gush of exhaled breath I didn't know I'd been holding. I felt heavy, and weak, and I didn't want to hear anymore. But I had to know everything so I could tell the police. I just wished I'd had my tape recorder with me in case Larry decided to change his story. I kept him talking and said, "But Nathan said there was no sign of a struggle. Didn't Doc put up a fight?"

"No," Larry said, lowering his voice. "It was dark. When he crawled in beside Becker he thought something bit him, or that he'd leaned up against a nail or something."

"How did John know to use adrenaline?"

"Keeps the stuff around at his resorts, especially in Africa. People are allergic to all kinds of shit. John knew it would work because he told Becker there was a guy on safari once who had an allergic reaction to a bee sting. The guy ended up dying. But not from the sting; from the allergy shot. Guy had a heart condition. They didn't have one of those pen things. They had, like, a vial of it and John figures they probably gave him too much. The adrenaline made his heart go all out of whack. Sped it up and then, like, it popped."

Larry put his hands out. "Hey, don't look at me like that, Hellie. I didn't do it. I just put that pen thing in the bin. John had a bunch more. Listen to me. After I phoned the Doc, I took off. It was all too freaky for me."

I was staring at him in disbelief. I was staring at a murderer. "But you knew," I said. "You knew what they were going to do, Larry. You knew! How could you let it happen?" I cocked an ear for any sign of Nathan. None came. I considered bolting. Larry had gone along with killing the Doc. But … he'd kept Arthur alive. I'd wait a few more minutes for Nathan. He'd be along any minute, I assured myself.

"So you must have seen Suzanna," I said.

"Yeah, I saw her go in and out of the hotel. After she left, I called the Doc." Now there was deep regret in Larry's voice. "Anyway, we set things up with Sandy and Doug."

"Sandy and Doug are in on this?"

"No. I made up all that stuff about the guy wanting to buy their freakin' fudge. When we needed a key to your place, I thought up the bogus will thing. Told Suzanna there might be a copy in the house. Figured she'd steal a key from you. But she already had one from a long time ago. So then I thought up the dog."

"You thought up the dog? Des said Suzanna put you up to getting it for me."

He shook his head. "That's what I told Nathan after they arrested her. See, we wanted her in there snooping around, but not too much."

"Why?"

"If someone got suspicious, or something happened and one of us got caught, we could say we thought we saw someone prowling around. It'd just be Suzanna getting the dog, or Sandy and Doug. John made a copy of Suzanna's key."

"Was it you hanging around the Doc's backyard at night?" He nodded. "So it was you who put all that stuff in with the fudge."

"Yeah."

"Why the Doc's house? Why couldn't you store it someplace else?"

"I guessed it was a safe bet. Who would think to look in Doc Rivard's house? And I got the impression John liked the idea of having it there."

"Ah. Revenge. So he's into smuggling liquor now too? I don't get this, Larry. Who smuggles liquor?"

Larry shook his head. Shame contorted his face.

"What? What is it, Larry?"

"They're doin' some weird shit."

"What kind of weird shit? Where?" I thought I heard the front door open. Nathan! Larry didn't seem to notice. I kept him talking. "What are they doing, Larry, making moonshine?"

"I wish they were. Those bottles are full of — " Something caught Larry's eye. I saw it too: a flicker in the glass panelled ceiling. There was a creak — a footfall on hardwood.

"Nathan?" I said.

Larry gasped. My eyes snapped to him. Shock and fear animated his face. At the same moment, I heard the sing of an arrow and watched in horror as it struck Larry's chest. Larry grabbed for it with both hands. Air escaped his lung in a whoosh. A low guttural noise rose in his throat. I reached out for him. The scene played out in slow motion. Larry crumpled to the floor. I went down with him.

A shadow stretched across the ceiling. I looked up. John Morrow's reflection splintered and multiplied in the mirrored walls.

CHAPTER 26

IN THE SPLIT SECOND JOHN FUMBLED FOR SOMETHING IN HIS POCKET, I ran. Jumped over the gate, and made my legs carry me down the stairs. Footsteps thundered behind me.

"Hellie, stop or I'll shoot you."

I knew he'd have a pretty hard time running and shooting me at the same time with a bow and arrow. At least that's what I was counting on.

I charged across the expansive foyer. I heard my self-defense instructor's voice: *Don't ever let them take you to another location. Fight for your life where you are.*

He caught me at the front door, threw an arm around my neck and stuck something hard in my back. I hadn't counted on him having a gun. He hauled me to the garage. I was certain he would kill me. For the second time that week, I pleaded for my life.

"Don't be a fool, Hellie," John said struggling to unlock the driver's door of Larry's Land Rover. "I'm not going to hurt you. Get in."

Never, ever let them take you ...

I got in. My first thought was to lock the doors. John had the keys. He'd shoot his way in if he had to. I was letting him take me.

The garage door went up after John hit the remote on the dash. He leaned over and turned the key in the ignition. "Move it," he said.

I inched the Rover down the drive. My heart leapt when I spied an RCMP cruiser parked on the street. John saw it too.

"If you touch that horn or do anything to attract attention, I will kill you now. I'm going to take you to the camp for a short time. Then I'll let you go. Co-operate, you live. It's simple."

Nathan was not in the cruiser. I'd left the front door open for him. We'd just missed each other. Sergeant Delaware would be climbing the stairs right about now.

"John, they'll know it was you."

"No they won't. They'll know it was Arthur Elliott. Just like they know it was Arthur who killed Daniel Peterson."

We were travelling down Banff Avenue Tourists strolled along the street, sipping coffees and peeking in shop windows. And I was about to die. I wanted to scream at them to help me. But I couldn't. He had the gun trained on me. I was paralyzed.

"Don't even think about jumping, Hellie. I won't hesitate to shoot you."

"I wasn't planning to," I said petulantly.

"Just drive the car."

We left Banff and retraced the route to the Ghost River Wilderness Reserve. As we did, pieces of the sordid puzzle fell into place. John Morrow killed the Doc, Daniel and now Larry. There were three other murders I could also think of that were probably linked to John: Marianna Rock, her daughter and the agent. The list was long, and it was about to get even longer. I suspected the only reason he hadn't already killed me was because he might need a hostage if we ran into Arthur or the police.

For my part, I probably would have jumped out at a light and taken my chances. But I was betting Arthur was on his way to getting himself killed. And maybe, just maybe I could help him, or he me. If … he was still alive. I decided to test my suspicions about the other three murders. If I was right, it might put John Morrow off kilter and give me a little leverage.

"I think Ansel knows what you did in Tanzania. Or he suspects at any rate." I braced myself and waited for John to tell me to shut up and drive, or shoot me. He did neither.

"What does he suspect?"

Gotcha! My fingers relaxed their grip on the steering wheel, and I ran with my theory. "I was with Ansel last night, at his hotel room." I paused and let him fill in the details. "During a little pillow talk Ansel and I started chatting about a few things."

"Don't play games with me. What things?"

"Nothing specific, really. Ansel just mentioned something about his wife and you. And, you know, the unusual circumstances surrounding her death. How she called your safari company. How the poachers seemed to know she was on her way to your camp." Out of the corner of my eye I could see the wheels turning in John Morrow's mind. "Ansel will put it together when they find Larry."

He was silent for a moment, then said, "You're lying, Hellie. Ansel would never think such a thing."

"Ansel was asking questions, John. And if I show up dead, he'll put it together." John shifted in his seat. I kept going, making educated guesses as I went. "Marianna found out what you were up to, didn't she?" He didn't answer. "She found out that you were nothing but a common poacher who was smuggling weapons in and forging customs documents to get your illegal ivory out of Tanzania. She discovered you were one of the very people she and Arthur were fighting so hard to stop. You turned out to be the enemy, John. But you were also her husband's best friend and godfather to her child."

I stole a glance in his direction. John still had the gun trained on me, but his eyes stared straight ahead. "Marianna was on her way to tell her husband about you so he wouldn't have to hear it from someone else," I continued. "Or perhaps Marianna Rock was being loyal to you and was going to give you the opportunity to do the honourable thing and tell Ansel yourself." John ran a nervous hand over his mouth and licked his lips. "But she never got the chance. Because you had your goons — "

He stopped me when he pressed the gun to my side. "Marianna would still be alive today if she hadn't got herself mixed up with Arthur Elliott. Keep your mouth shut and drive."

The rest of the drive seemed shorter, much shorter this time. Minutes really. But then time always does seem to speed up when you're trying to buy a little more.

We pulled onto the service road, then bumped our way down the dry creek bed to the end, where we abandoned the vehicle. Two others before us had done the same thing. A green Ford Bronco and an old, light blue Dodge pickup were parked at the trailhead. I didn't recognize the Bronco, but I could have thrown myself on the hood of the old truck and hugged it — the Dodge belonged to Miriam Bauer, which meant Miriam, Arthur or both had to be somewhere nearby.

"Do you recognize either of these?" John asked.

I let out the breath I had been holding. "No."

"Are you sure one of these isn't Arthur's?"

"I'm sure. Arthur doesn't own a vehicle," I said, willing my eyes not to blink.

John scrutinized the two trucks. "Could be hikers," he mumbled to himself. He looked up the trail and back down the creek bed. "If we do see anyone, Hellie, you better smile and keep your comments to the weather."

We headed up the trail and after what seemed like only seconds instead of half an hour, the chain link fence surrounding the Deifenbunker came into view, and I wished with all my heart that those motorcycle guys had bought it. In my desperate mind I saw dozens of leather-clad toughs sitting around the enclosure drinking beer just waiting to save me.

"Stop," John said as I passed the locked gate. Keys rattled behind me. Metal scraped against metal.

I peered back over my shoulder and watched the gate swing open. "You! You're the owner!" I said.

"That's right. I'm the owner."

Run! The voice screamed in my head. I couldn't. My legs wouldn't let me. He would shoot me in the back. But the thought of being forced down a dark shaft on my belly drew panic from the pit of my stomach. I had seen pictures of bomb shelters. Some were nothing more than a shaft dug into the ground like a storm sewer. I knew there was just such a shaft waiting for me behind those doors. John would shoot me and stuff my body or ... stuff me down there alive! Please God never that. Never! I readied myself to run. Larry's words came back in a rush: *One near Ottawa is like a small city.* I took a breath. I didn't run.

John fit a key in the bunker door and opened it to reveal a concrete tunnel high and wide enough to drive a truck through. I exhaled and took in a ragged breath. He told me to get going. But my legs still wouldn't let me move. I searched for an escape.

"Don't bother, Hellie. There are four big men down there who will find you. Just go." John's voice was softer. "I'm not going to hurt you. I just need you out of the way for a little while. It's not too far down."

I entered the tunnel. The door closed behind me. We were in pitch darkness. The gun barrel pressed against my spine. I shifted my weight and put my hand on my chest over the crystal, and I prayed it would protect me again. At the same moment, my arm brushed against something hard in my jacket pocket. Bear spray. Thank you my dear, dear friend! I seized the opportunity and slipped the palm-sized canister from my pocket and tucked it into the front of my pants under my shirt.

"Move," John commanded.

I took hesitant steps letting only the very tips of my fingers follow the cool concrete wall, waiting with dread for them to brush up against something furry and hanging upside down.

The tunnel was suddenly illuminated. John had the gun in one hand and in the other hand a huge flashlight he must have picked up at the entrance. Now John had two deadly weapons. He could either shoot me or bludgeon me to death. All I had was a can of deterrent. We walked on, passing under dripping pipes, each step taking us deeper and deeper into the earth.

At the end of the tunnel was a steel door, thick as a bank vault's. John opened it and we entered another tunnel. This one was narrower, but well lit. We took a right. Down a little further, then a left. I was trying to keep track of the turns.

We walked on, and it felt as if I was passing through a thick fog. Nothing seemed real. We turned a corner. Damp earthy smells permeated the dense stale air and assaulted my senses. We went deeper into the bunker. I was Poe's Fortunato descending the catacombs to my own grave.

CHAPTER 27

A MUFFLED CRY CAME FROM SOMEWHERE DEEP IN THE BOWELS OF THE shaft and arrested my steps. Musty smells rose in the stagnant air. Hay. Manure. Circus smells. Animal smells. More strange noises, low moans and growls floated toward us.

A brightly lit entrance lay ahead.

"Move, Hellie."

I walked on. With each step the terrible sounds — howls, cries, growling — grew and filled our subterranean world.

I stopped. "What is that?" I hissed.

John pressed the gun to my back to keep going. The howls grew louder. Rage. I was listening to cries of rage.

We stepped over the threshold and entered a cavernous room — a white room lit up like an operating theatre with white walls, white light. Those were the first things I saw. The rest took more time to absorb.

Cages.

Five, six, seven cages were spread around the room, each one holding a grizzly or its black cousin hostage. And every wretched creature was fitted with a tube jutting from a gaping wound in its side and running out to a bottle collecting the bear's precious bile.

Some of the cages were not big enough for the animals stuffed inside them. The larger ones had their paws sticking outside the cramped quarters.

I had glimpsed a scene like this once before when I was still working at *The Star*. A news story and pictures came in about a lab in China. The headline read: "Dishonourable Trade In Bear Parts." I tsk, tsked it and thought how lucky I was to live in a country where such a terrible thing could never happen. Then I forgot about it. Now I was standing in the middle of that hellish picture.

Some of the bears were rocking their heads, banging their skulls against the bars. My attention was drawn to a small black bear nearest us. His head weaved and banged at the bars. But it wasn't his head that held my gaze. It was his paws. Or, I should say, where his paws should have been. Bloody stumps were wrapped in bandages so red with blood they looked almost black. The China lab story spoke of this: They remove the paws, sell them for soup and keep the creature alive to extract more bile.

The room shifted. Rocked. I put my hand out against the wall to steady myself. In the far corner of the room, a man was crouched in front of one of the cages. He was wearing Larry's blue Gore-Tex jacket. "Melwheeler's Mountain Adventures" was stitched across the back.

I knew who the man was and what he was doing; he was talking to the bear.

The room righted itself as shock morphed to rage sending bile up my own throat. What he'd done to the Doc, to the others ... What he was doing to these animals ... I wanted to kill John Morrow. If I'd had a gun I believe I would have. But I hung on to my own life and didn't lash out. Not yet.

"Larry?" John called out. He corrected himself when he realized it couldn't possibly be Larry. "Mike? That you?"

Arthur turned and faced us. He stepped away from the cage. I saw the bear. It was Lulu. Her two cubs were on either side in their own cages.

"They're gone," Arthur said.

I felt John shift behind me. "Becker?" John called out. There was less certainty in his voice.

Arthur took a step toward us. "Hellie, are you — "

"Stay where you are," John said. He called out for his helicopter pilot. "Vince?"

"They've gone," Arthur repeated. "All of them. Your pilot, your technician, Becker and the other fellow. You are alone, John Morrow."

I sensed John's confusion and panic rise in unison with my own courage.

"I don't believe you. How did you get in here?"

"Larry gave me a key," Arthur said.

"I'll shoot her, Arthur. I swear to God I will. Unless you tell me what you've done with them."

The bears were quiet during this exchange. As if they sensed the tension and knew something was about to happen.

"Arthur," John said sharply. "Where are the others?"

"I convinced them of the wrong they were doing and impressed upon them that they would pay for their misdeeds; if not in this life, certainly in the next."

"You and Hellie are about to experience your next life if you don't start talking some truth."

"I also told them the police are on their way. Which is the truth. So, John Morrow, there is no sense making things any worse for yourself."

John pushed me forward with another nudge of the gun barrel. "Get over by your friend," he said.

I didn't move. He was going to execute us. He had to. It was his only chance. Larry was dead. The others probably wouldn't talk.

Arthur read the situation. "I've told someone else," he said. "Larry told me everything. The liquor bottles filled with the bile. The gall bladders wrapped in with the chocolate fudge, to get them past the security dogs' noses. I know it all, and I went to a friend and I told that friend what you have done, John."

"Then why aren't the police here? You're bluffing, Arthur. You couldn't call the police because you knew they'd pick you up and it'd take forever to convince them to get up here."

"I told my friend to wait half an hour after I left so that I'd get here first. I used my friend's truck. It's at the trailhead. They are coming."

John didn't believe him, and I wasn't sure I did either. We were out of time. He was going to kill us. I looked across the room to Arthur standing quietly, unarmed among his bears and about to die. I'd made a promise to the Doc that I'd look after Arthur. I intended to keep it. My hand moved to the canister. I found the nozzle, my finger slipped over the trigger.

Slowly and deliberately, I turned and faced John Morrow.

Our eyes met. Mine said: *I win.* His were merely a question mark. I lifted the can and sprayed the iris-frying pepper directly in his eyes. The next thing I heard was an explosion in my ear. I was on the ground, certain I'd been shot. Someone was screaming. I thought it was John Morrow, but it sounded as if his cries were coming from far away. I turned my head. The volume went up.

"My eyes! My eyes!"

The bears were howling in concert. Metal cages rattled. I kept my eyes closed, and waited for the next shot to rip through my head and finish me off. I felt someone pass in front of me. My eyes snapped open.

John was on his knees in front of me. Arthur reached down and picked up John's gun from where it was lying beside him and placed it next to me. I touched my head and felt for blood. There was none.

"Help me!" John screamed. "Get me water. Get water for my eyes."

Arthur moved toward the cages. I grabbed the gun and knelt beside John. I leaned in close to his ear. "Look. Look at them you pig," I said. "Look at what you've done to them."

"Get me water. Please."

Arthur knelt beside John and splashed water into the man's eyes until John was able to do it himself.

I held the gun to John Morrow's head. I wanted to pull the trigger. God, how I wanted to.

"Get up," I said. "And take out every one of those tubes. Or I'll blow your stinking head off."

"I can't," John whimpered. "I don't know how. My technician did it. I can't see."

"You won't be able to breathe in a minute."

Boots on concrete echoed down the shaft and filled the chamber. Nathan's voice boomed over a police bullhorn. "This is the police. Drop your weapons. We're coming in."

At the entrance, Nathan and Ansel stood with their mouths agape at the terrible, unspeakable scene before them. A half-dozen more constables followed and froze in their stride when they entered the chamber.

I kept my eyes on Ansel. He was staring down at his oldest and most trusted friend. John was still nursing his eyes. Ansel took a couple of steps forward and cast the older man in his looming shadow. Ansel's jaw jutted with anger, his eyes so dark blue they looked black as death.

"You responsible for this filth, John?" Ansel said.

John Morrow continued to splash water in his eyes.

"You tell me the truth now, John. I want to hear it from you. You do this?"

John wouldn't look at his friend. His silence was answer enough for Ansel.

"Why, John? Damn it. Be a man and answer me."

John splashed more water in his eyes. "You'll never understand, Ansel."

"There is not a doubt in my mind about that. Did you kill Michael Rivard? You did, didn't you? Was it because he knew about this?"

"Yes, Ansel," I said softly. "And because John was afraid the Doc may have found out what he's been doing in Tanzania all these years. John was worried the Doc finally learned about all the ivory he's poached and the illegal arms he smuggled in through the Doc's clinic."

Ansel's eyes snapped to me, to John then to Arthur. "No. He's the one," Ansel said pointing to Arthur.

"No, Ansel," I said. "Marianna found out that John was poaching. That he was bringing in illegal weapons. I suspect the agent they found murdered alongside your wife is the one who told her."

Arthur looked confused, then said, "Yes, that must have been it. I was waiting for a message from that agent. We thought the poachers followed him and saw Marianna."

"That's right," I said. "They were John Morrow's poachers."

"John?" Ansel swayed and put a hand out to steady himself against a beam. "John?" It was as though each time he said his friend's name he was uttering a foreign word. "You bastard!"

Tears were streaming down John's cheeks, not all of them caused by the pepper spray. John Morrow was afraid for his life and for good reason.

"Ansel, you've got to believe me. It wasn't supposed to happen like that. They weren't supposed to hurt Nici."

"No? They were just supposed to murder my wife?" In a flash of blind rage Ansel grabbed the gun from my hand and locked John Morrow's throat in the crook of his arm. He trained the gun on John's temple.

"Please, Ansel, don't ... don't do it. Don't shoot," John pleaded.

Nathan stepped forward. "Drop the weapon, Mr. Rock."

Ansel ignored him. "You killed my baby girl. Your own god-daughter."

"Oh, Ansel. Please. I didn't mean for it to happen."

"Shut your mouth you filthy, disgusting liar. It's your turn now." Ansel's eyes were those of a deranged man.

"Drop the weapon, Rock," Nathan said and drew his revolver.

Ansel didn't respond. I doubted he even heard the order. Six years of pent-up guilt, fear and rage made him deaf to reason.

"Count to three you sonofabitch because that's how much time you've got to live."

"One," Ansel said.

"Rock, drop your weapon!"

"Ansel, please listen to Nathan," I begged.

"Two."

John's eyes squeezed shut. His face contorted with pain. Tears leaked from his eyes.

Arthur spoke. "Marianna didn't believe in killing, Ansel. Please honour her now."

Ansel blinked and looked up at his old enemy. With his eyes still on Arthur, Ansel said, "Three."

CHAPTER 28

IT WAS TEN THIRTY IN THE MORNING AND I WAS STILL IN BED. NOT sleeping, just lying there with the weight of the previous day anchoring me to the mattress. I could still hear John scream when he thought Ansel would pull the trigger. Still hear the sound of metal scraping against rock as Ansel let the gun slip from his hand. And I would never forget the shell-shocked look on Ansel's face when he released his grip on his true enemy and let John Morrow fall to his knees whimpering.

The phone rang. I let the machine pick it up. After a few minutes it rang again, then a third time. I dragged myself up on one elbow and picked up the receiver. It was Des letting me know that Becker and his confreres had all been apprehended.

"And the bears?" I asked. When the wardens and a vet showed up at the bunker, Ansel, Arthur and I did what we could to help them tranquilize the bears, remove the tubes and prepare them to be flown to a rehab centre in Calgary.

Des sighed. "Had to destroy the black bear, the one with the bandaged legs. There was nothing anyone could do. Poor thing," Des whispered.

I felt ill as the image of that wretched creature filled my mind. "Those bastards," I said through clenched teeth. "How could anyone be so cruel?"

"I don't know," Des said. "At least the rest will be okay. But now the problem is ... " he paused, " ... what will we do with Lulu?"

I sat up. "Why? What's wrong with her?"

"We're afraid she's too used to people. You know Arthur's been feeding her. And with her history of coming into town ... " Des trailed off. "There's talk of putting her in the zoo."

"They can't," I said.

"Yeah, they can," Des said sadly. "I'm fighting it. If it were up to me, I'd rather put a bullet in her head."

"Arthur would agree," I said. "And so do I."

"I'll keep you posted," he said. "How are you doing, Hellie?"

"Fine. Uh, Des," I said tripping over my words. "About the other day, when you came by and I said I'd been out late ... uh and then Ansel — "

"It's okay, Hellie. None of my business."

"Yes it is. We're friends, aren't we?"

Silence stretched between us, until Des finally said, "You bet. And I want you to know I think you did a great job finding out what's been going on. You took some pretty big risks and, well, I'm just glad you're okay."

"Thanks," I said.

We rang off, and I went directly back to bed with the intention of staying there for the rest of the day. No sooner were the covers back over my head than the phone rang again.

It was my editor from *McMillan* magazine, who, unlike myself, was in a fine, upbeat mood. He'd been talking with Ansel that morning and got the gist of what happened.

"This is good, Hellie. This is very good. We'll run the two stories together: the Ansel Rock bighorn hunt and the poaching piece. You'll get a lot of space."

"Sounds good," I said trying to put some enthusiasm in my voice.

He was thrilled. And in keeping with his high spirits and charitable mood he said, "Take your time with the Ansel Rock story. Fix it up. Get the personal stuff in there. Then use a lot of ink on the poaching piece. This'll be your issue, Hellie."

"No." I said. "This one belongs to the bears."

After we hung up, I looked back at my pillow and gave up the idea of going back to bed. I dragged myself to the bathroom, showered and then threw on a pair of jeans and a sweater.

Tiger was with Bernie, and Arthur was in Calgary with his bears, so I was alone. I spent the rest of the morning and the better part of the afternoon staring out the kitchen window, sipping coffee. When someone knocked at the back door, I was relieved.

"Arthur! You're home." When I saw him standing there in the crisp autumn air wearing one of his orange and red kikois, I wept. But this time, my tears were not of sadness, nor loss, nor grief. These were tears of hope. I swiped at my eyes. "I'm so glad you're back so soon.

I've been waiting."

"I know," he said. "Your wish was on the wind and it spoke to me." He smiled and tugged at one of the silver earrings in his ear. "I'm making tea. Will you join me?"

"Love to."

"Good." He rubbed his hands together. "The truth is out, Hellie. Now we may celebrate."

I grabbed my coat and followed him down the wooded path. But just as we neared the river, Arthur's words about truth sparked a thought, and I stopped.

"There's something I need to do," I said.

Arthur just smiled. "I'll have the tea waiting," he said and went on his way.

As I started back up the path toward the house, my courage quickly gave way to fear and worry. This wasn't going to be easy. My pace slowed to a near crawl, and I felt like tearing down to Arthur's cabin and forgetting the whole thing. But my legs kept carrying me to the back door, through the kitchen and down the hall where I picked up the phone. I took a deep breath and then made the call I should have made a year ago.

When it was over, I ran back down the path feeling like my life had just been switched from *hold* and back to *on*.

***

Inside Arthur's little cabin the welcoming smells of spiced tea and woodsmoke enveloped me like a hug.

"Ah, Hellie," Arthur said. "You look so refreshed."

"I'm going home for awhile," I said. Aside from Bernie, Arthur was the only other person I had confided in about my failed marriage and my little brother Danny.

Arthur just nodded. "Will you come back?"

"Yes."

"Good," he said. "Because I believe you are needed here." He turned away and busied himself with the tea things.

I sat down at the pine table and looked up at the picture of Lulu.

Arthur set the pot of tea on the table and followed my gaze. "The bears are doing remarkably well," he said. "And our Lulu and her cubs will be back to continue their fall feeding in no time."

Des obviously hadn't told him what fate may be awaiting Lulu, or more likely, Arthur wasn't allowing himself even to consider it.

"I'm going back to the city tonight," Arthur said. "But I needed to take care of some business here first. And, of course, I wanted to see how you are managing, Hellie. What a terrible ordeal you have been through. I'm very sorry you have had to go through this." He handed me a steaming cup of green tea.

"I'm just relieved it's over," I said accepting the tea. "John Morrow is a disgusting excuse for a human being."

"Greed is a terrible burden," Arthur said solemnly. "And we must pity those who have to carry it."

"It'll be a long time before I pity John Morrow." I sipped my tea. "I don't get it, Arthur. He went to impossible lengths to bottle that bear bile and ship out a few gall bladders. How much could he possibly make?"

"Oh, heavens. Millions. One pound of bear gall bladders can sell for thirty, forty thousand dollars on the black market. Some people believe the bladders have miraculous curative powers. The belief is unfounded, of course. And the bile, same thing, it's supposed to work magic, and it can fetch as much as a thousand dollars a gram. US dollars."

"Worth more than gold," I said.

"Absolutely. And the paws ... in Japan a bowl of bear-paw soup can cost as much as eight hundred dollars."

"John Morrow destroyed human and animal lives. I hate him," I said flatly.

Arthur smiled kindly. "No you don't. You don't know how to hate."

He was giving me a whole lot more credit than I deserved. "By the way, how did Larry kidnap you?"

"After you left that day at Miriam's cabin, Becker and Larry came to get me. Poor Larry. He was a child, you know."

"Yes. I do know," I said.

"He was supposed to do away with me."

"But he couldn't."

"No. He couldn't. Larry was doing all right. He was planning to keep me hidden until he could get away himself. But he got scared that he might get caught, so he started to scheme. He made me put my prints on the adrenaline pen. I told him not to do it, that it was foolish. But he was insistent. He wanted to make sure the police were absolutely positive it was I who had killed our dear friend Michael. Then John Morrow frightened him, of course."

I nodded. "The night of his party. John was upstairs."

"Yes. Larry told me John was looking around. He was suspicious of Larry. Once my prints were found on that adrenaline pen, John knew I was alive."

"Didn't he clue in that John would know you were alive?"

"Larry wasn't thinking clearly. All he was concerned about was not going to jail."

I stirred the fire in the pot-bellied stove and slipped in another log. When I knelt on the carpet I felt the trapdoor under my knee. "Arthur, why did you keep all that ivory and those skins?"

He gave me a sad smile. "I begged Michael to tell the truth about his time in Africa, to give that ivory and those skins to a museum. We all make mistakes, I would tell him. But he was too proud. He didn't want people to think he was a hypocrite."

"Why didn't he just get rid of them?" I said.

"He couldn't bear to waste them. Neither could I. And chances were, if he threw them out, someone would have discovered them somehow. Murphy's Law," Arthur said.

We sat and watched the fire burn in the little stove and I know we were both giving the Doc a moment of silence. After a while I said, "Did you suspect John Morrow?"

"No. I was too busy watching the Petersons. But Michael did. I should have made the connection. Once I'd told Michael that Ansel was in town, Michael asked me if he'd come alone. Naturally, I said John Morrow was with him. The next thing I know Michael is on his way home."

"Did you know John in Africa?"

"I knew of John through his safaris, of course. We used to protest against them. When we had the time," he added. "But mostly we left him alone. He had a pretty good reputation as an honest businessman who ran his safaris well. And I knew Michael had been on safari with him years ago. I'd warned Michael when we first met that his ivory was probably from poached sources, but I did not know he got the ivory from John. After I moved here, Michael spoke about the ivory and the skins only once. I never saw them. I only knew they were down there." He pointed a finger to the cellar. "They were Michael's conscience. I left it alone.

"Ah, and by the way, Hellie, Miriam tells me Michael has left his beautiful house to us. I don't want it, of course, so I'm passing it along to you." He said it as if we were discussing a piece of pottery. "I'm going back to Africa."

My heart sank. "Arthur, I don't — "

He held up a hand to quiet me.

I closed my mouth and looked closely at this odd little man who dressed like a brightly-clad Tibetan monk and lived among the animals like St. Francis of Assisi. I noticed the deep lines around his eyes, how thin he was, how the bones in his shoulders protruded like sharp knives. He'd somehow grown more fragile, more elderly over these past few days. Or perhaps I just hadn't noticed before.

Something occurred to me.

I narrowed my gaze at him and wondered just how old Arthur really was. He'd told the Doc they were the same age, seventy-one. But Arthur had told us all a lot of things ...

"Arthur," I said. "How old are you?"

A mischievous smile spread across his face, lifting his bushy beard at the corners of his mouth. "I am as old and as young as I need to be."

"That's about what I thought," I said, returning his smile. "I'll keep the cabin for you, always."

"I was hoping you would," he said. "The bears might need me again."

There was a knock at the door. "Ah, good. Mr. Rock has arrived," Arthur said.

"Ansel? Here?" I said.

He opened the door. Ansel took off his cowboy hat before he stepped over the threshold. He nodded and said, "Hello." Inside the tiny cabin, the big Texan looked like Gulliver in the land of the little people.

"Thank you for coming, Ansel," Arthur said.

Ansel kneaded his hat in his hands and averted his eyes from Arthur.

"Please have a seat, if you like," Arthur said.

"No thanks. I won't be staying long. I'm sure I know why you asked me here. So let's just get it over with."

"I'm sure you do not," Arthur said. "So I'd like to speak first, if that would be all right."

Ansel shifted uncomfortably from one foot to the next. "Shoot."

"I'm sorry," Arthur said. " It seems a completely inadequate thing to say. But this is all I have to offer you: I am very, very sorry for everything I have done to you, and the pain I have caused you."

The younger man kicked the toe of his boot at a knot in the wood floor. He shook his head and said, "What the hell are you talking about, old man? I thought you'd asked me here to give me the lecture I deserve. I'm the fool who's been chasing after you for the past half-dozen years. I'm the one who got you run out of Tanzania. And I've been working double-time trying to get you thrown in jail here."

"You needn't have gone to so much trouble," Arthur said. "Once I shot at you, I'd done most of your work for you."

Ansel chuckled. "Yeah, I guess you did. Since we're on the topic, why did you do that? Hellie here figured it was because you thought I really was going to shoot that ram."

"Oh, yes, she's quite right. I've been keeping an eye on you just as long as you've been watching me," Arthur said shyly. "I had a good feeling about the way you were handling your grief. Each time you came for the auction you stayed in Kananaskis. It was clear to me what you were doing, that you were saving that ram for Marianna. But then this time you decided to come here to Banff looking for me. I thought you were acting erratically. Up there on that mountain I thought the temptation might have overtaken you. And I couldn't take the chance."

"So you figured you'd better take a shot at me just in case I decided to take home my ram."

"Marianna's ram," Arthur corrected him.

"Yeah. Well, any damn poacher could have got it. I just wish it hadn't been that bastard Morrow. Anyway, it's over." He looked down at the floor then back to Arthur. "For the record, I want you to know that I am sorry for what I've done to you. But know this, too: I do not agree with how you go about doing what you do. I have always been in agreement with putting an end to poaching." His shook his head in disgust. "Now isn't that the most goddamned ironic thing you've ever heard? My best friend — ”

Arthur cut in. “Ansel, please listen to me. I am telling you that I am sorry. Sorry for putting your wife in jeopardy. Sorry for putting Hellie in danger, and the bears, and Michael, of course. I am sorry I made them vulnerable. I deceived Hellie. I encouraged your wife to get involved in a very dangerous business, and I spoiled Lulu. All have had to pay dearly for my selfishness.”

Ansel let out a low, rumbling laugh. “You always give yourself this much credit, old man? My shrink calls that an overly inflated sense of self-importance. That's what I apparently suffer from. Guess you got it too.”

Arthur smiled at the younger man.

“My wife,” he stopped himself. “Marianna had a mind of her own. A good mind. It was up to her if she wanted to work with you or anyone else she chose. Her right. You didn't coerce her. Hell, I'm the one who pushed her out the door. And Hellie, no one forced her.” He turned to me. “Isn't that right?”

“If you say so,” I said with a wry smile.

He gave me a dour look that said, *Very funny.*

“As for the bears,” Ansel went on. “I heard what you were up to. And yeah, you were stupid there. No question. But then I was stupid for being blind to the truth, and I'm responsible for bringing John Morrow here. So I'm going to stick around a while and do the best I can to make sure those bears are fixed up and returned to the woods. And I don't care what it costs.”

“Good,” Arthur said. “Good for you. And I'll continue to make sure they don't end up on some rich hunter's basement floor.”

Ansel studied his adversary. A thin smile tugged at the corners of his mouth. He reached out a hand. Arthur accepted it. As I watched the men shake hands, I believed they both did so in the knowledge that they were much more alike than either would ever care to admit.

CHAPTER 29

THIRTY MILES OUTSIDE THE TOWN OF BANFF, BERNIE, PAUL AND I WERE waiting in a clearing. A week had passed, and Ansel would be leaving the next morning. I hadn't seen much of him during that time, but he'd left me with a couple of questions. Today he'd want answers.

Between writing my articles and putting the Doc's estate in order, I had been able to avoid Ansel and his questions. But now final drafts of the two stories were done and sent off to the editor, who said he was certain the pieces would be up for an award. The Doc's lawyers were handling everything else. My time was up.

Ansel pulled his truck up and I went over to meet him. He got out, and the big Texan put his hands on my shoulders. I looked up into his quiet, peaceful eyes. It was clear Ansel's time in the mountains had been productive. He had brought his own ghosts to Banff. Now he could leave them behind. Ansel Rock had found a little of that closure he'd so desperately needed.

"Well?" he said.

"I've considered it, Ansel. I really have. The answer is still no. You cannot see the final draft. The only time you'll read about yourself is when you buy a copy of the magazine."

He tilted his back and let out a good laugh. "I should hire you," he said. "You deal a tough hand, Ms. MacConnell."

"I told you, Ansel, I was going to write the truth, and I have."

He nodded thoughtfully. "Man can't ask for more than that."

His eyes were fixed on mine and the hope in those eyes was killing me. If we stayed like that much longer, I'm sure I would have said yes to question number two. Ansel, ever the negotiator, saw what was coming.

"You'd love my house, Hellie. Swimming pool. Tennis courts. Nice dogs. Bring that little hound of yours. You could use a holiday. Your friends could come, too." He waved to Bernie and Paul who waved back. "Hell, I'll fly 'em all up."

"How about a compromise?" I said.

"Hmm. I've taught you well," he said, trying to conceal his disappointment.

"I'm going home for a little while," I said. "Thought it was time to straighten things out. I might bring my brother, Danny, back here with me. We'll see how it goes."

"That sounds like a good plan," Ansel said. "And I've just come up with another one. How about when you're done in Toronto, I fly you and your brother to my place?"

I laughed. "Why don't we try writing first?" I said. "Maybe a few phone calls … "

He looked away and I thought he was going to press me. He didn't. "Well, I'm not a particularly patient man," he said. "Guess I'll have to be one now, though. And I'm not much of a writer. So we'll leave the letters to you. I'll use the phone, a lot."

"I have something for you," I said. From around my neck I took off the crystal necklace and put it around Ansel's neck. "This seems to have brought me some good luck. Bernie says it has some kind of protective powers. I think she's right, so I'd like you to have it."

Ansel put his big hand over the crystal. "Well, that's about the best present anyone's ever given me." He leaned down, put his firm lips to mine and kissed with warm, gentle passion. I wrapped my arms around him and returned his kiss, and I felt my heart swell.

When he drew back he said, "I've got a little something for you, too. Just picked it up on my way over here." He took me by the hand and led me to the back of his truck. I was expecting more journal pages, but as he flipped open the hatch I nearly fell over when I saw what he had back there.

"Ansel," I gasped. "You can't be serious. I can't take this."

"Oh yes you can, and you will. Because I cannot take one hundred pounds of alabaster grizzly bear on the plane with me. She's yours. You've earned her. And I want you to have her."

"How do you know she's a she?" I said.

"Just do."

Thank you," I whispered, and he folded me into his arms.

We held on to each other until we heard the sound of a vehicle rumbling behind us. A Parks Canada truck bounced along the ruts. Des was at the wheel, taking it slow to minimize the impact on his passenger in the back. Arthur was next to him.

The truck came to a stop. Des and Arthur got out, and Des told us to move back. His words were a formality, though, an unnecessary precaution. No one expected trouble.

Above us, the sun cast a brilliant fall shine across the cerulean sky. To the west, however, clouds were gathering, moving in like steamships sailing in on a dark ocean. It was now November. The few remaining poplar leaves fluttered on bare branches like copper butterfly wings in the late autumn breeze. Snow would come any time now and the barren meadow would be put to rest under layers of cold, pristine blankets. I was looking forward to the snow. To when it would repaint the mountain peaks and transform their monochrome dusky grays to sharp blue-blacks, deep forest-greens and rich ochre-golds. Fall is a time of endings. Winter a time of rest. The snow would bring the ice climbers and skiers. It would send the bears to bed and the hunters home. Fall, the season of waiting, was over. This year it seemed we had all waited too long. The snow would be a welcome friend.

Des loaded his rifle and handed a second one to Arthur. Des was going against regulations. But, as he would say later, "I figured it was only right that he should do it."

"It" was the moment we had all been waiting for and dreading. But no matter how painful the next few minutes would be, we all knew it was for the best. Des told us to stay close to our vehicles. Ansel and I joined the others near Bernie's car.

"Open your doors," Des said. "If she breaks back, get in."

The Parks truck rocked. Des moved in behind, took hold of the rope and pulled it until the door of the culvert trap slid open. A dark, silver-tipped head poked out and was followed by 400 pounds of grizzly bear. Lulu sniffed the air then lumbered down the ramp on slightly unsteady legs. She stopped at the bottom and turned her massive head to Arthur.

Lulu was the last one. All the other bears had been successfully treated and released. For the past week, the wardens had agonized over the fate of Lulu and her cubs. "She is too used to humans," they said. "A danger." Arthur tirelessly corrected them, "We humans are the danger."

Lulu looked both ways, as if checking for traffic. Arthur was talking to her the entire time. But I could make out only one word: "Sorry."

The great bear fixed her beady eyes on her old friend. She moved toward him. Des raised his rifle and followed her. Arthur shook his head and held out a hand pointing toward the forest across the clearing. Lulu's cubs had been released earlier in the same area. I wondered if they were watching their mother from the woods now. I hoped not.

Arthur stamped his foot and shooed her away. The big bear moved off, then stopped and looked back.

Lulu the grizzly stood on her hind legs and surveyed the land. Again my eyes played the same trick: I was staring at a giant human being. I shook away the image.

The massive cloud ships sailed in and docked above our heads. Lulu looked up to them as though checking the weather. She ambled back toward her trusted companion. Arthur stamped his foot again. She moved a little farther away. Let out a cry and turned.

Arthur raised the rifle. I wondered how he could see. Tears glistened in his eyes. Des gave the signal.

Arthur pulled the trigger.

I shut my eyes. I think we all did, including Arthur. Lulu let out another howl, a howl of indignation when the rubber bullet made contact with her hide. Des sent a flare into the air. It went up and over the bear's head in a fiery, smokey explosion. Paul moved up and set off a series of bear bangers that sent rapid percussions like gunfire at the startled bruin's retreat.

Lulu charged forward toward the woods where her cubs were waiting. She turned and took another look back at her old friend. Cotton-ball-sized snow puffs began to fall from the sky creating a thick gauzy curtain across the meadow. The clouds shifted and let a ray of sun filter in to set the heavy puffs in a dazzling fire-white light. Lulu stopped at the edge of the bush to look back one last time at her old friend. Then she was gone into the cover of the Rocky Mountain forest.